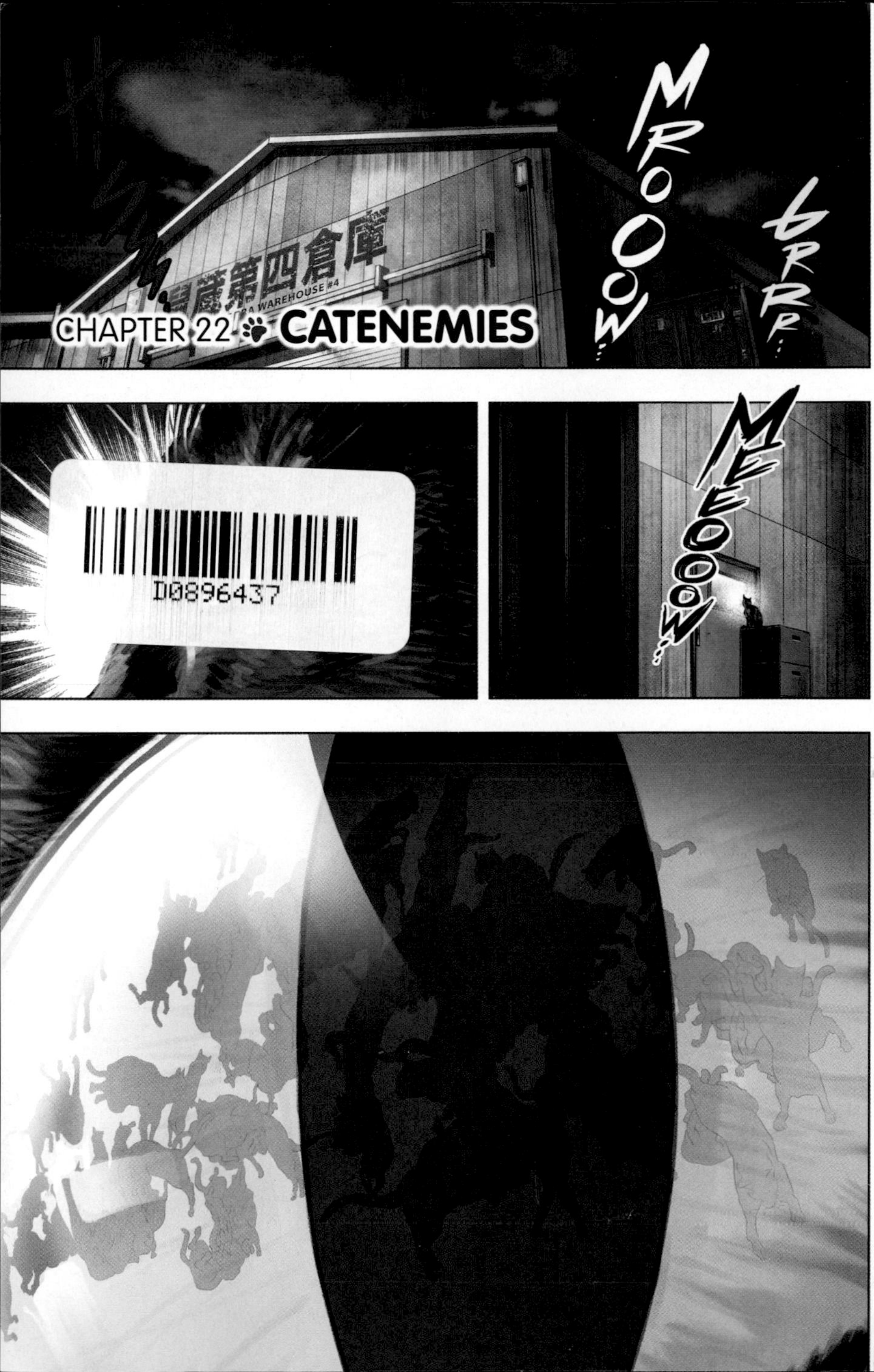
CHAPTER 22 CATENEMIES
蔵第四倉庫
RA WAREHOUSE #4
GRRR...
MROOOW...
MEEOOOW...

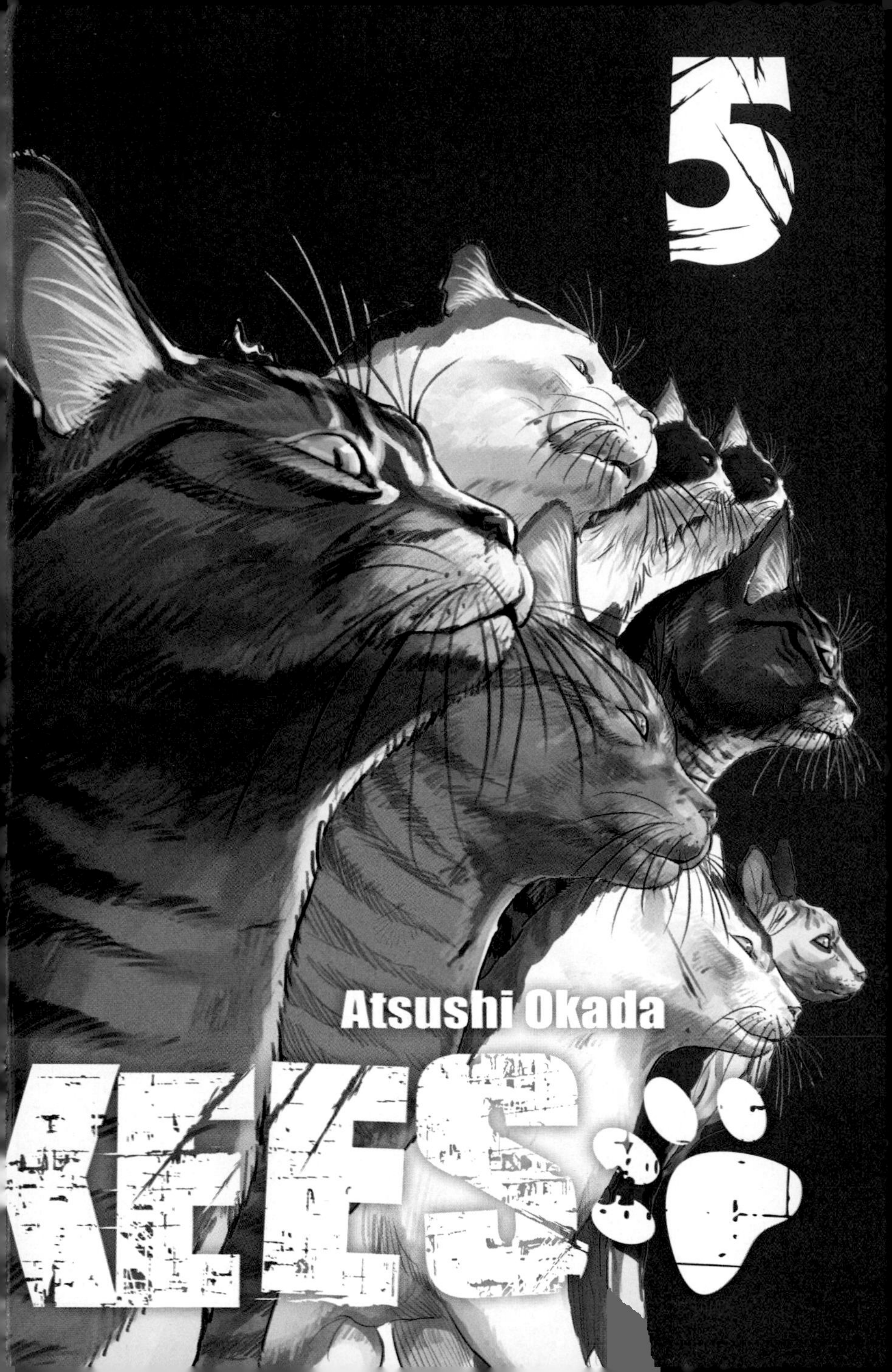
5
Atsushi Okada

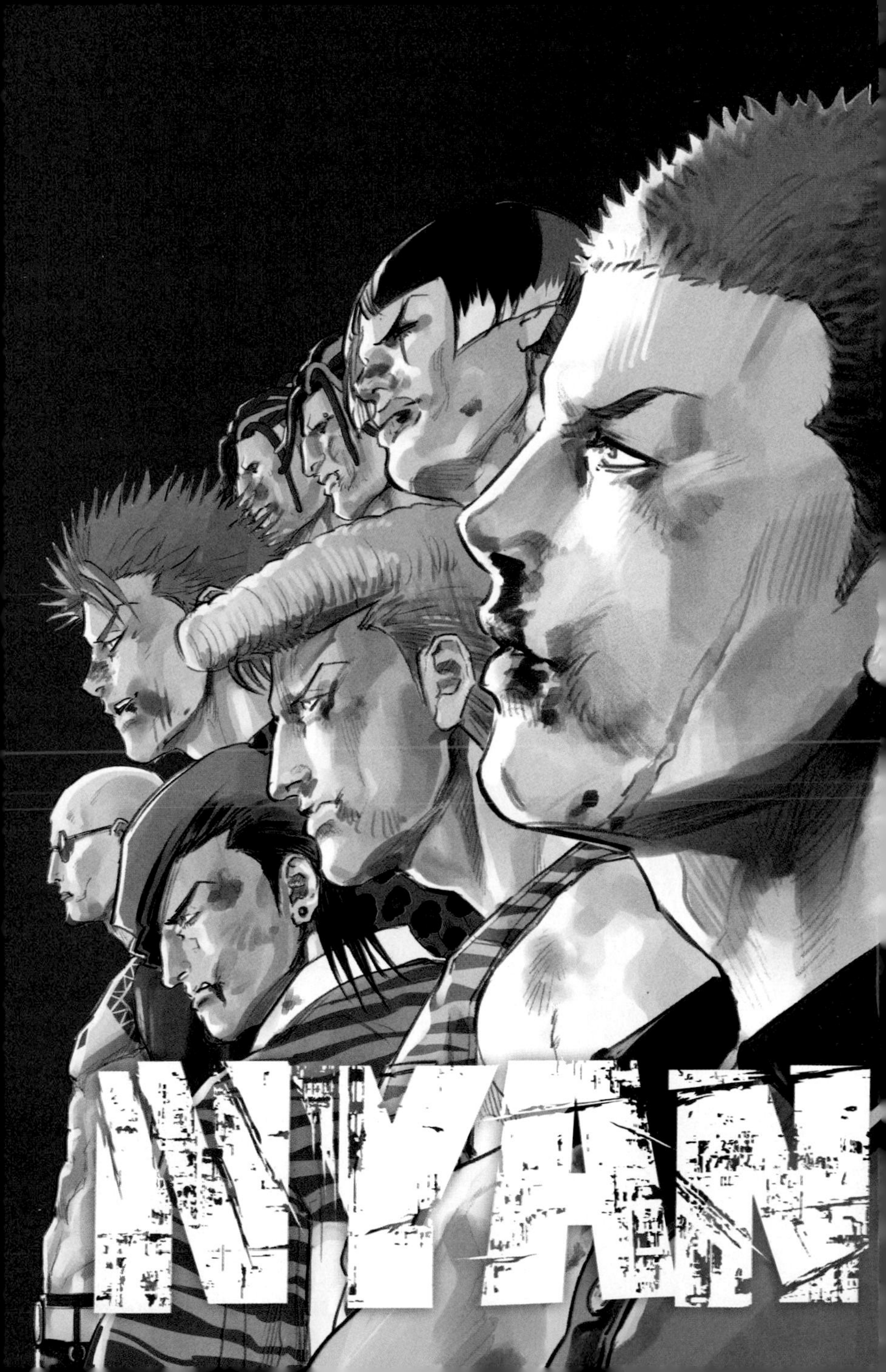

C O N T E N T S

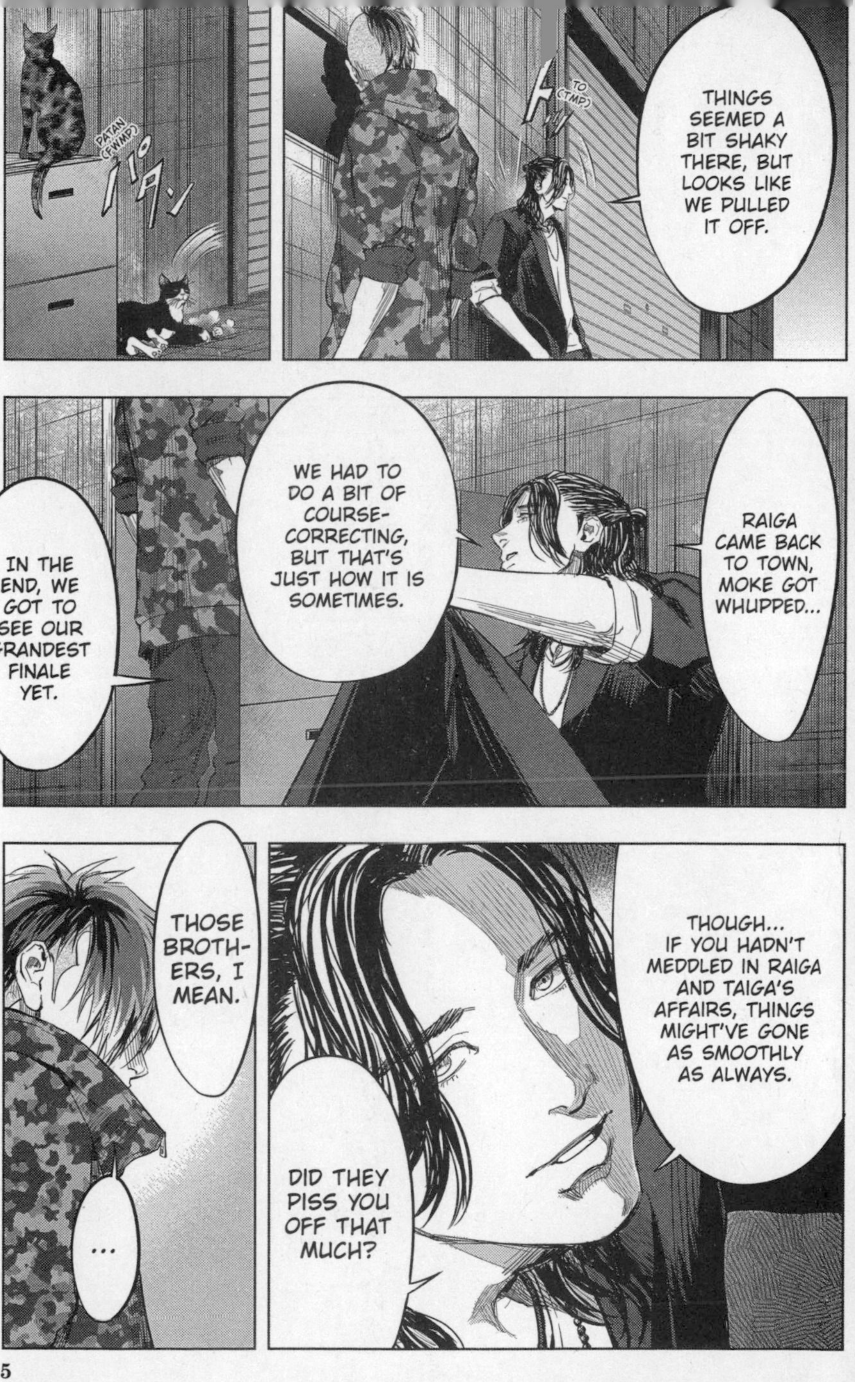
トッ
TO (TMP)
THINGS SEEMED A BIT SHAKY THERE, BUT LOOKS LIKE WE PULLED IT OFF.
パタン
PATAN (FWMP)
RAIGA CAME BACK TO TOWN, MOKE GOT WHUPPED...
WE HAD TO DO A BIT OF COURSE-CORRECTING, BUT THAT'S JUST HOW IT IS SOMETIMES.
IN THE END, WE GOT TO SEE OUR GRANDEST FINALE YET.
THOUGH... IF YOU HADN'T MEDDLED IN RAIGA AND TAIGA'S AFFAIRS, THINGS MIGHT'VE GONE AS SMOOTHLY AS ALWAYS.
DID THEY PISS YOU OFF THAT MUCH?
THOSE BROTHERS, I MEAN.
...

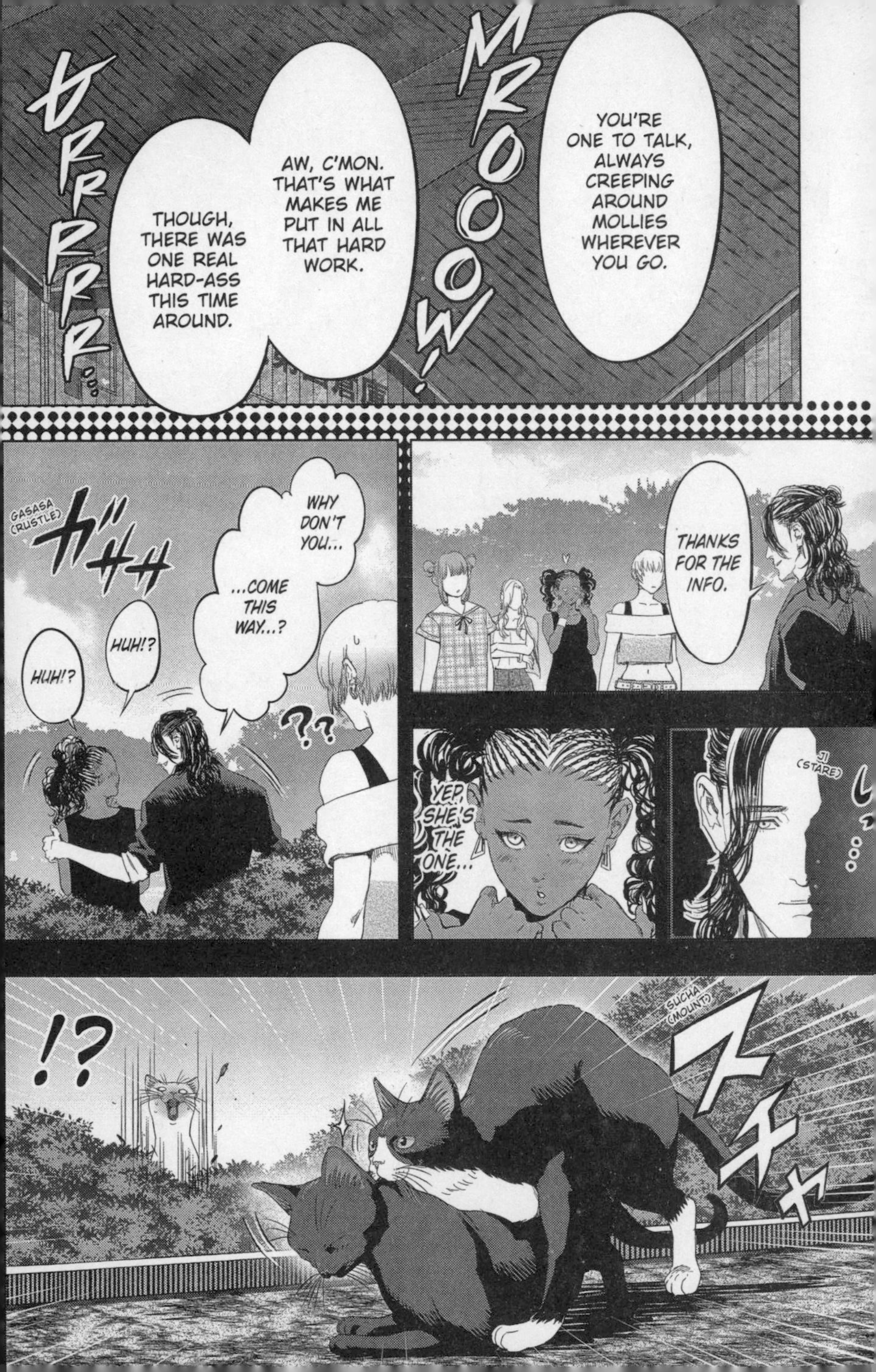
YOU'RE ONE TO TALK, ALWAYS CREEPING AROUND MOLLIES WHEREVER YOU GO.
MROOOW!
AW, C'MON. THAT'S WHAT MAKES ME PUT IN ALL THAT HARD WORK.
THOUGH, THERE WAS ONE REAL HARD-ASS THIS TIME AROUND.
THANKS FOR THE INFO.
JI (STARE)
YEP, SHE'S THE ONE...
WHY DON'T YOU...
...COME THIS WAY...?
HUH!?
HUH!?
GASASA (RUSTLE)
SUCHA (MOUNT)
!?

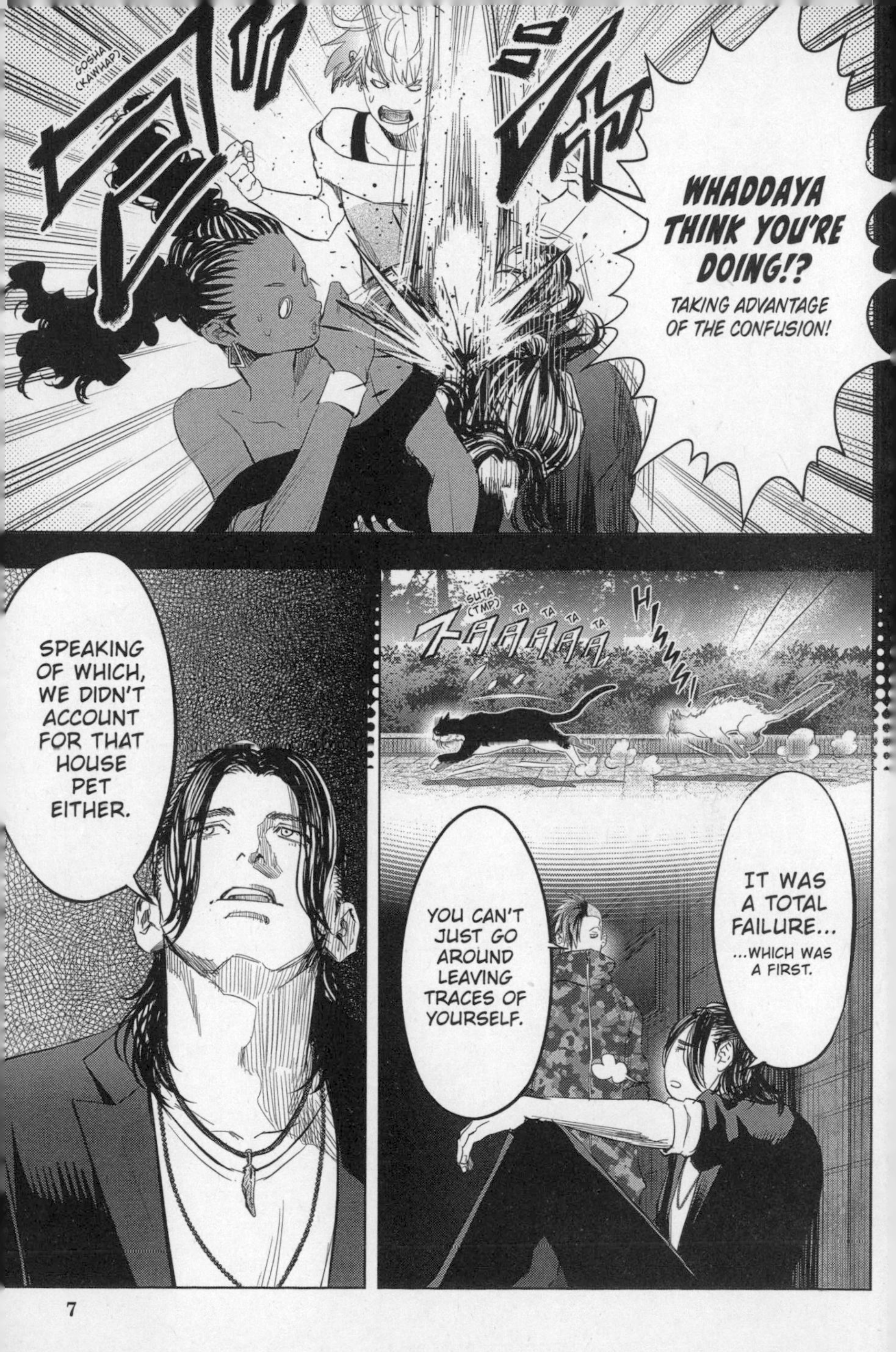
WHADDAYA THINK YOU'RE DOING!?
TAKING ADVANTAGE OF THE CONFUSION!
GOSHA (KAWHAP)
SUTA (TMP)
TA TA TA TA TA
IT WAS A TOTAL FAILURE...
...WHICH WAS A FIRST.
YOU CAN'T JUST GO AROUND LEAVING TRACES OF YOURSELF.
SPEAKING OF WHICH, WE DIDN'T ACCOUNT FOR THAT HOUSE PET EITHER.

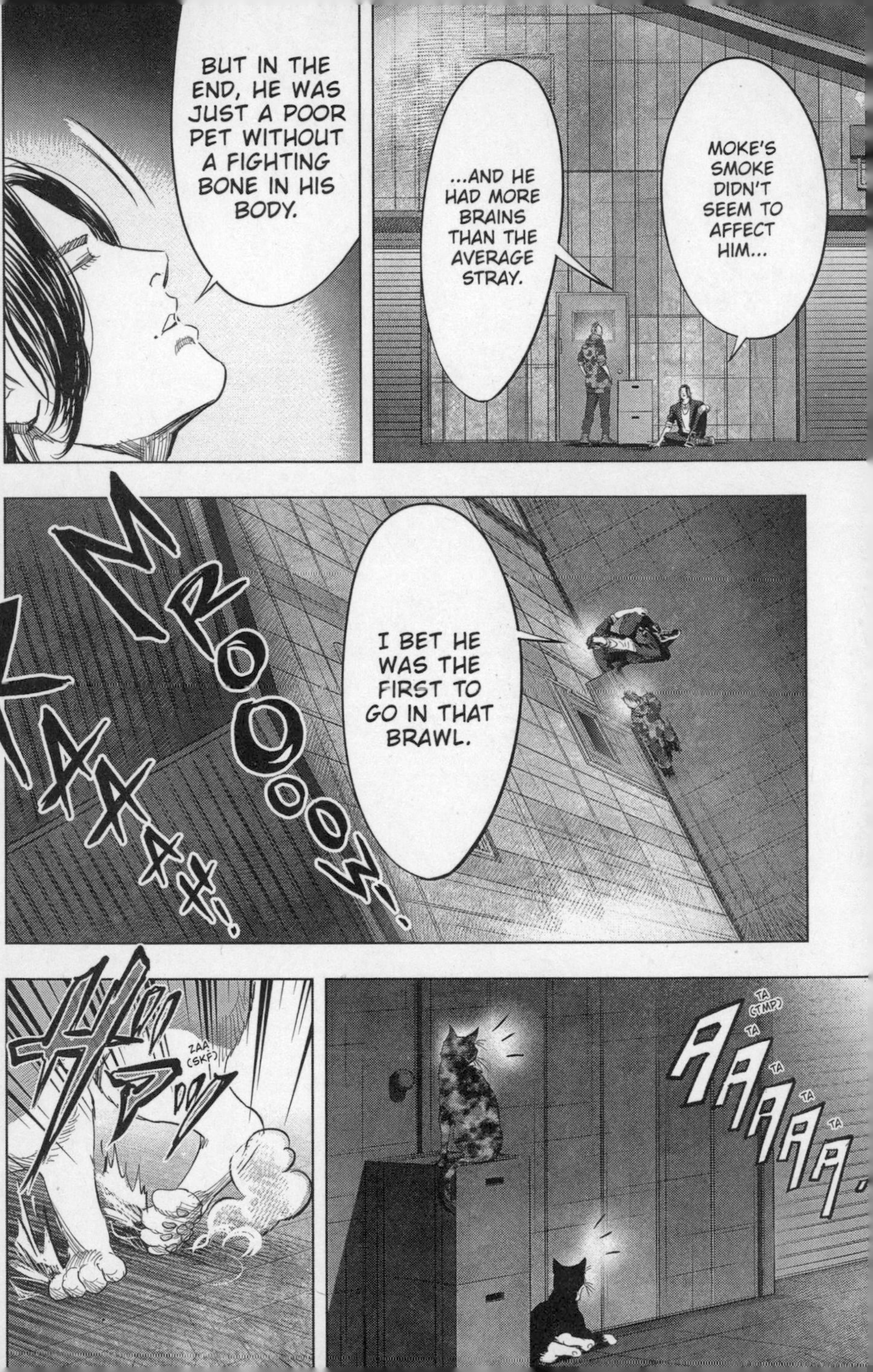
MOKE'S SMOKE DIDN'T SEEM TO AFFECT HIM...
...AND HE HAD MORE BRAINS THAN THE AVERAGE STRAY.
BUT IN THE END, HE WAS JUST A POOR PET WITHOUT A FIGHTING BONE IN HIS BODY.
I BET HE WAS THE FIRST TO GO IN THAT BRAWL.
MROOOOW!
TA (TMP)
TA
TA
TA
TA
TA
AAAAA
ZAA (SKF)

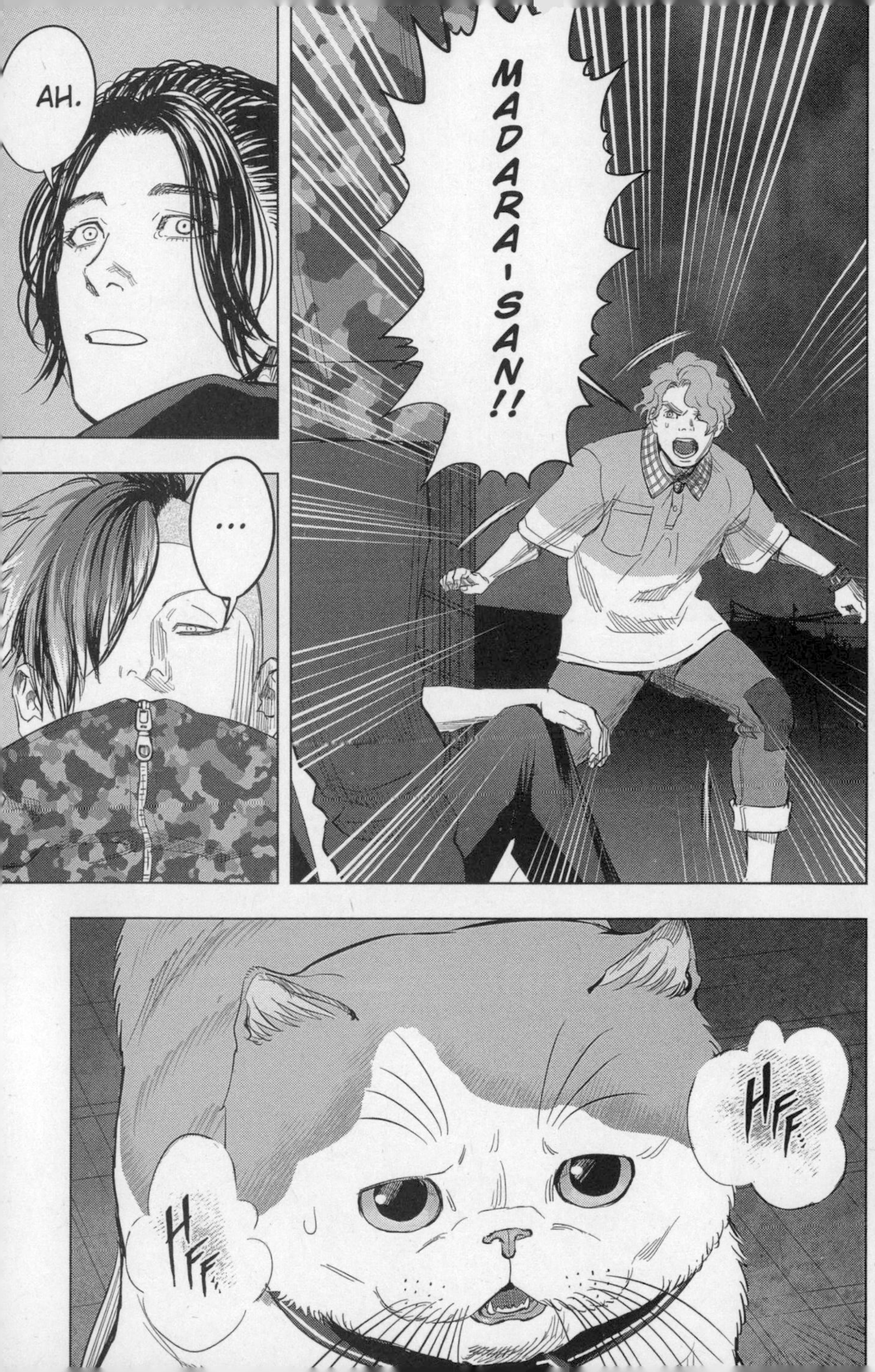
MADARA-SAN!!
AH.
...
HFF
HFF

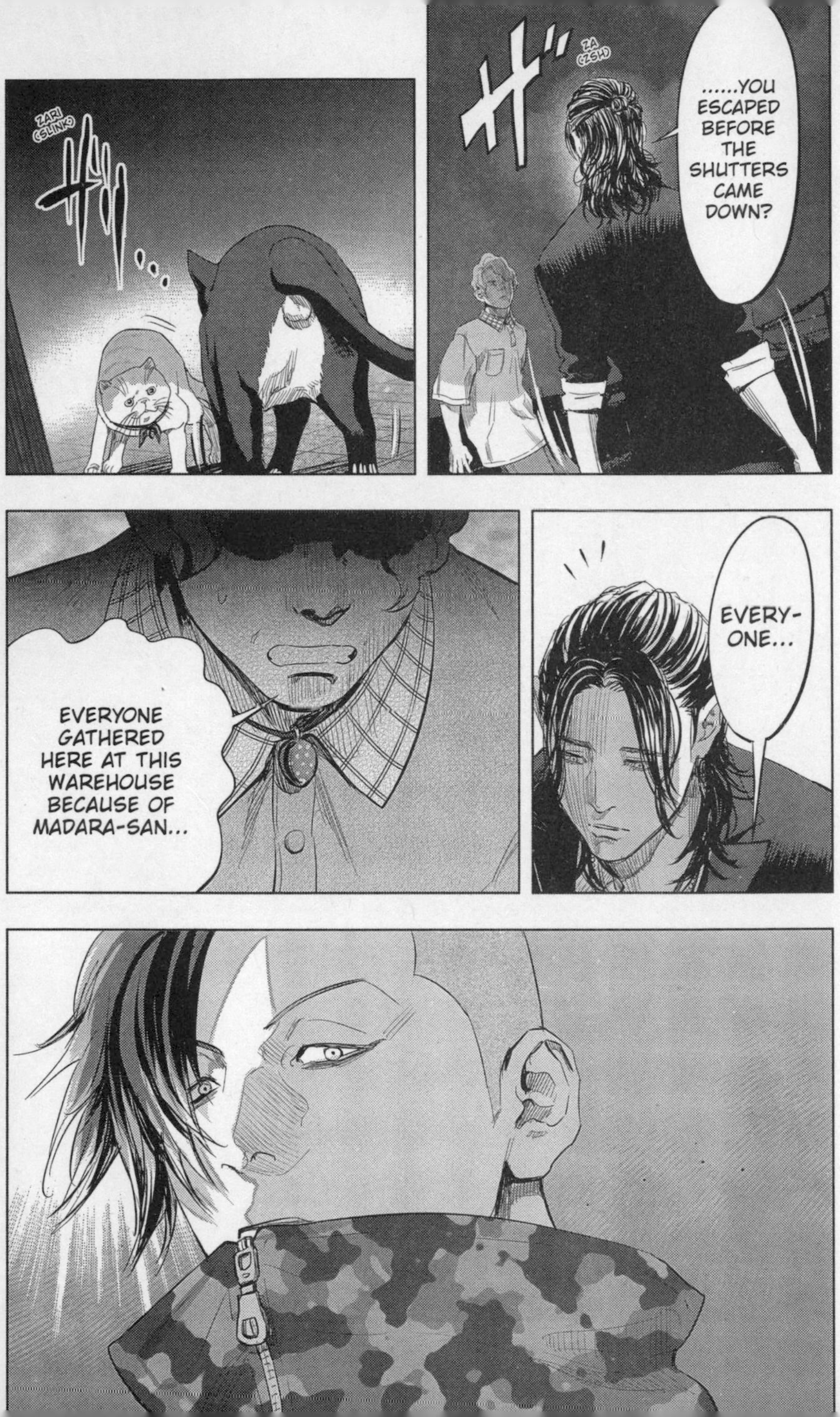
ZA (ZSH)
......YOU ESCAPED BEFORE THE SHUTTERS CAME DOWN?
ZARI (SLINK)
EVERY-ONE...
EVERYONE GATHERED HERE AT THIS WAREHOUSE BECAUSE OF MADARA-SAN...

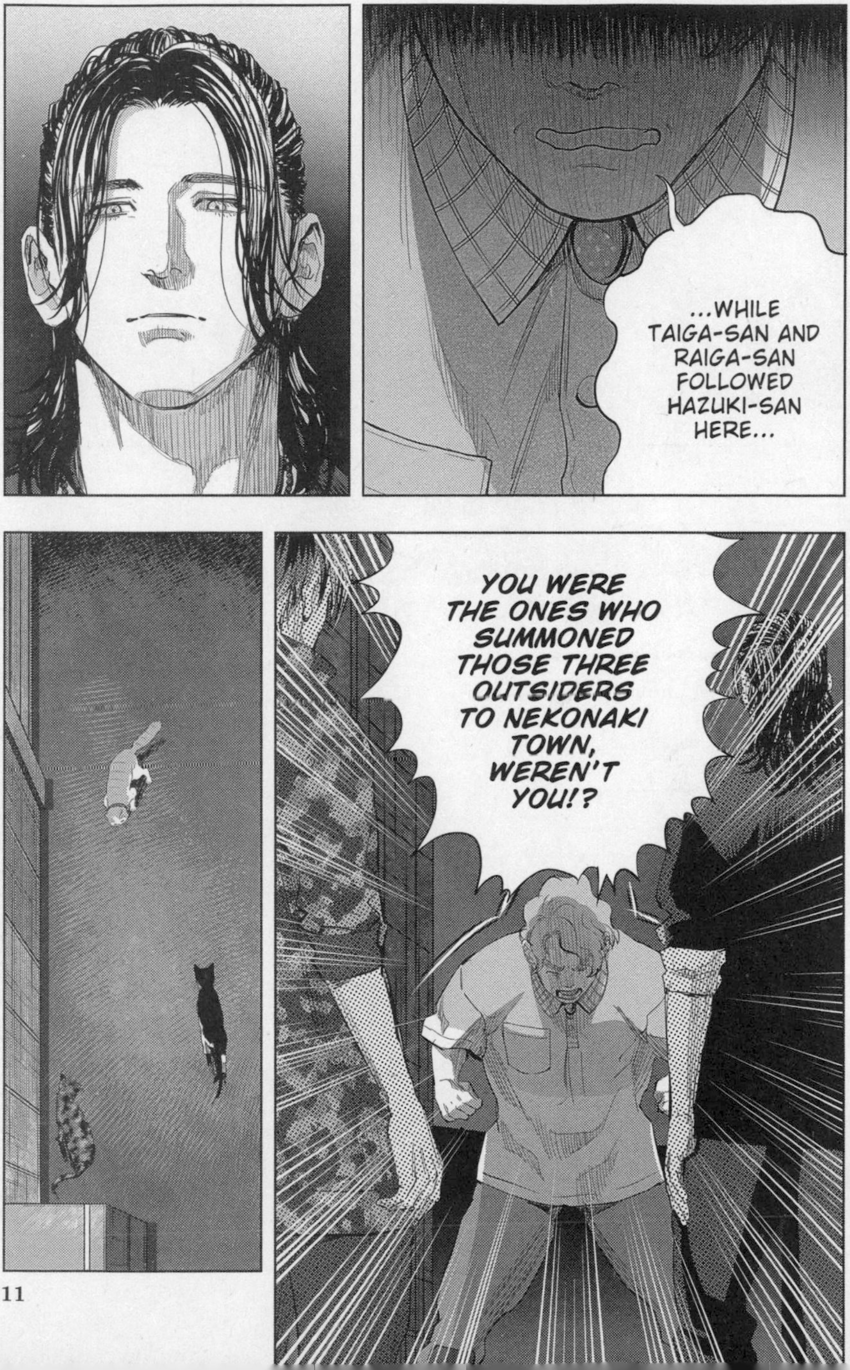
...WHILE TAIGA-SAN AND RAIGA-SAN FOLLOWED HAZUKI-SAN HERE...
YOU WERE THE ONES WHO SUMMONED THOSE THREE OUTSIDERS TO NEKONAKI TOWN, WEREN'T YOU!?

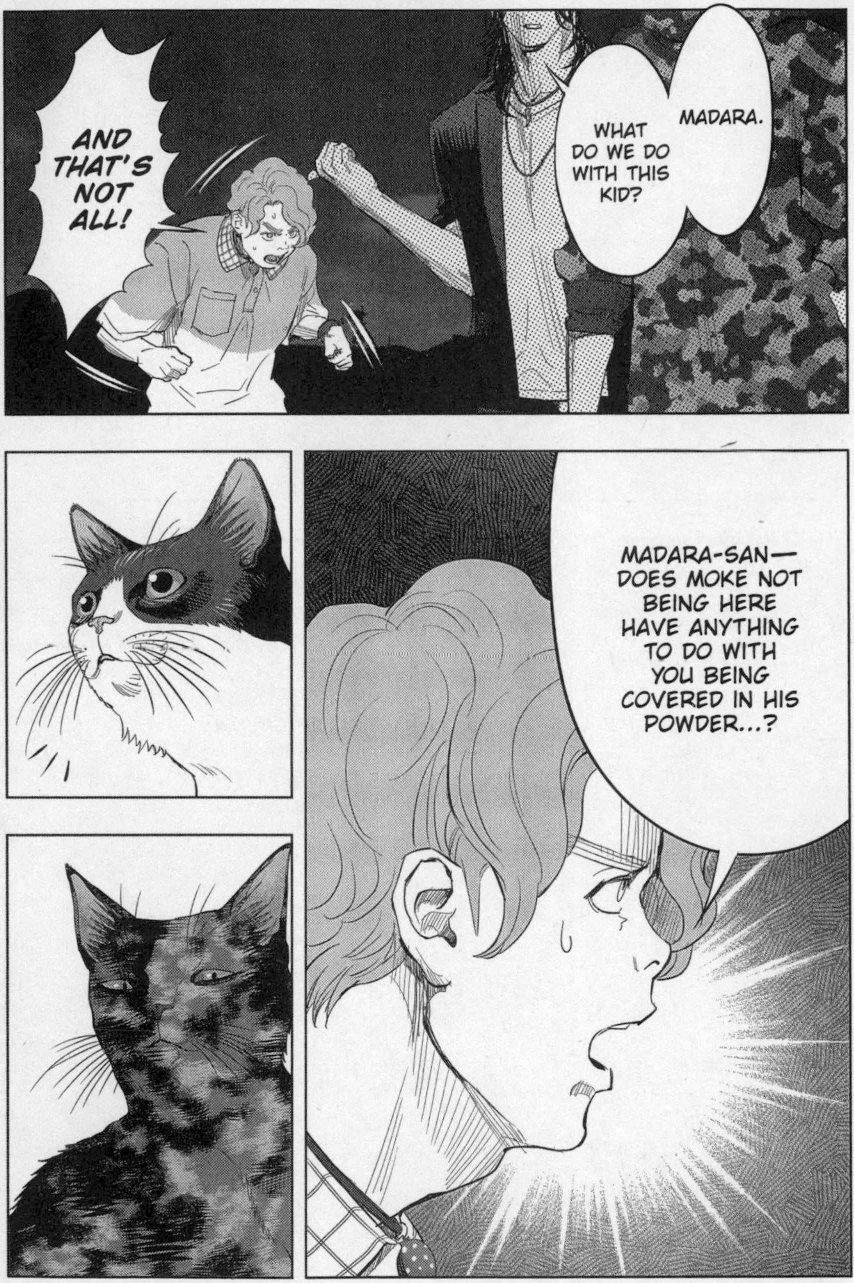
MADARA.
WHAT DO WE DO WITH THIS KID?
AND THAT'S NOT ALL!
MADARA-SAN— DOES MOKE NOT BEING HERE HAVE ANYTHING TO DO WITH YOU BEING COVERED IN HIS POWDER...?

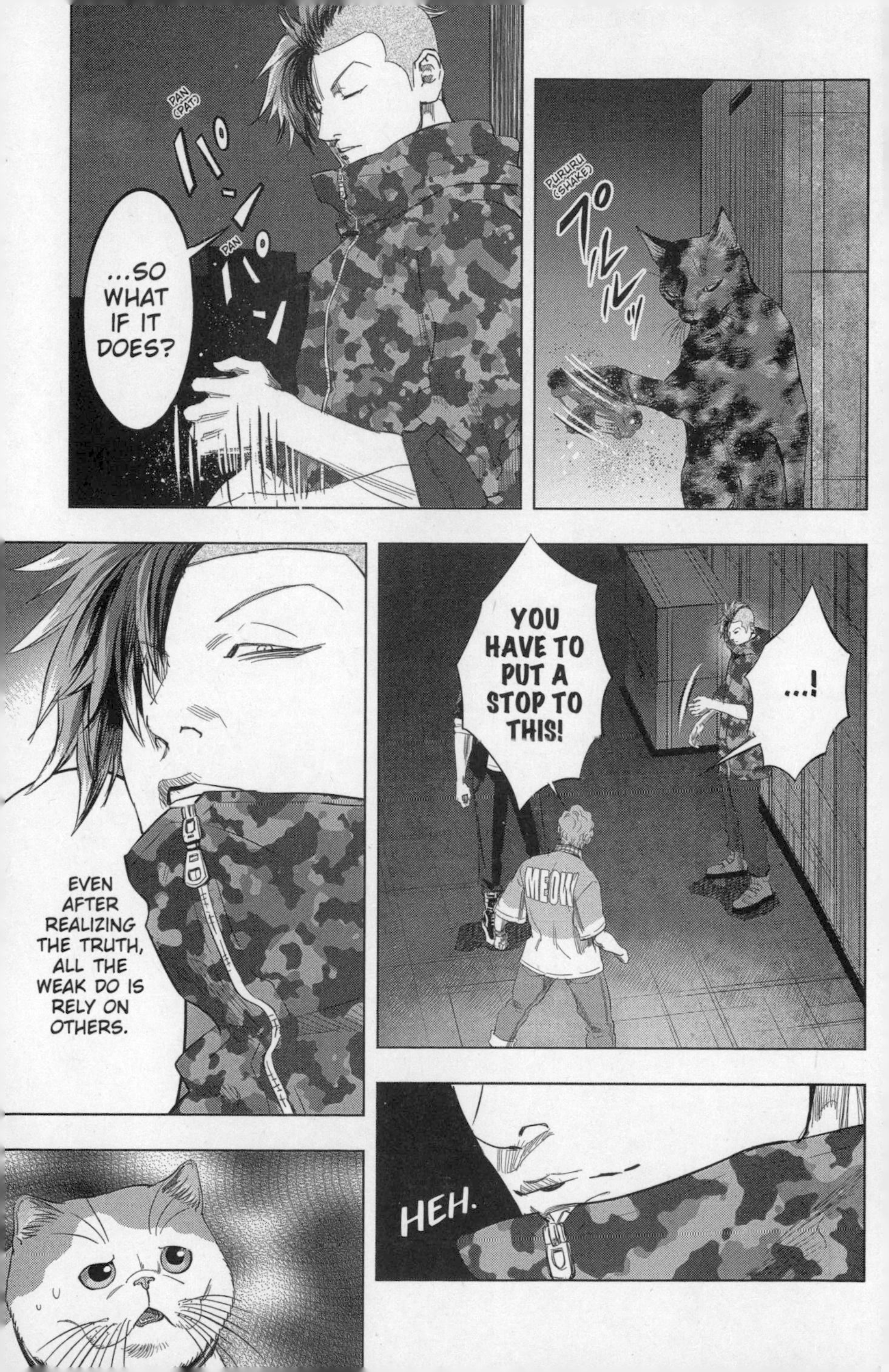

PURURU (SHAKE)
PAN (PAT)
PAN
...SO WHAT IF IT DOES?
YOU HAVE TO PUT A STOP TO THIS!
...!
MEOW
EVEN AFTER REALIZING THE TRUTH, ALL THE WEAK DO IS RELY ON OTHERS.
HEH.

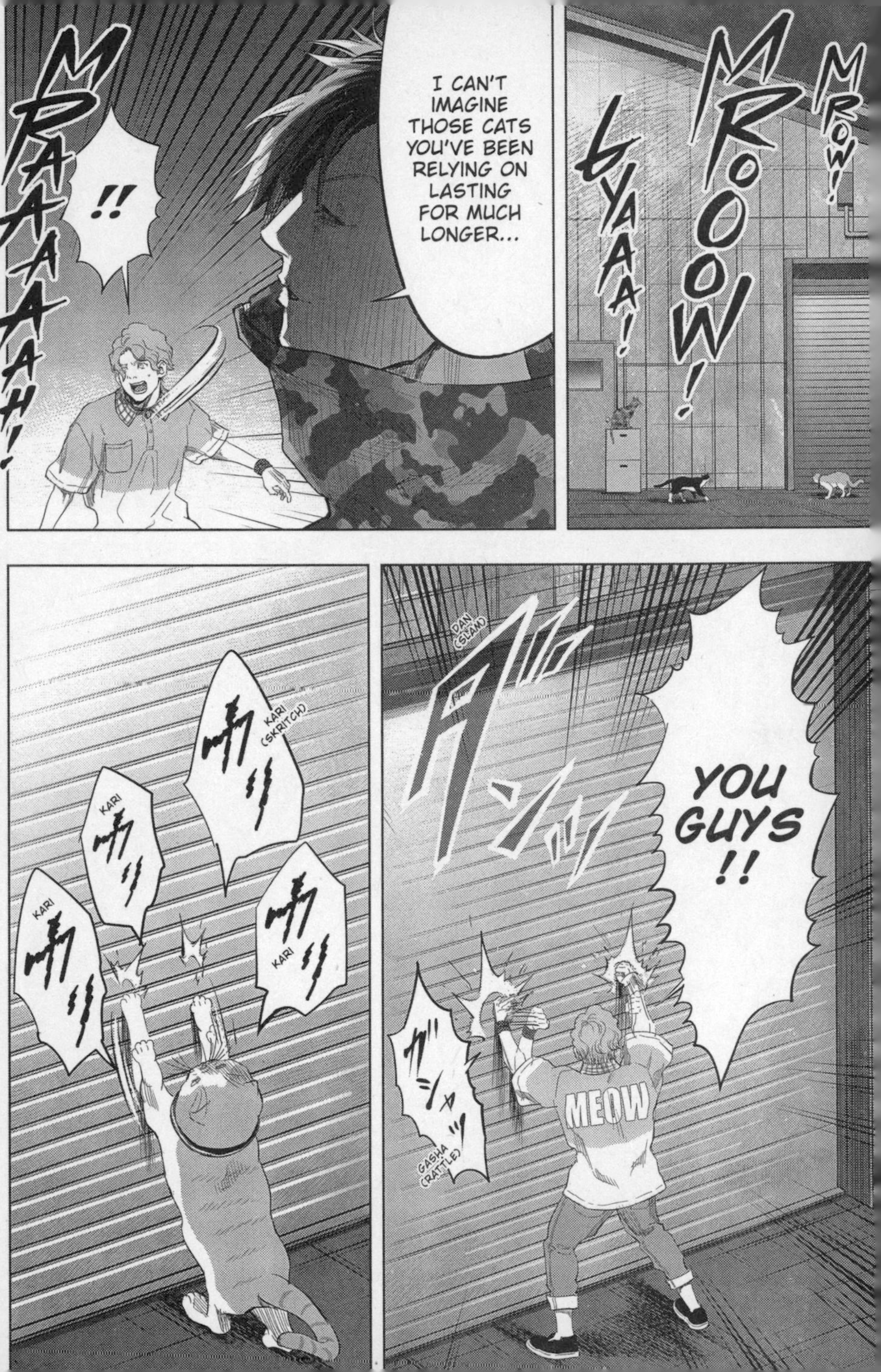

MROW!
MRROOOW!
GYAAA!
I CAN'T IMAGINE THOSE CATS YOU'VE BEEN RELYING ON LASTING FOR MUCH LONGER...
!!
MRAAAAAAH!!
DAN (SLAM)
YOU GUYS!!
GASHA (RATTLE)
MEOW
KARI (SKRITCH)
KARI
KARI
KARI

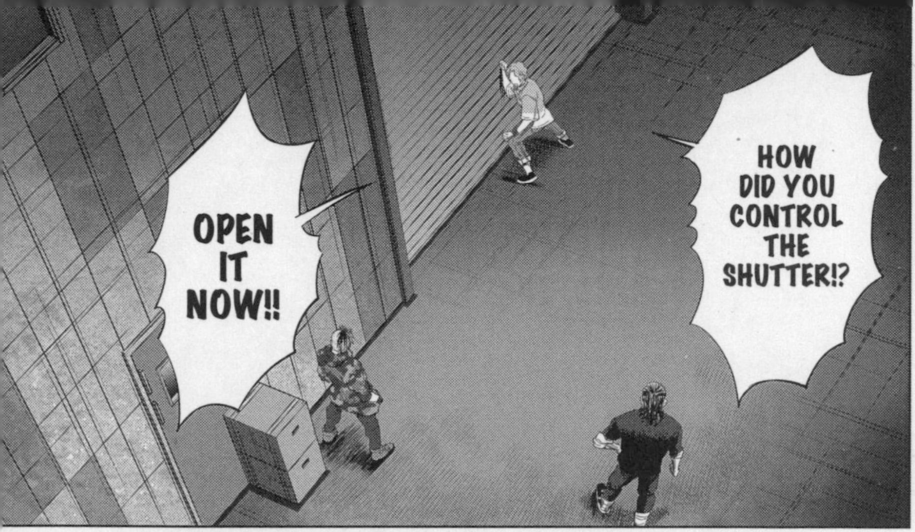
HOW DID YOU CONTROL THE SHUTTER!?
OPEN IT NOW!!

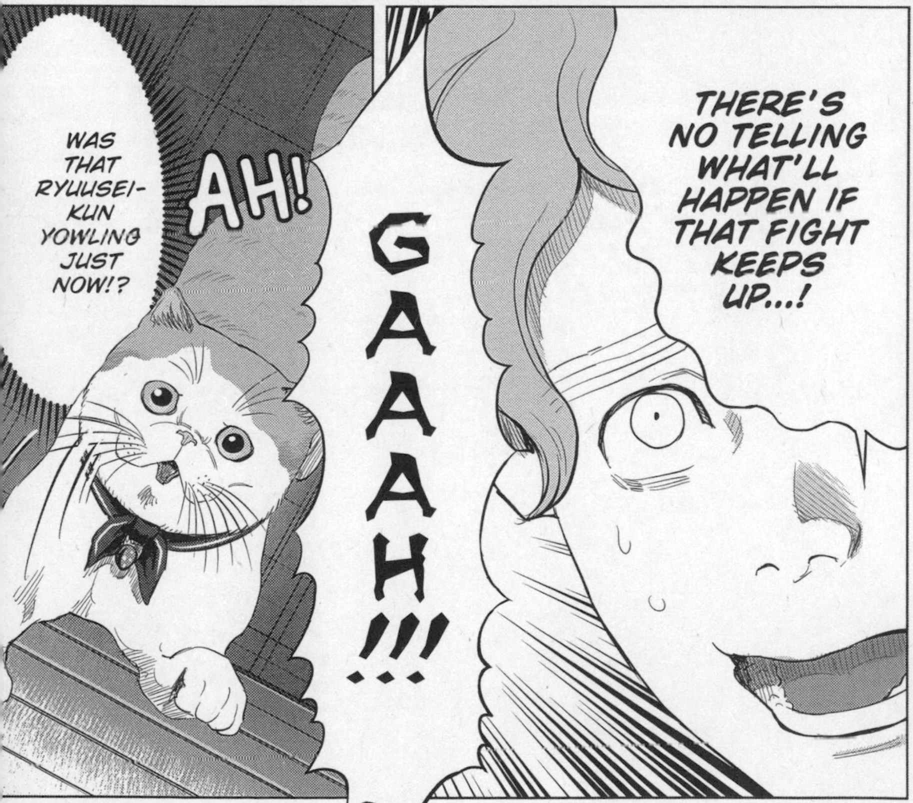
THERE'S NO TELLING WHAT'LL HAPPEN IF THAT FIGHT KEEPS UP...!
GAAAH!!!
AH!
WAS THAT RYUUSEI-KUN YOWLING JUST NOW!?

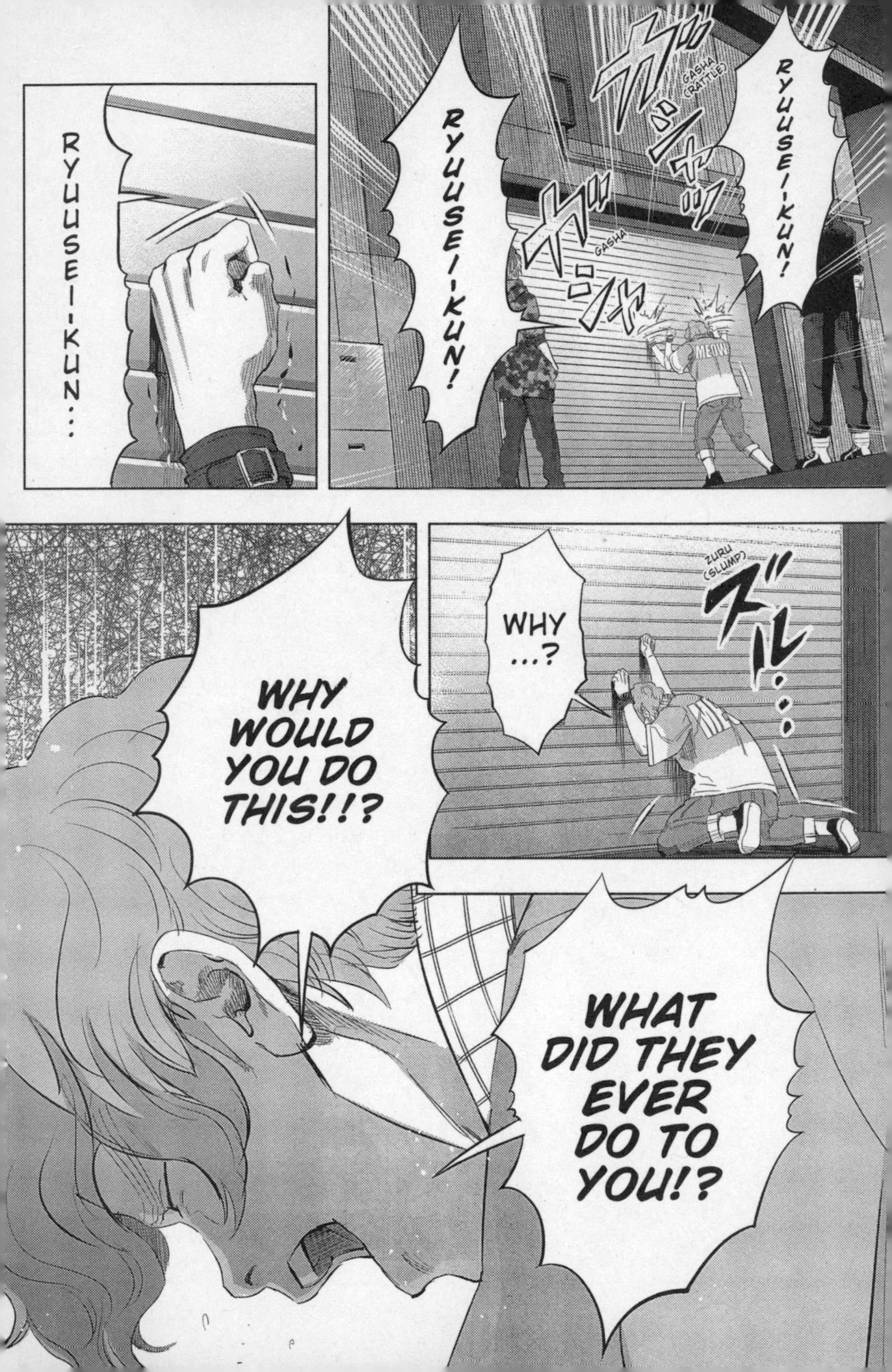
RYUUSEI-KUN!
GASHA (RATTLE)
GASHA
RYUUSEI-KUN!
RYUUSEI-KUN...
ZURU (SLUMP)
WHY...?
WHY WOULD YOU DO THIS!!?
WHAT DID THEY EVER DO TO YOU!?

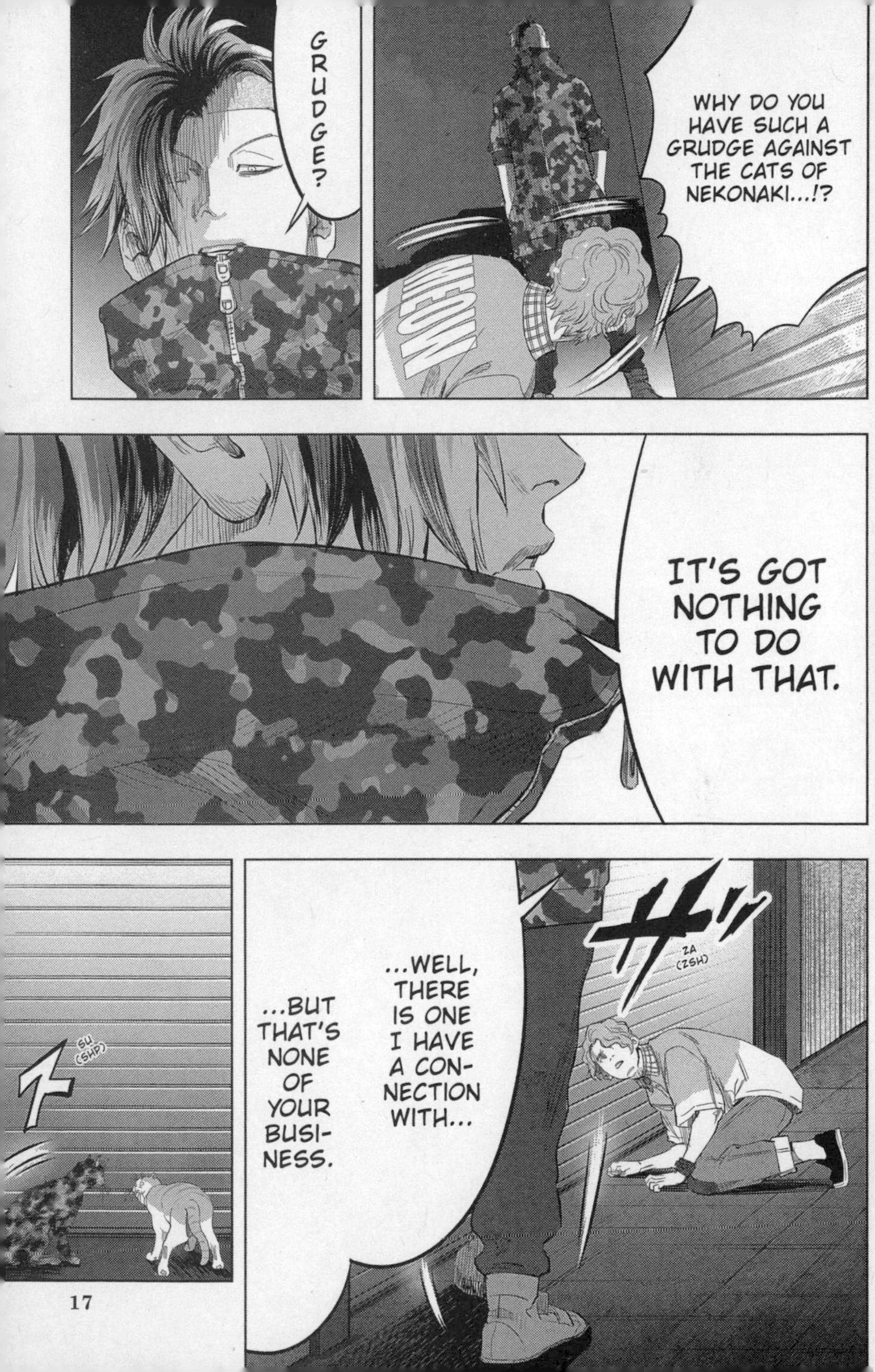
WHY DO YOU HAVE SUCH A GRUDGE AGAINST THE CATS OF NEKONAKI...!?
GRUDGE?
MEOW
IT'S GOT NOTHING TO DO WITH THAT.
ZA (ZSH)
...WELL, THERE IS ONE I HAVE A CONNECTION WITH...
...BUT THAT'S NONE OF YOUR BUSINESS.
SU (SHP)

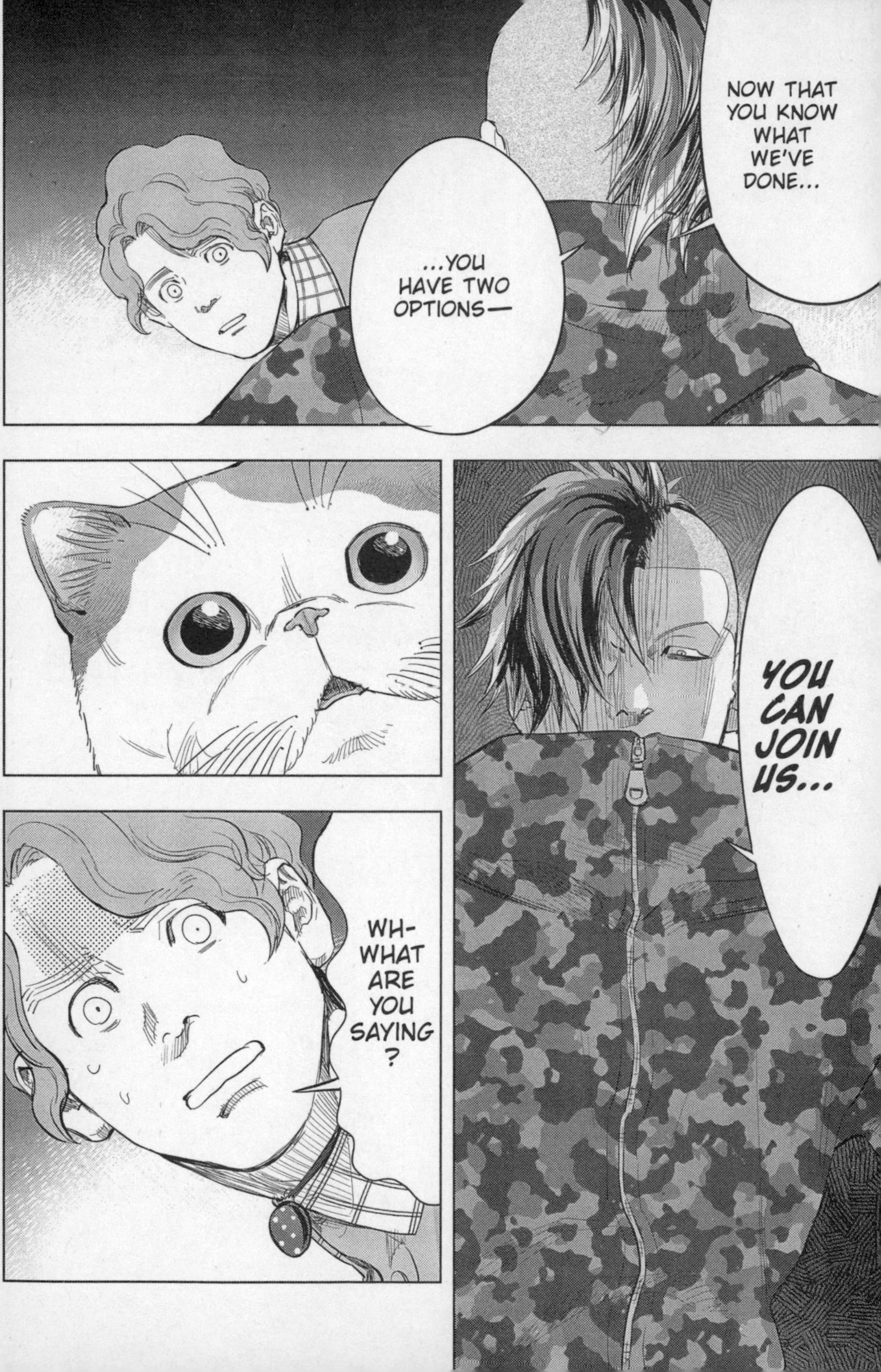
NOW THAT YOU KNOW WHAT WE'VE DONE...
...YOU HAVE TWO OPTIONS—
YOU CAN JOIN US...
WH-WHAT ARE YOU SAYING?

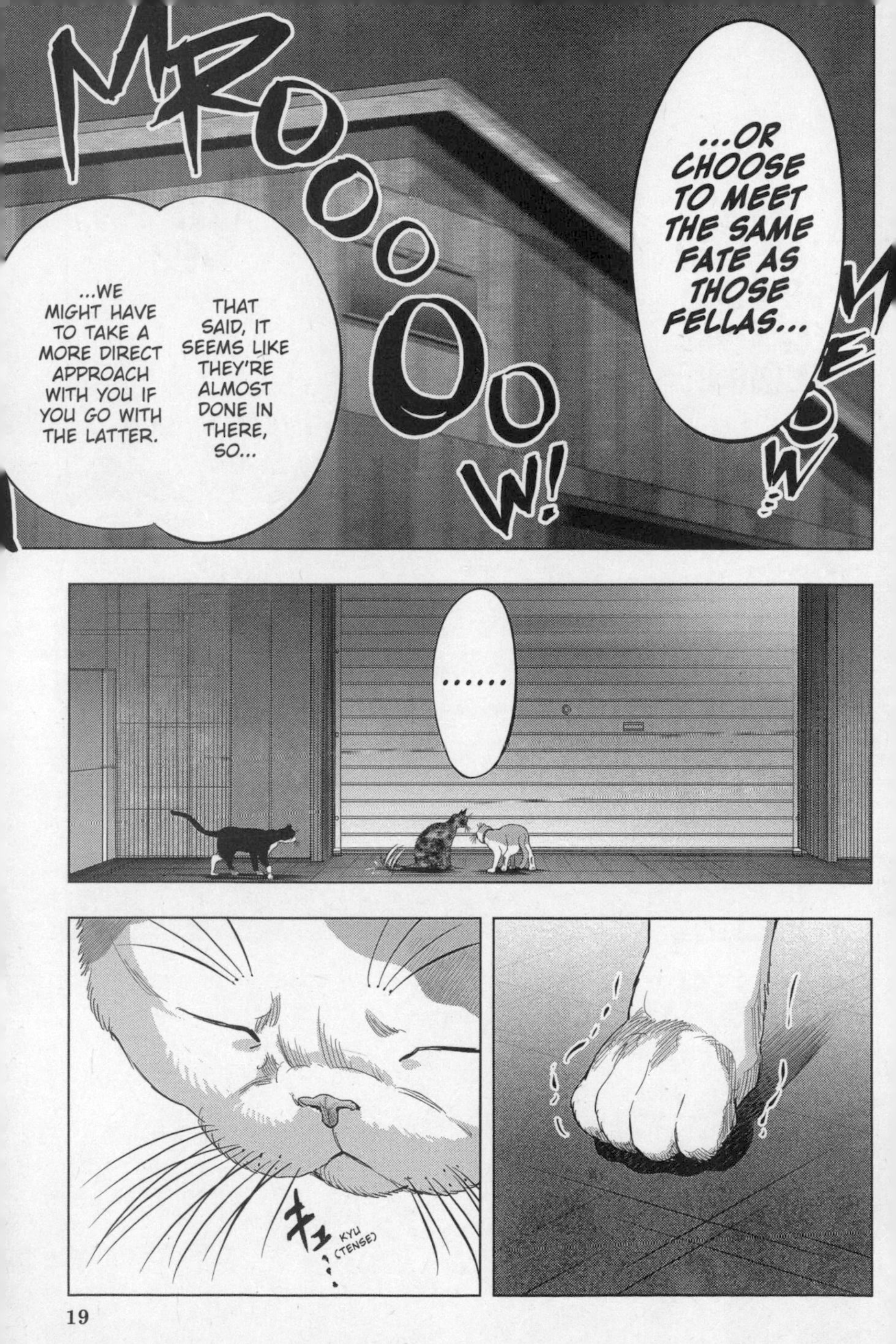
...OR CHOOSE TO MEET THE SAME FATE AS THOSE FELLAS...
MEOW...!
MROOOOOOOW!
THAT SAID, IT SEEMS LIKE THEY'RE ALMOST DONE IN THERE, SO...
...WE MIGHT HAVE TO TAKE A MORE DIRECT APPROACH WITH YOU IF YOU GO WITH THE LATTER.
......
KYU (TENSE)

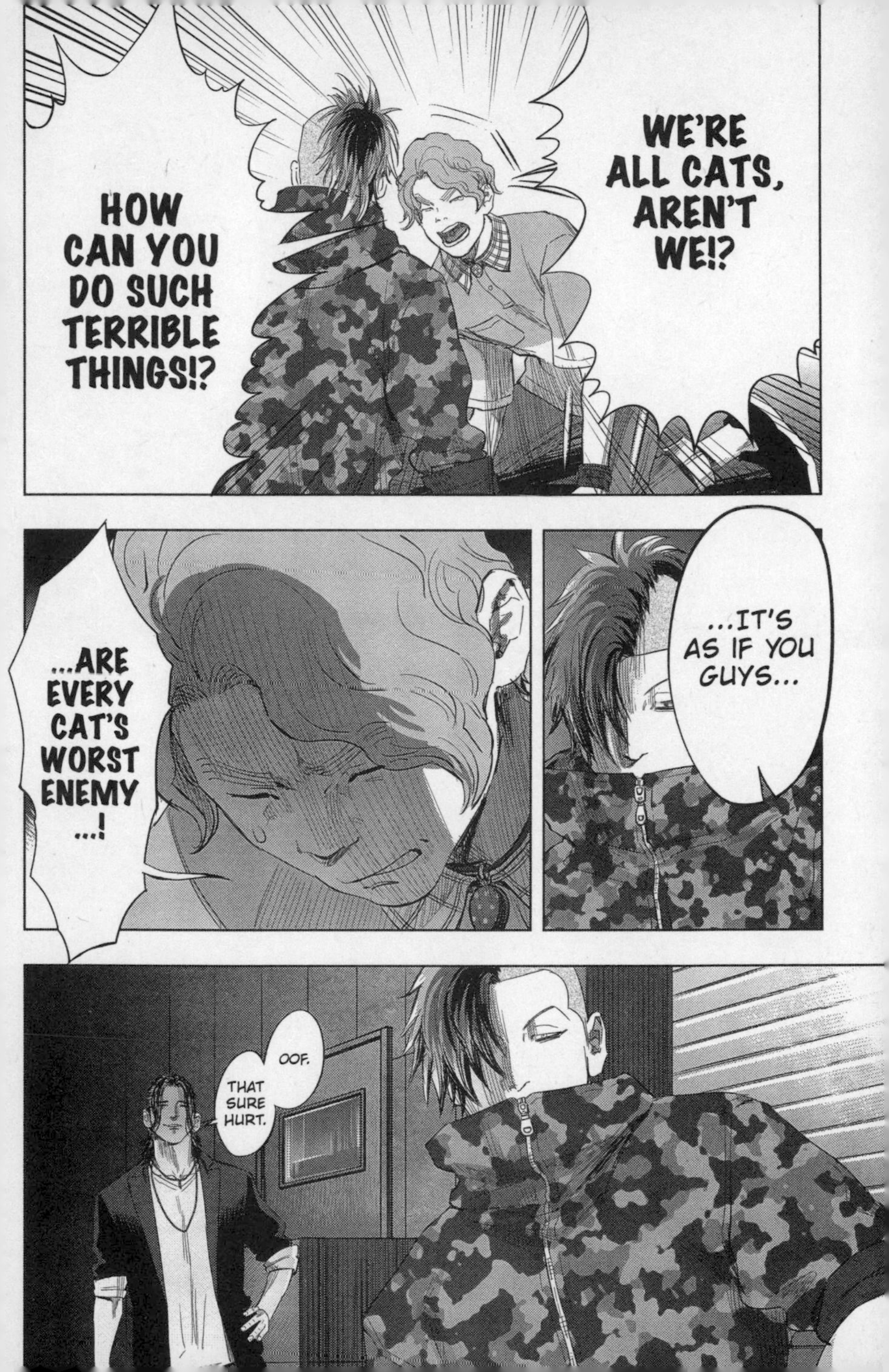
WE'RE ALL CATS, AREN'T WE!?
HOW CAN YOU DO SUCH TERRIBLE THINGS!?
...IT'S AS IF YOU GUYS...
...ARE EVERY CAT'S WORST ENEMY ...!
OOF.
THAT SURE HURT.

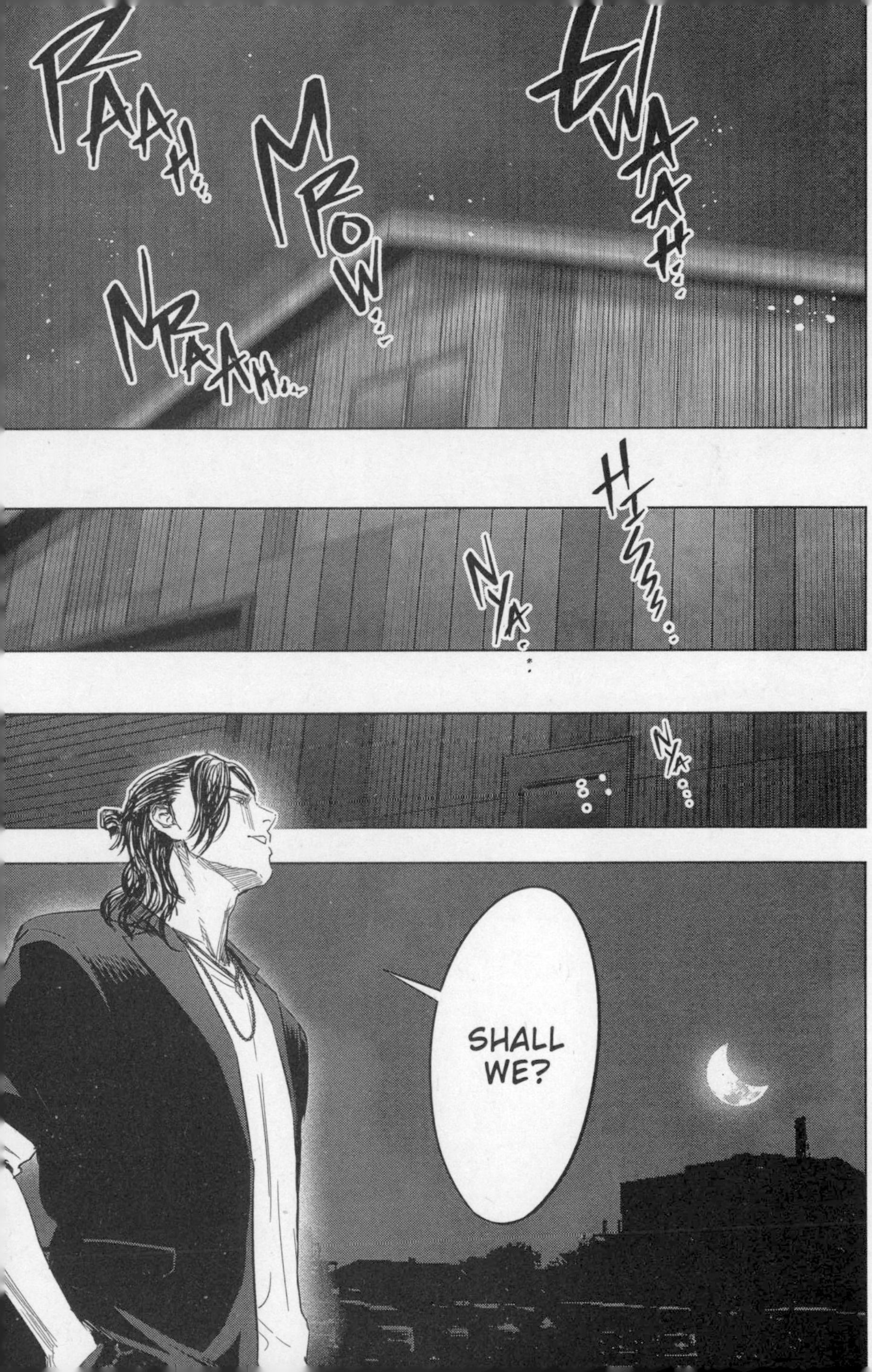
WAAAH...
MROW...
RAAH...
MRAAH...
HISSS...
NYA...
NYA...
SHALL WE?

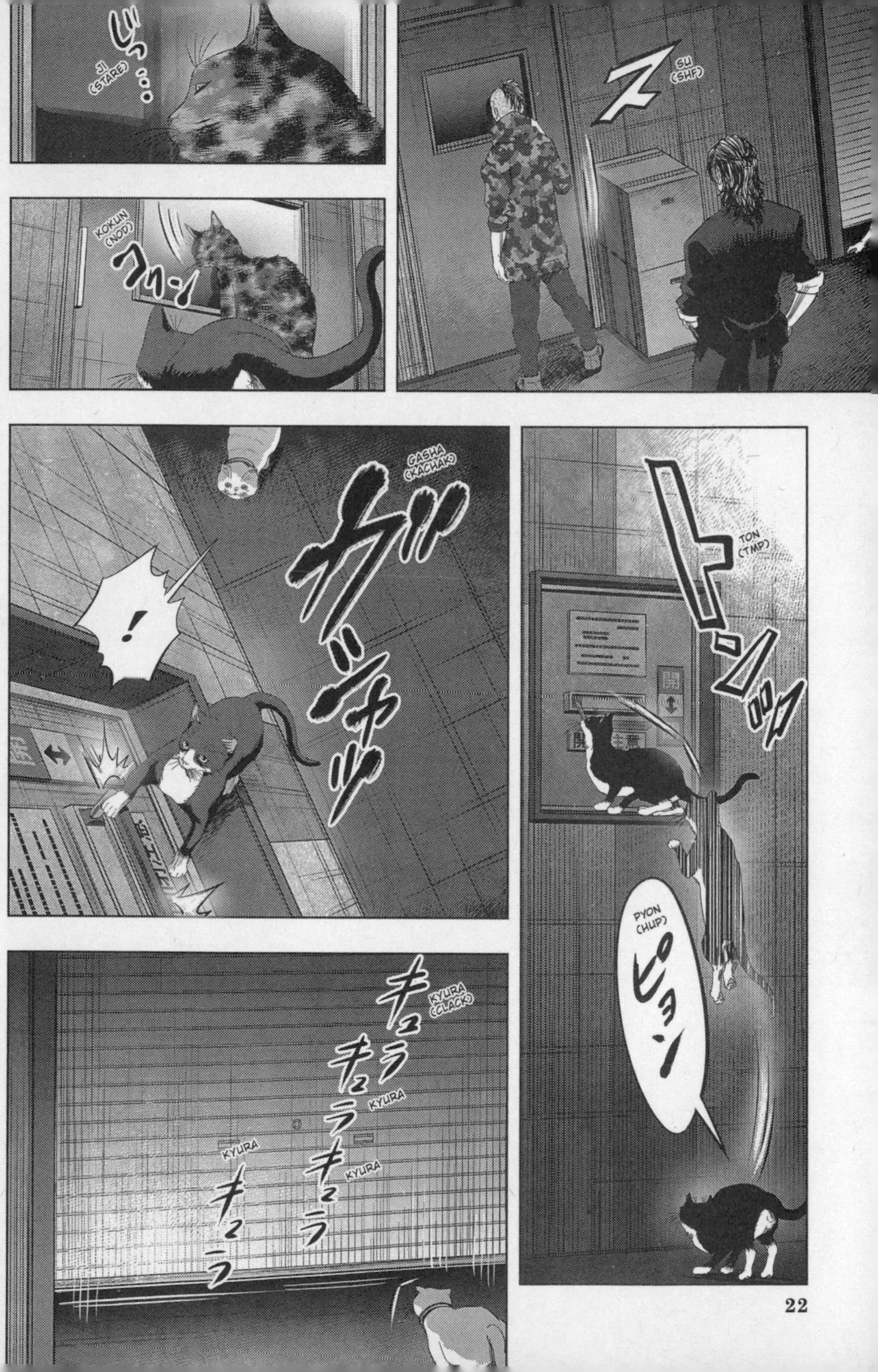
SU (SHF)
JI (STARE)
KOKUN (NOD)
TON (TMP)
PYON (HUP)
ピョン
GASHA (KACHAK)
!
KYURA (CLACK)
KYURA
KYURA
KYURA

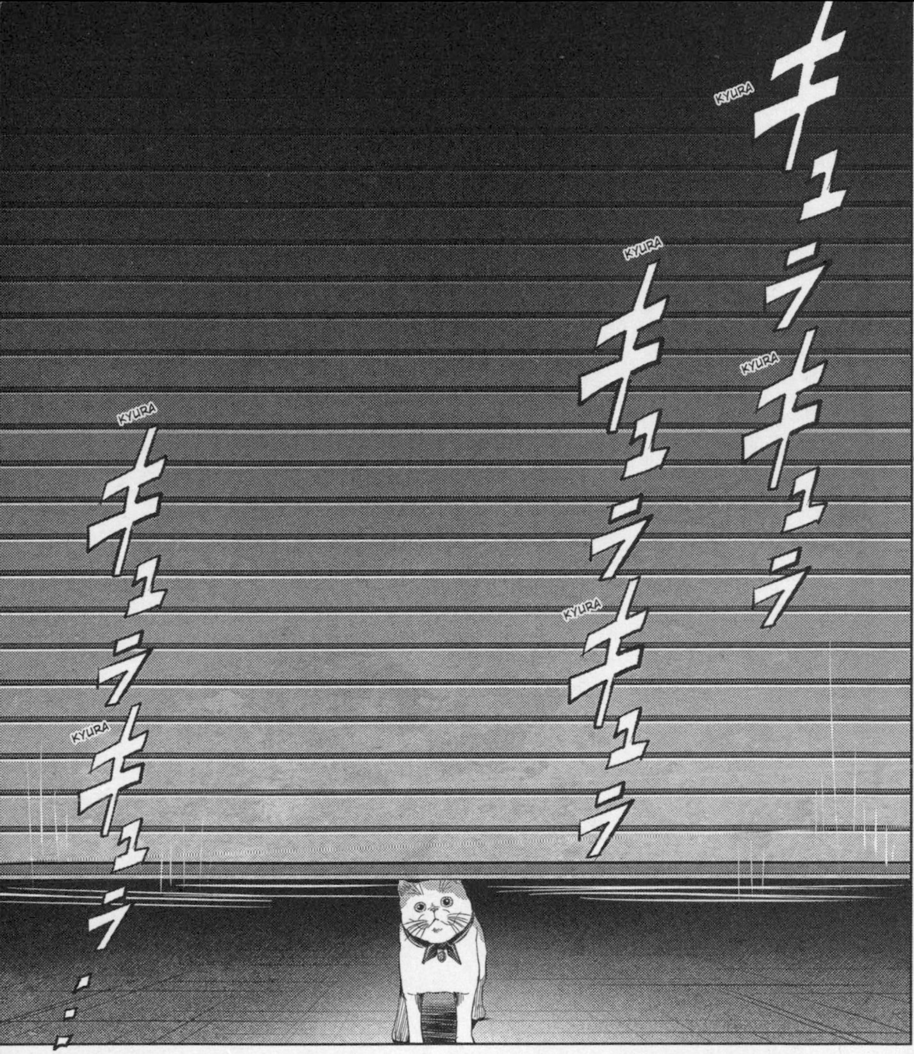
キュラ
KYURA
キュラ
KYURA
キュラ
KYURA
キュラ
KYURA
キュラ
KYURA
キュラ……
KYURA
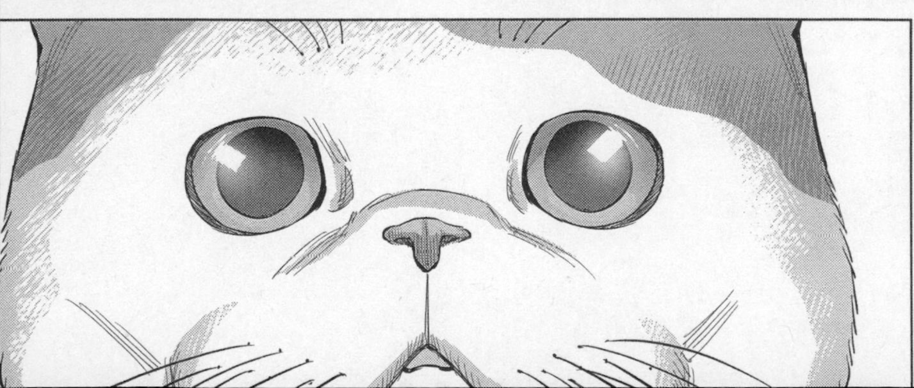

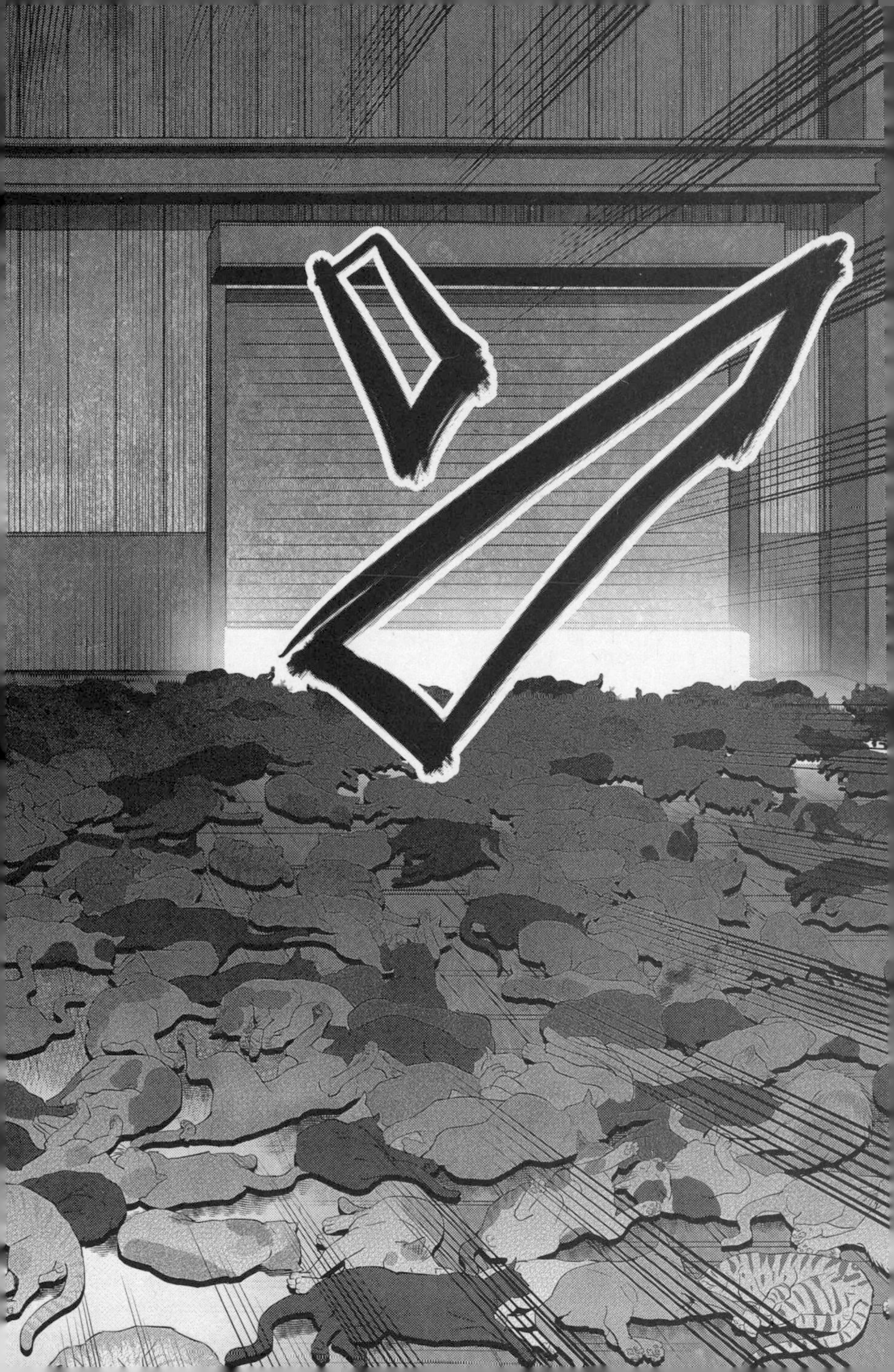
ン

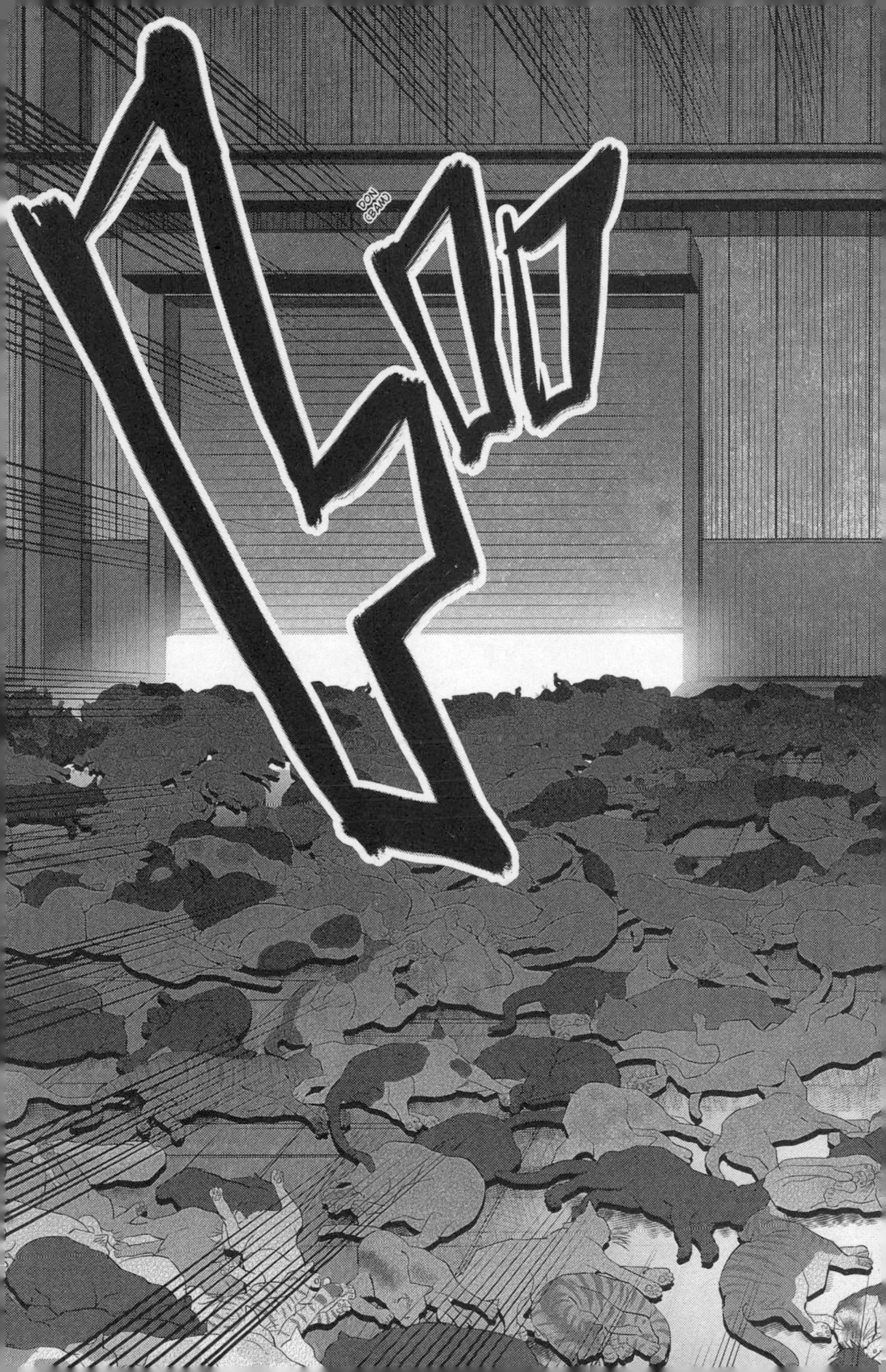
DON
(BAM)

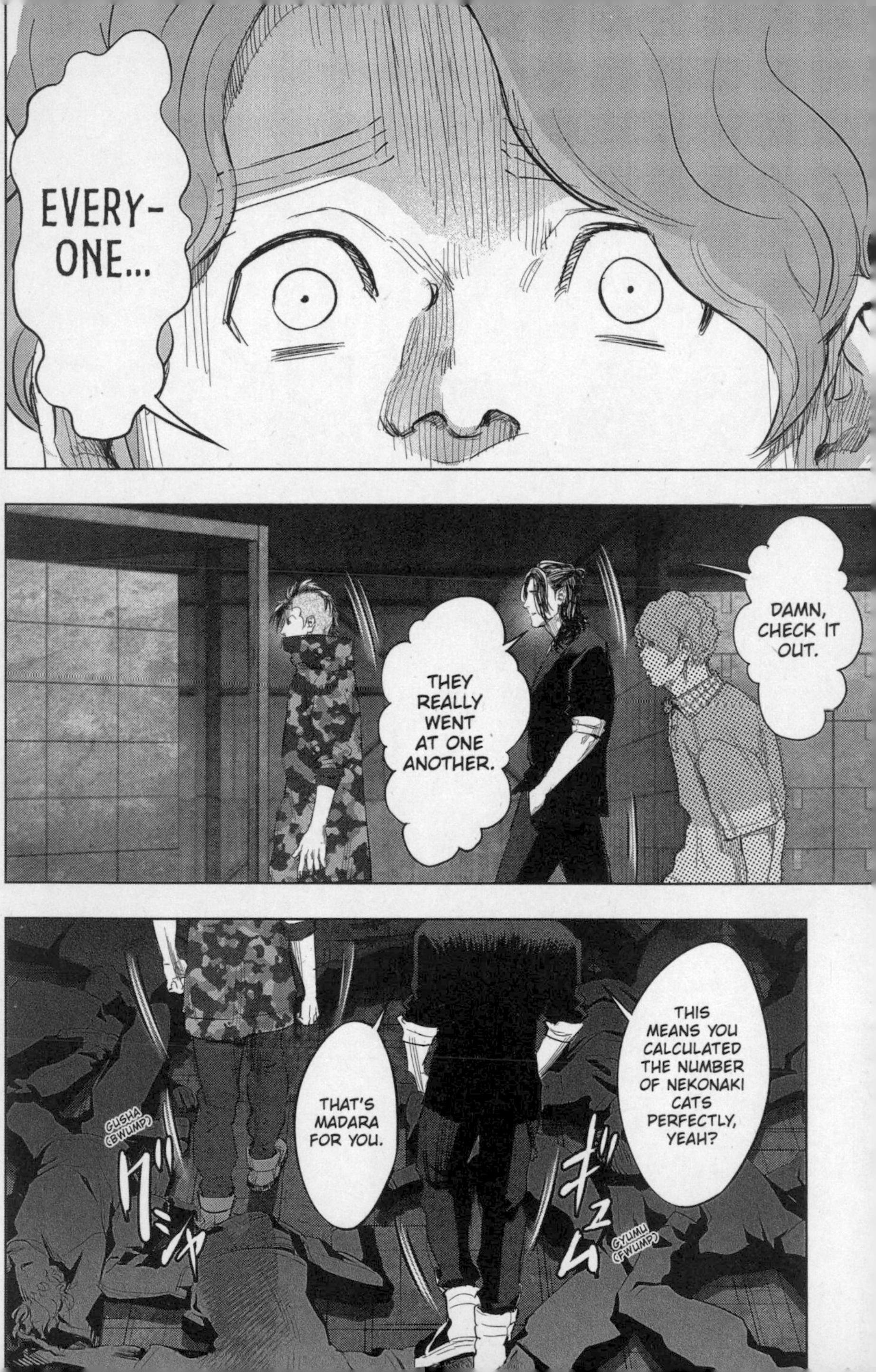
EVERY-ONE...
DAMN, CHECK IT OUT.
THEY REALLY WENT AT ONE ANOTHER.
THIS MEANS YOU CALCULATED THE NUMBER OF NEKONAKI CATS PERFECTLY, YEAH?
GYUMU (FWUMP)
THAT'S MADARA FOR YOU.
GUSHA (BWUMP)

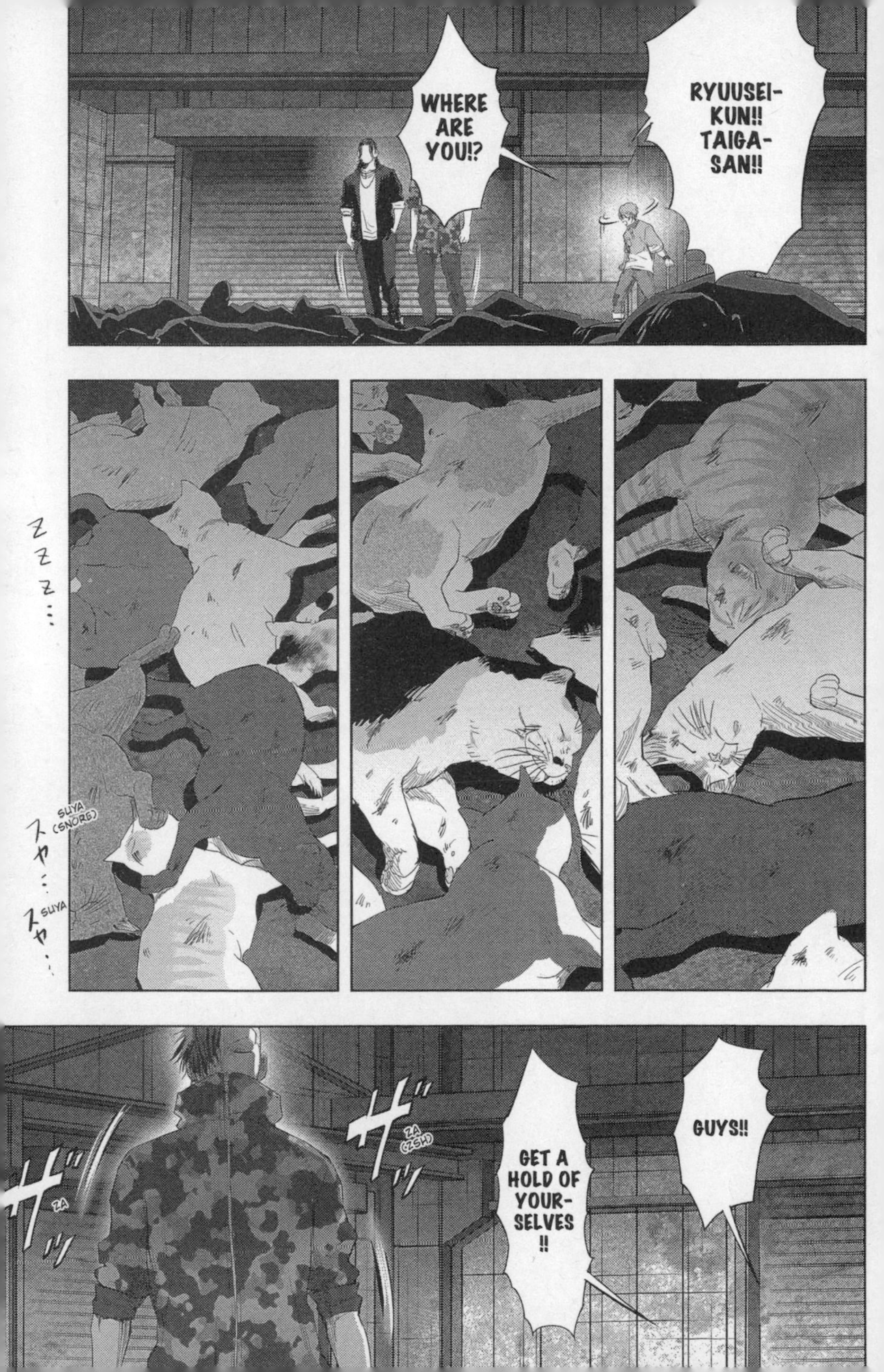RYUUSEI-KUN!! TAIGA-SAN!!
WHERE ARE YOU!?
Z Z Z...
SUYA (SNORE)
スヤ…
SUYA
スヤ…
GUYS!!
GET A HOLD OF YOURSELVES!!
ZA (ZSH)
ザッ
ZA
ザッ

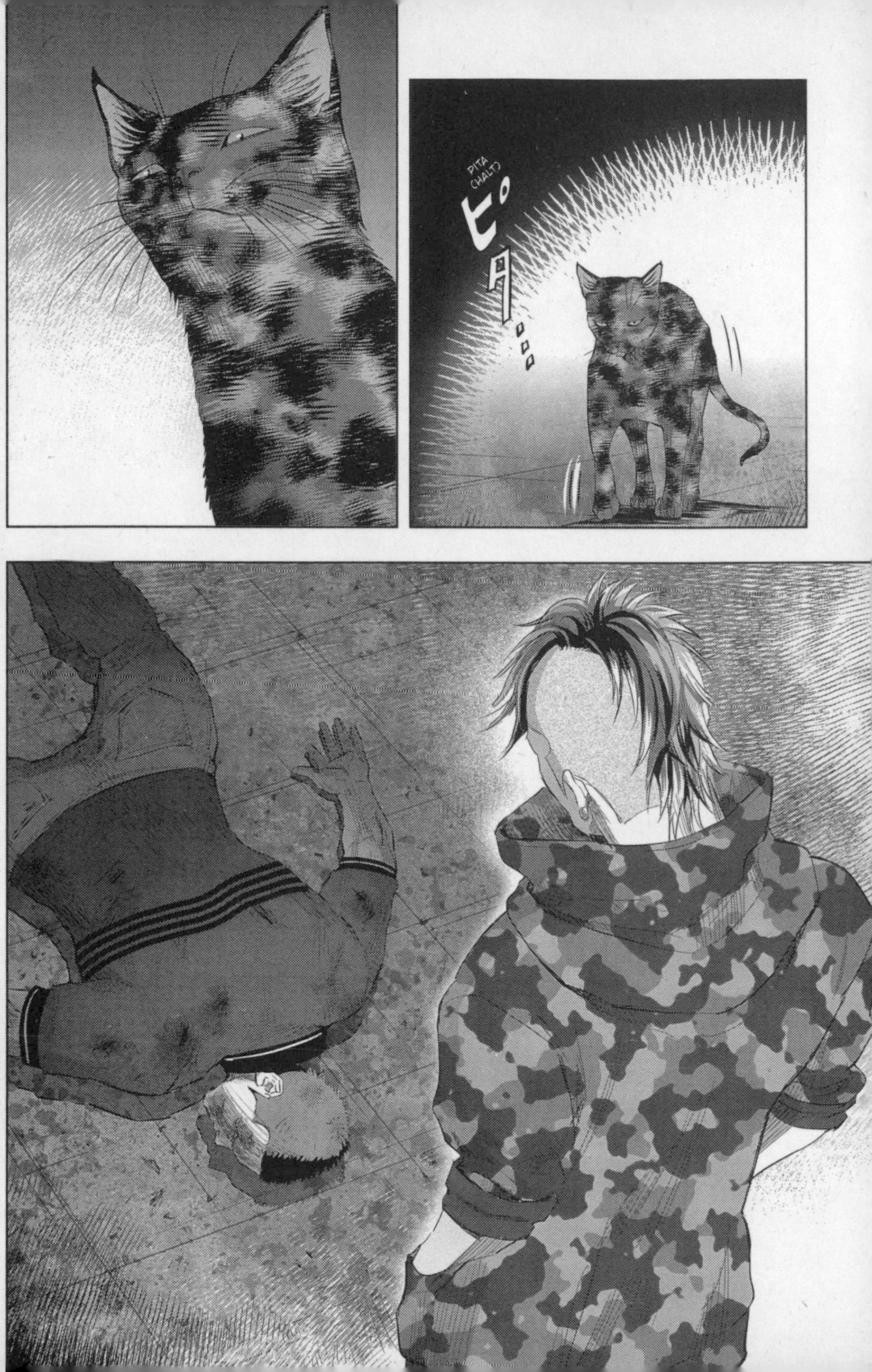
ピタ…
PITA (HALT)

RYUUSEI-KUN!!

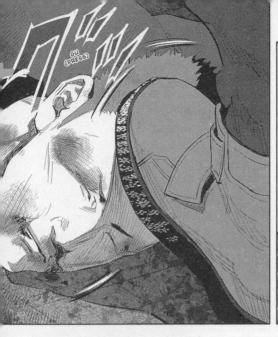

GU
(PRESS)

SEEMS YOU'RE STILL CONSCIOUS.

...

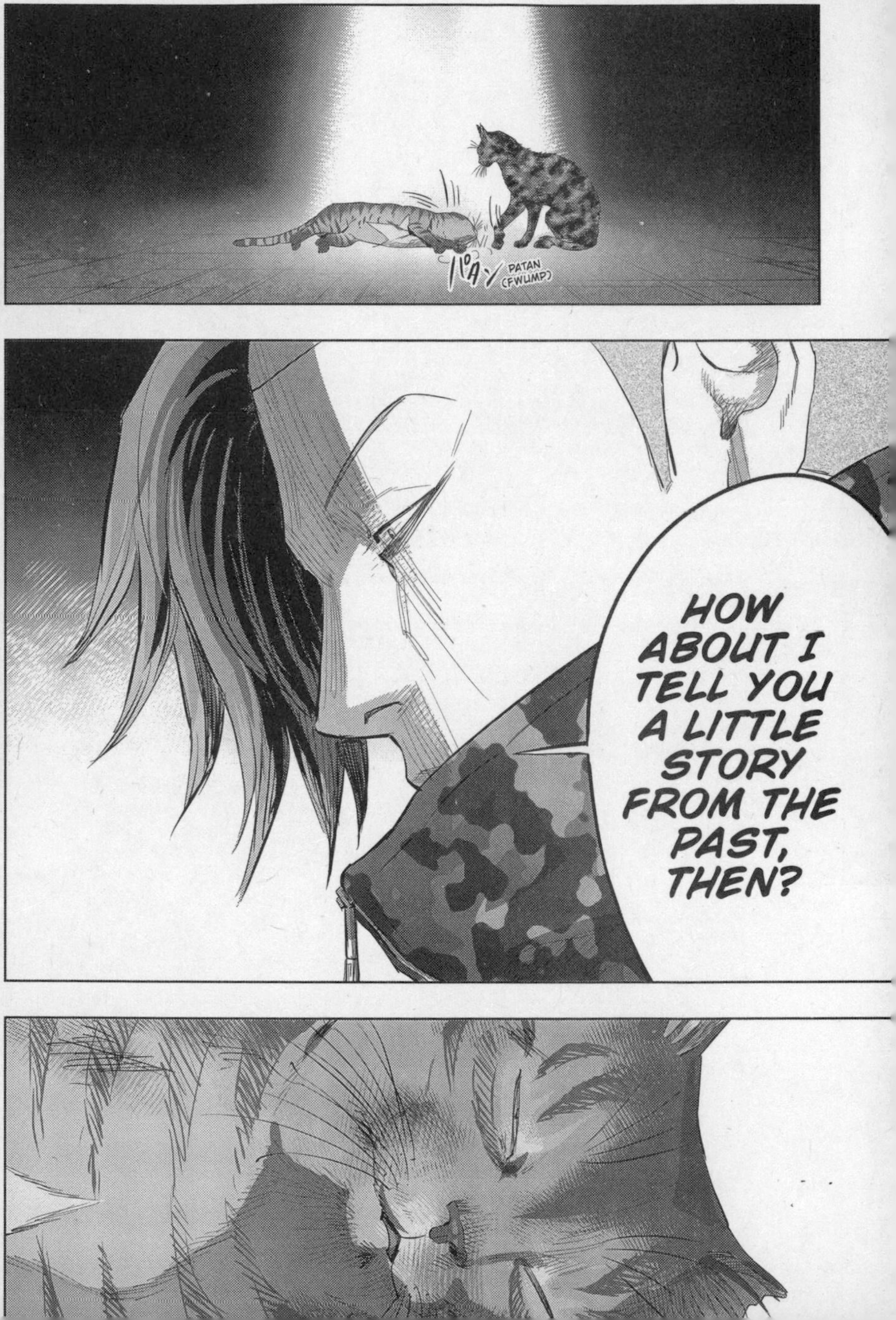
パタン
PATAN (FWUMP)
HOW ABOUT I TELL YOU A LITTLE STORY FROM THE PAST, THEN?

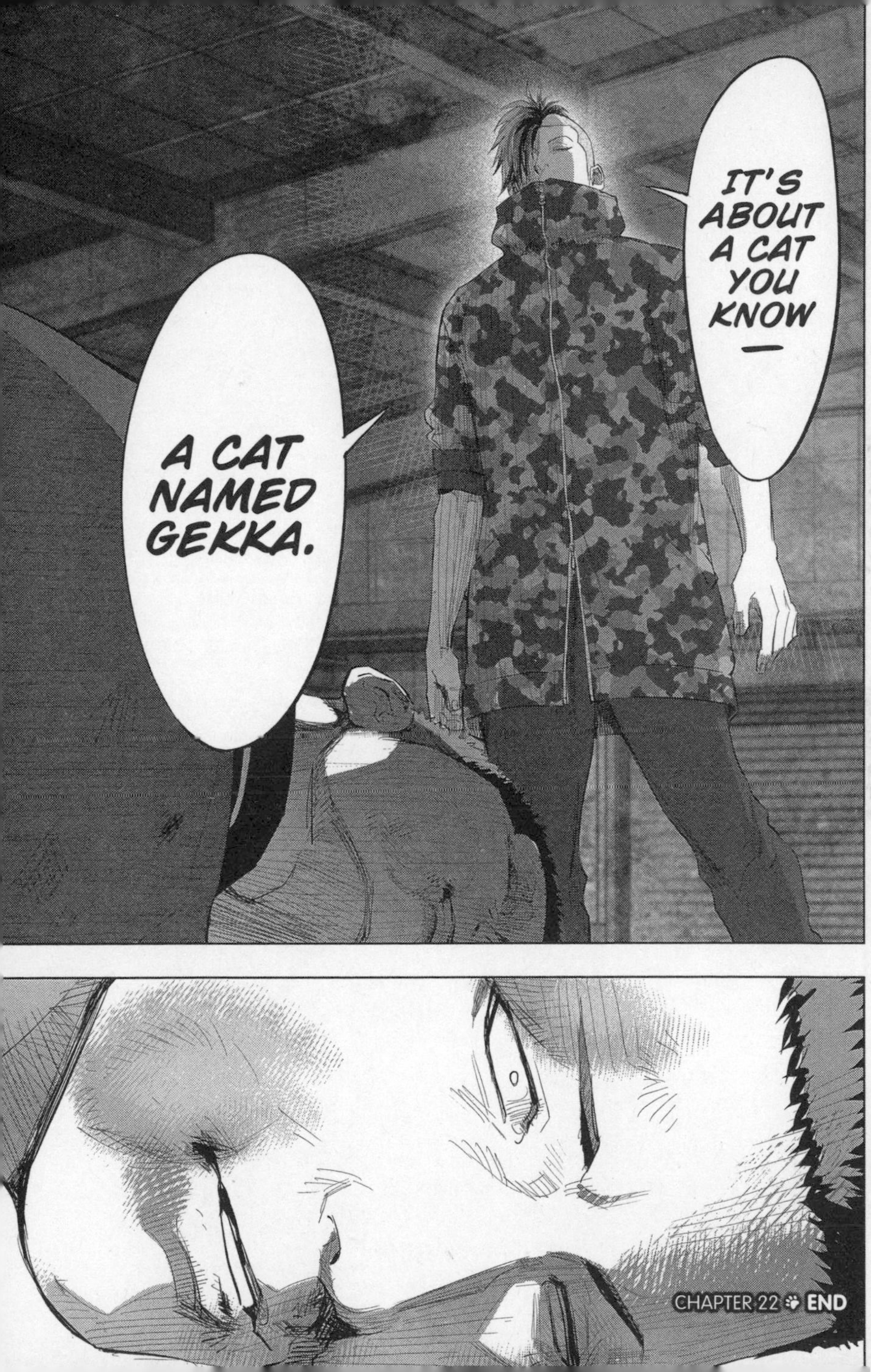
IT'S ABOUT A CAT YOU KNOW —
A CAT NAMED GEKKA.
CHAPTER 22 END

RYUUSEI

MOCCHI

NYANKEES

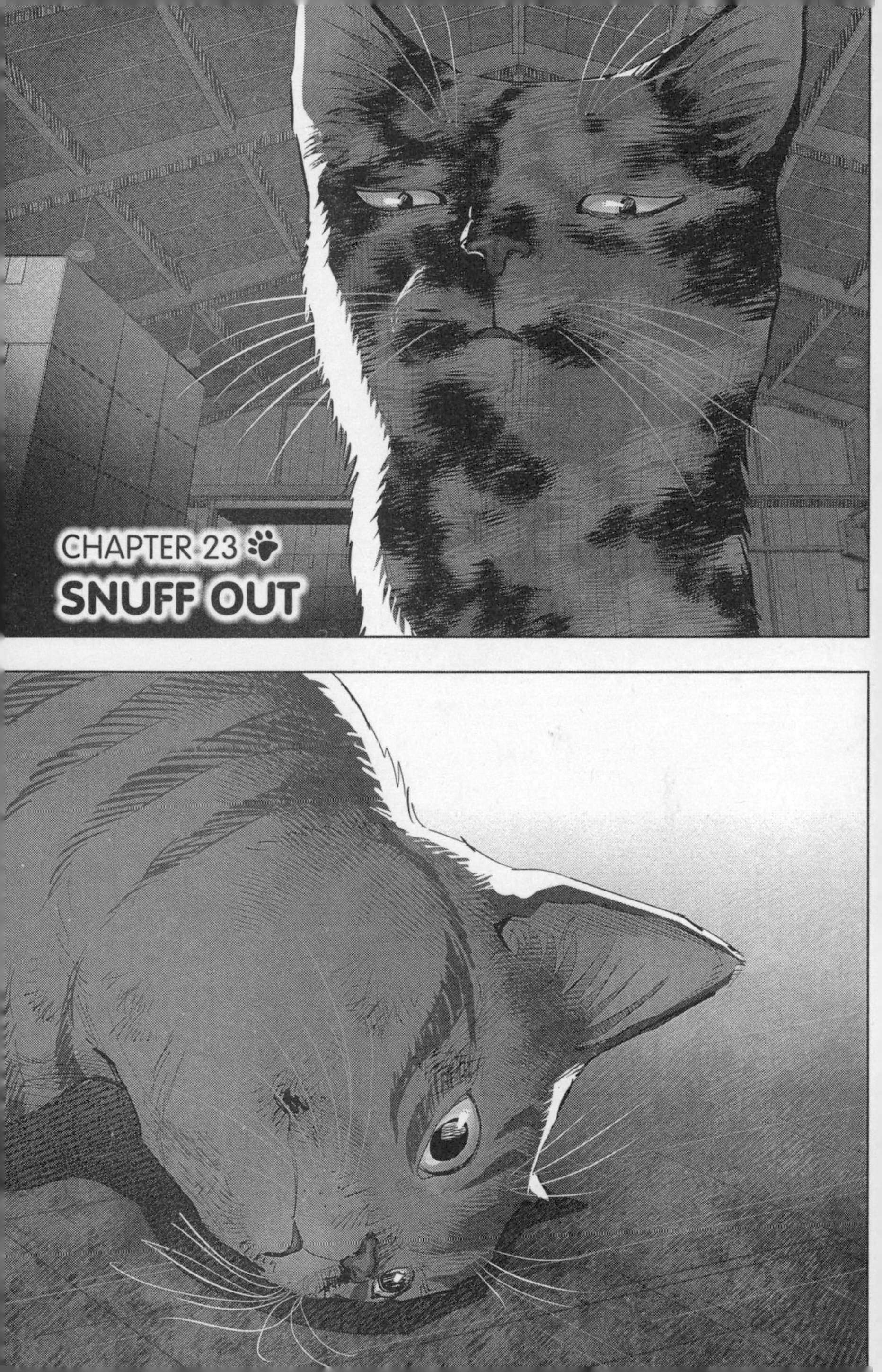
CHAPTER 23
SNUFF OUT

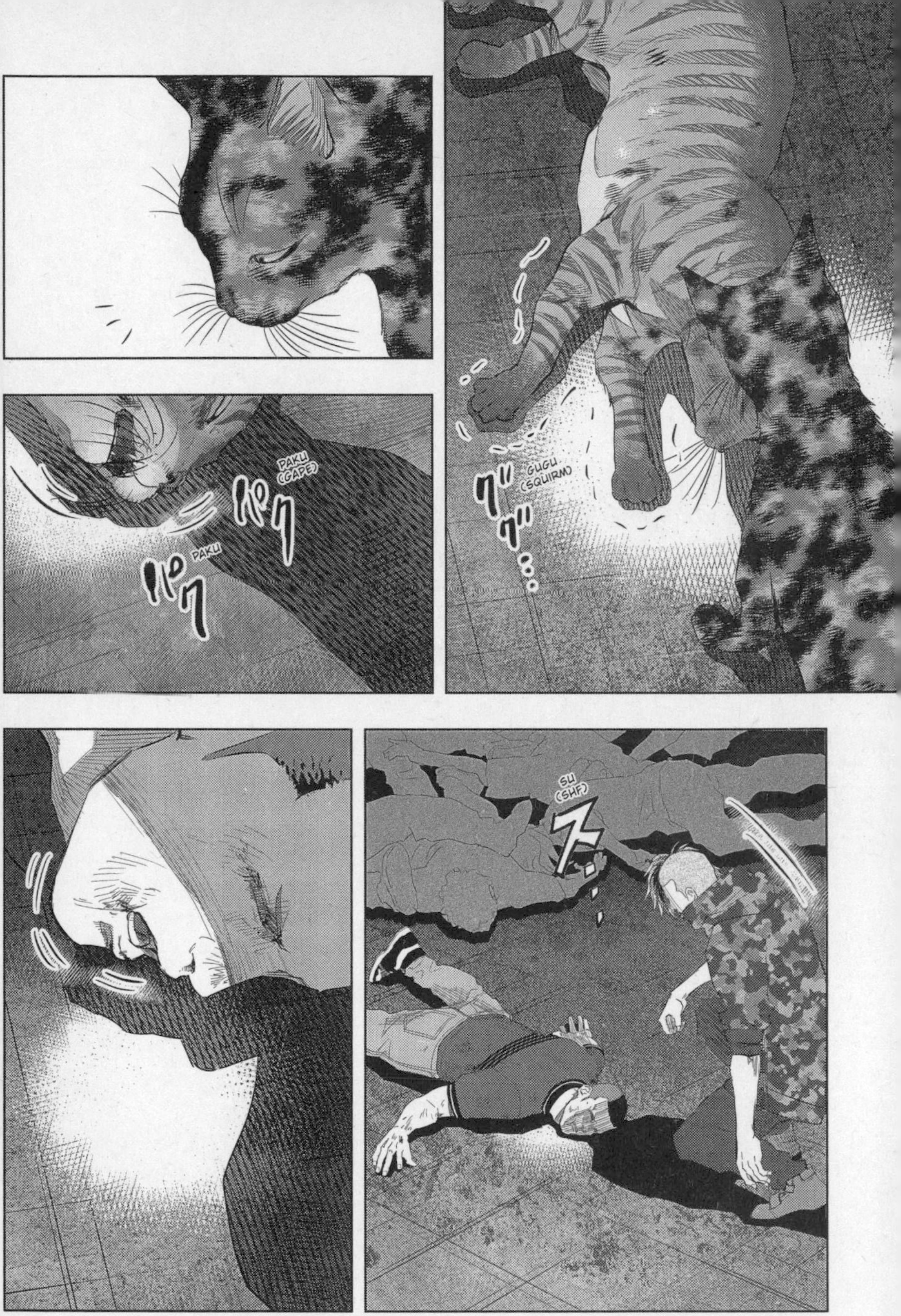
GUGU (SQUIRM)
PAKU (GAPE)
PAKU
SU (SHF)

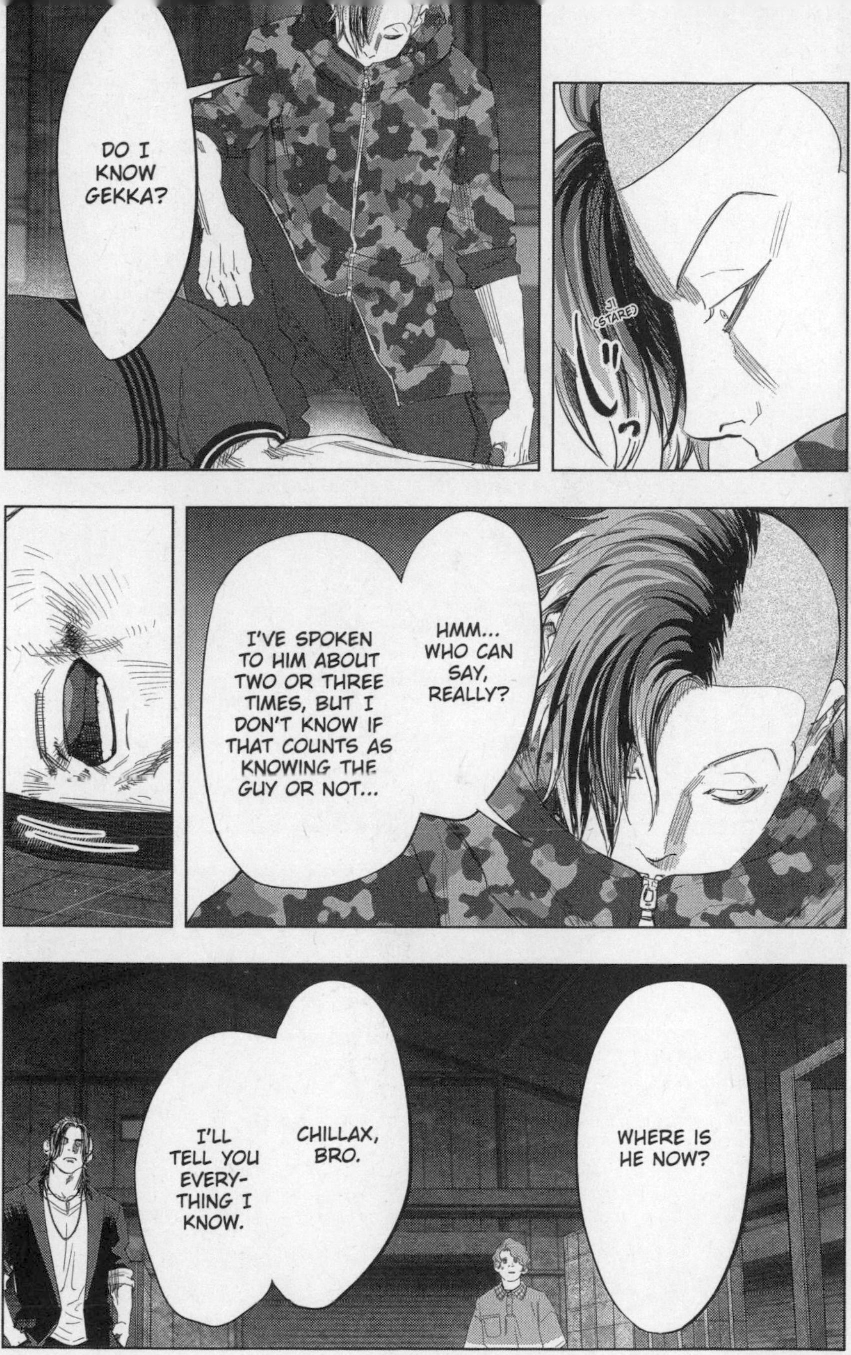
JI (STARE)
DO I KNOW GEKKA?
HMM... WHO CAN SAY, REALLY?
I'VE SPOKEN TO HIM ABOUT TWO OR THREE TIMES, BUT I DON'T KNOW IF THAT COUNTS AS KNOWING THE GUY OR NOT...
WHERE IS HE NOW?
CHILLAX, BRO.
I'LL TELL YOU EVERY-THING I KNOW.

IT WAS IN KEDAMA TOWN WHERE YOU FIRST MET GEKKA AND BEFRIENDED HIM.

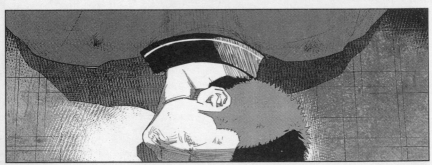

YOU WERE TIGHT WITH THE OTHER LOCAL CATS AND ENJOYED SOME PEACEFUL TIMES...

...BUT AT SOME POINT, GEKKA BEGAN REJECTING YOU.

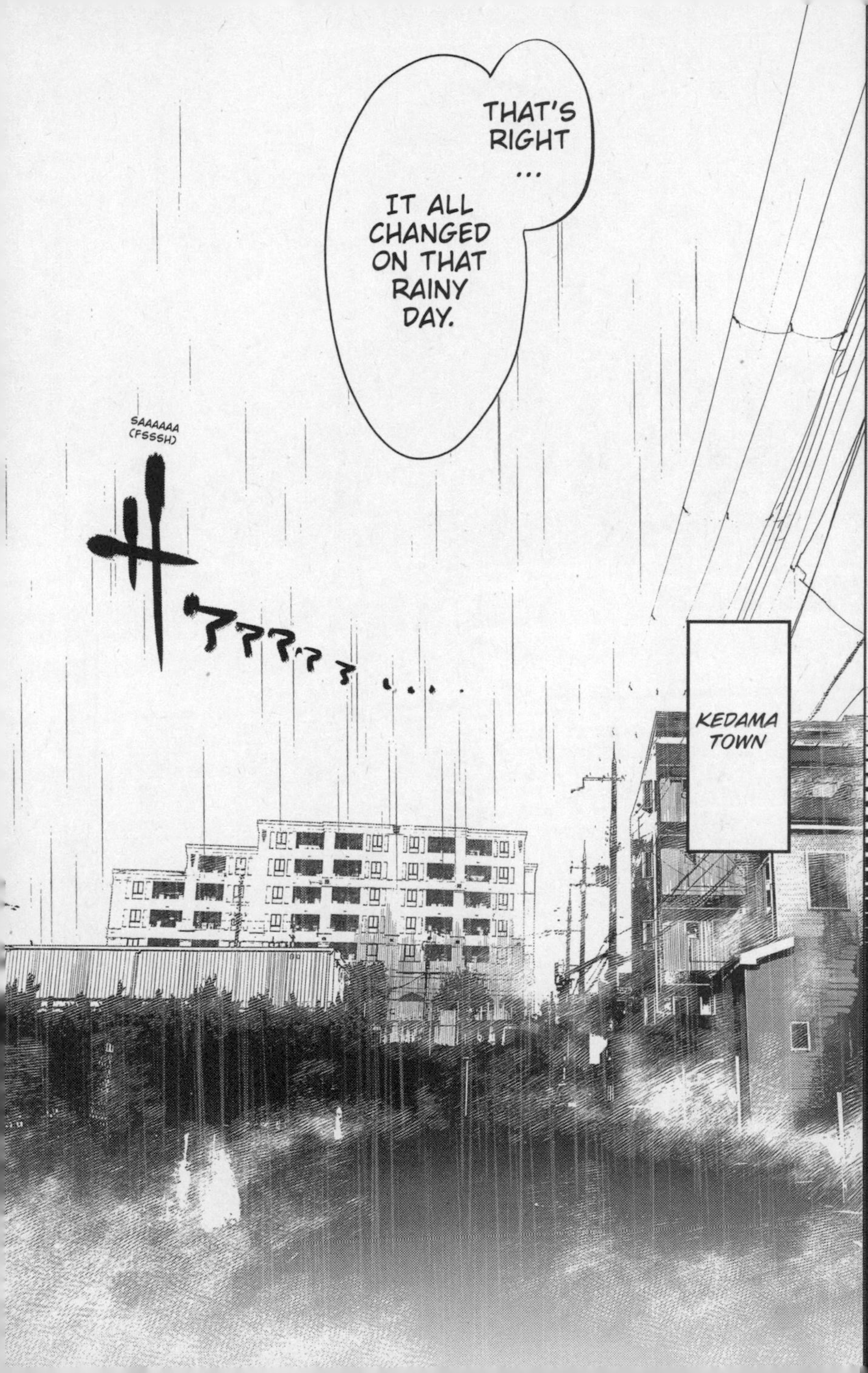
THAT'S RIGHT ...
IT ALL CHANGED ON THAT RAINY DAY.
KEDAMA TOWN
SAAAAAA (FSSSH)

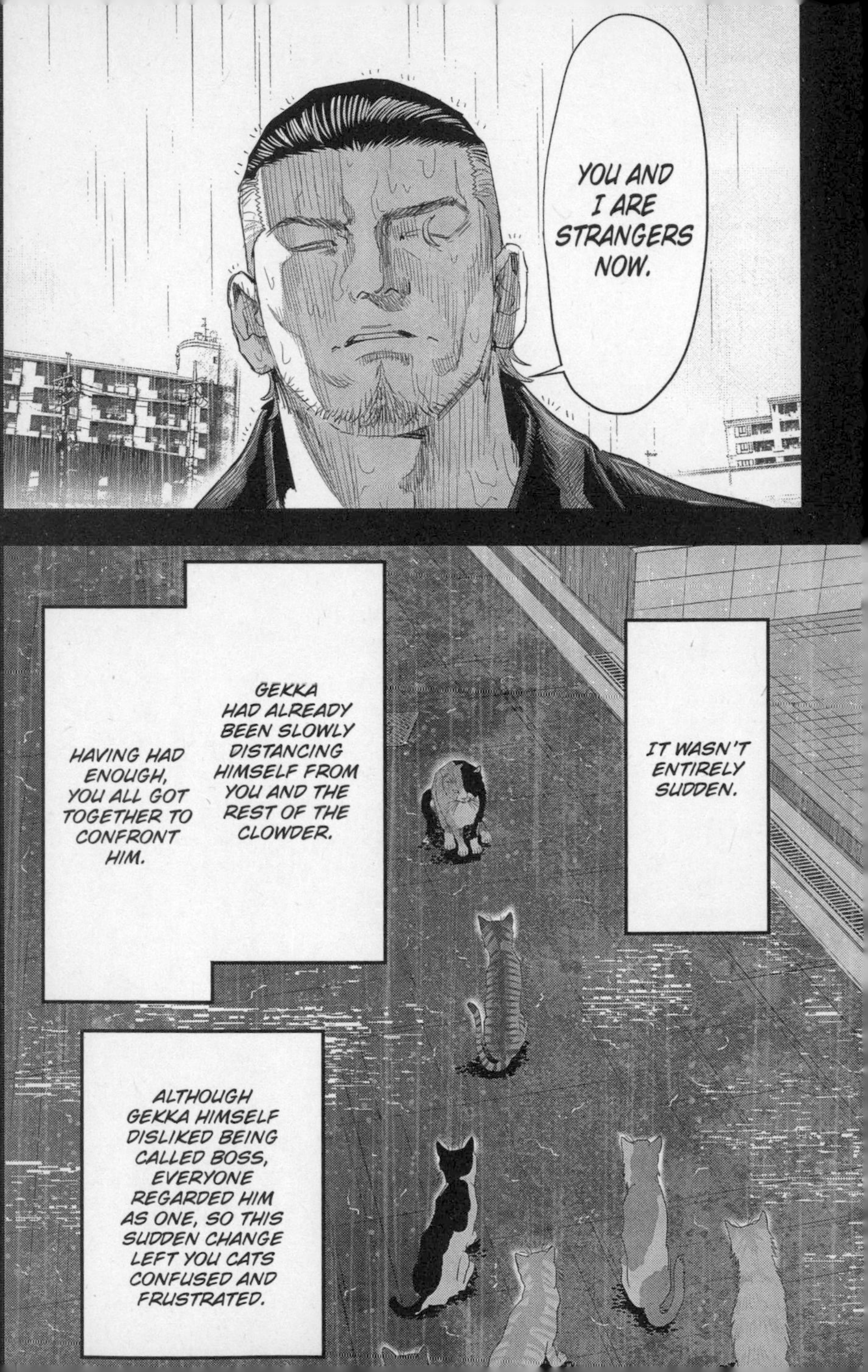
YOU AND I ARE STRANGERS NOW.
IT WASN'T ENTIRELY SUDDEN.
GEKKA HAD ALREADY BEEN SLOWLY DISTANCING HIMSELF FROM YOU AND THE REST OF THE CLOWDER.
HAVING HAD ENOUGH, YOU ALL GOT TOGETHER TO CONFRONT HIM.
ALTHOUGH GEKKA HIMSELF DISLIKED BEING CALLED BOSS, EVERYONE REGARDED HIM AS ONE, SO THIS SUDDEN CHANGE LEFT YOU CATS CONFUSED AND FRUSTRATED.

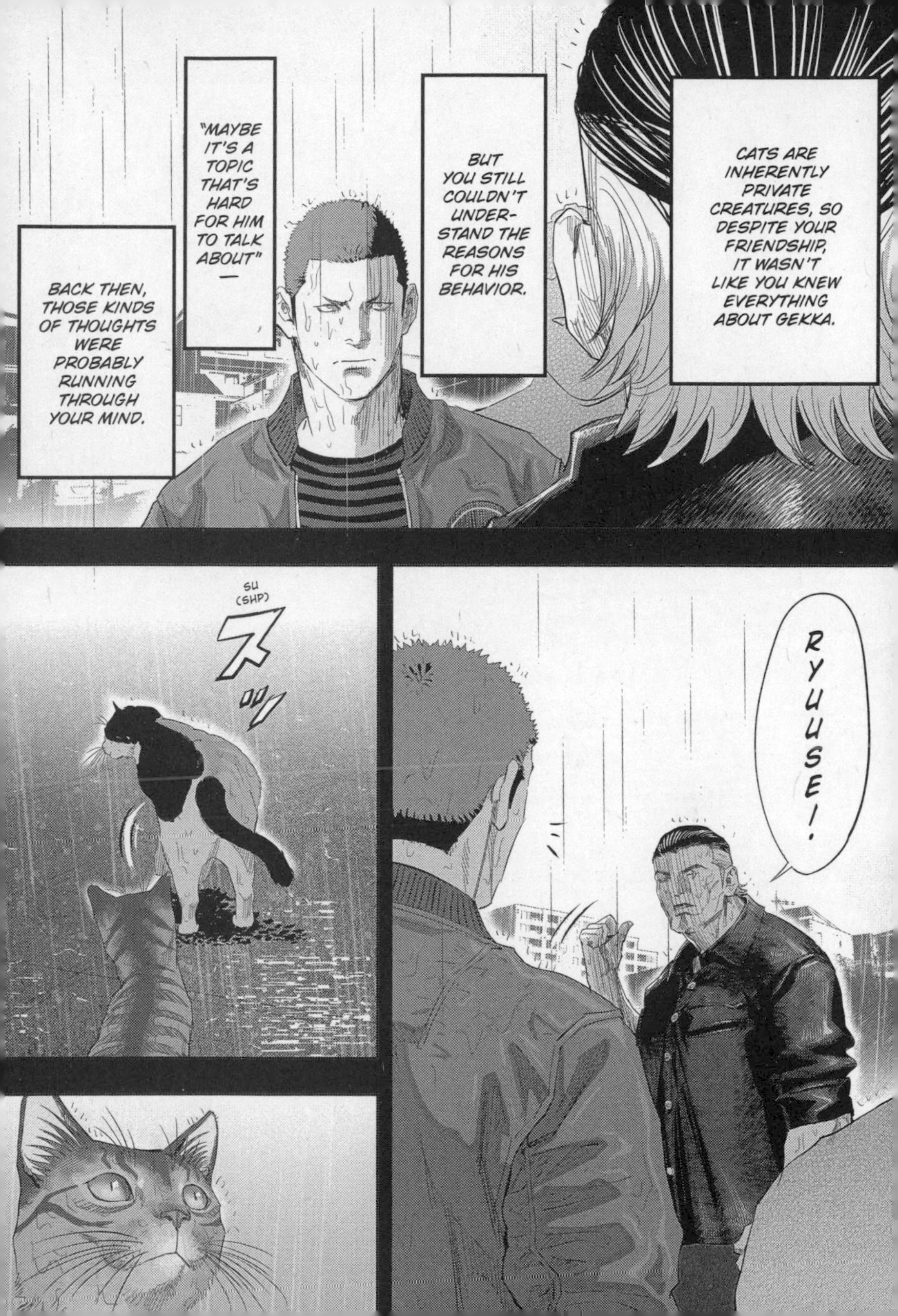
CATS ARE INHERENTLY PRIVATE CREATURES, SO DESPITE YOUR FRIENDSHIP, IT WASN'T LIKE YOU KNEW EVERYTHING ABOUT GEKKA.
BUT YOU STILL COULDN'T UNDER-STAND THE REASONS FOR HIS BEHAVIOR.
"MAYBE IT'S A TOPIC THAT'S HARD FOR HIM TO TALK ABOUT"—
BACK THEN, THOSE KINDS OF THOUGHTS WERE PROBABLY RUNNING THROUGH YOUR MIND.
RYUUSE!
SU (SHP)
ス

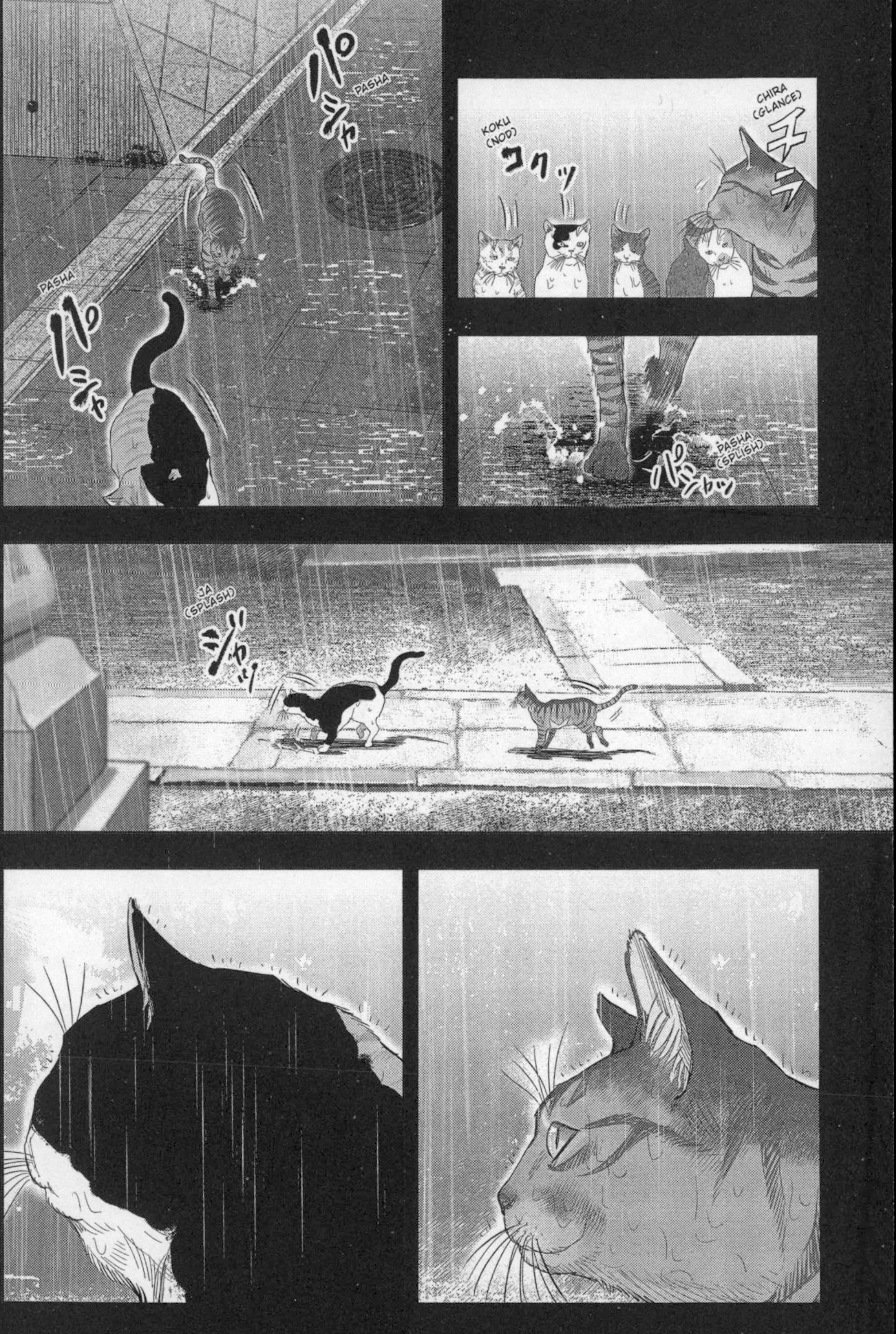
CHIRA (GLANCE)
KOKU (NOD)
PASHA (SPLISH)
PASHA
PASHA
JA (SPLASH)

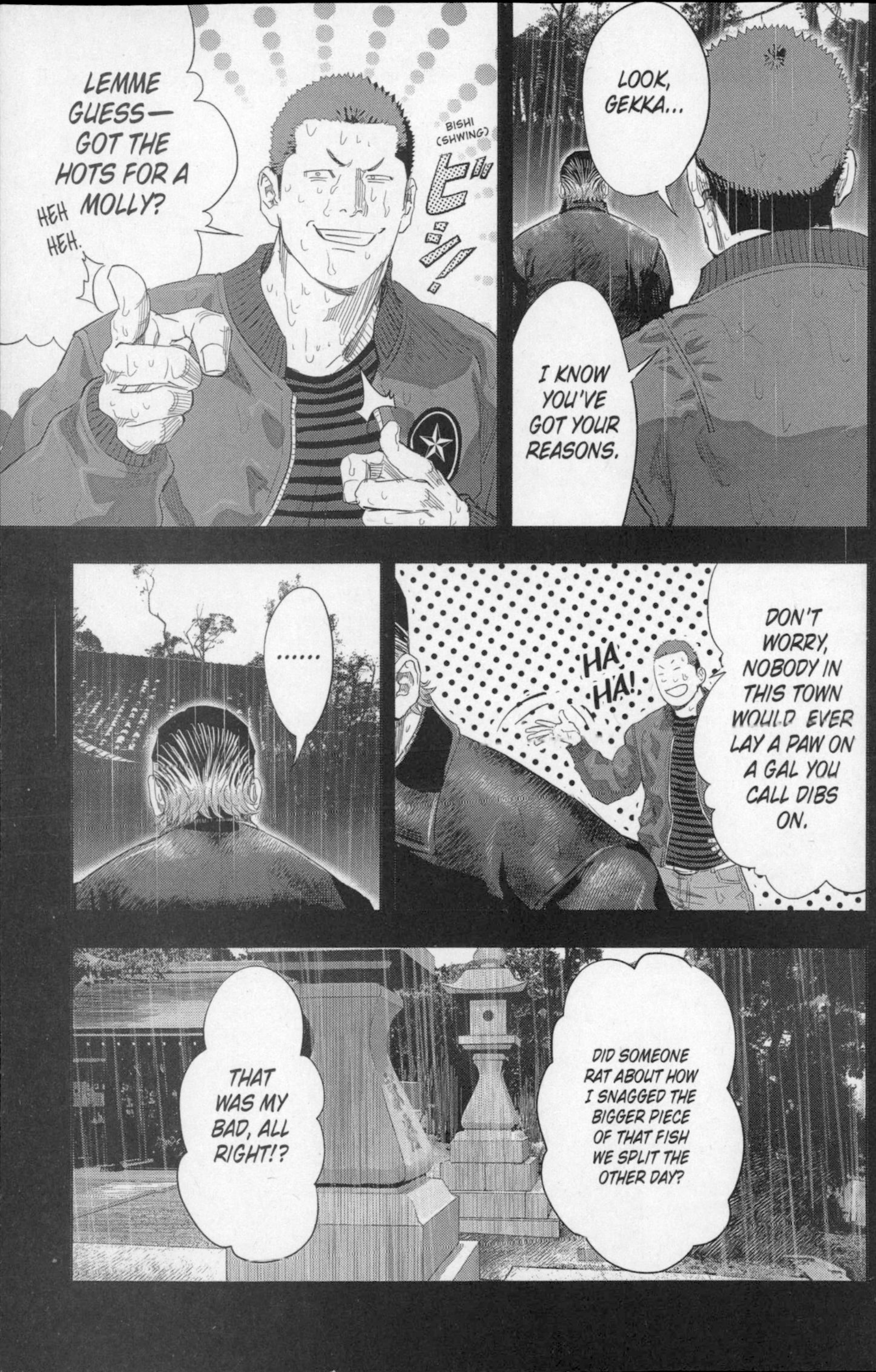
LOOK, GEKKA...
I KNOW YOU'VE GOT YOUR REASONS.
LEMME GUESS— GOT THE HOTS FOR A MOLLY?
BISHI (SHWING)
HEH HEH.
DON'T WORRY, NOBODY IN THIS TOWN WOULD EVER LAY A PAW ON A GAL YOU CALL DIBS ON.
HA HA!
......
DID SOMEONE RAT ABOUT HOW I SNAGGED THE BIGGER PIECE OF THAT FISH WE SPLIT THE OTHER DAY?
THAT WAS MY BAD, ALL RIGHT!?

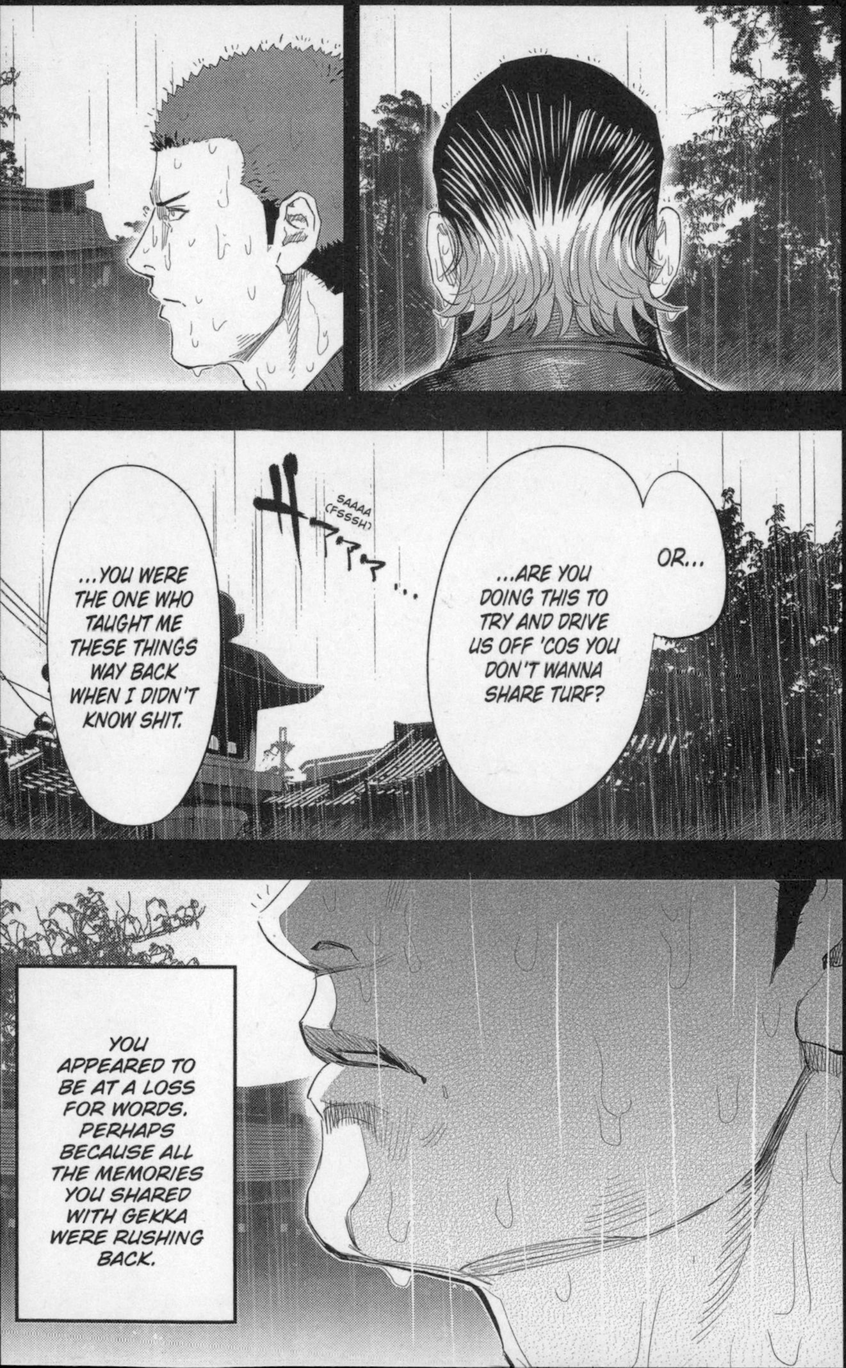
OR... ...ARE YOU DOING THIS TO TRY AND DRIVE US OFF 'COS YOU DON'T WANNA SHARE TURF?
SAAAA (FSSSH)
...YOU WERE THE ONE WHO TAUGHT ME THESE THINGS WAY BACK WHEN I DIDN'T KNOW SHIT.
YOU APPEARED TO BE AT A LOSS FOR WORDS. PERHAPS BECAUSE ALL THE MEMORIES YOU SHARED WITH GEKKA WERE RUSHING BACK.

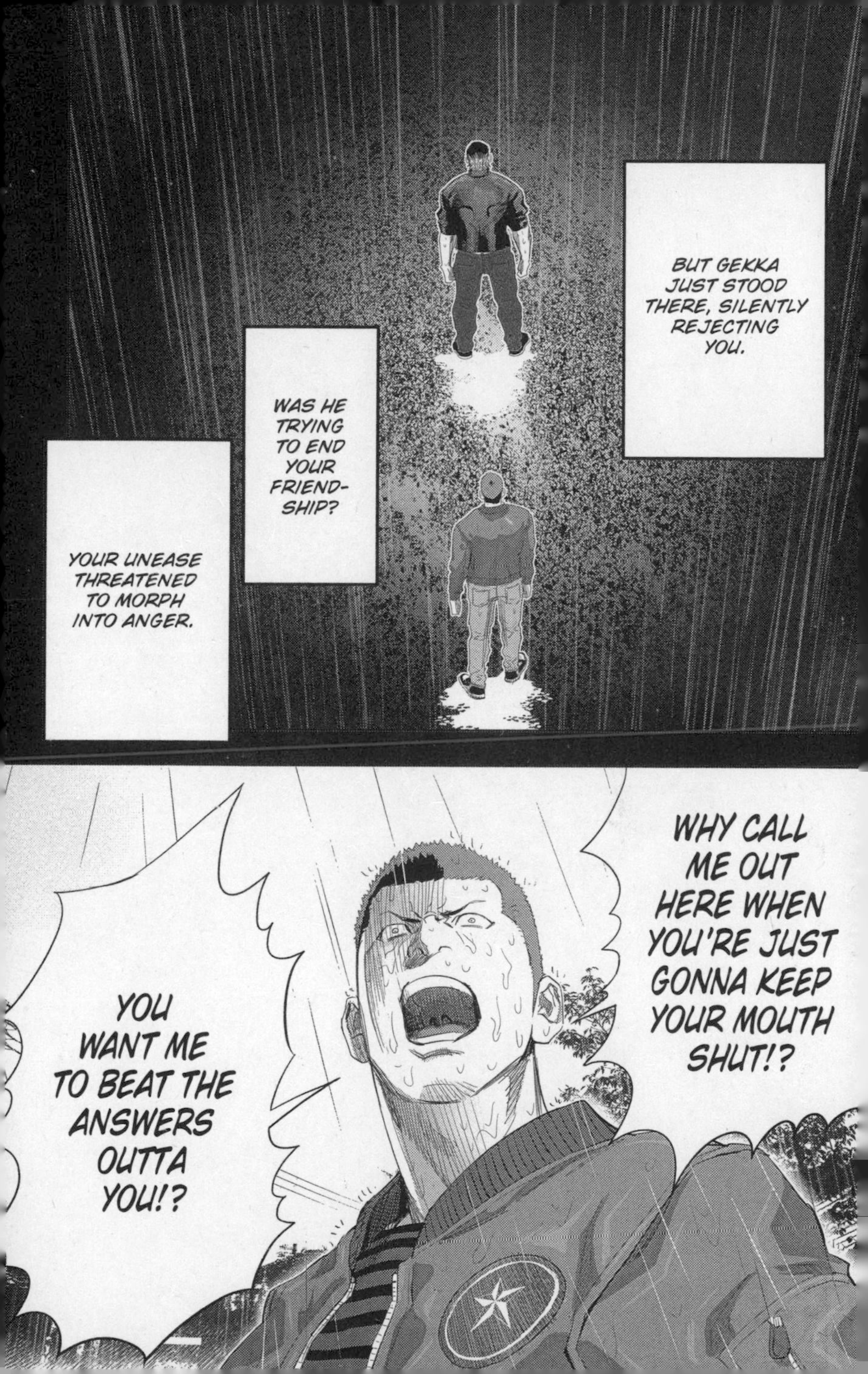
BUT GEKKA JUST STOOD THERE, SILENTLY REJECTING YOU.
WAS HE TRYING TO END YOUR FRIEND-SHIP?
YOUR UNEASE THREATENED TO MORPH INTO ANGER.
WHY CALL ME OUT HERE WHEN YOU'RE JUST GONNA KEEP YOUR MOUTH SHUT!?
YOU WANT ME TO BEAT THE ANSWERS OUTTA YOU!?

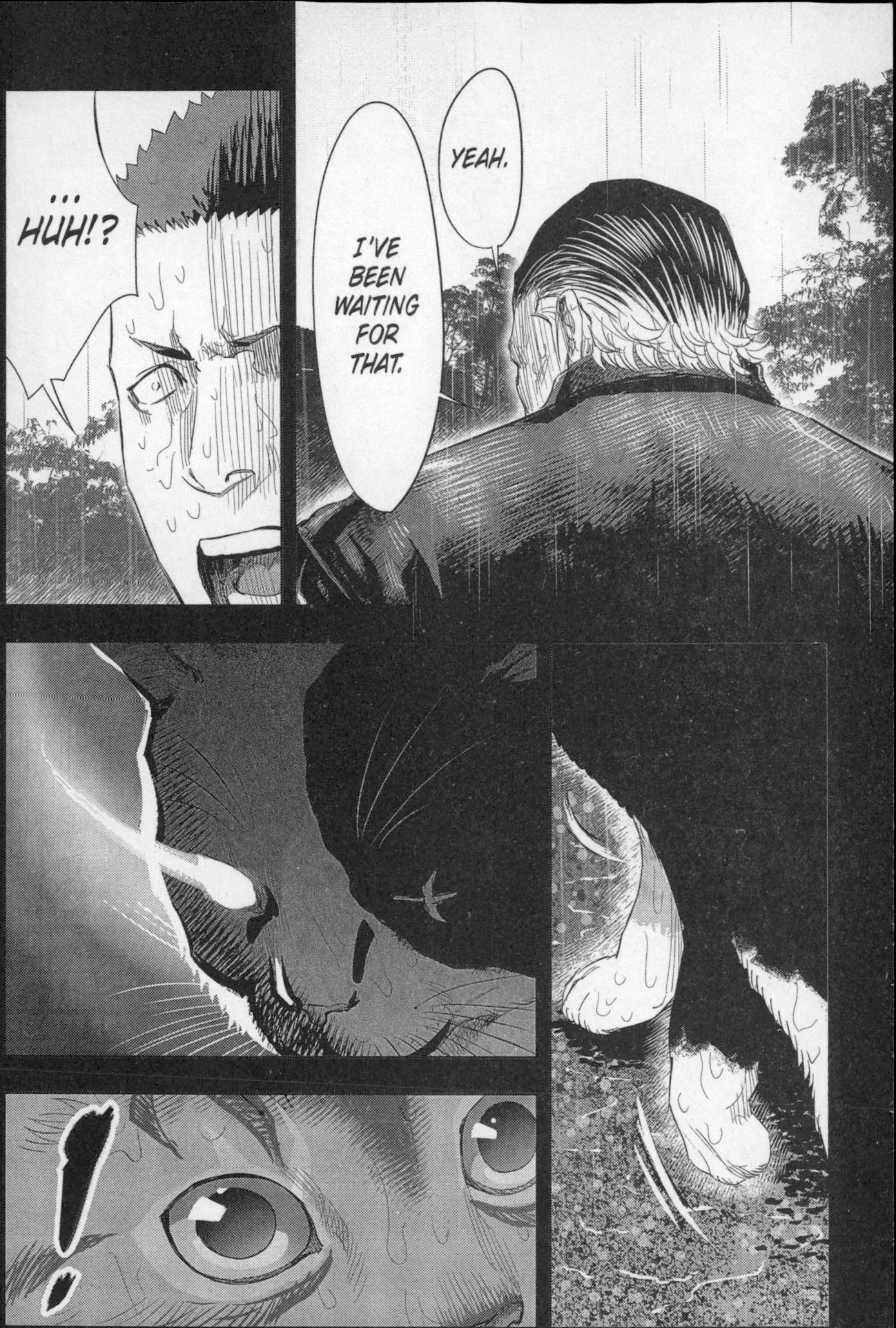
YEAH.
I'VE BEEN WAITING FOR THAT.
...HUH!?
!

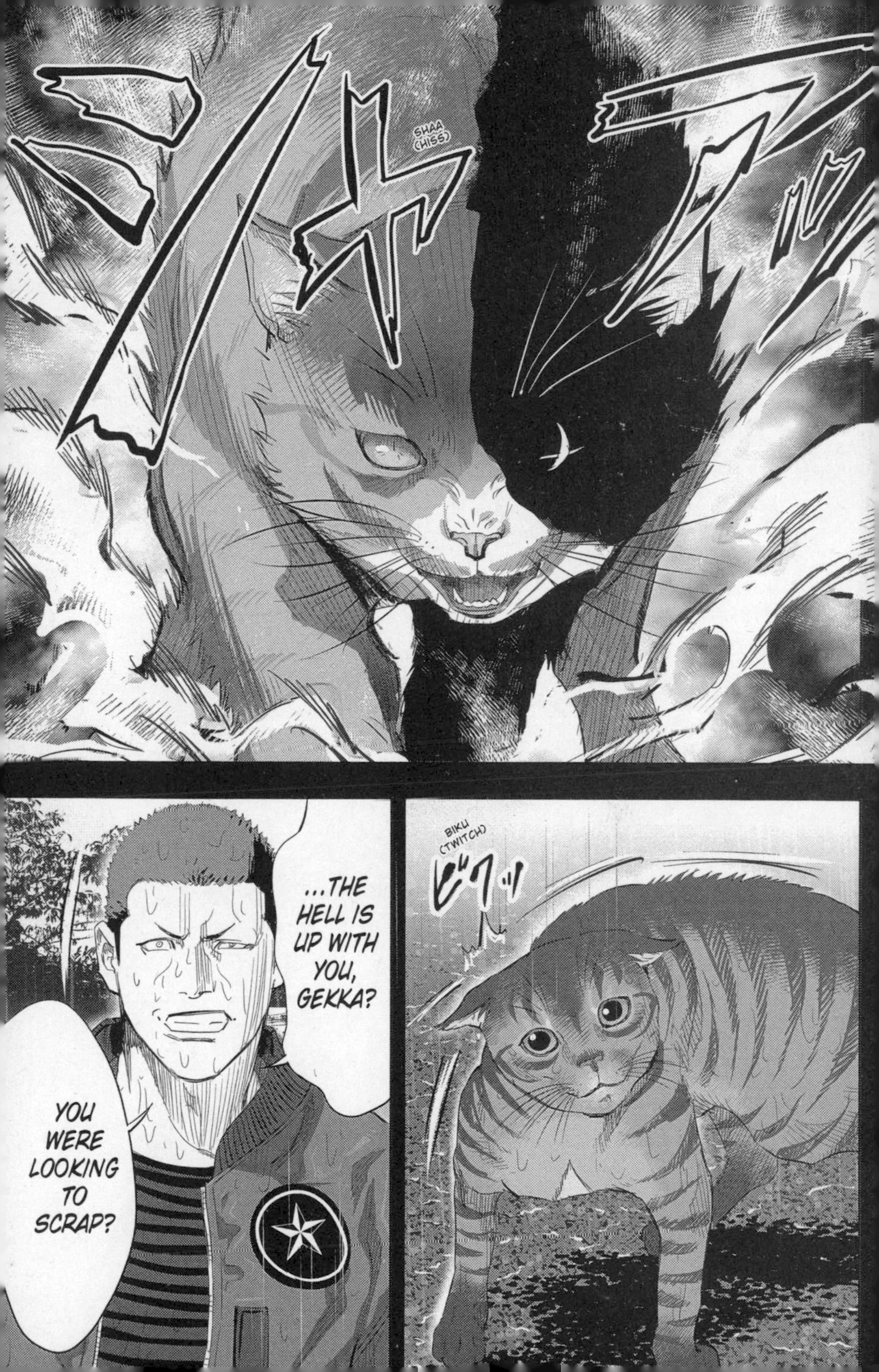
SHAA (HISS)
BIKU (TWITCH)
...THE HELL IS UP WITH YOU, GEKKA?
YOU WERE LOOKING TO SCRAP?

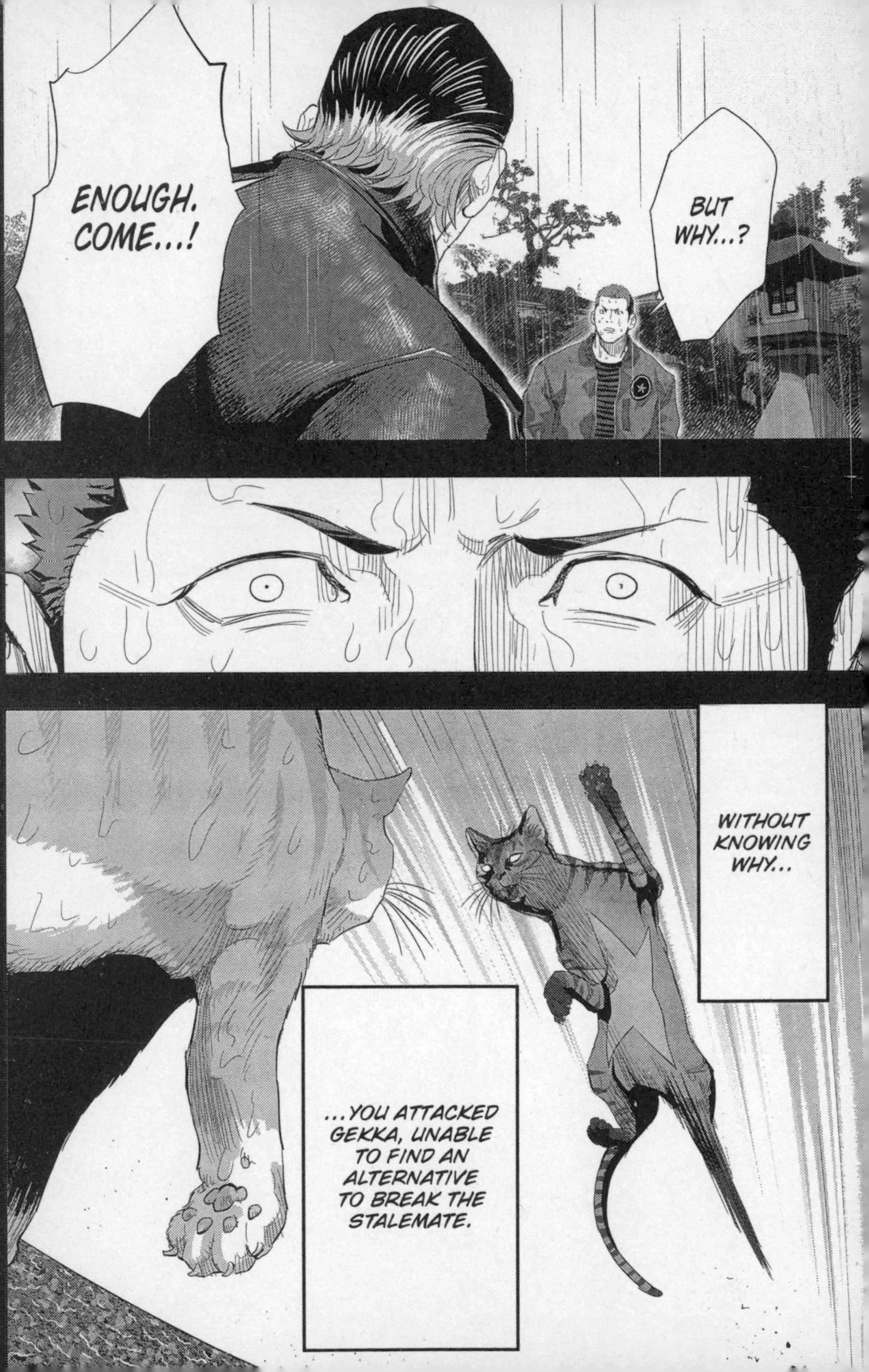
BUT WHY...?
ENOUGH. COME...!
WITHOUT KNOWING WHY...
...YOU ATTACKED GEKKA, UNABLE TO FIND AN ALTERNATIVE TO BREAK THE STALEMATE.

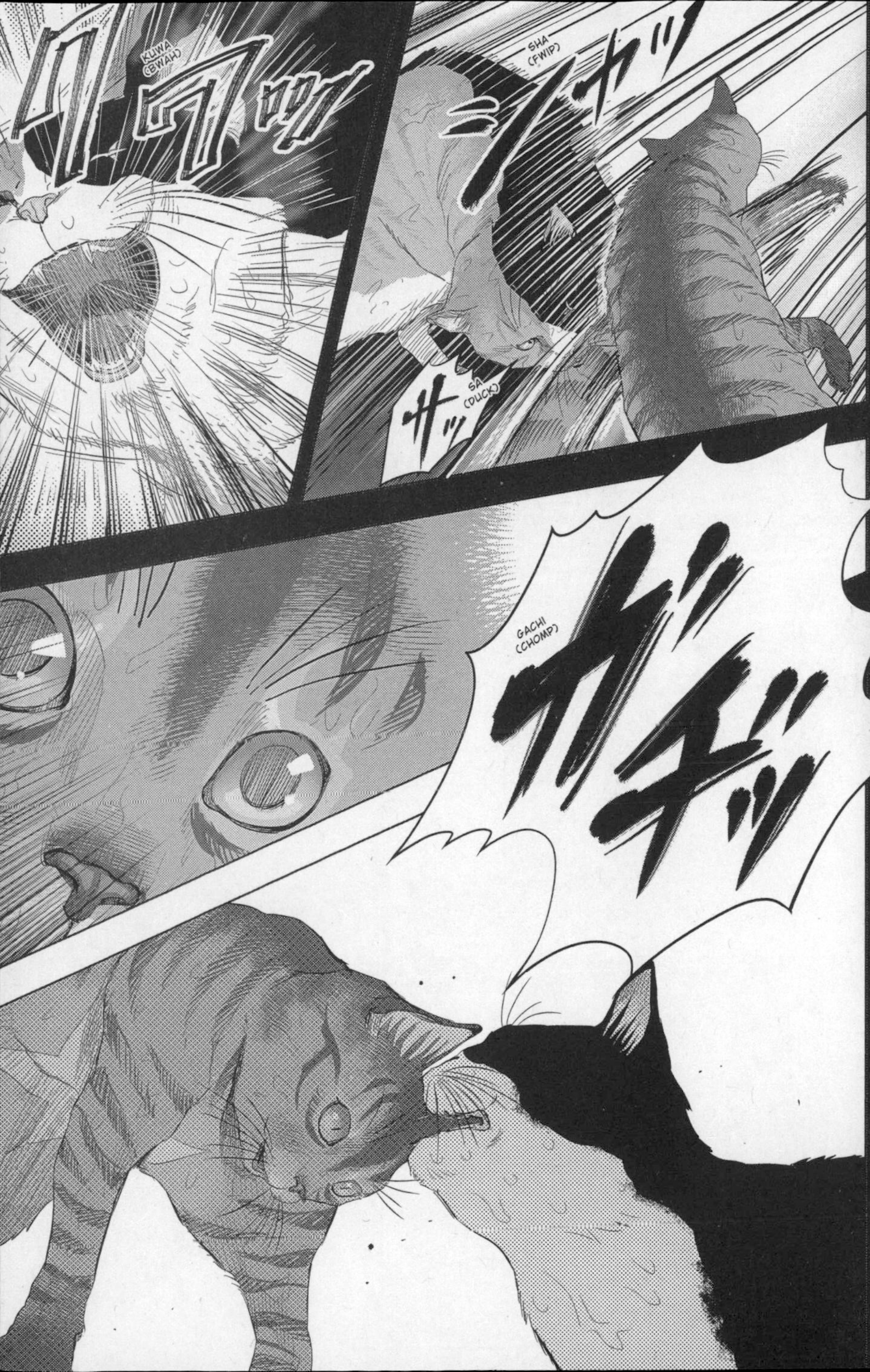
SHA (FWIP)
SA (DUCK)
KUWA (BWAH)
GACHI (CHOMP)

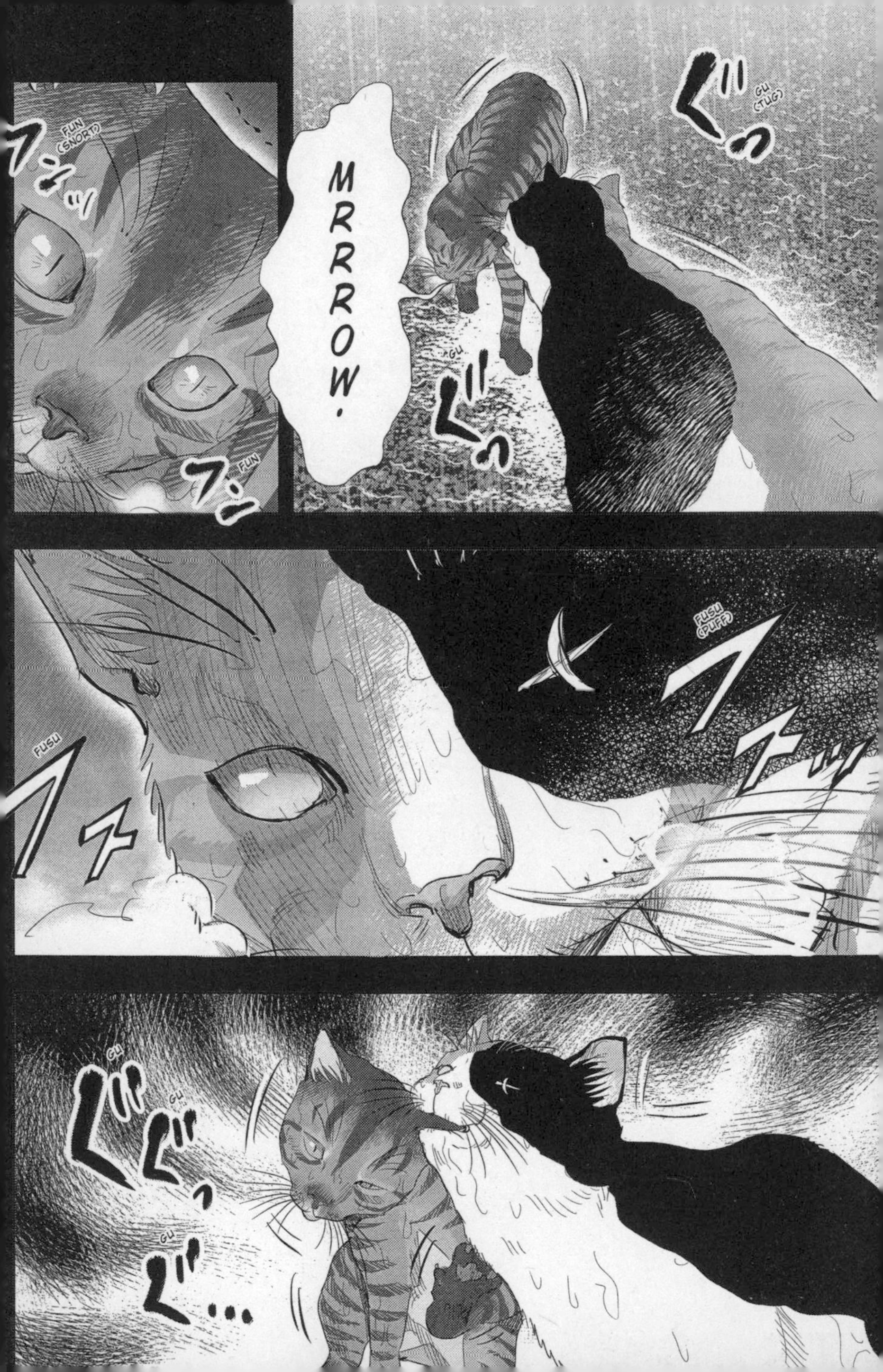
GU (TUG)
MRRROW.
GU
FUN (SNORT)
FUN
FUSU (PUFF)
FUSU
GU
GU
GU

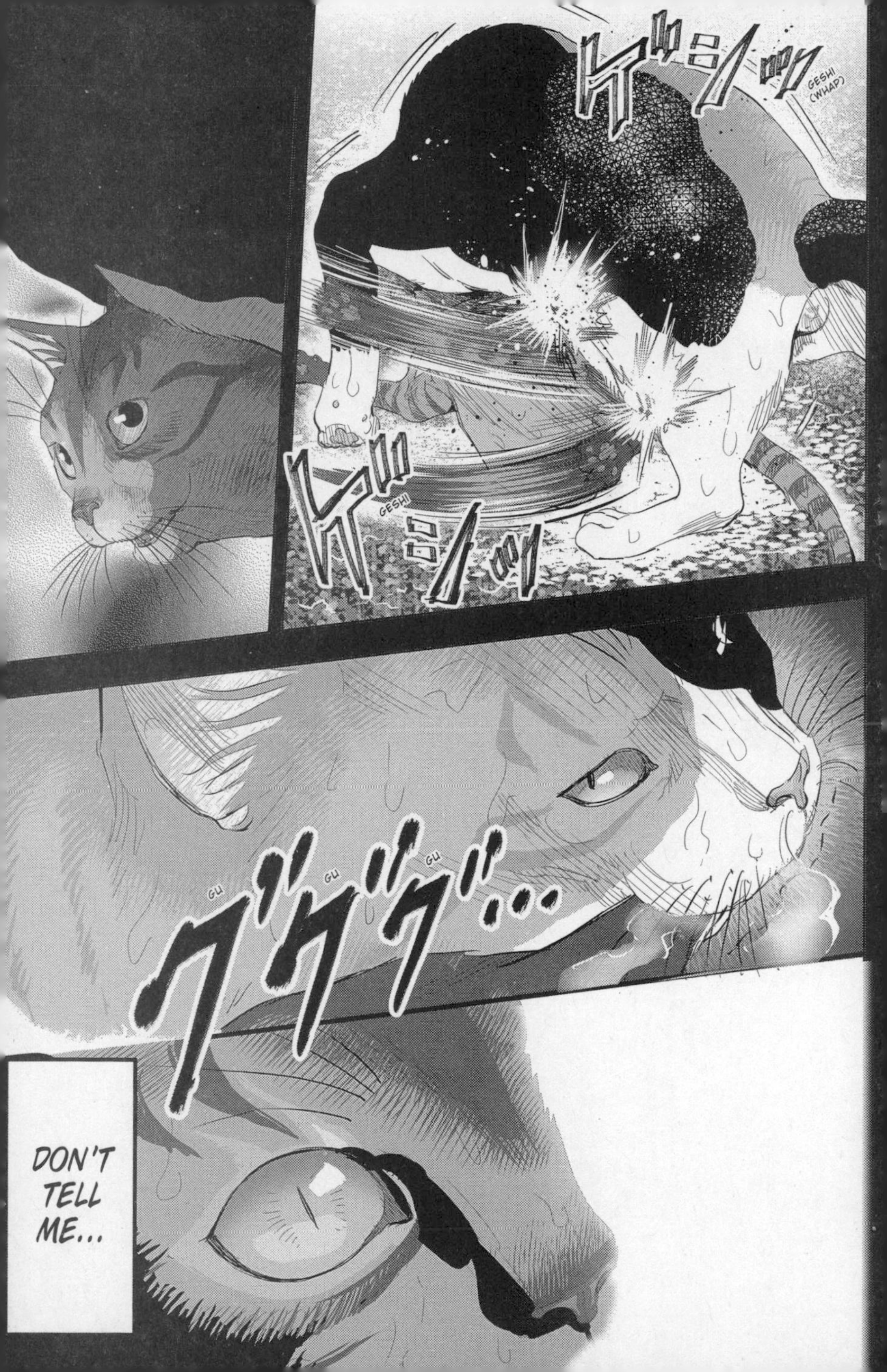
GESHI (WHAP)
GESHI
GU GU GU
DON'T TELL ME...

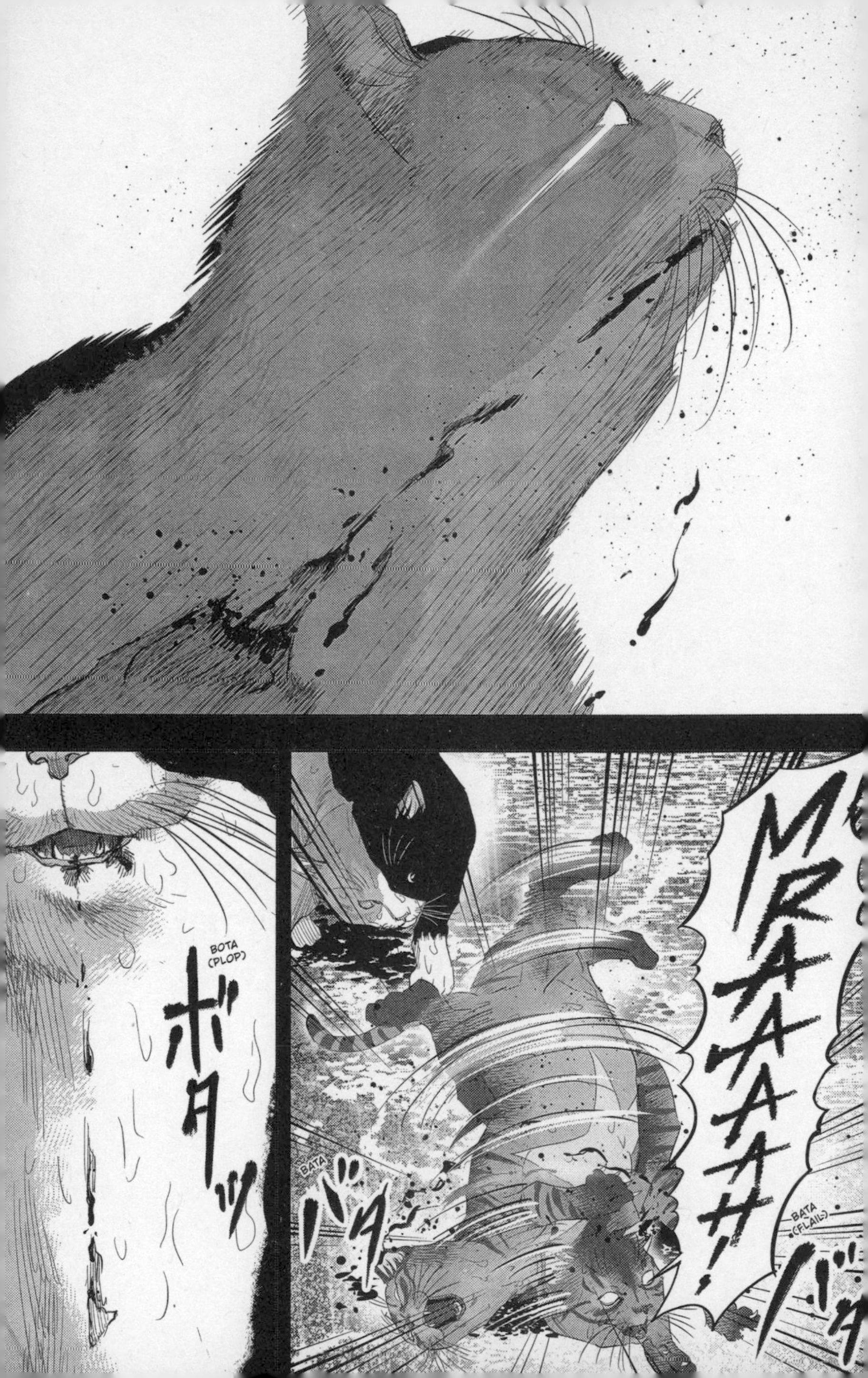
MRAAAAH!!
BATA (FLAIL)
BATA
BOTA (PLOP)
ボタッ

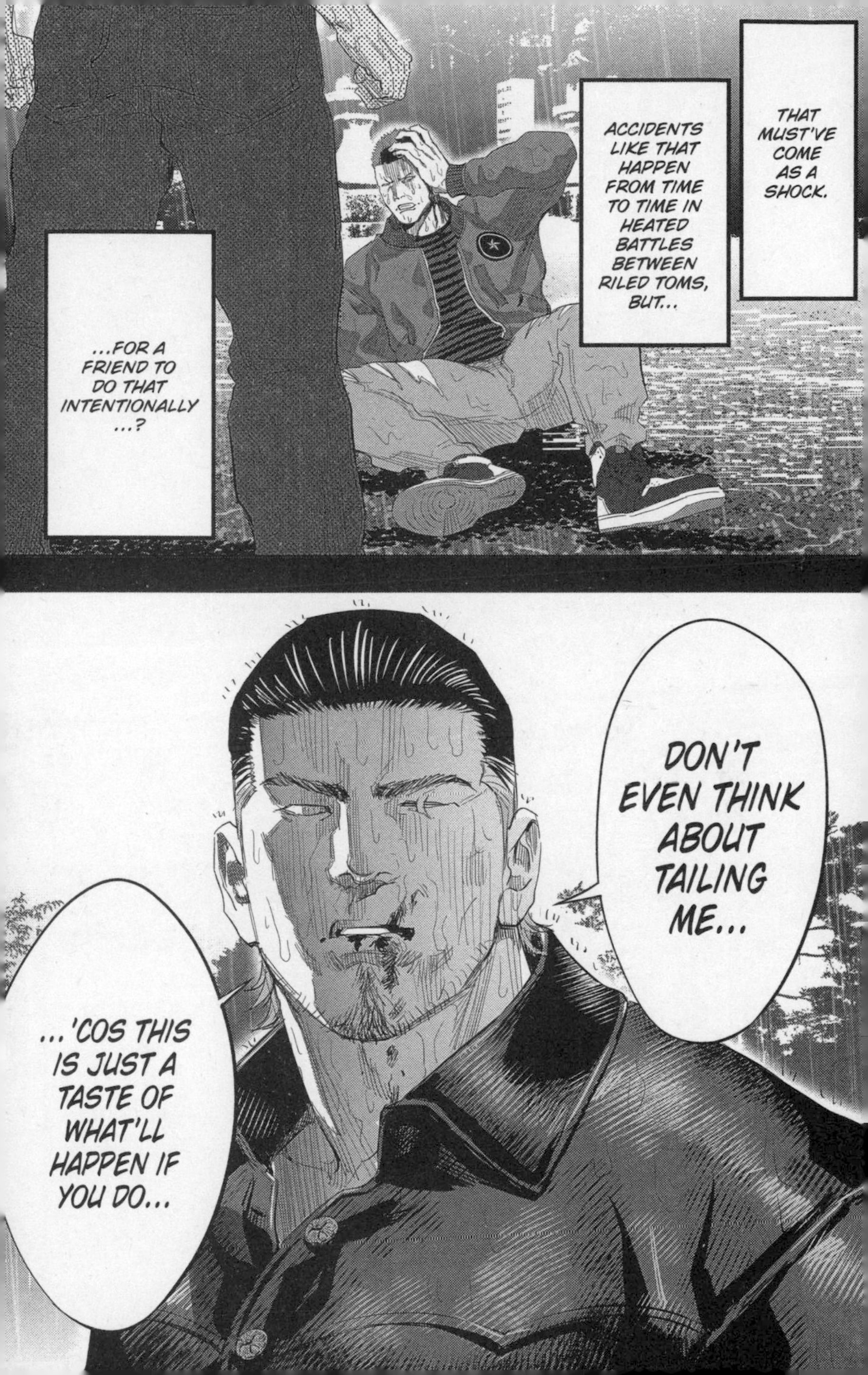
THAT MUST'VE COME AS A SHOCK.
ACCIDENTS LIKE THAT HAPPEN FROM TIME TO TIME IN HEATED BATTLES BETWEEN RILED TOMS, BUT...
...FOR A FRIEND TO DO THAT INTENTIONALLY ...?
DON'T EVEN THINK ABOUT TAILING ME...
...'COS THIS IS JUST A TASTE OF WHAT'LL HAPPEN IF YOU DO...

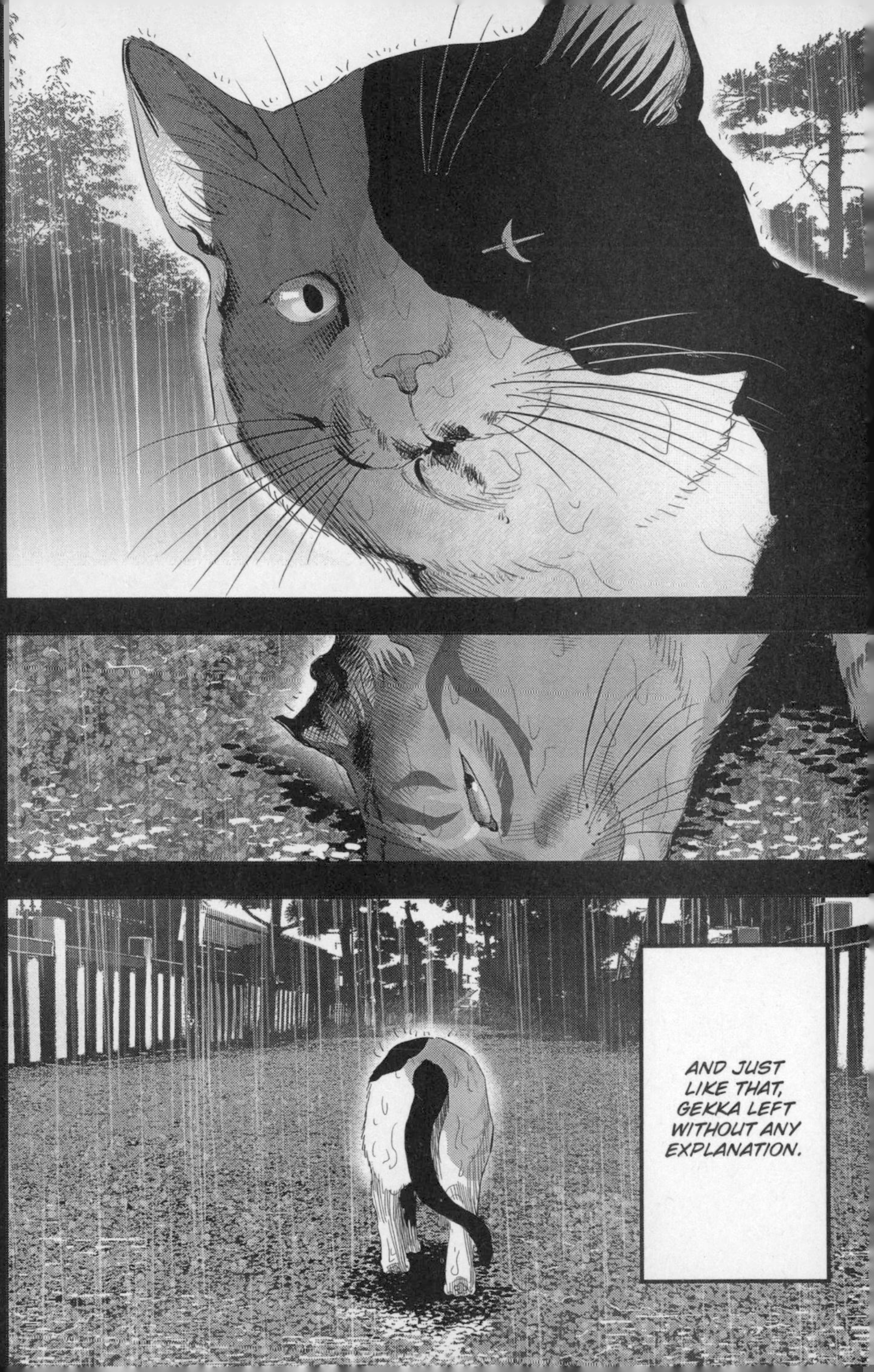
AND JUST LIKE THAT, GEKKA LEFT WITHOUT ANY EXPLANATION.

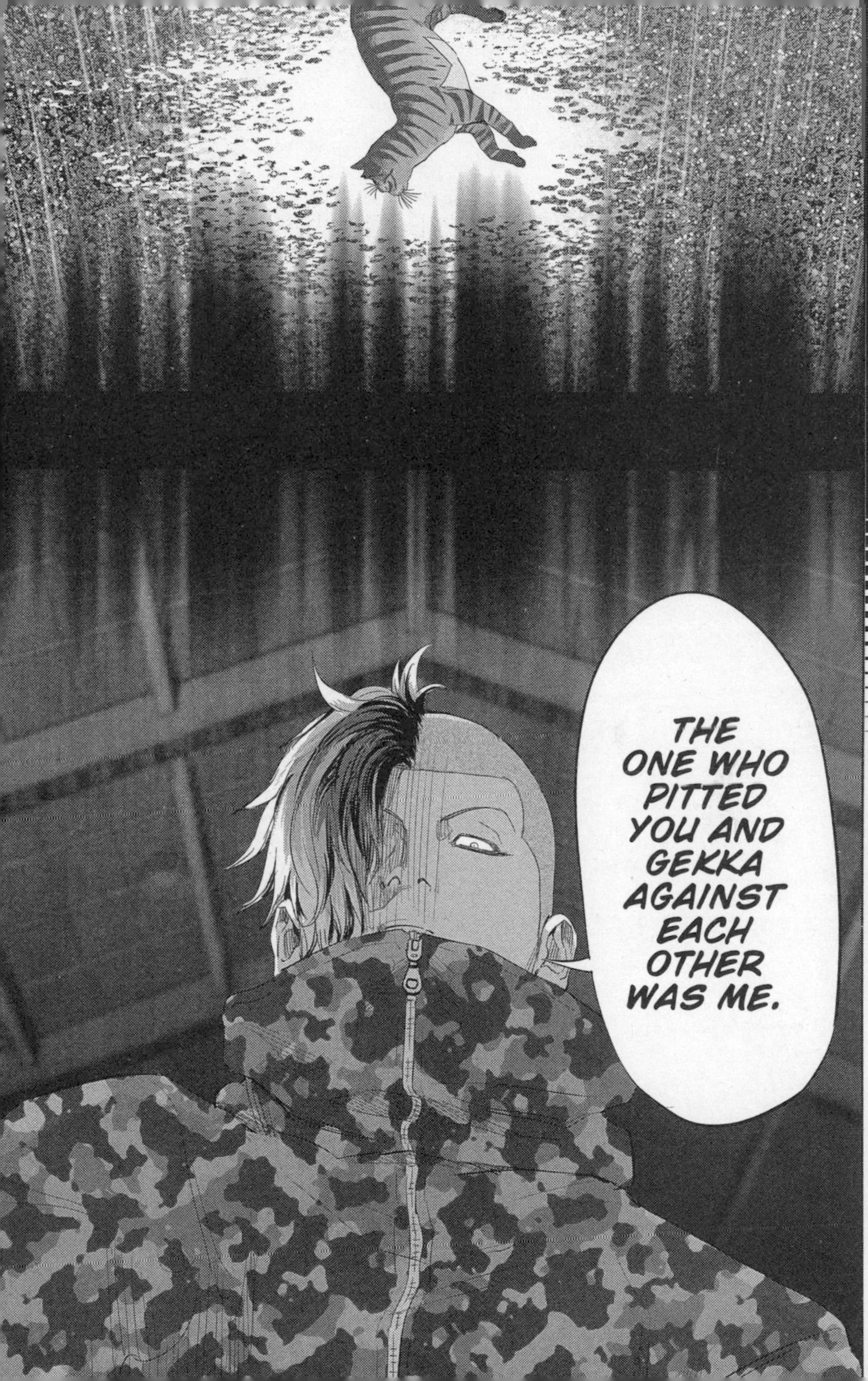
THE ONE WHO PITTED YOU AND GEKKA AGAINST EACH OTHER WAS ME.

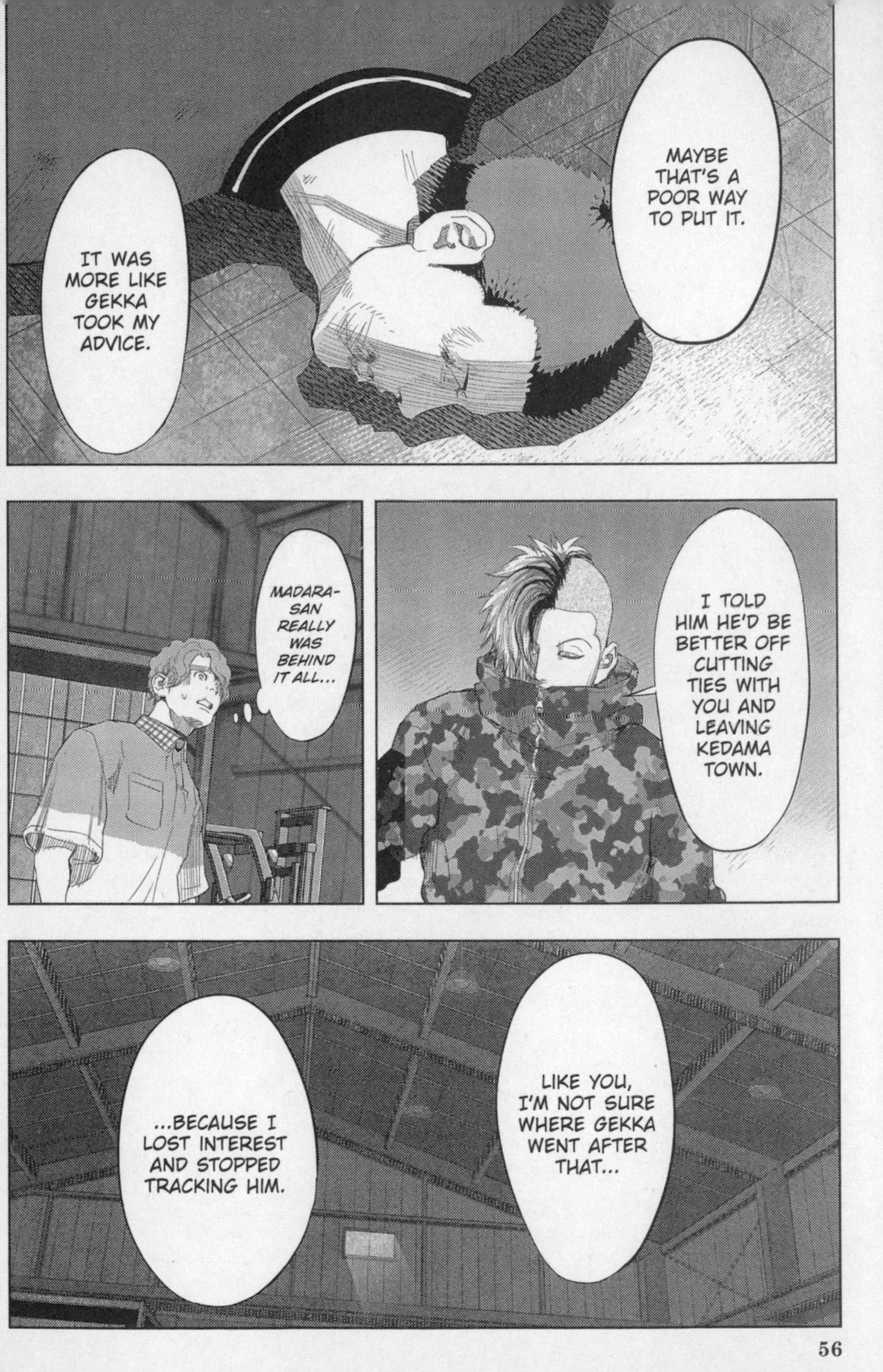
MAYBE THAT'S A POOR WAY TO PUT IT.
IT WAS MORE LIKE GEKKA TOOK MY ADVICE.
I TOLD HIM HE'D BE BETTER OFF CUTTING TIES WITH YOU AND LEAVING KEDAMA TOWN.
MADARA-SAN REALLY WAS BEHIND IT ALL...
LIKE YOU, I'M NOT SURE WHERE GEKKA WENT AFTER THAT...
...BECAUSE I LOST INTEREST AND STOPPED TRACKING HIM.

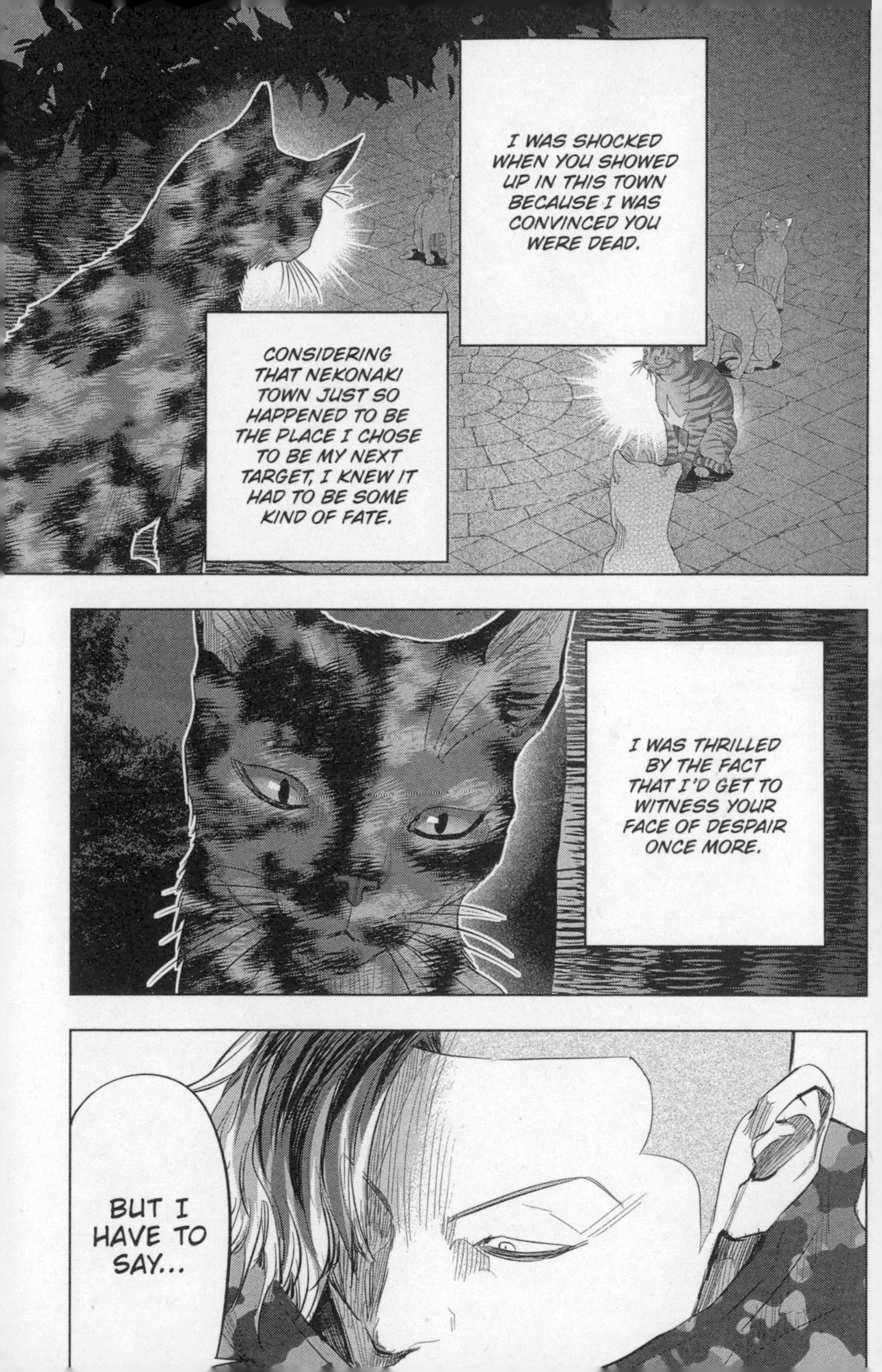

I WAS SHOCKED WHEN YOU SHOWED UP IN THIS TOWN BECAUSE I WAS CONVINCED YOU WERE DEAD.
CONSIDERING THAT NEKONAKI TOWN JUST SO HAPPENED TO BE THE PLACE I CHOSE TO BE MY NEXT TARGET, I KNEW IT HAD TO BE SOME KIND OF FATE.
I WAS THRILLED BY THE FACT THAT I'D GET TO WITNESS YOUR FACE OF DESPAIR ONCE MORE.
BUT I HAVE TO SAY...

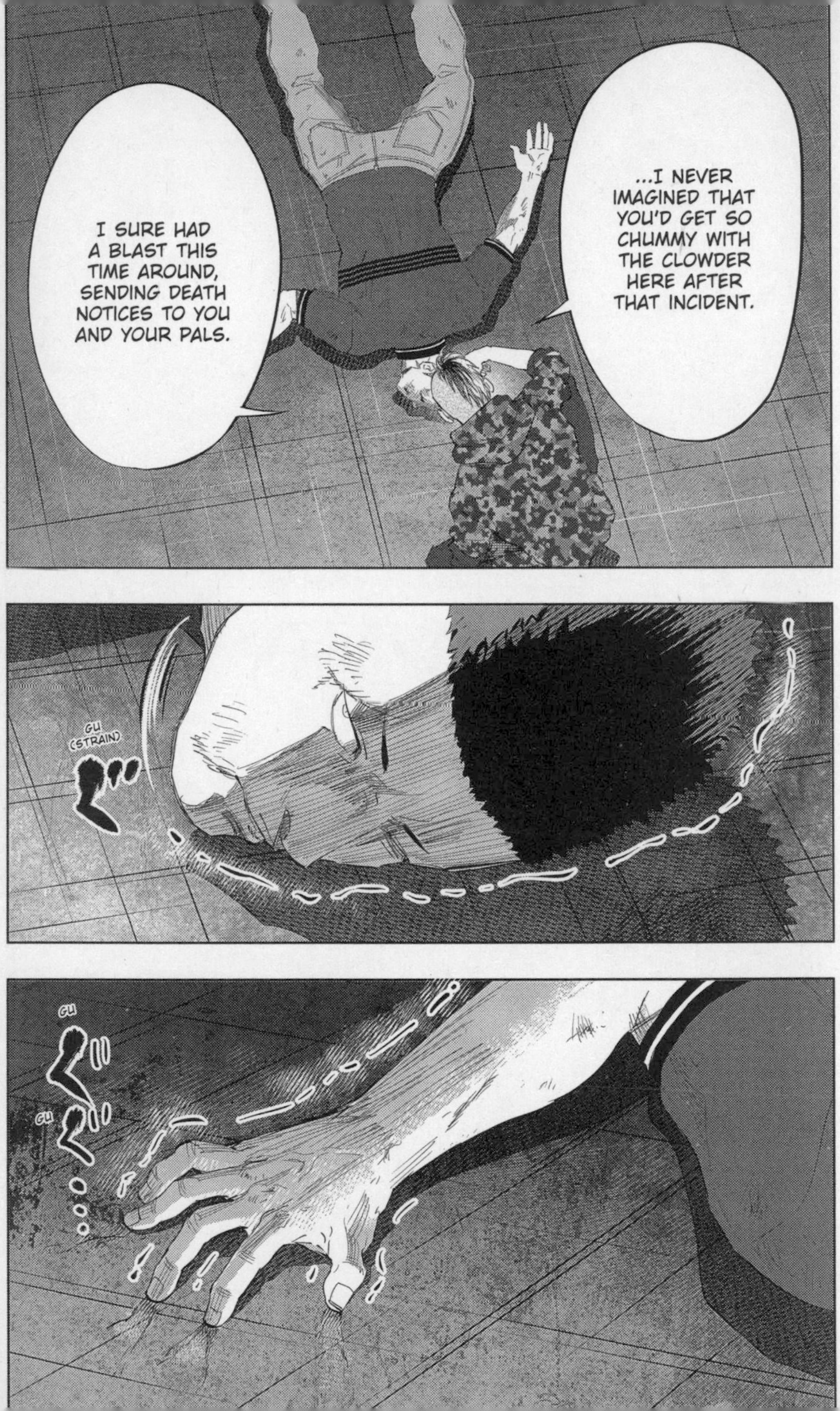
...I NEVER IMAGINED THAT YOU'D GET SO CHUMMY WITH THE CLOWDER HERE AFTER THAT INCIDENT.
I SURE HAD A BLAST THIS TIME AROUND, SENDING DEATH NOTICES TO YOU AND YOUR PALS.
GU (STRAIN)
GU
GU

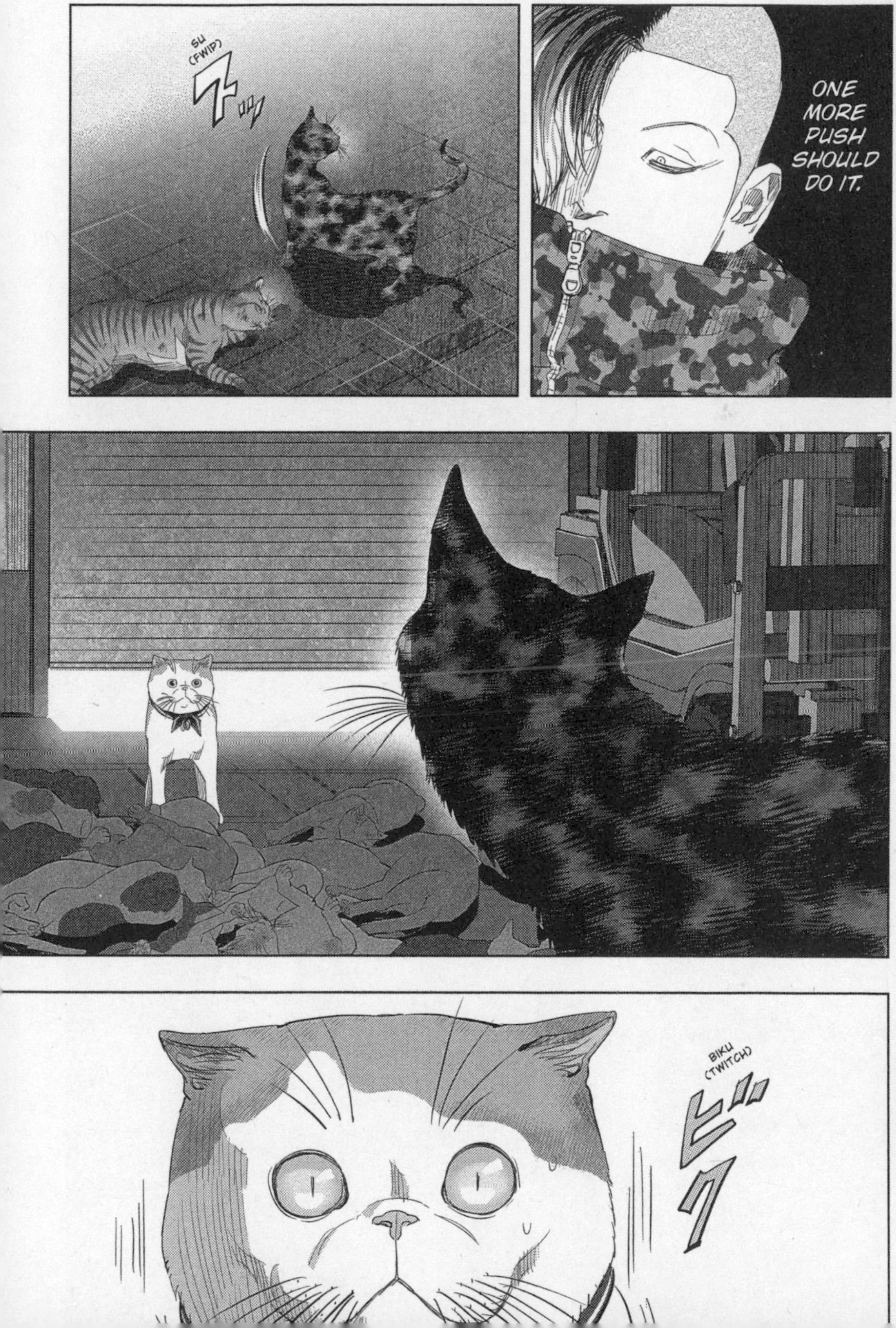
ONE MORE PUSH SHOULD DO IT.
SU (FWIP)
BIKU (TWITCH)

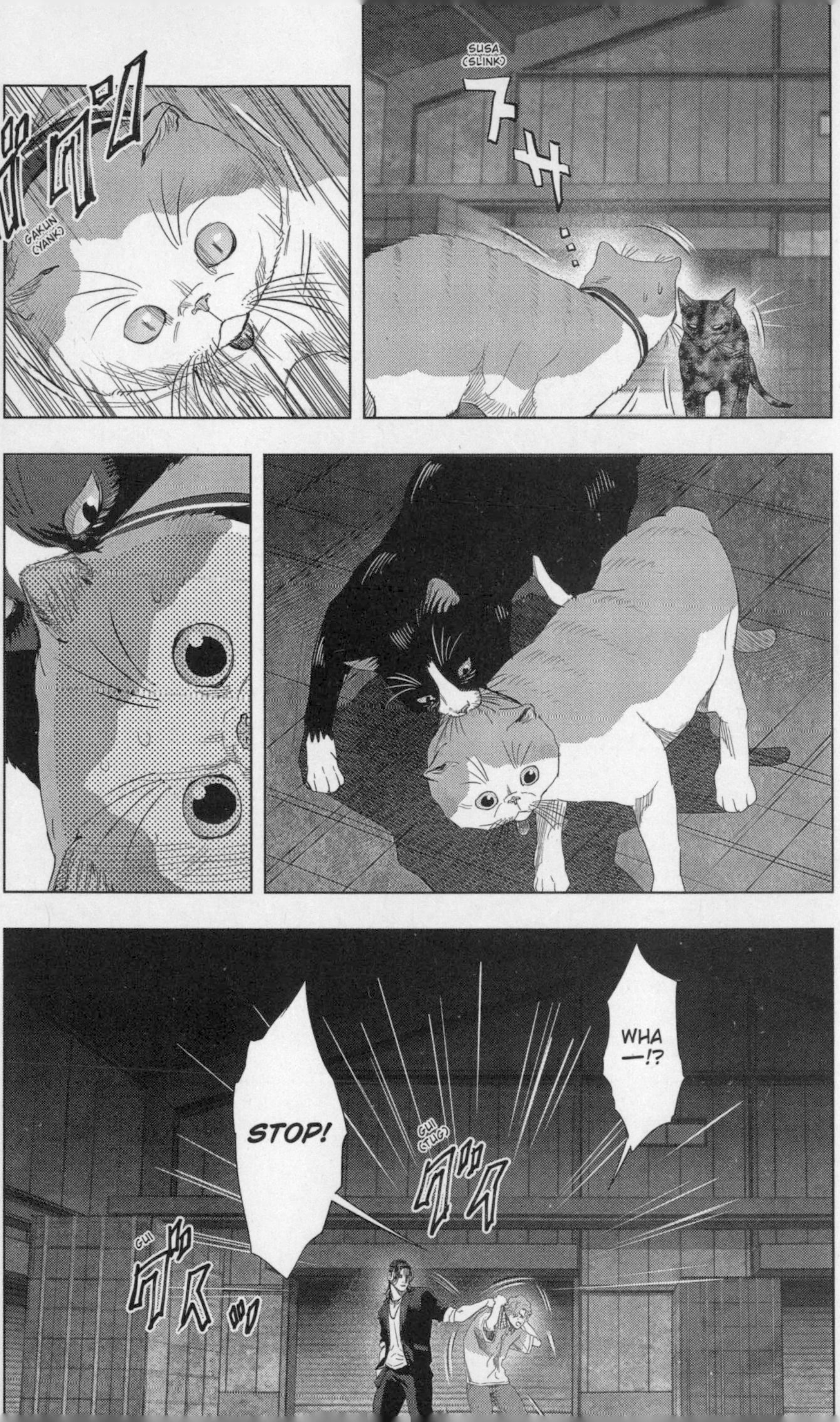
SUSA (SLINK)
GAKUN (YANK)
WHA—!?
GUI (TUG)
STOP!
GUI

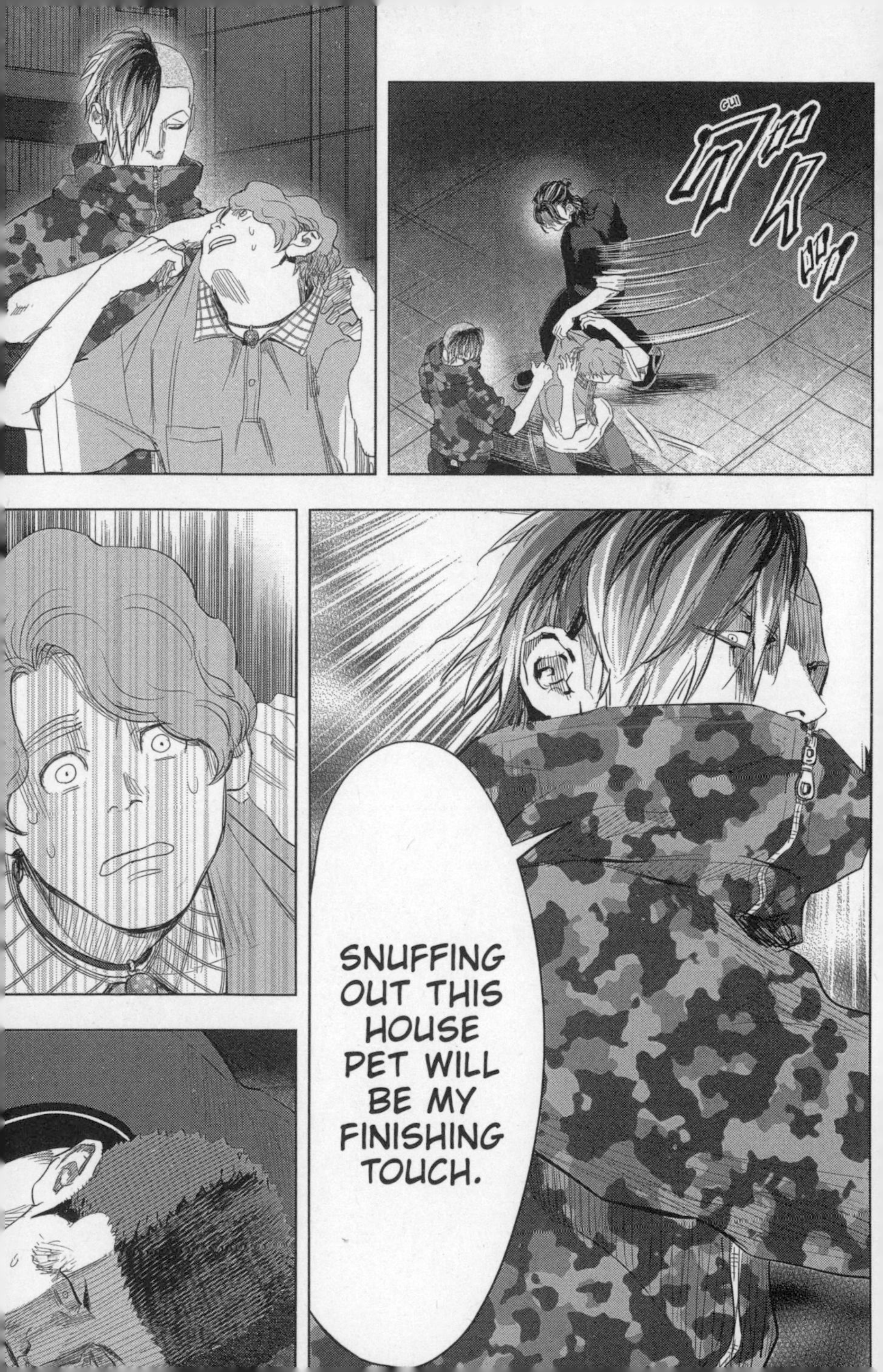
GUI
SNUFFING OUT THIS HOUSE PET WILL BE MY FINISHING TOUCH.

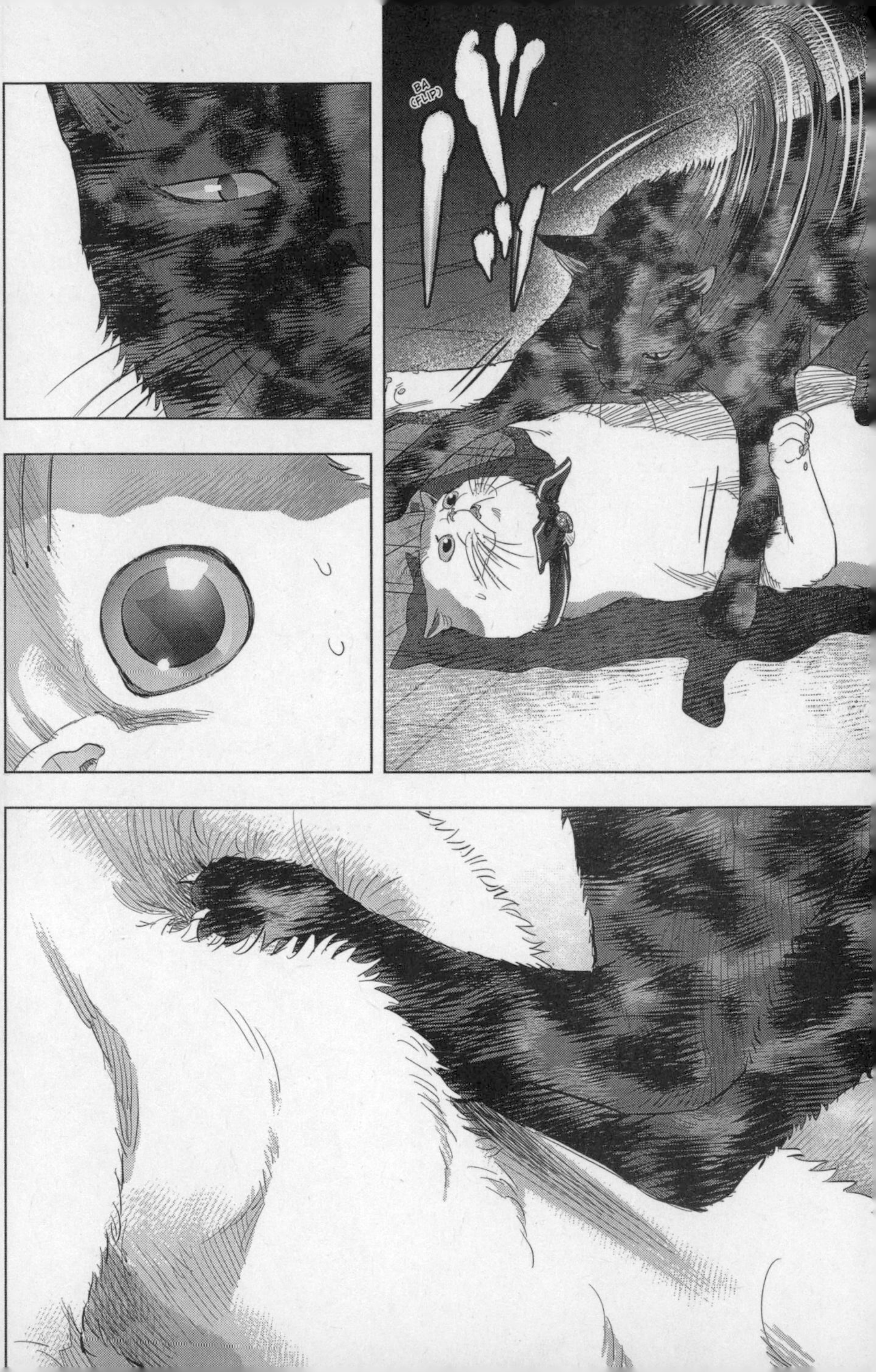
BA (FLIP)

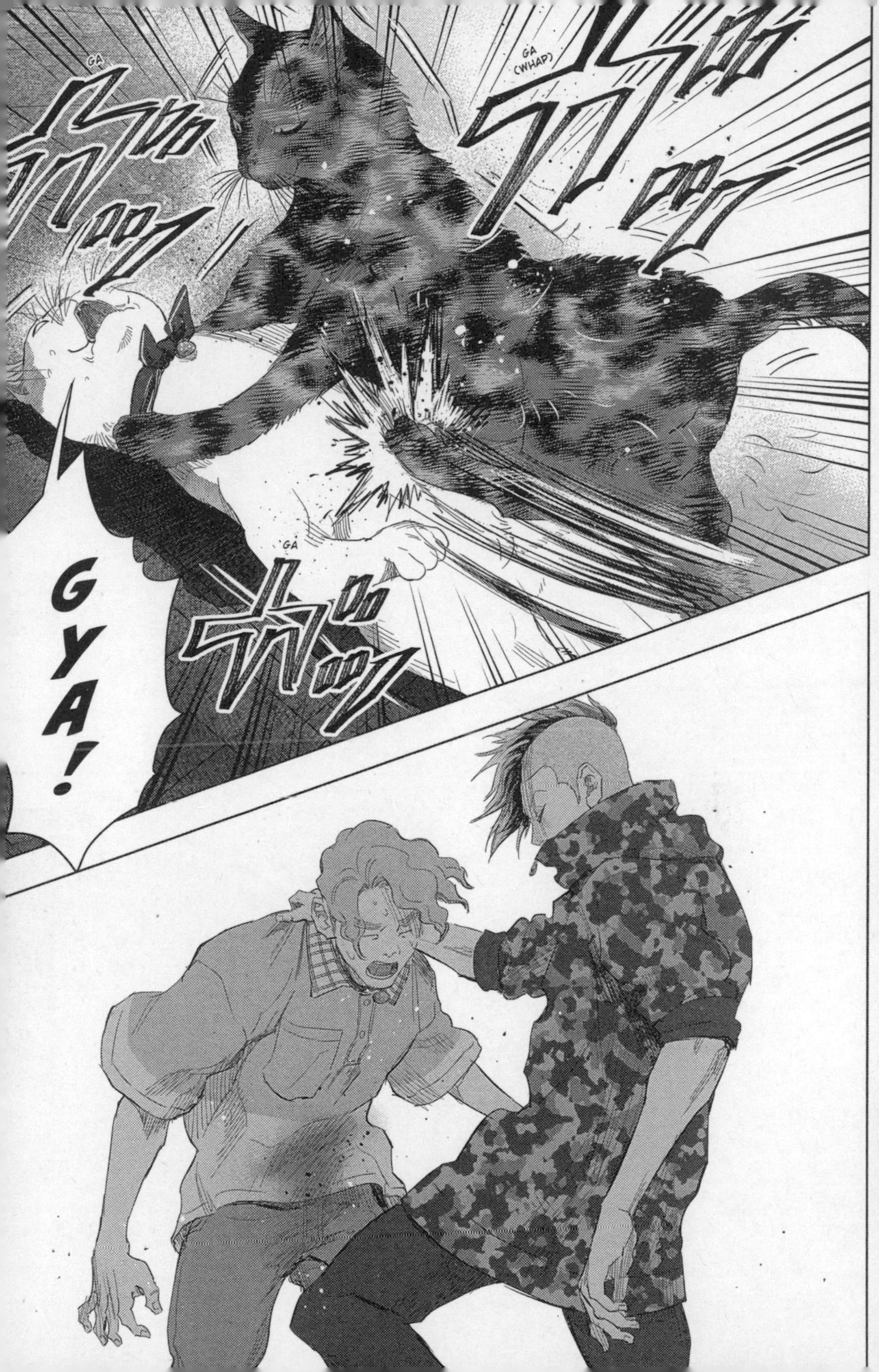
GA (WHAP)
GA
GA
GYA!

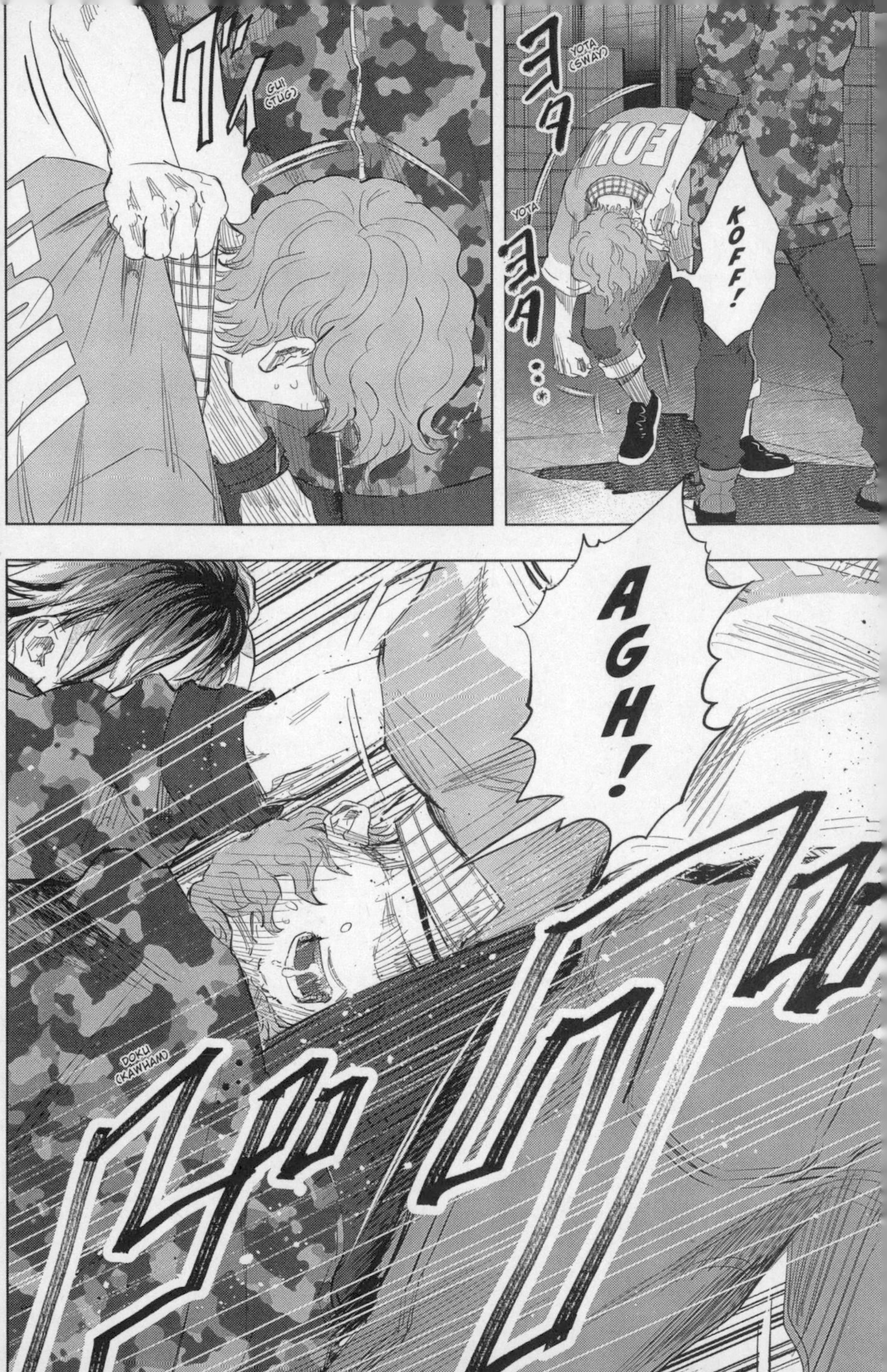
YOTA (SWAY)
YOTA
KOFF!
GUI (TUG)
AGH!
DOKU (KAWHAM)

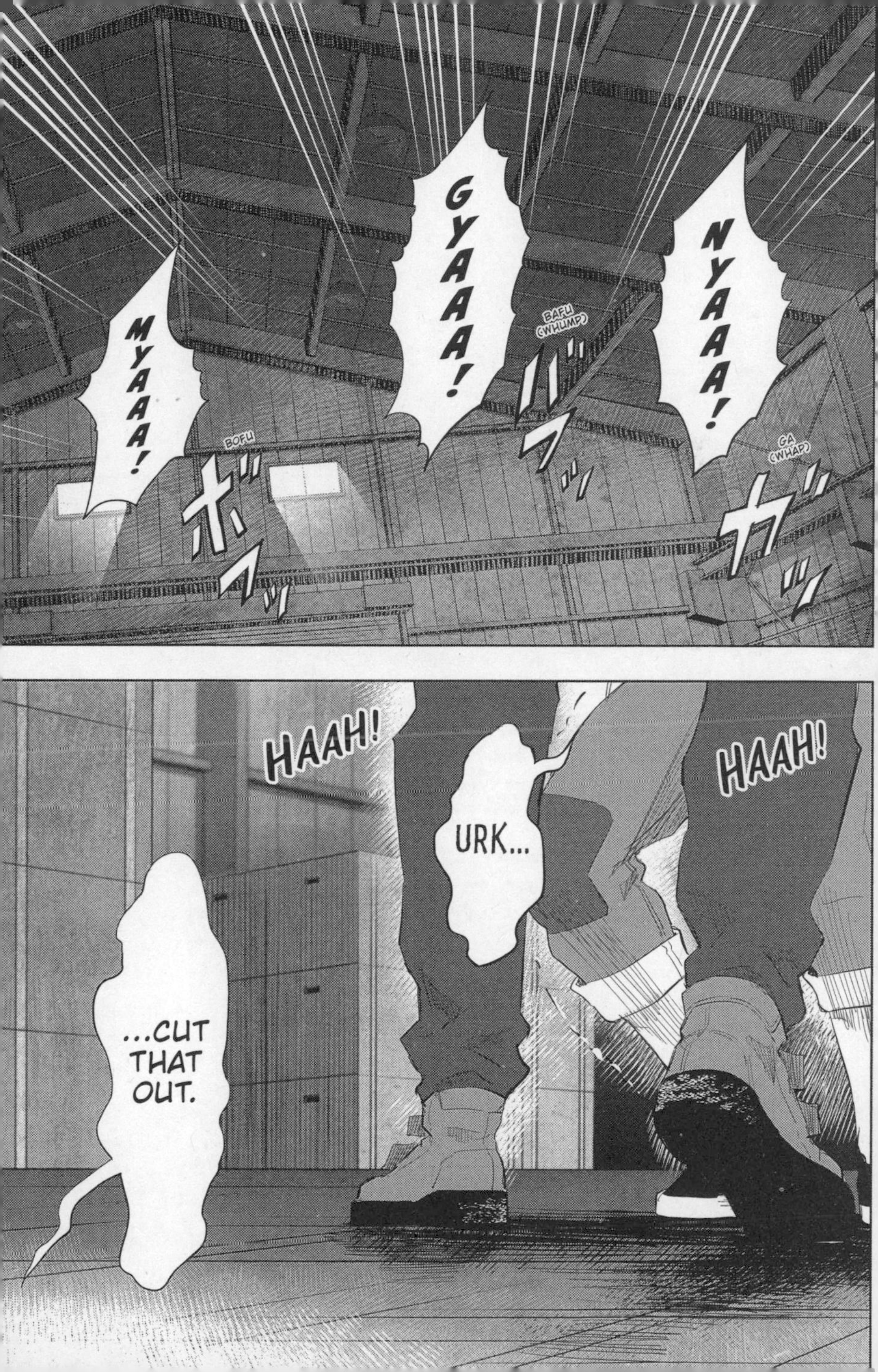
NYAAAA!
GA (WHAP)
BAFU (WHUMP)
GYAAAA!
BOFU
MYAAAA!
HAAH!
URK...
HAAH!
...CUT THAT OUT.

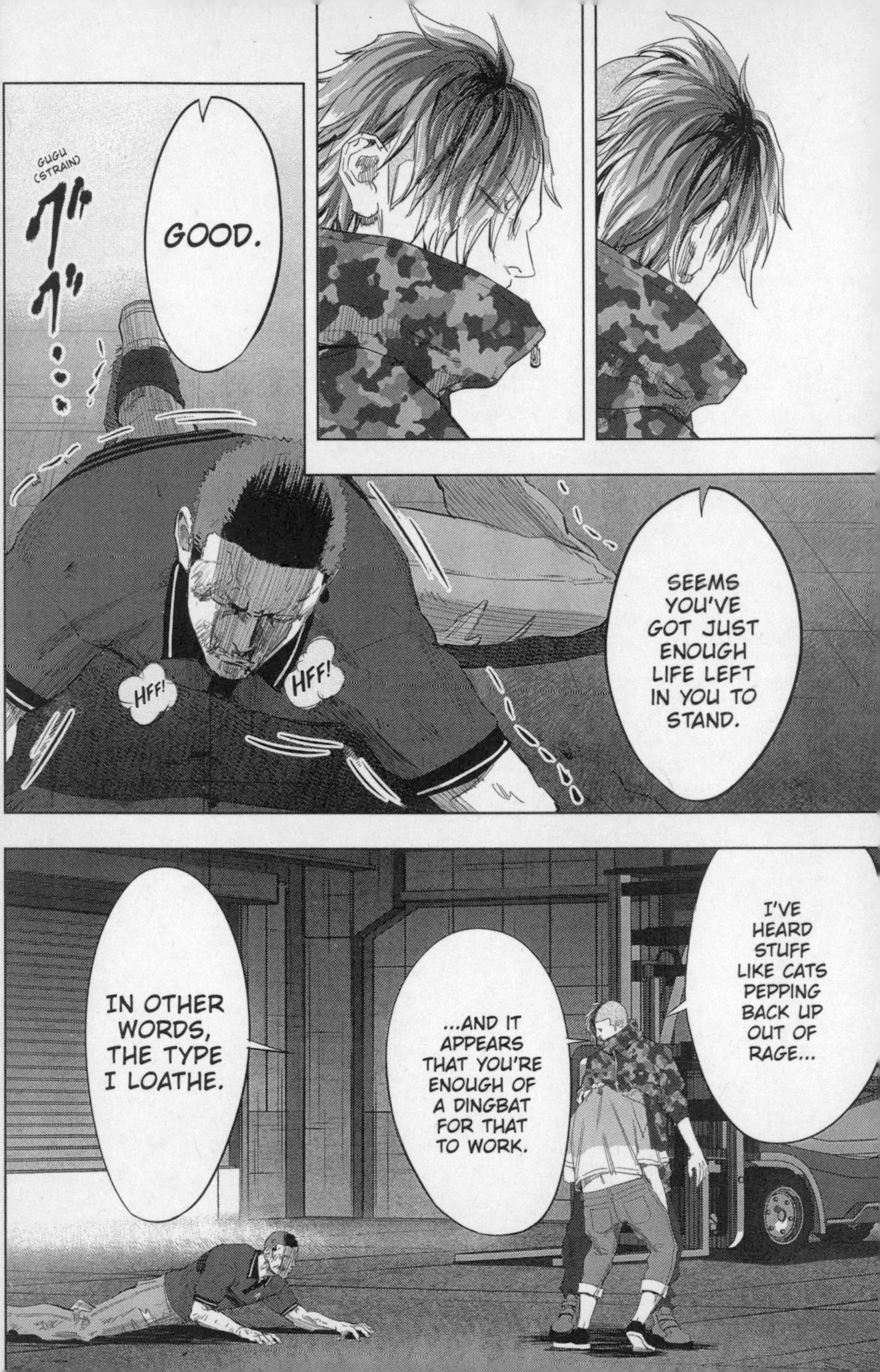
GUGU (STRAIN)
GOOD.
SEEMS YOU'VE GOT JUST ENOUGH LIFE LEFT IN YOU TO STAND.
HFF!
HFF!
I'VE HEARD STUFF LIKE CATS PEPPING BACK UP OUT OF RAGE...
...AND IT APPEARS THAT YOU'RE ENOUGH OF A DINGBAT FOR THAT TO WORK.
IN OTHER WORDS, THE TYPE I LOATHE.

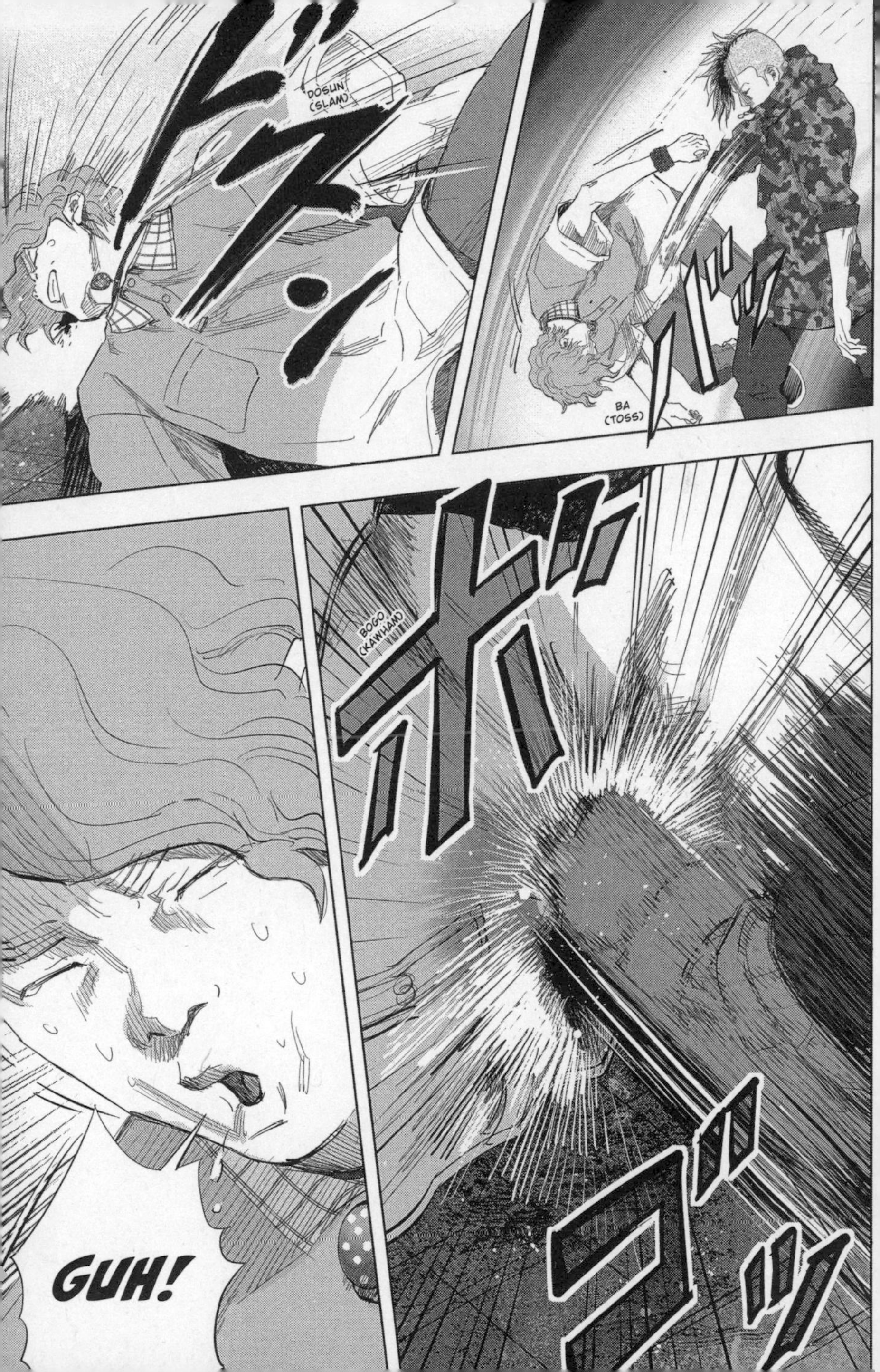
BA
(TOSS)
DOSUN
(SLAM)
BOGO
(KAWHAM)
GUH!

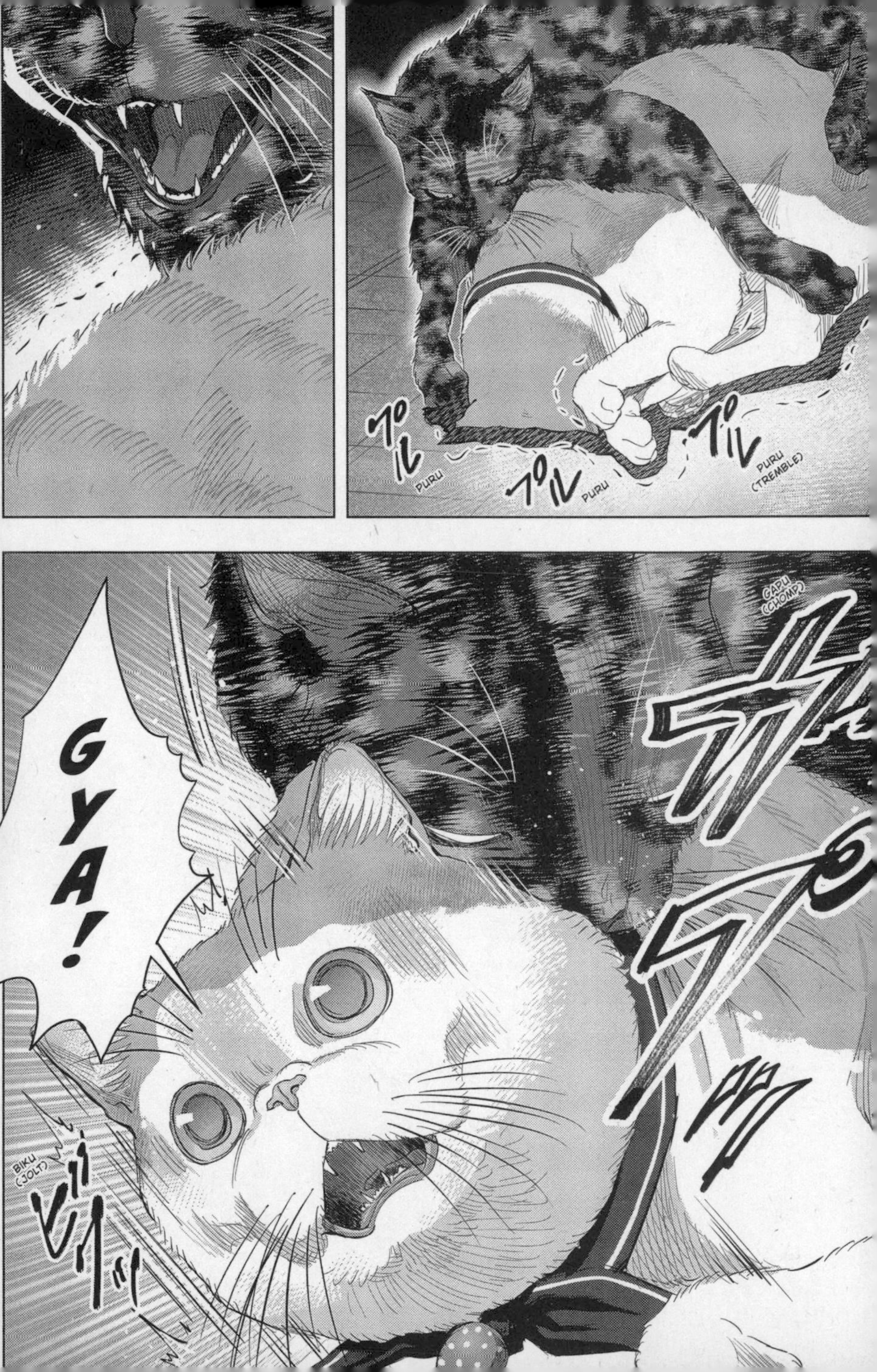

プル
PURU (TREMBLE)
プル
PURU
プル
PURU
GARU (CHOMP)
ガブッ
GYA!
BIKU (JOLT)
ビクッ

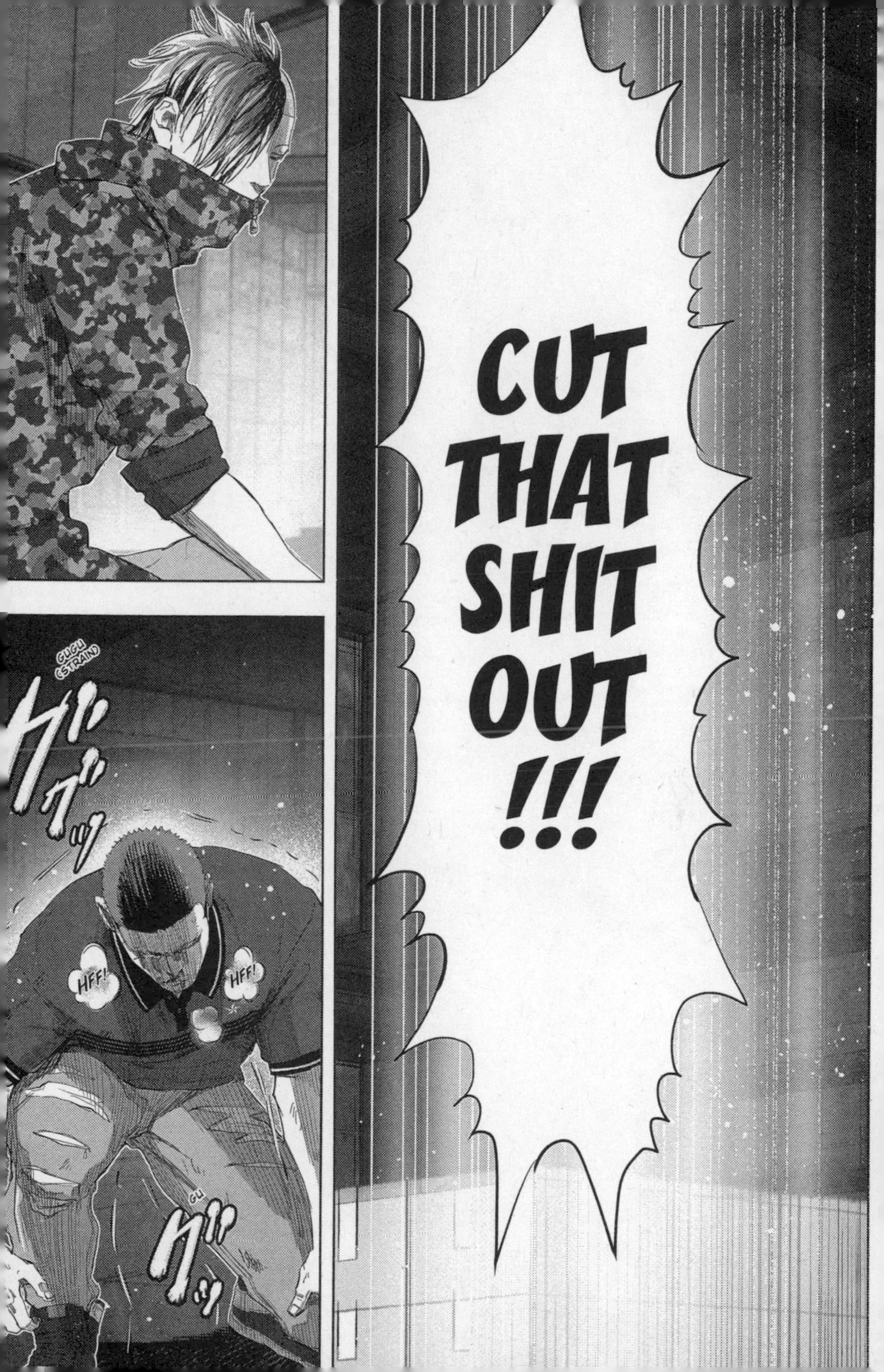
CUT THAT SHIT OUT!!!
GUGU (STRAIN)
HFF!
HFF!
GU

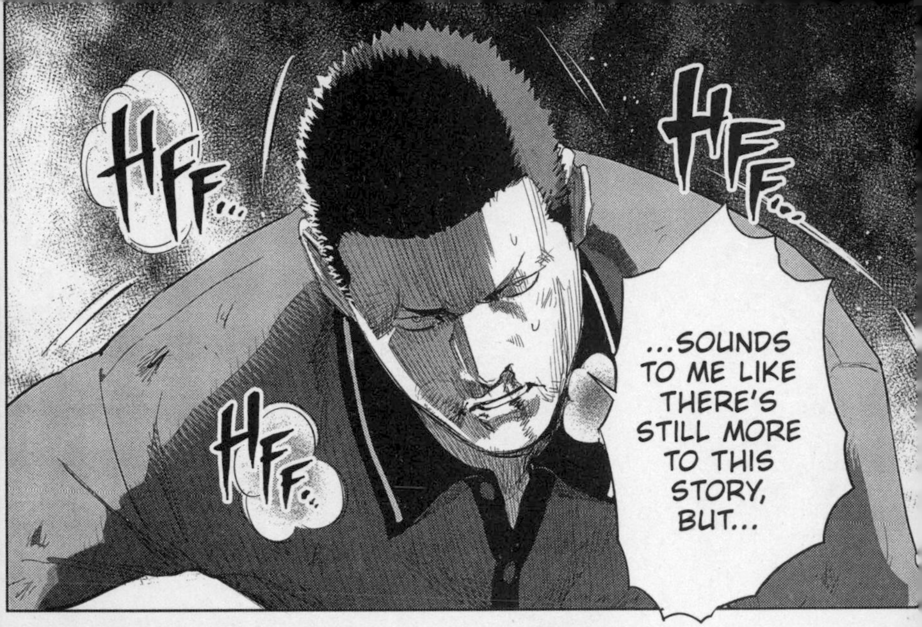
HFF...
...SOUNDS TO ME LIKE THERE'S STILL MORE TO THIS STORY, BUT...
HFF...
HFF...
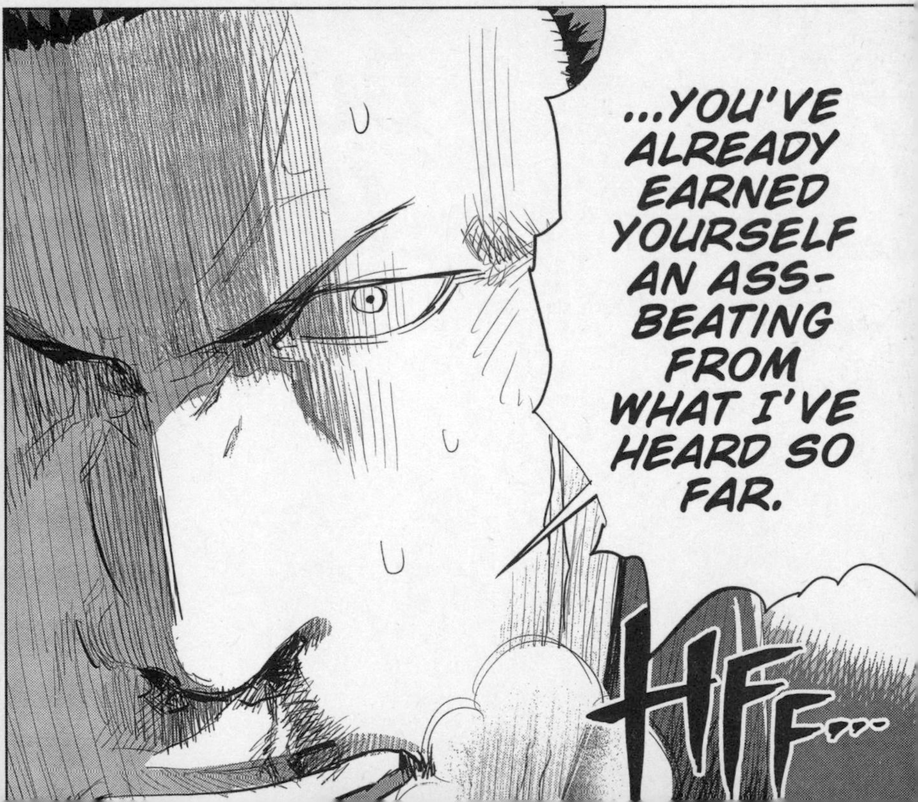
...YOU'VE ALREADY EARNED YOURSELF AN ASS-BEATING FROM WHAT I'VE HEARD SO FAR.
HFF...

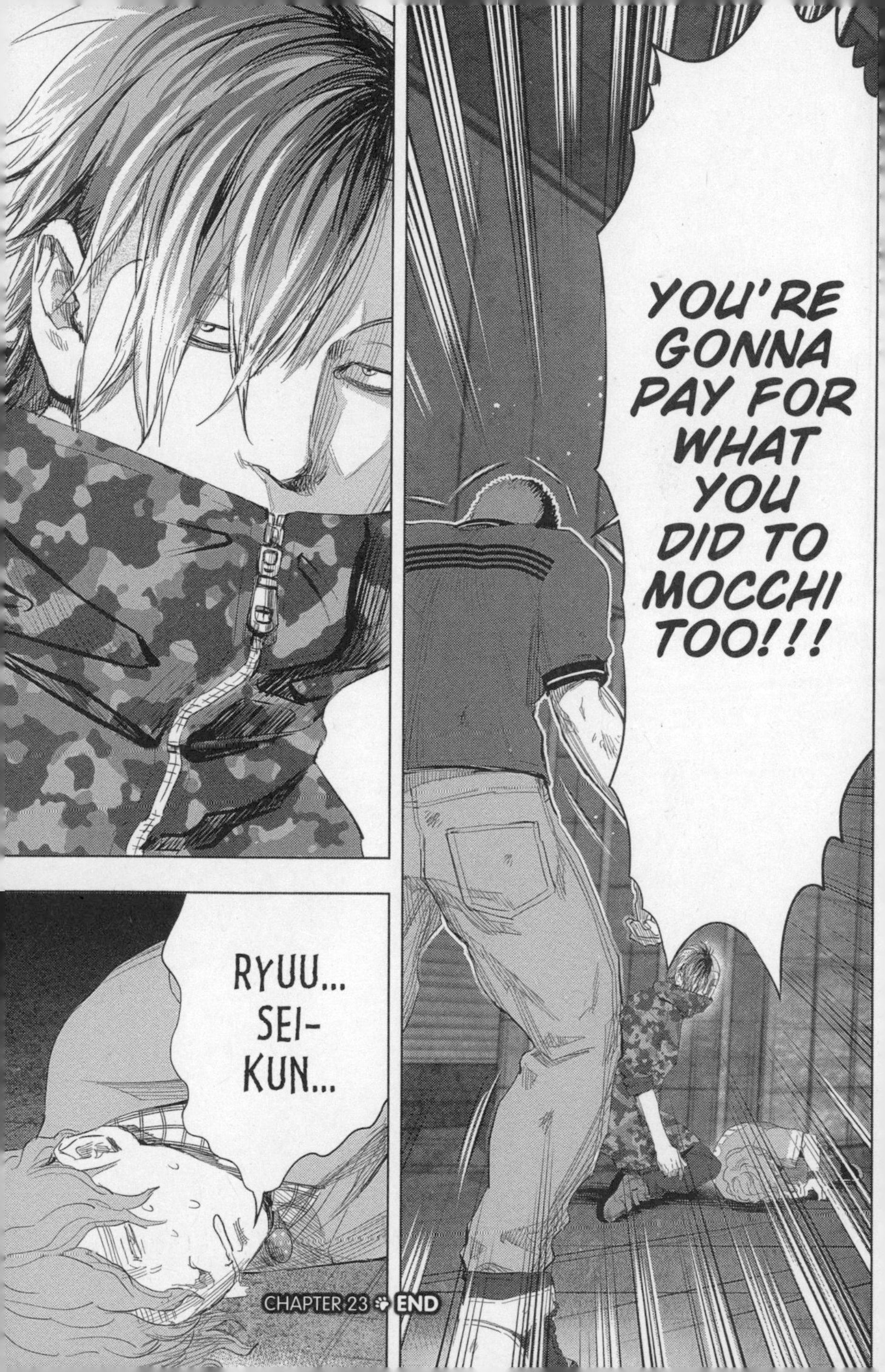
YOU'RE GONNA PAY FOR WHAT YOU DID TO MOCCHI TOO!!!
RYUU... SEI-KUN...
CHAPTER 23 END

TAIGA

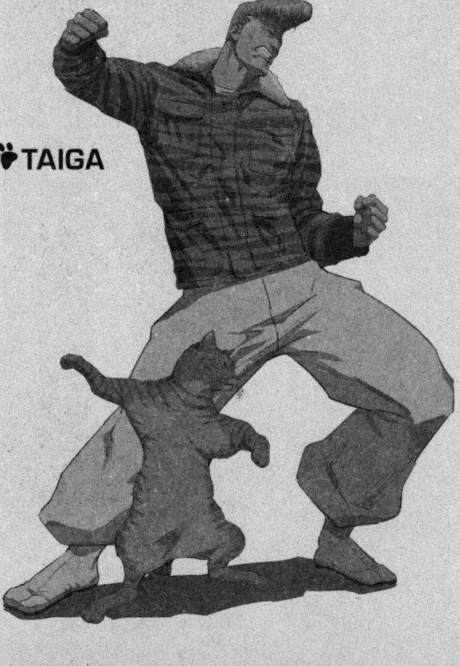

RAIGA

NYANKEES🐾

CHAPTER 24
FELINE INSTINCTS

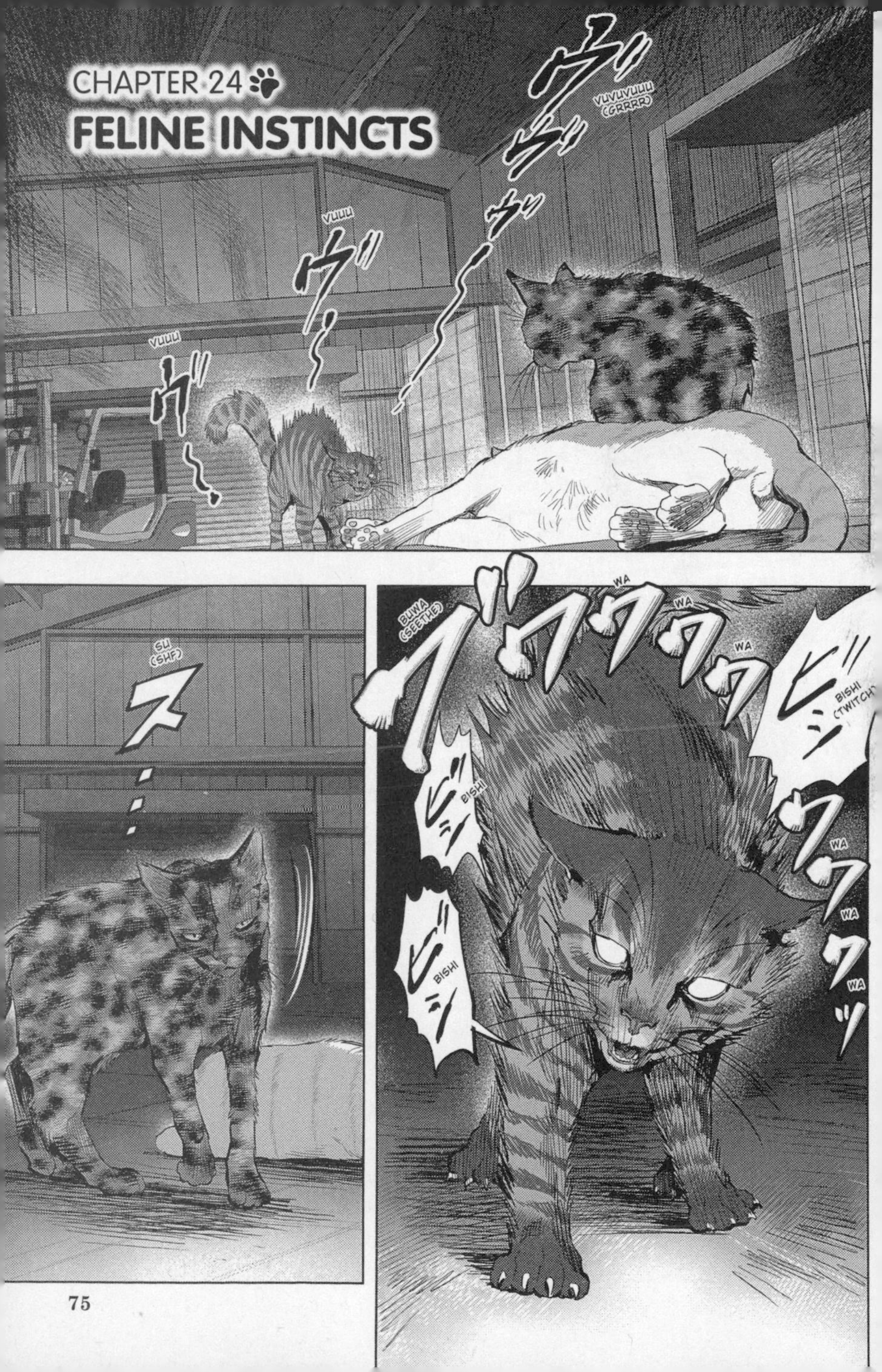
VUVUVUUU (GRRRR)
VUUU
VUUU
BISHI (TWITCH)
WA
WA
WA
BUWA (SEETHE)
WA
WA
WA
BISHI
BISHI
SU (SHF)

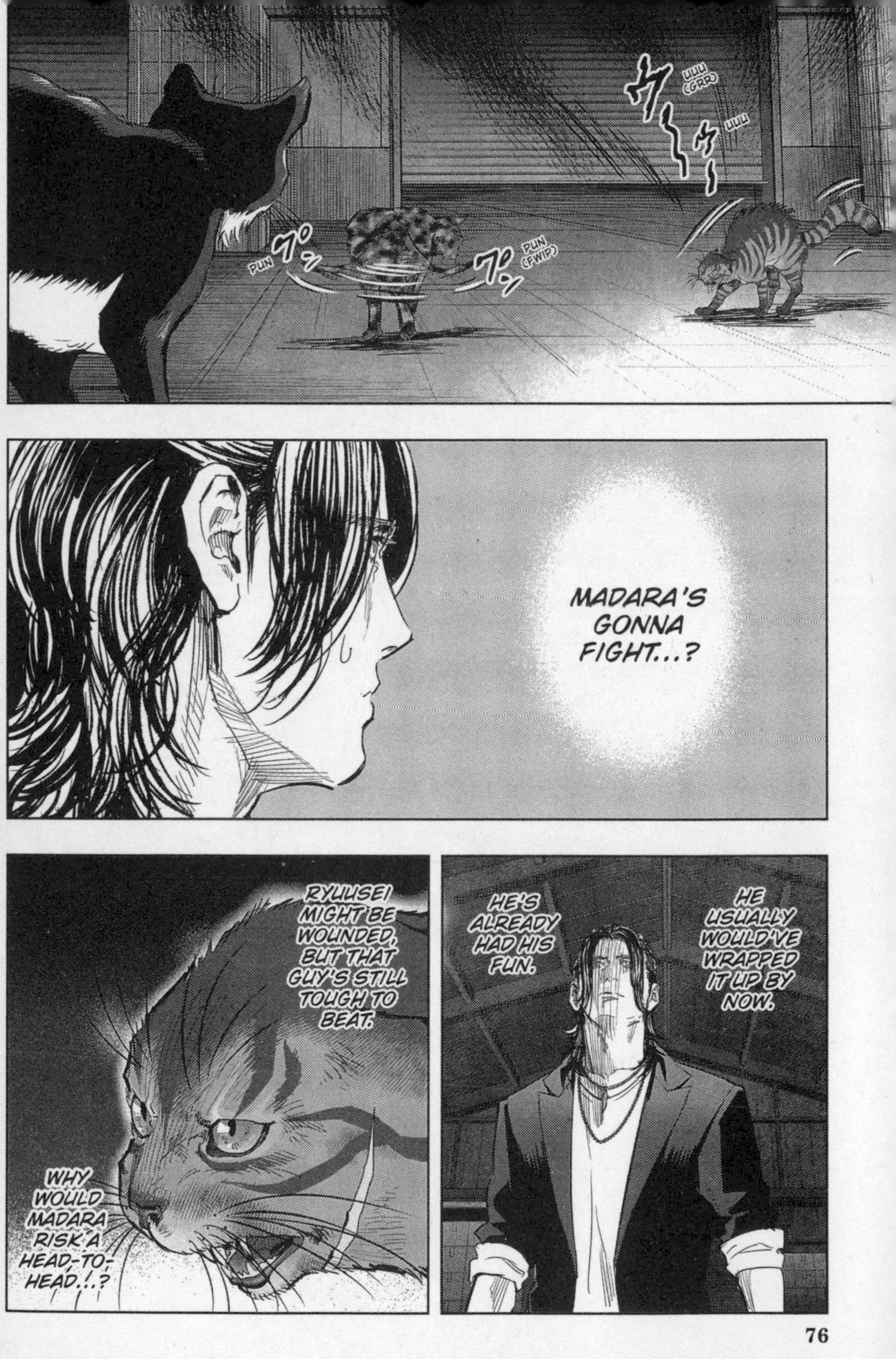
UUU (GRR)
UUU
PUN (FWIP)
PUN
MADARA'S GONNA FIGHT...?
HE USUALLY WOULD'VE WRAPPED IT UP BY NOW.
HE'S ALREADY HAD HIS FUN.
RYUUSEI MIGHT BE WOUNDED, BUT THAT GUY'S STILL TOUGH TO BEAT.
WHY WOULD MADARA RISK A HEAD-TO-HEAD..!?

WHY'S HE SO OBSESSED WITH THAT DARK TABBY...?

I WAS THE TARGET JUST LIKE BEFORE.

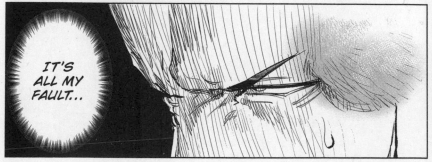

IT'S ALL MY FAULT...

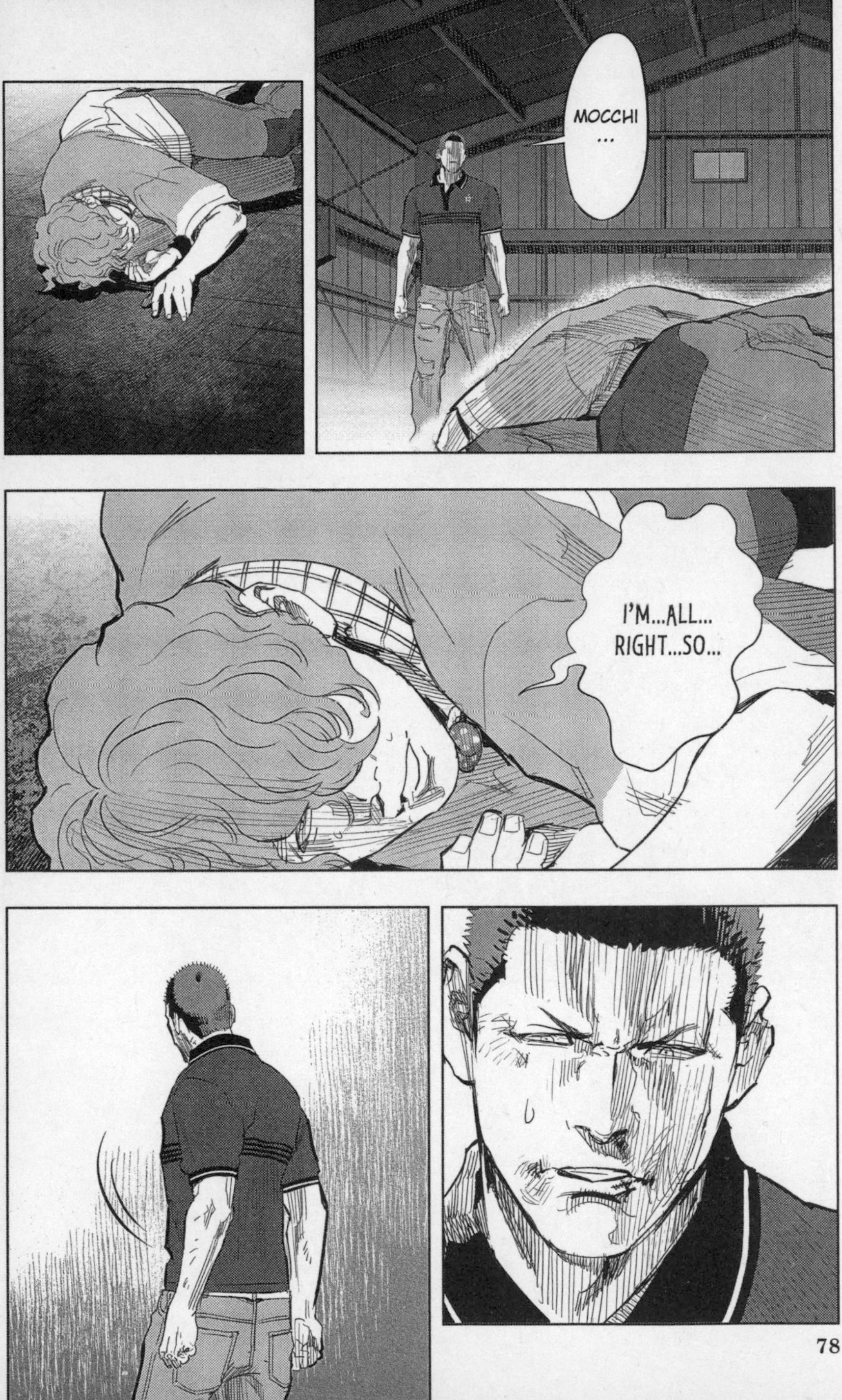
MOCCHI ...
I'M...ALL... RIGHT...SO...

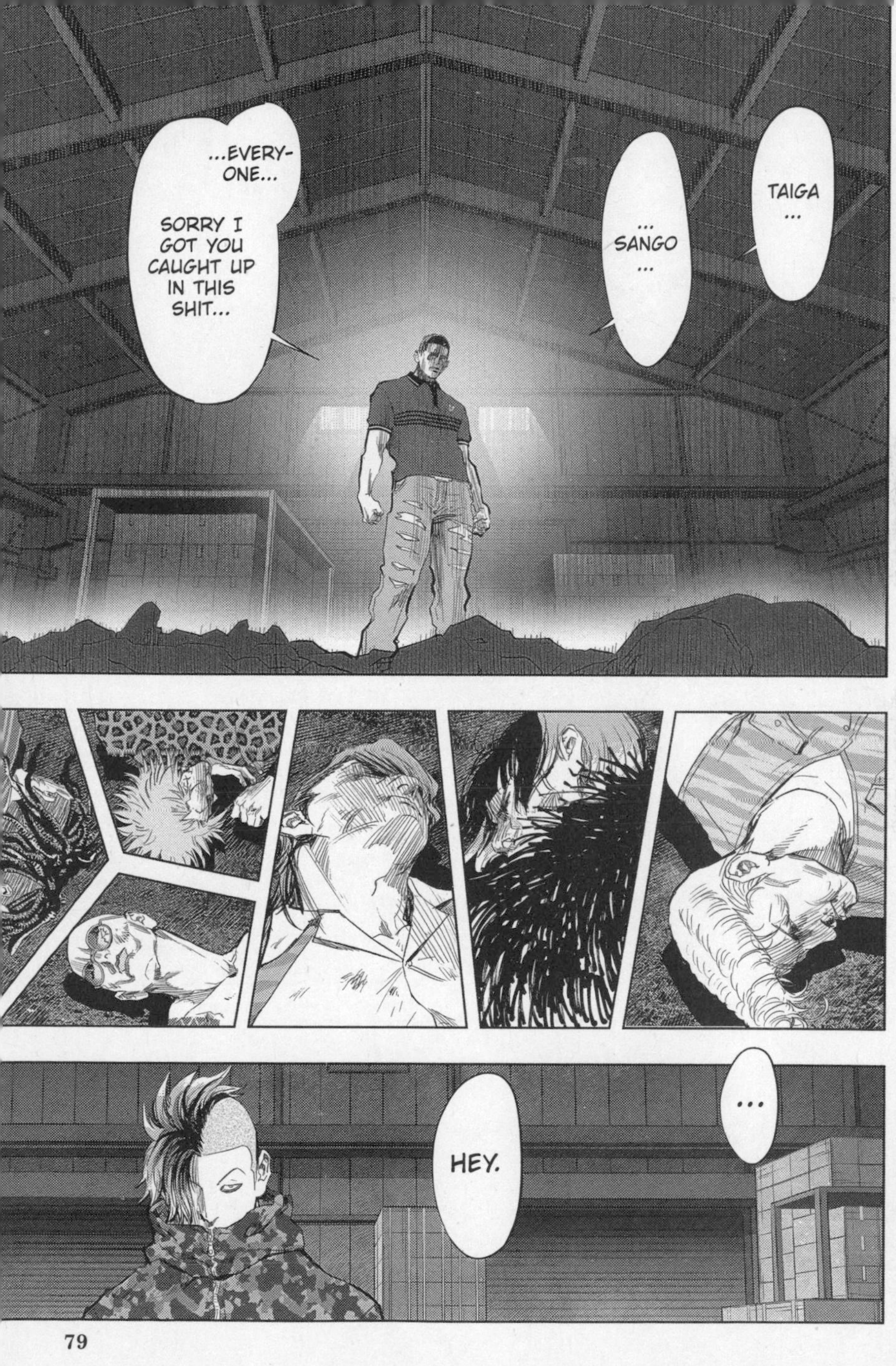
TAIGA ...
... SANGO ...
...EVERY-ONE...
SORRY I GOT YOU CAUGHT UP IN THIS SHIT...
...
HEY.

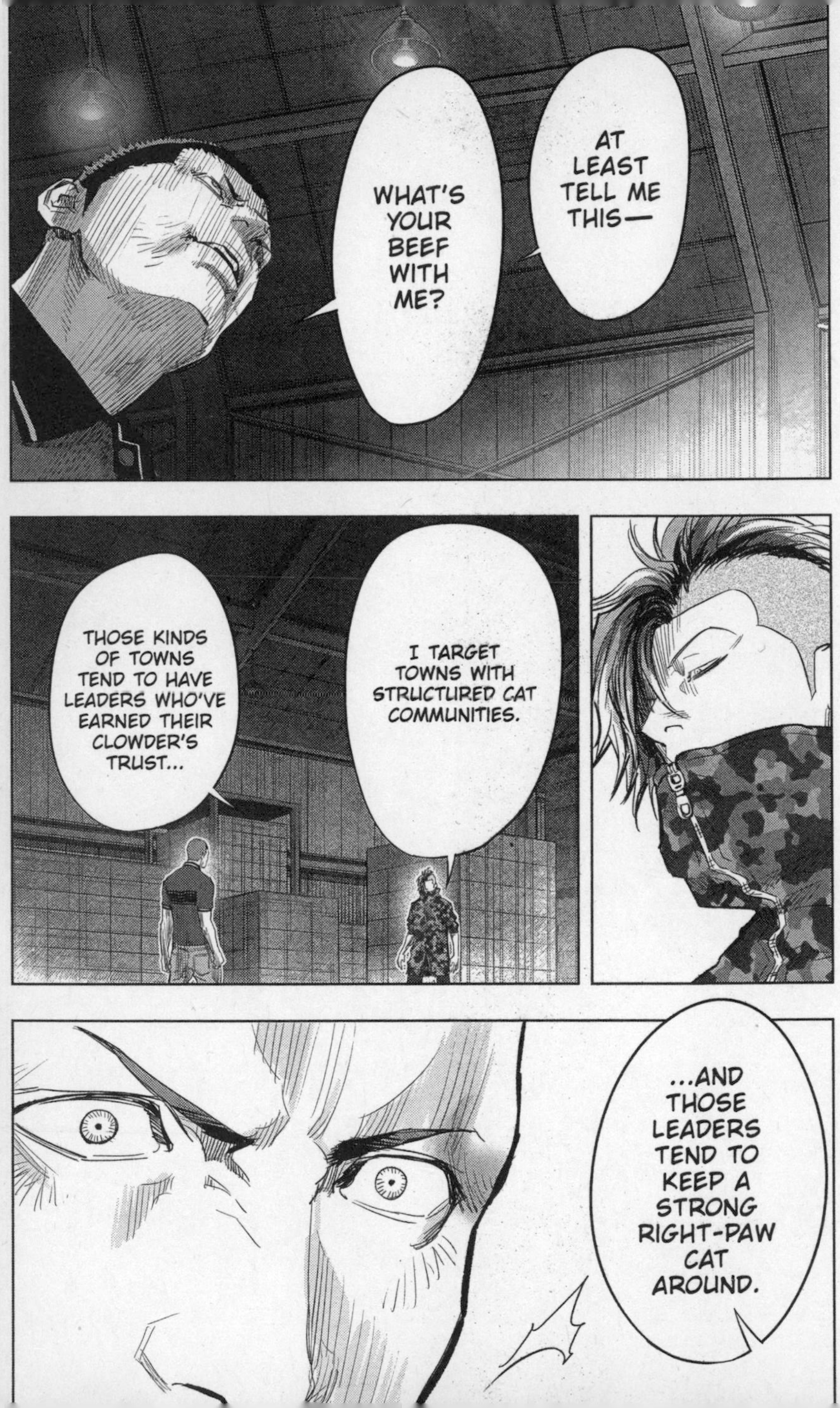
AT LEAST TELL ME THIS—
WHAT'S YOUR BEEF WITH ME?
I TARGET TOWNS WITH STRUCTURED CAT COMMUNITIES.
THOSE KINDS OF TOWNS TEND TO HAVE LEADERS WHO'VE EARNED THEIR CLOWDER'S TRUST...
...AND THOSE LEADERS TEND TO KEEP A STRONG RIGHT-PAW CAT AROUND.

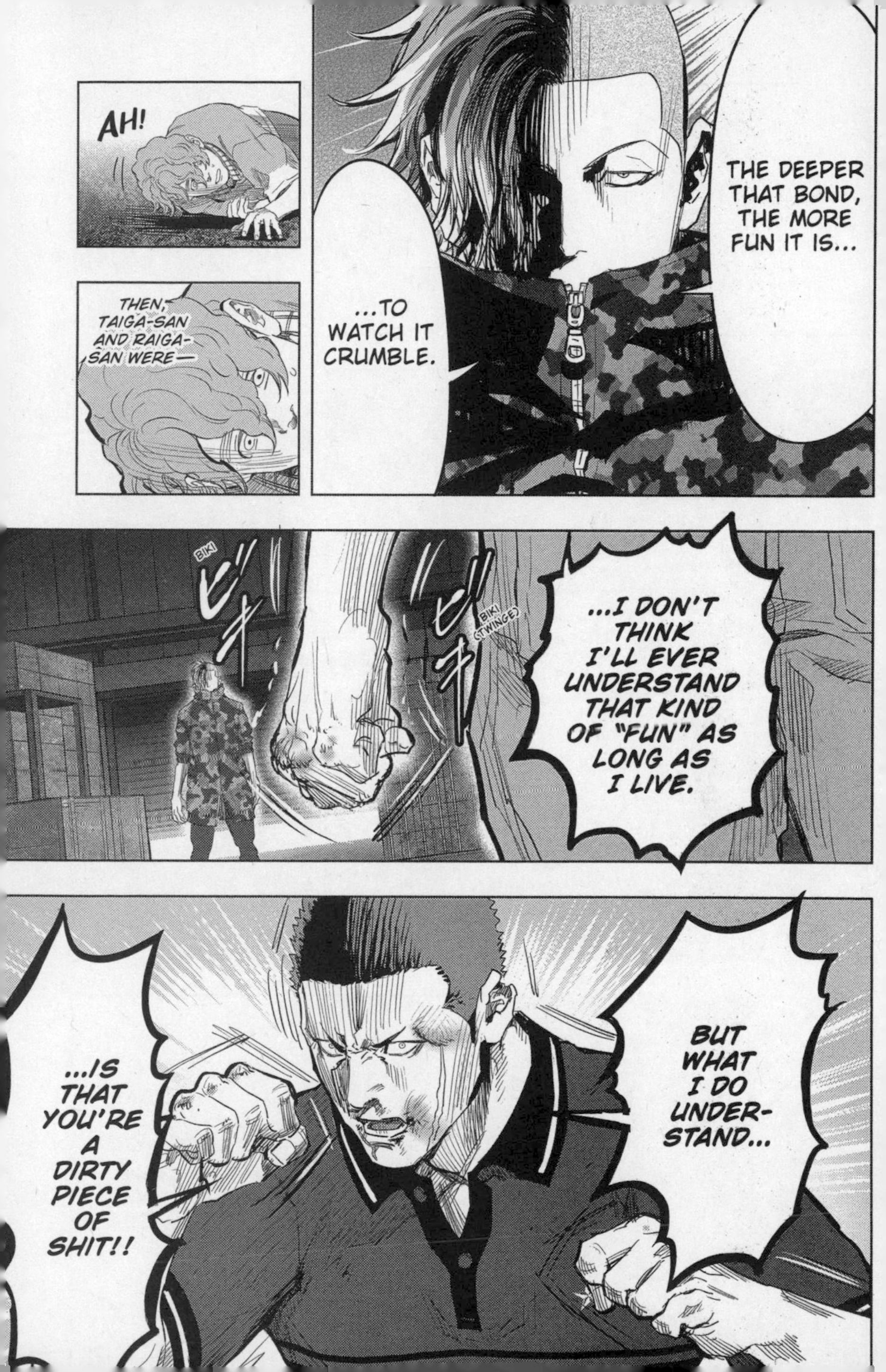
THE DEEPER THAT BOND, THE MORE FUN IT IS...
...TO WATCH IT CRUMBLE.
AH!
THEN, TAIGA-SAN AND RAIGA-SAN WERE—
...I DON'T THINK I'LL EVER UNDERSTAND THAT KIND OF "FUN" AS LONG AS I LIVE.
ビキ
BIKI (TWINGE)
ビキ
BIKI
BUT WHAT I DO UNDER-STAND...
...IS THAT YOU'RE A DIRTY PIECE OF SHIT!!

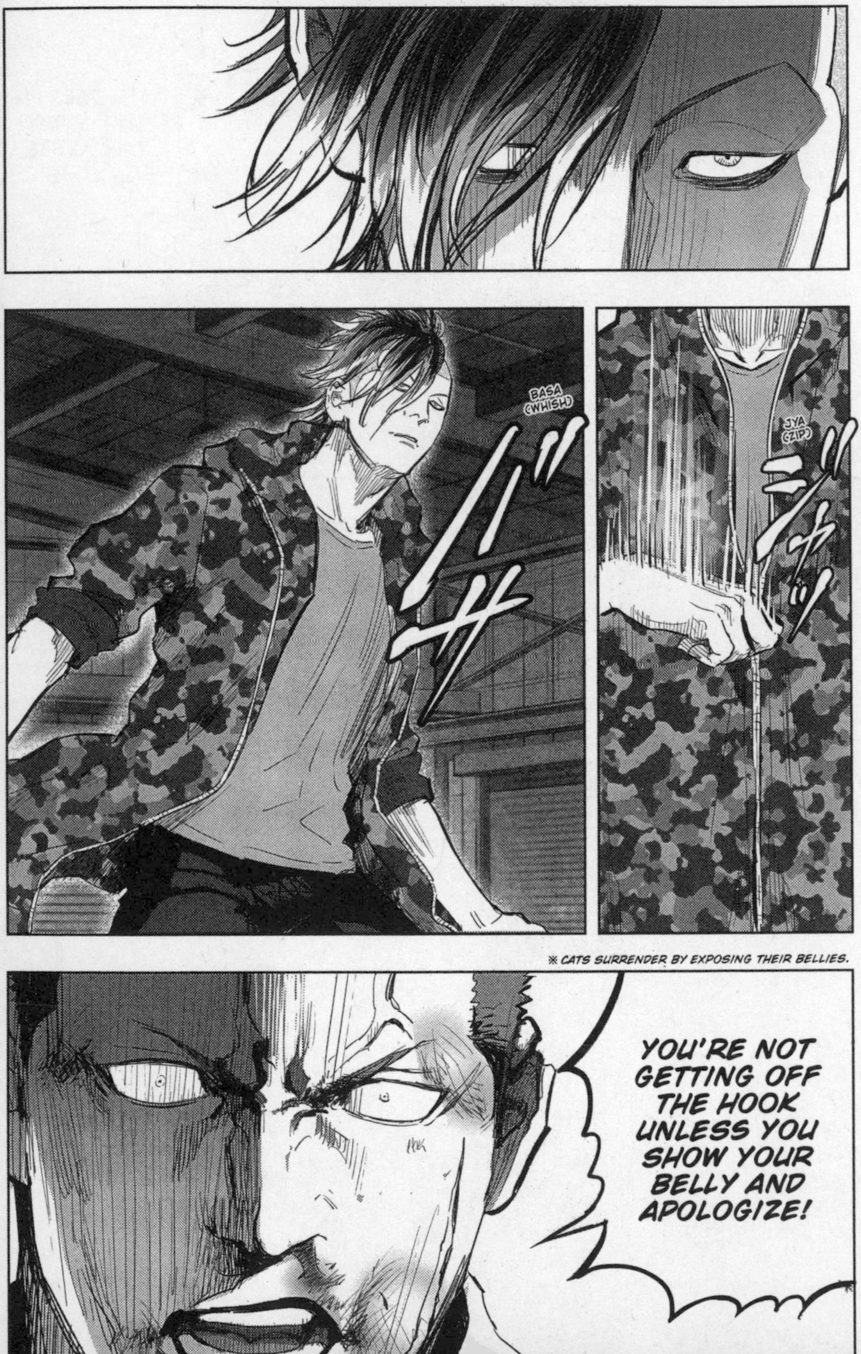
JYA (ZIP)
BASA (WHISH)
※ CATS SURRENDER BY EXPOSING THEIR BELLIES.
YOU'RE NOT GETTING OFF THE HOOK UNLESS YOU SHOW YOUR BELLY AND APOLOGIZE!

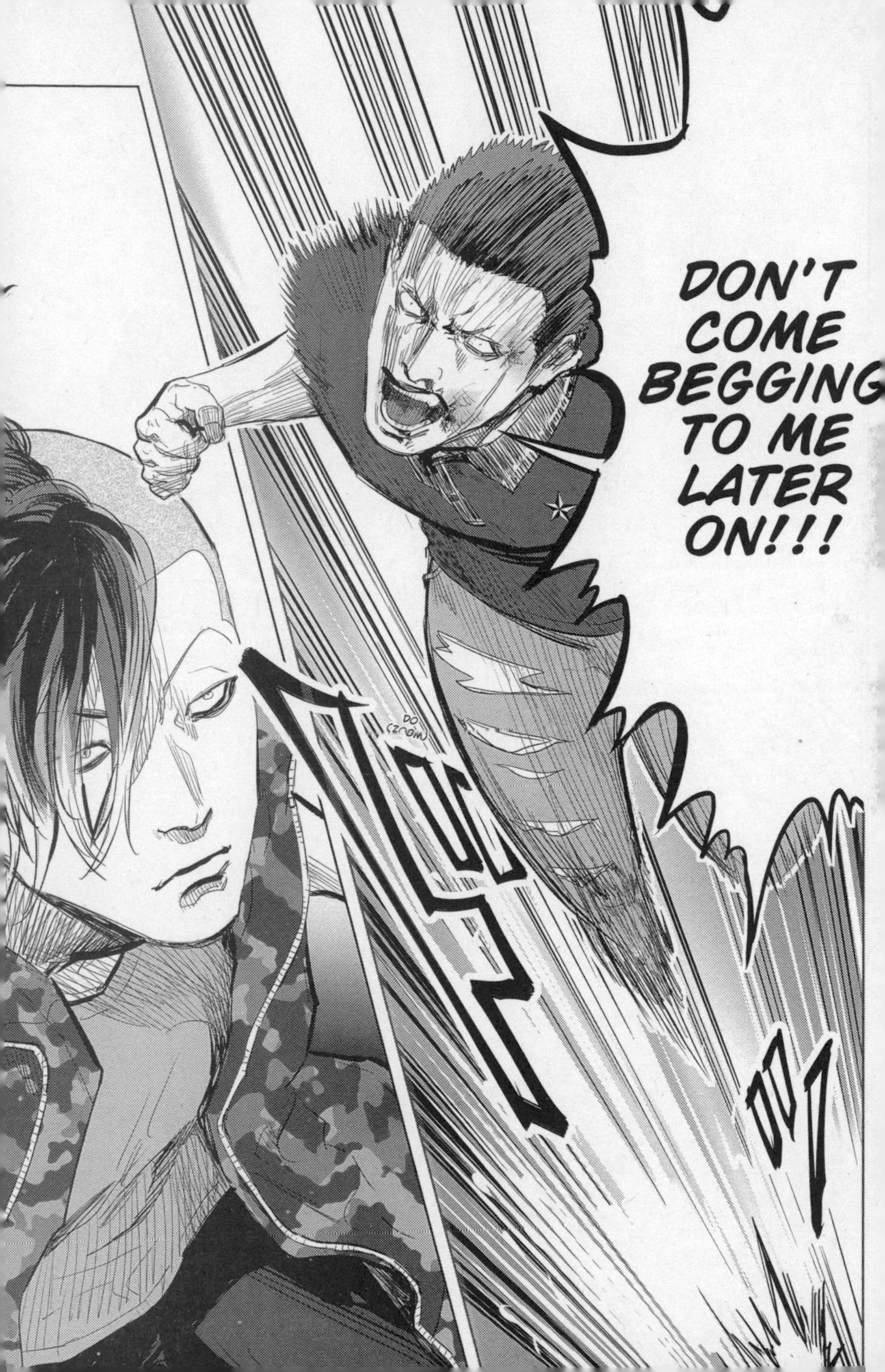
DON'T COME BEGGING TO ME LATER ON!!!
DO (ZOOM)

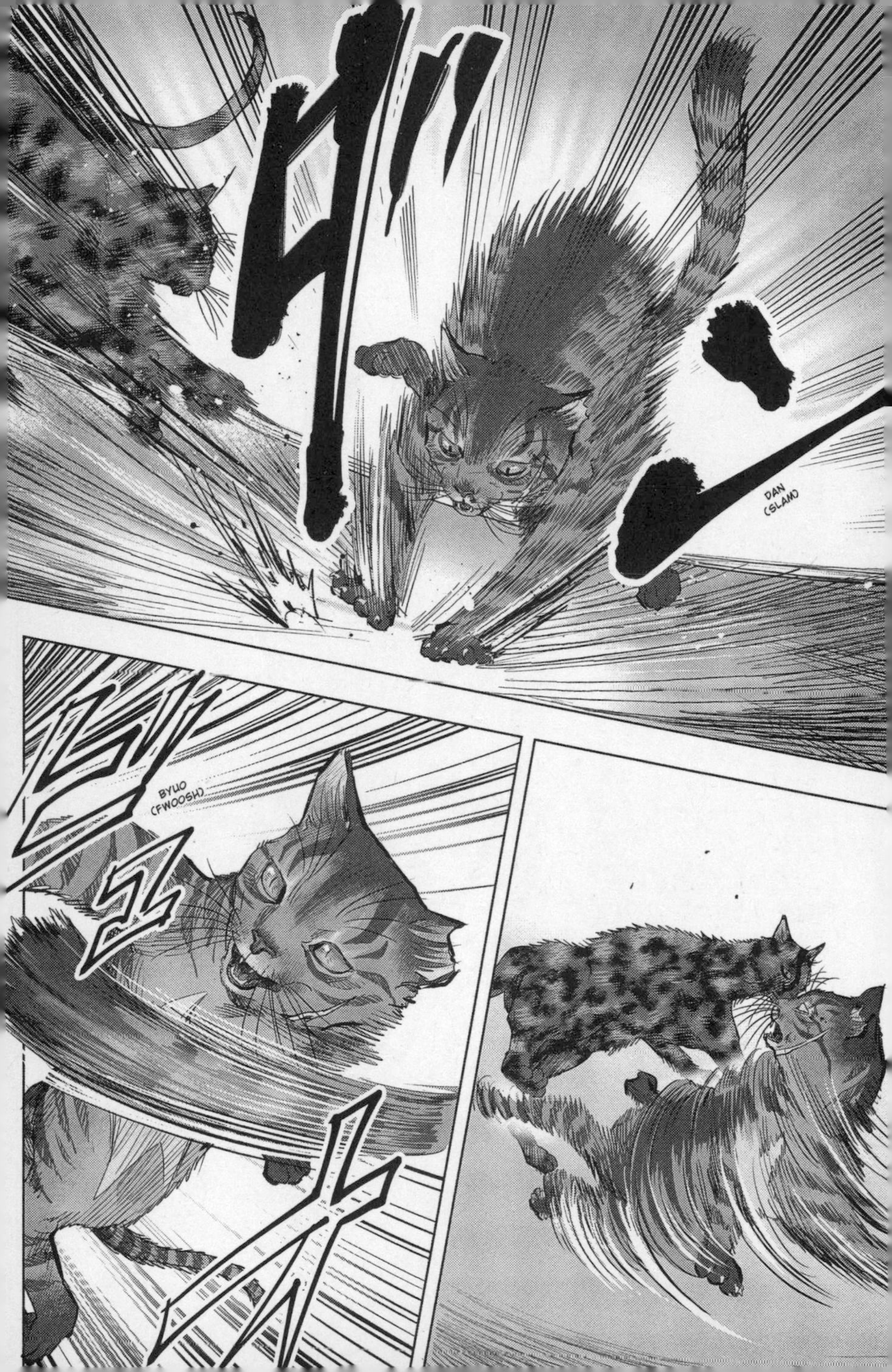
DAN
(SLAM)
BYUO
(FWOOSH)

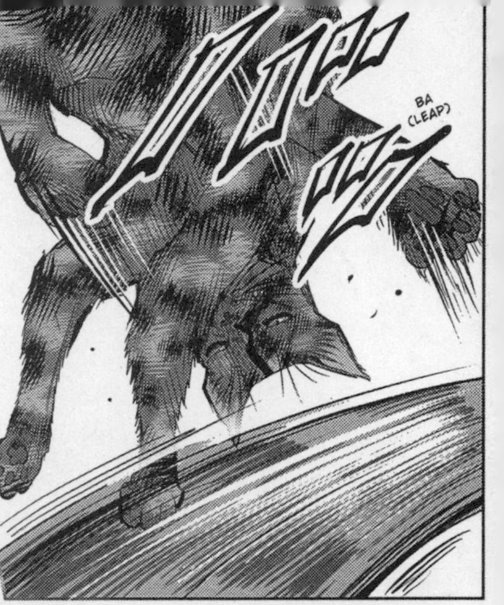
BA
(LEAP)
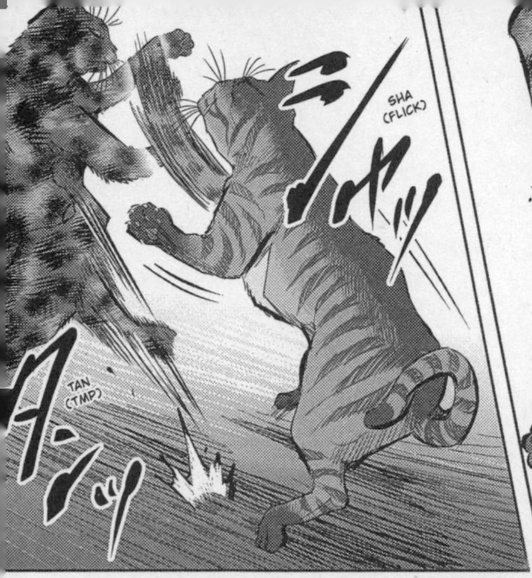
SHA
(FLICK)
TAN
(TMP)
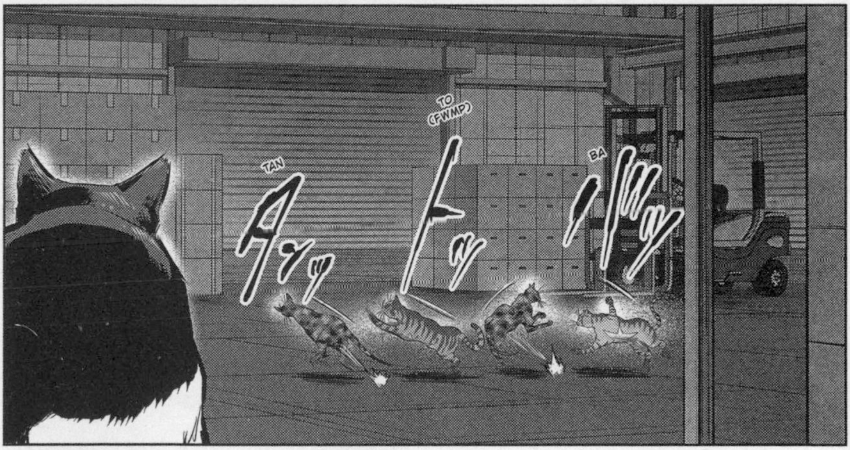
BA
TO
(FWMP)
TAN
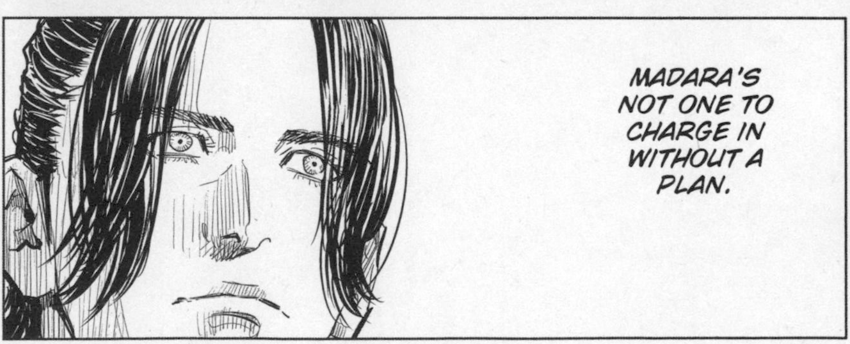
MADARA'S NOT ONE TO CHARGE IN WITHOUT A PLAN.

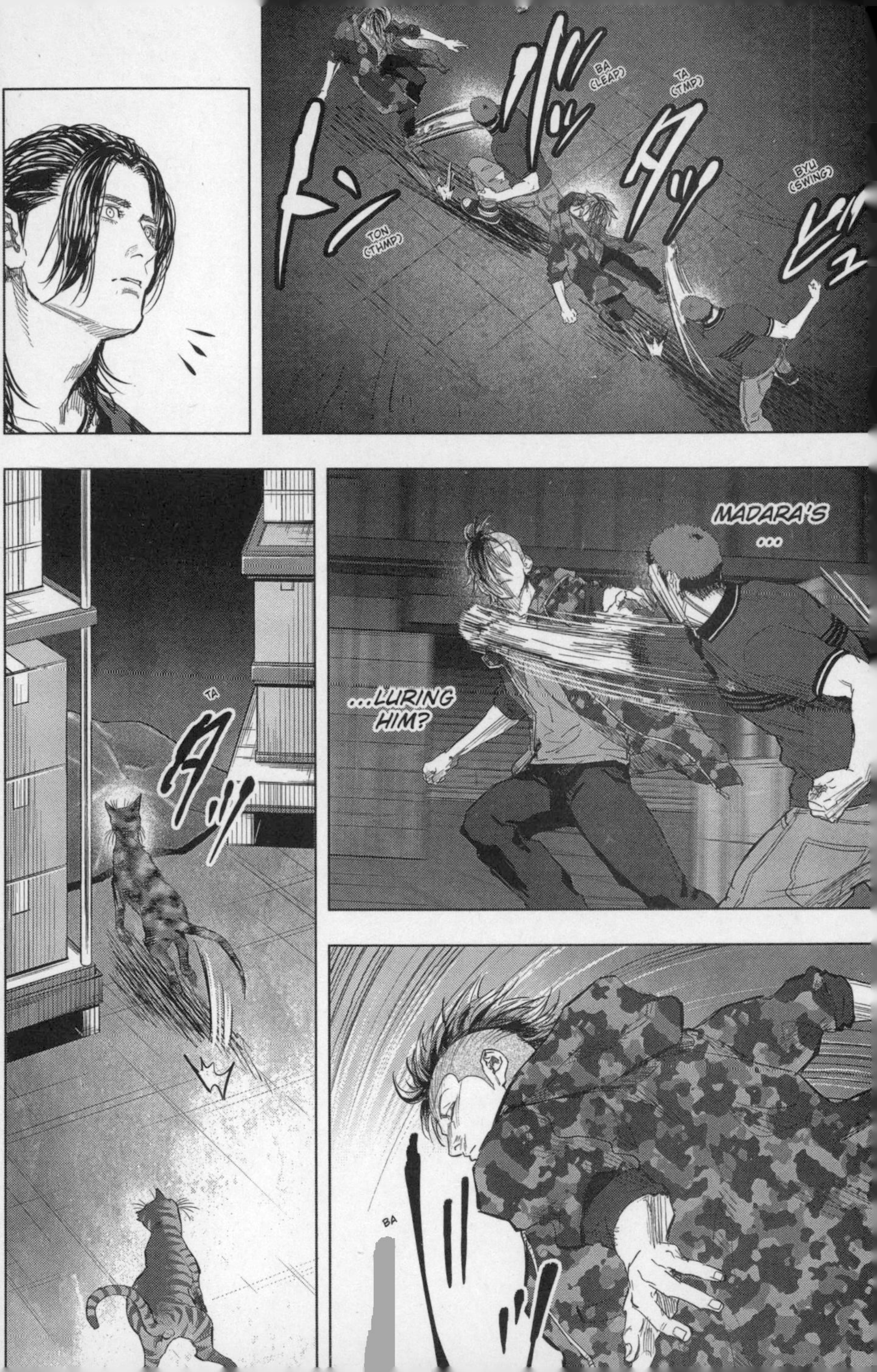
BYU (SWING)
TA (TMP)
BA (LEAP)
TON (THMP)
MADARA'S...
...LURING HIM?
BA
TA

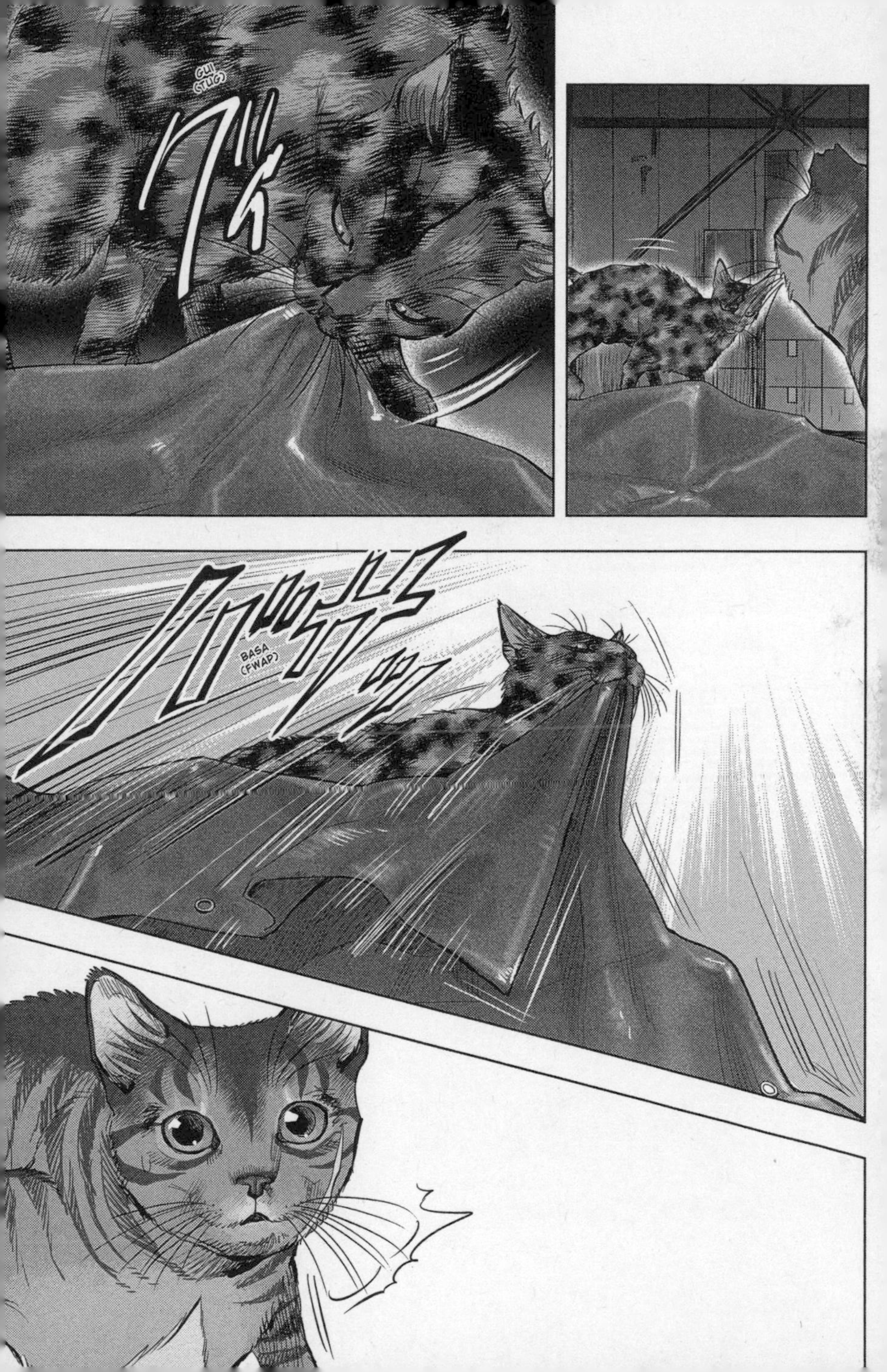
GUI
(TUG)
BASA
(FWAP)

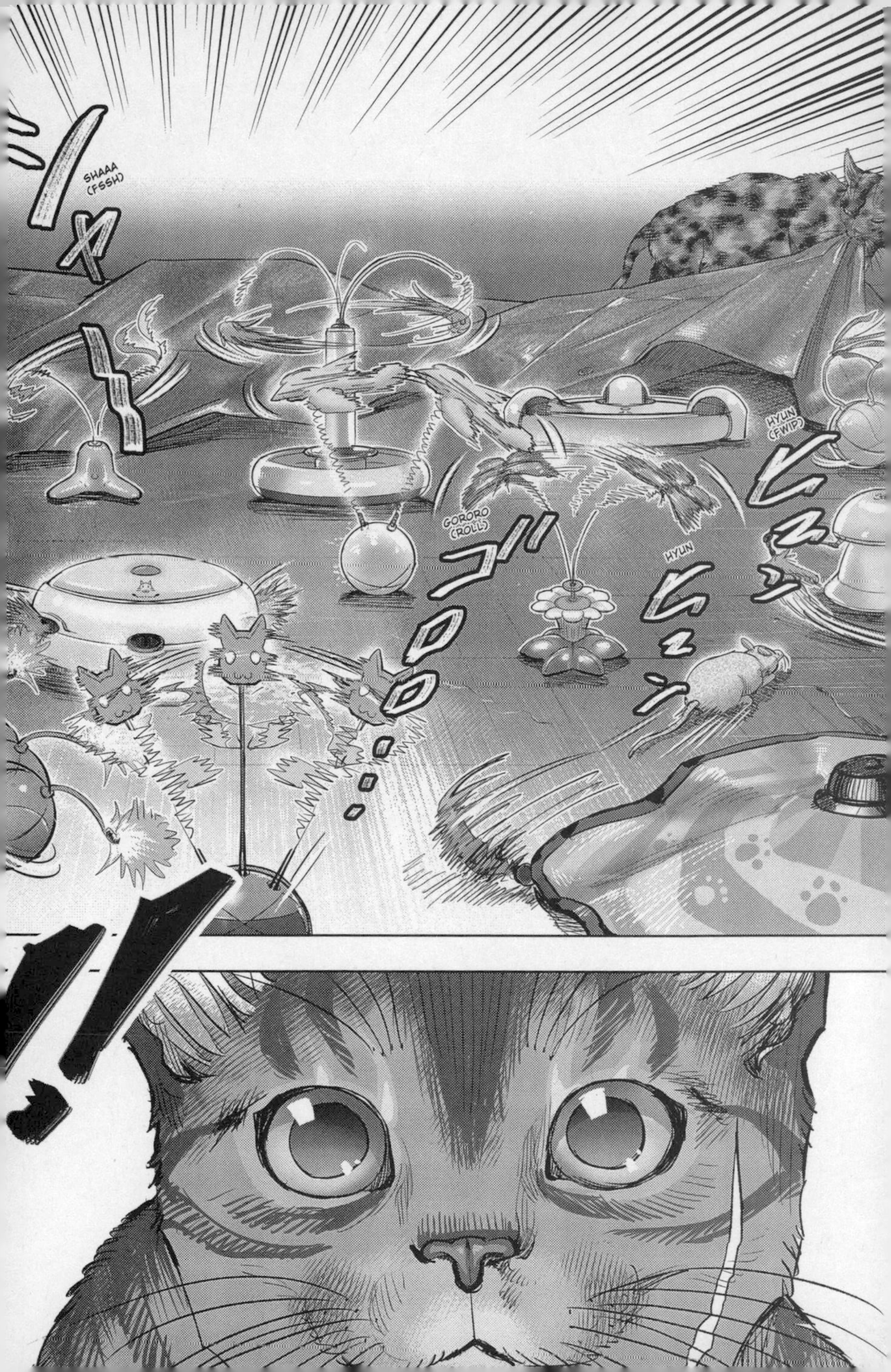
HYUN (FWIP)
HYUN
GORORO (ROLL)
SHAAA (FSSH)

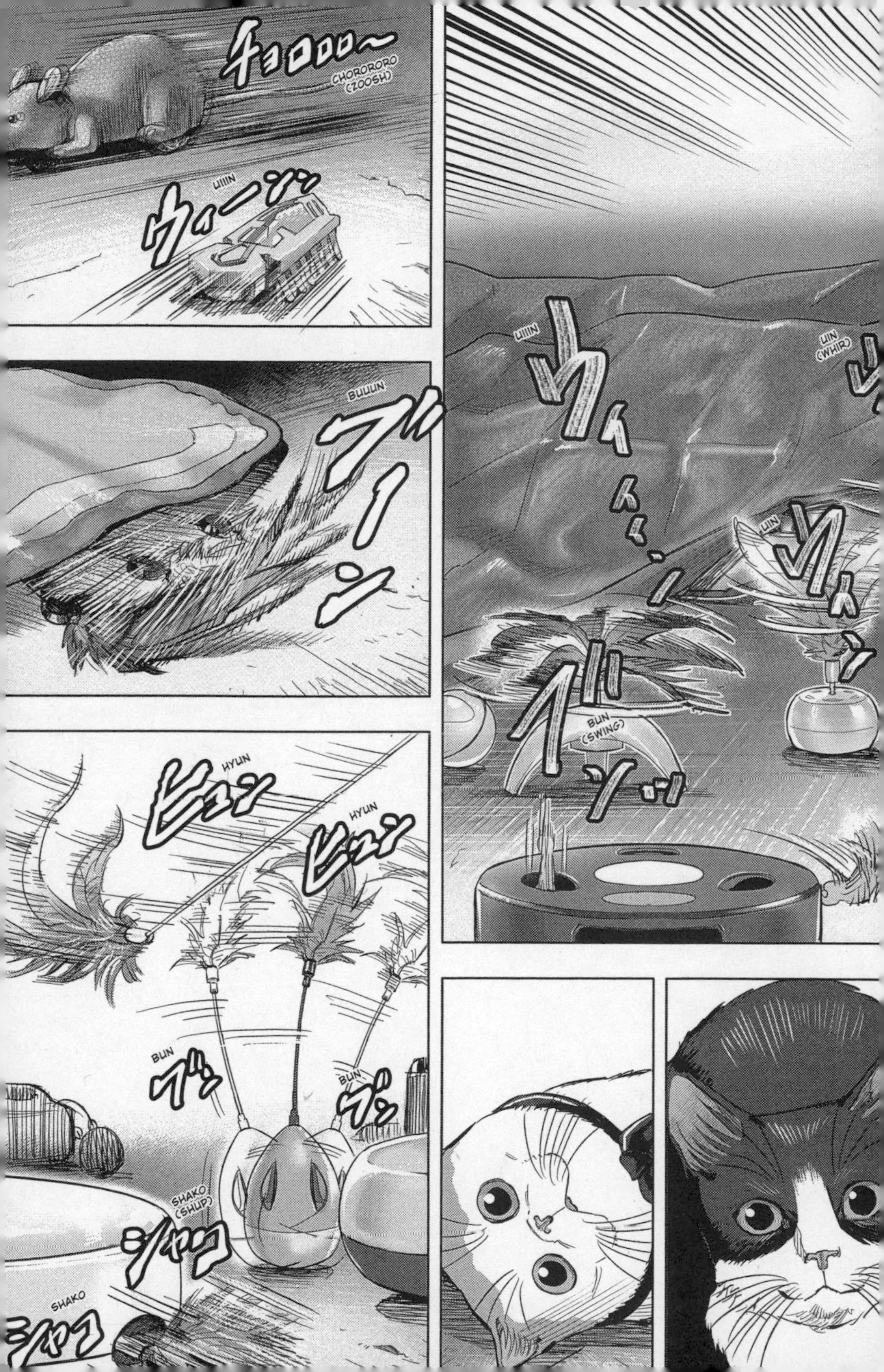
UIN (WHIR)
UIIIN
UIN
BUN (SWING)
CHOROROR0 (ZOOSH)
UIIIN
BUUUN
HYUN
HYUN
BUN
BUN
SHAKO (SHUP)
SHAKO

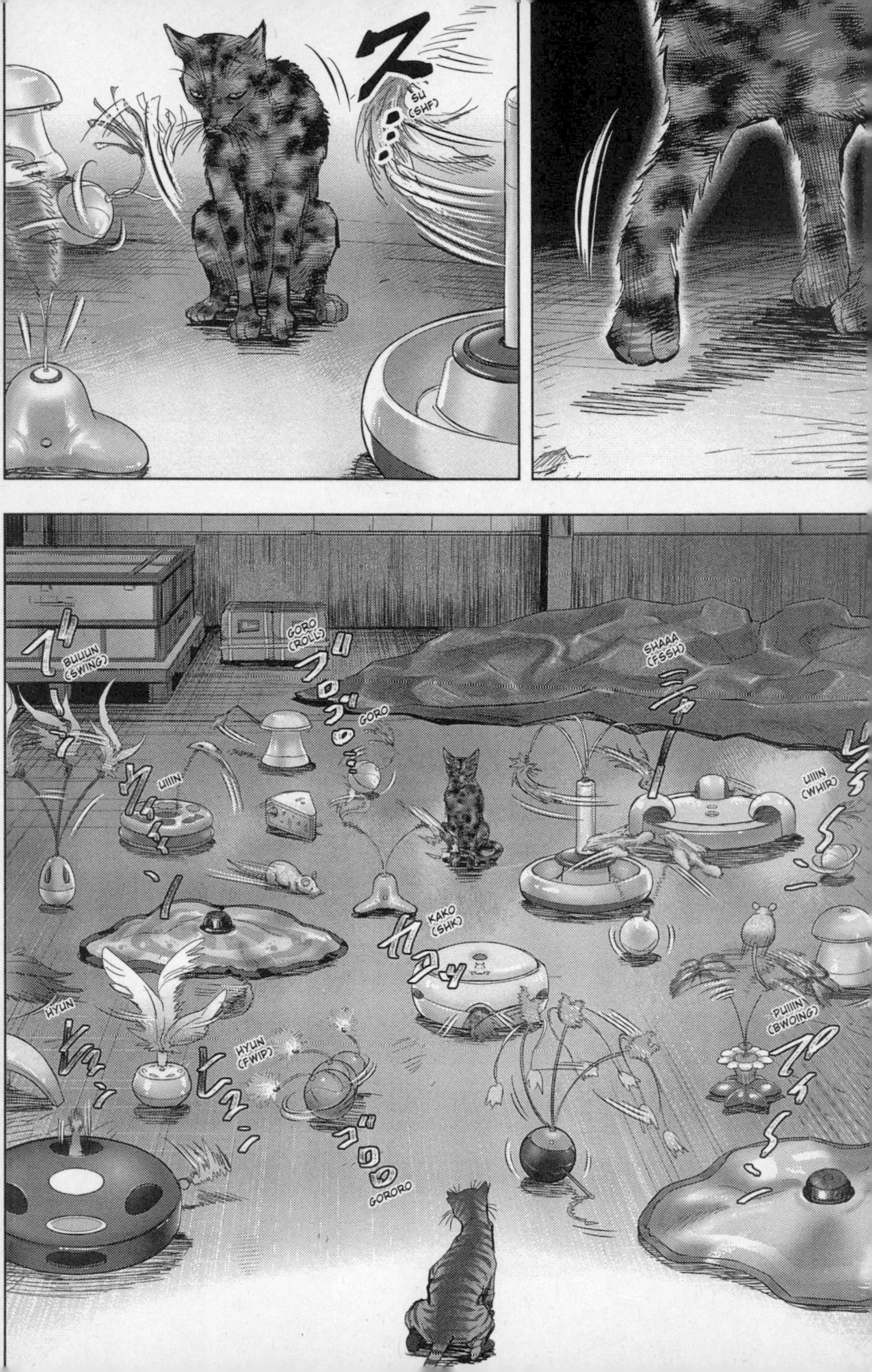
SU (SHF)
SHAAA (FSSH)
UIIIN (WHIR)
GORO (ROLL)
GORO
BUUUN (SWING)
UIIIN
KAKO (SHK)
PUIIIN (BWOING)
HYUN (FWIP)
HYUN
GORORO

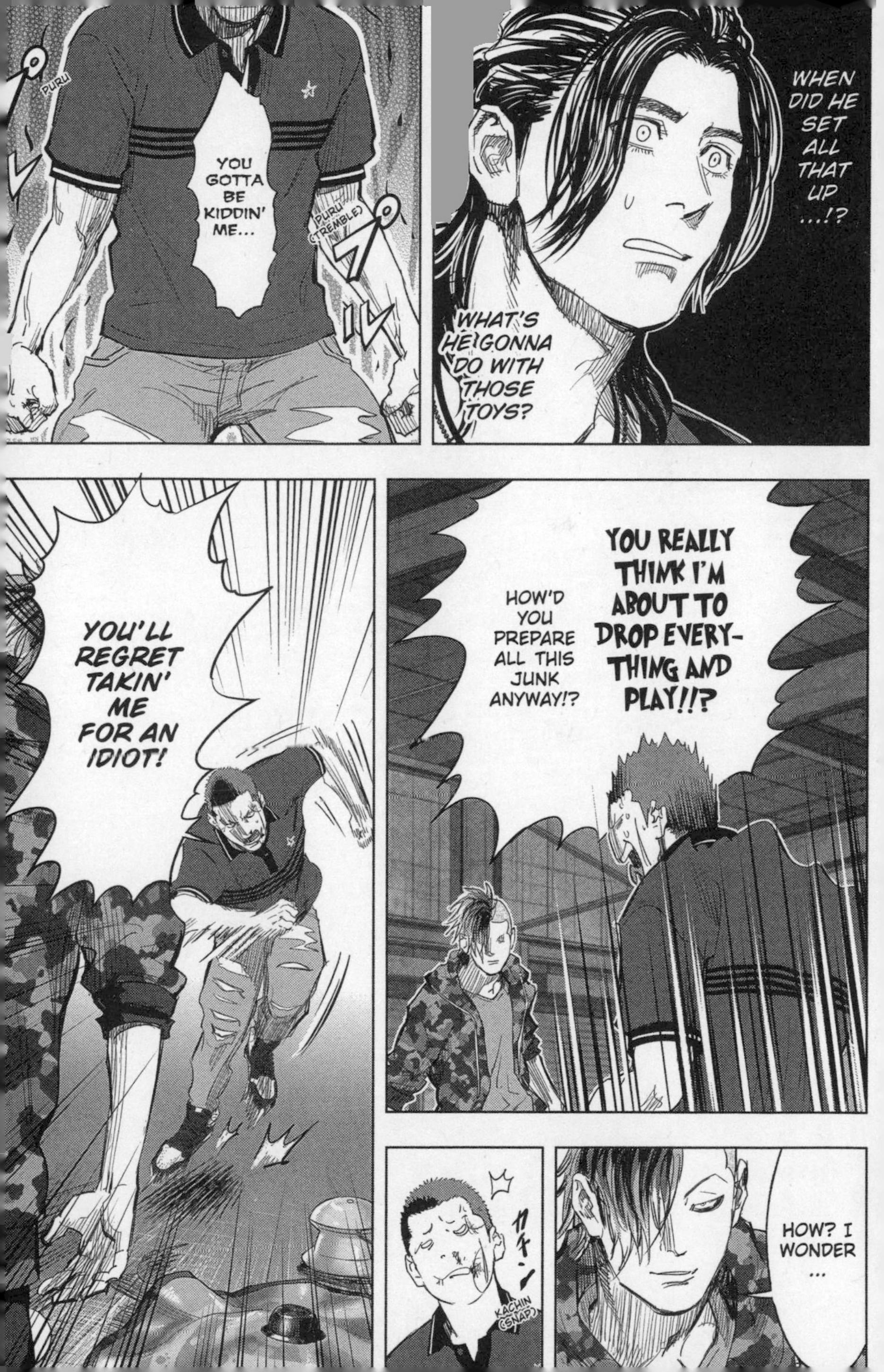
WHEN DID HE SET ALL THAT UP ...!?
WHAT'S HE GONNA DO WITH THOSE TOYS?
PURU
YOU GOTTA BE KIDDIN' ME...
PURU (TREMBLE)
YOU REALLY THINK I'M ABOUT TO DROP EVERY-THING AND PLAY!!?
HOW'D YOU PREPARE ALL THIS JUNK ANYWAY!?
HOW? I WONDER ...
KACHIN (SNAP)
YOU'LL REGRET TAKIN' ME FOR AN IDIOT!

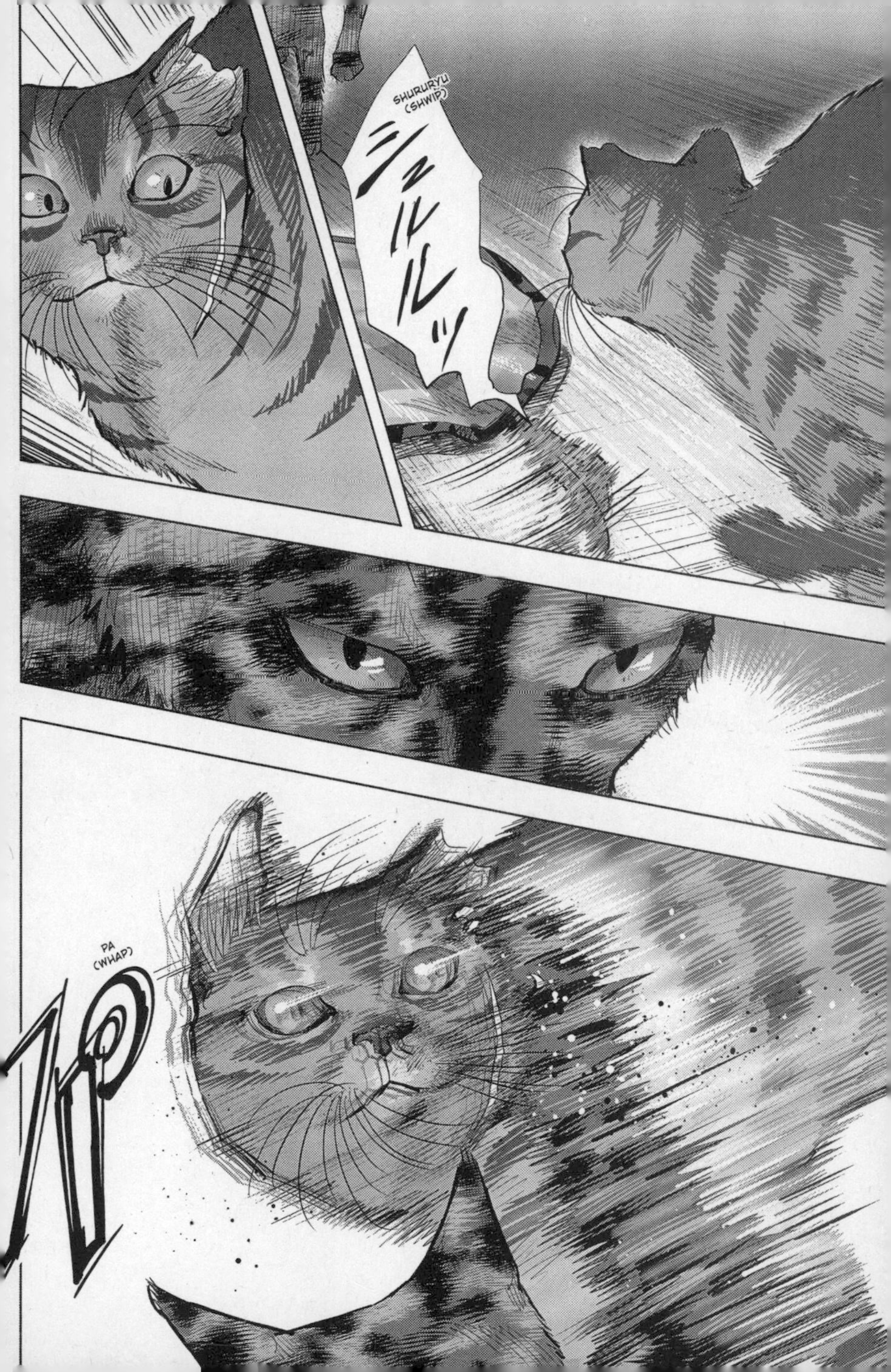
SHURURYU (SHWIP)
シュルルッ
PA (WHAP)
パ

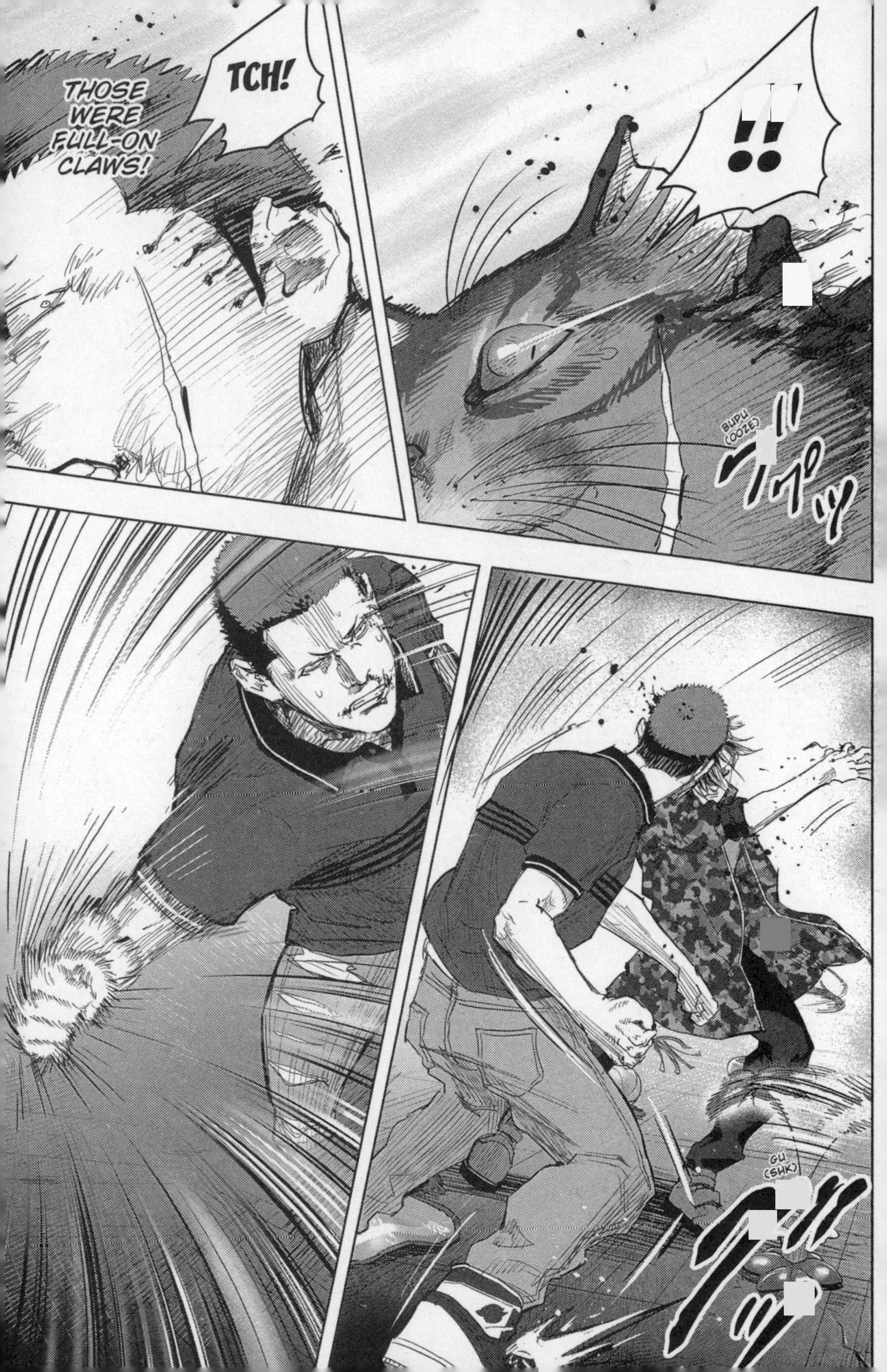
!!
BUPU (OOZE)
TCH!
THOSE WERE FULL-ON CLAWS!
GU (SHK)

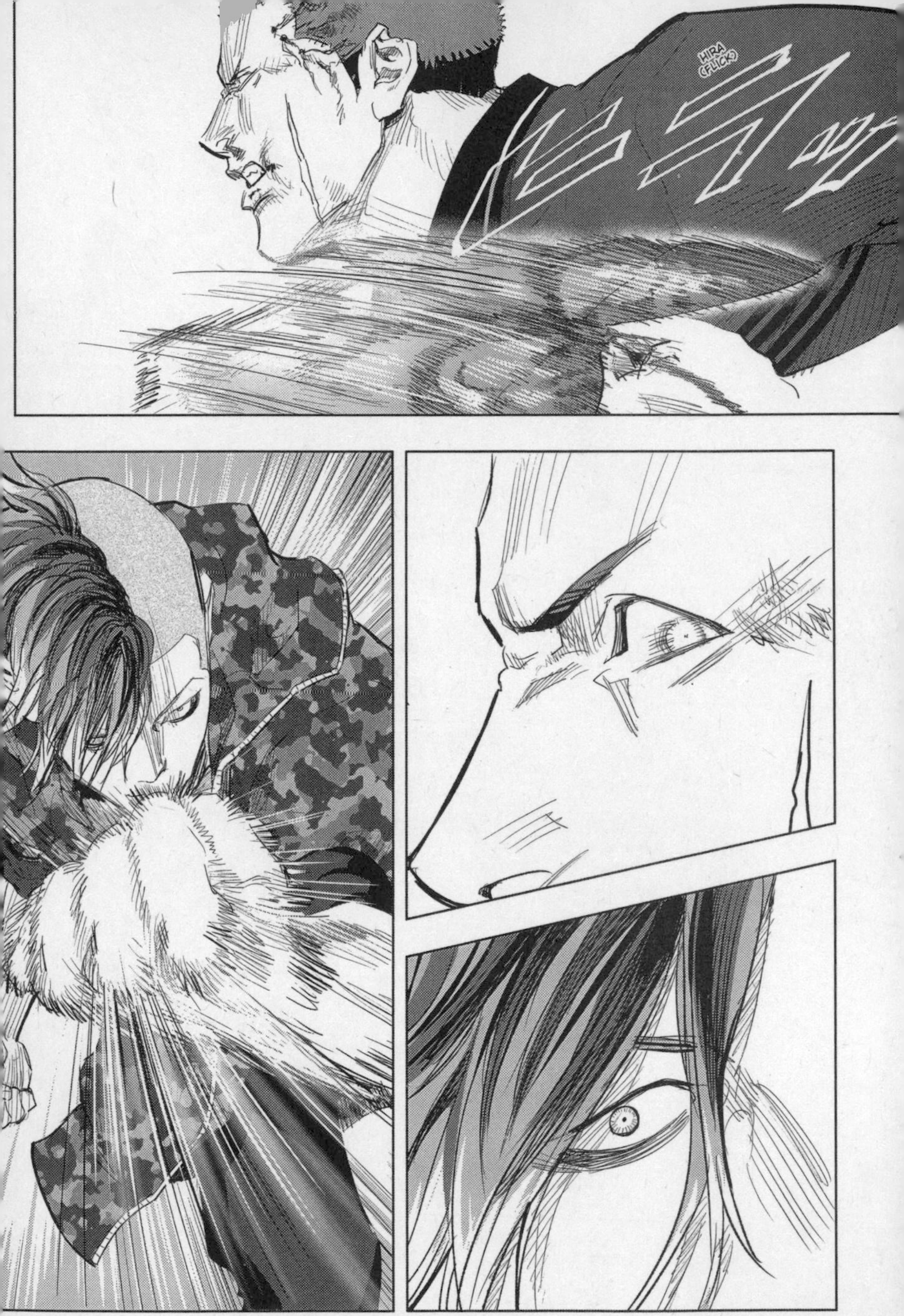
HIRA (FLICK)

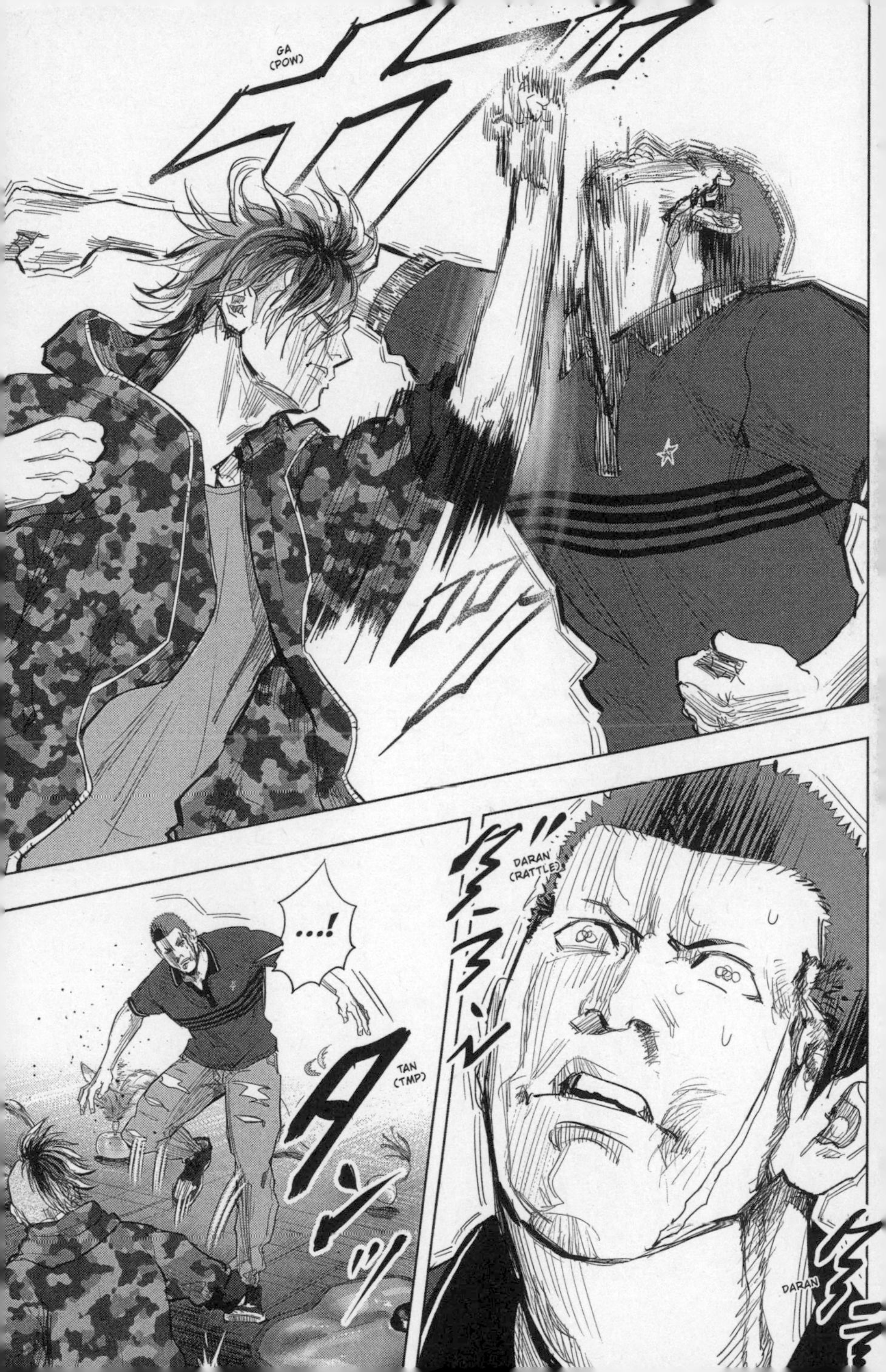
GA
(POW)
DARAN
(RATTLE)
DARAN
...!
TAN
(TMP)

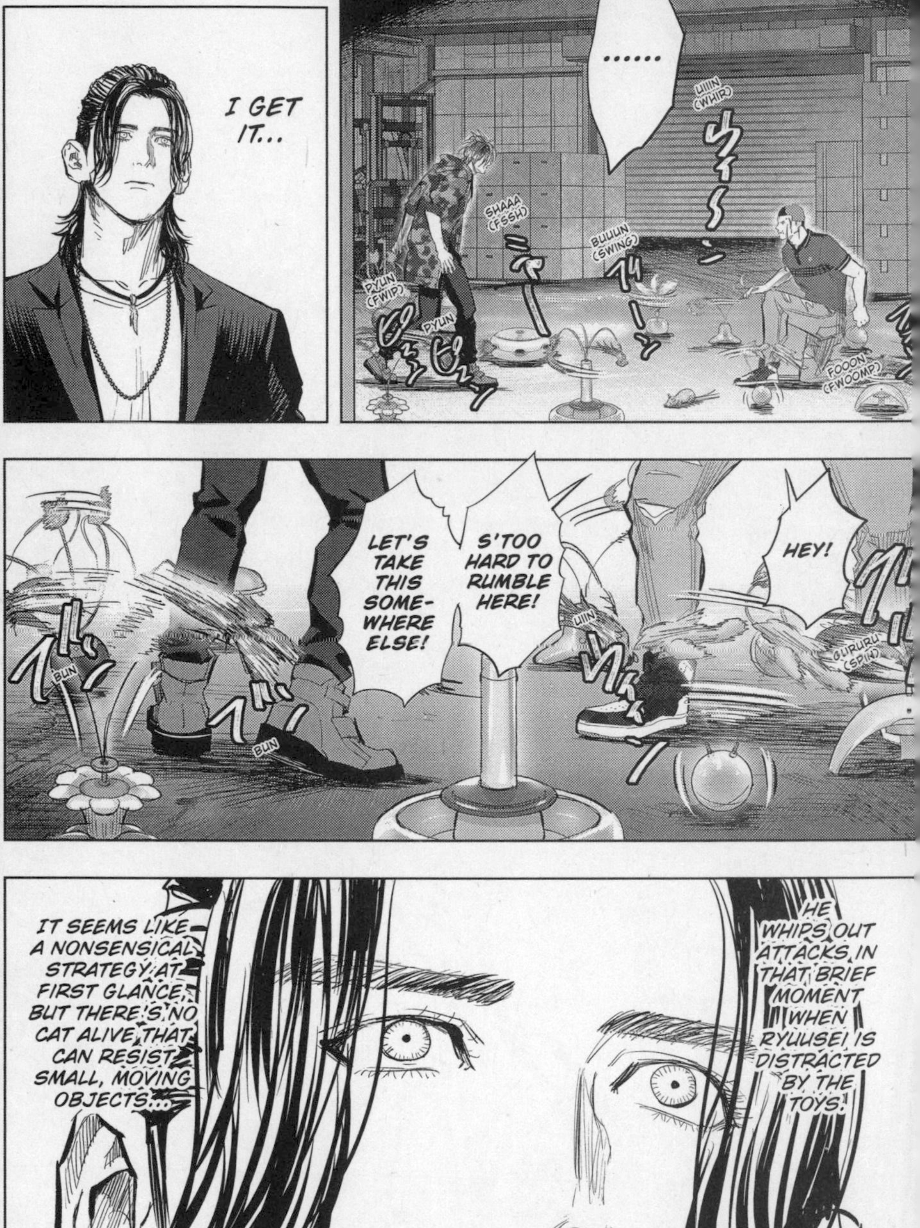
......
UIIIN (WHIR)
FOOON (FWOOMP)
BUUUN (SWING)
SHAAA (FSSH)
PYUN (FWIP)
PYUN
I GET IT...
HEY!
GURURU (SPIN)
UIIN
S'TOO HARD TO RUMBLE HERE!
LET'S TAKE THIS SOMEWHERE ELSE!
BUN
BUN
HE WHIPS OUT ATTACKS IN THAT BRIEF MOMENT WHEN RYUUSEI IS DISTRACTED BY THE TOYS!
IT SEEMS LIKE A NONSENSICAL STRATEGY AT FIRST GLANCE, BUT THERE'S NO CAT ALIVE THAT CAN RESIST SMALL, MOVING OBJECTS...

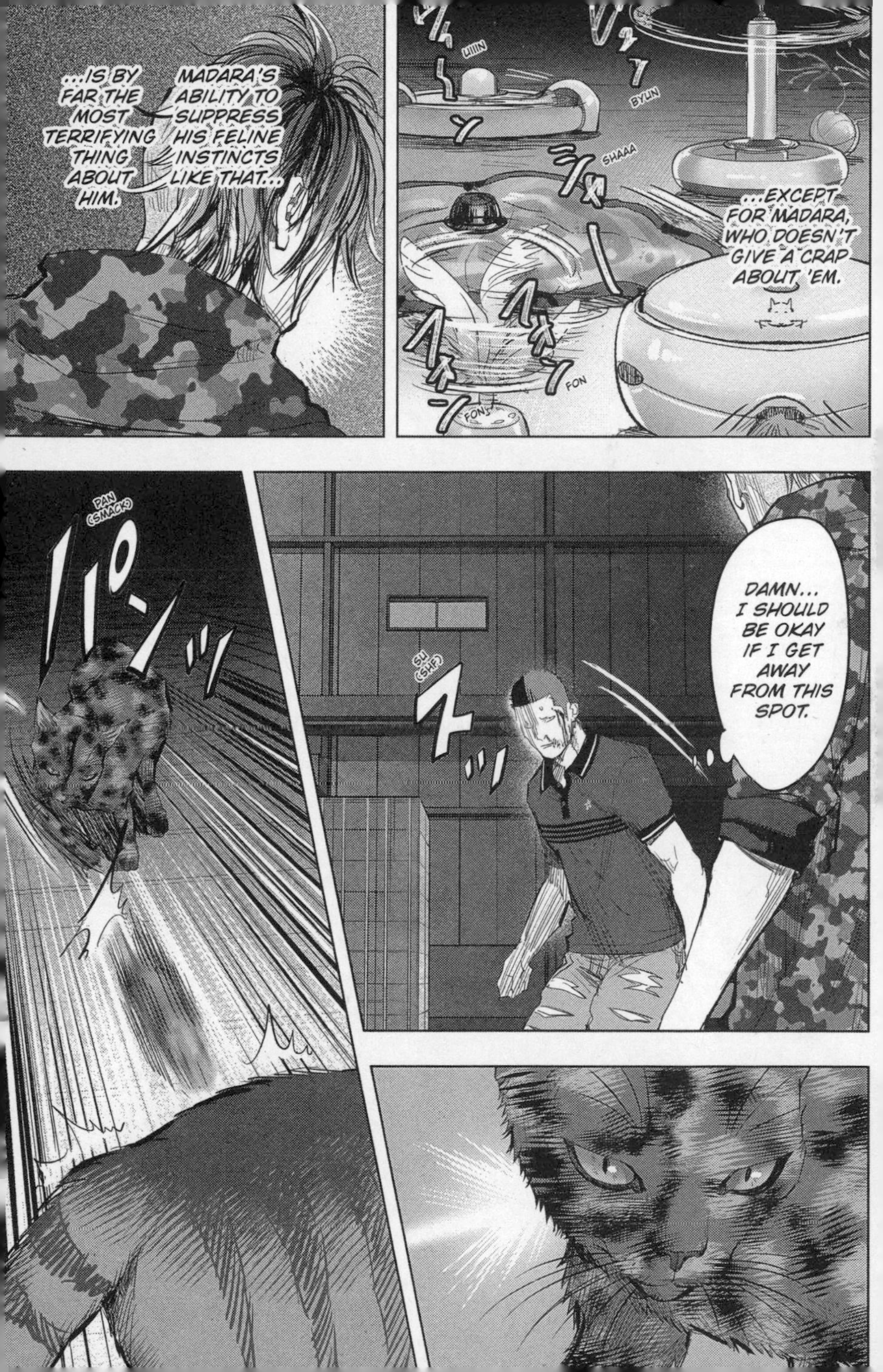
UIIIN
BYUN
SHAAA
FON
FON
...EXCEPT FOR MADARA, WHO DOESN'T GIVE A CRAP ABOUT 'EM.
MADARA'S ABILITY TO SUPPRESS HIS FELINE INSTINCTS LIKE THAT...
...IS BY FAR THE MOST TERRIFYING THING ABOUT HIM.
SU (SHF)
DAMN... I SHOULD BE OKAY IF I GET AWAY FROM THIS SPOT.
PAN (SMACK)

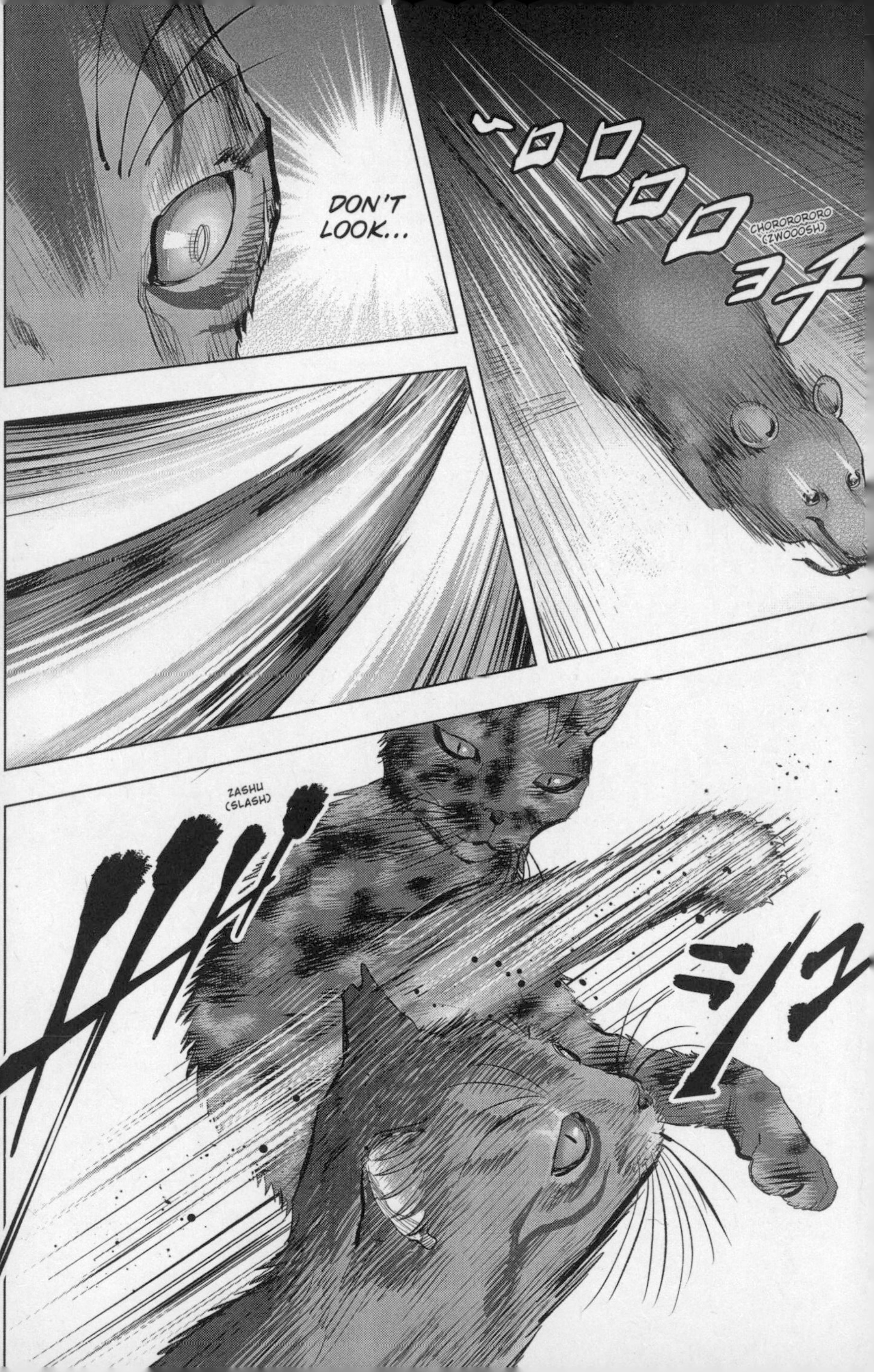
CHORORORORO
(ZWOOOSH)
DON'T LOOK...
ZASHU
(SLASH)

SHIT!!
HE WENT
FOR MY
EYES.

TSUUU
(OOZE)

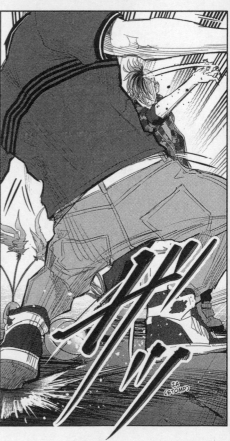

THE
BLOOD...

ZA
(STOMP)

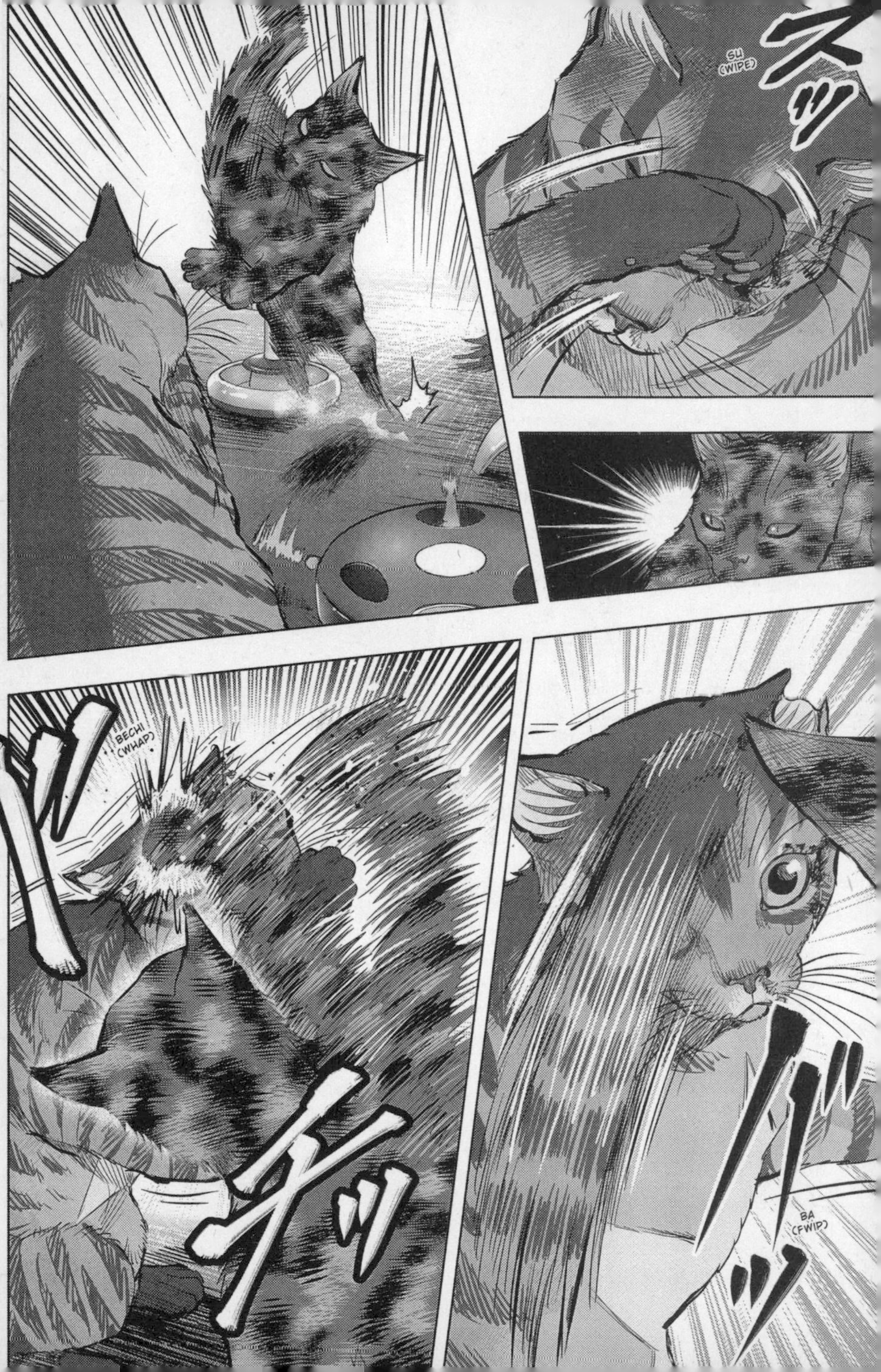
SU
(WIPE)
BA
(FWIP)
BECHI
(WHAP)

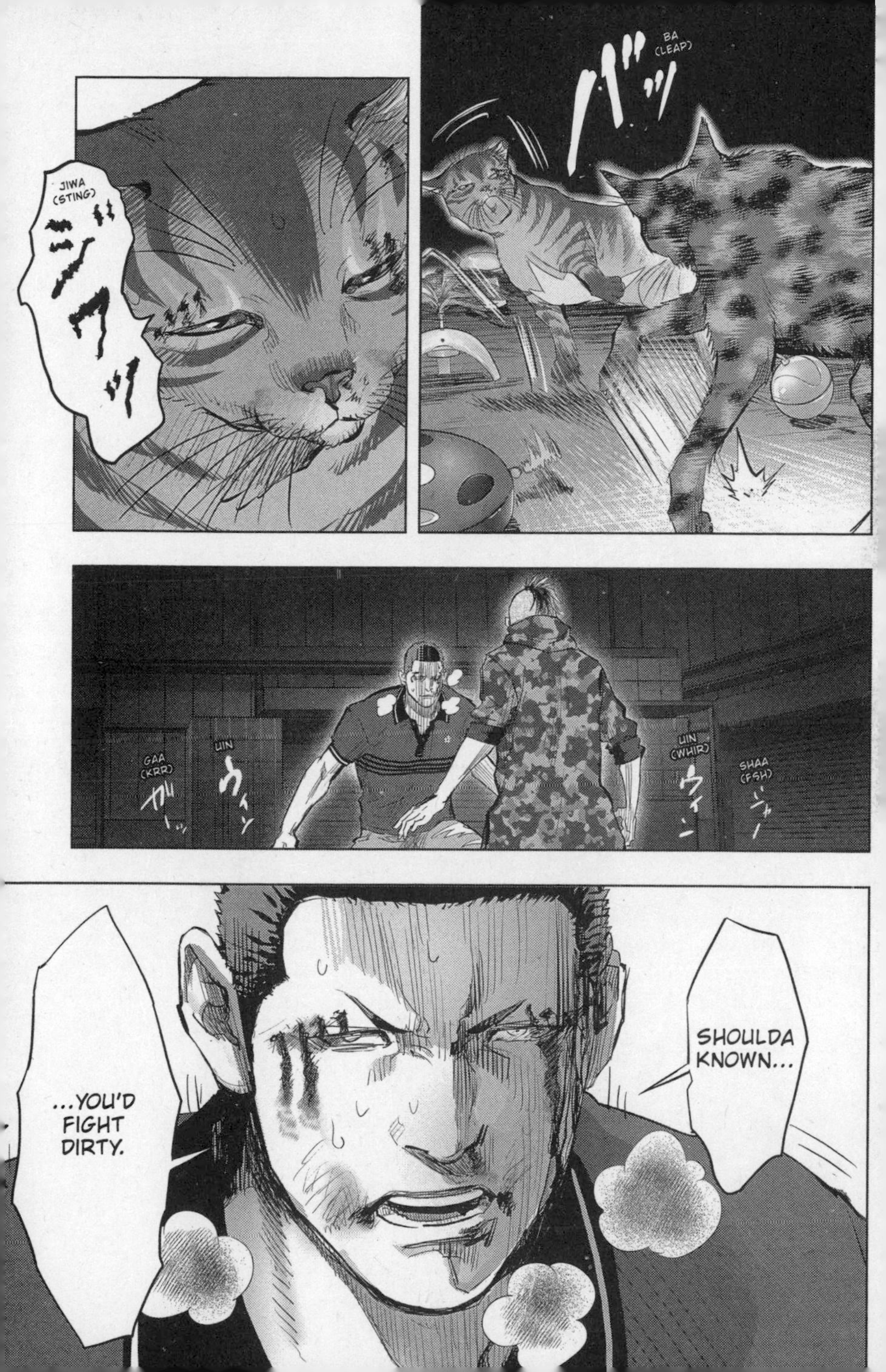
BA (LEAP)
JIWA (STING)
SHAA (FSH)
UIN (WHIR)
UIN
GAA (KRR)
SHOULDA KNOWN...
...YOU'D FIGHT DIRTY.

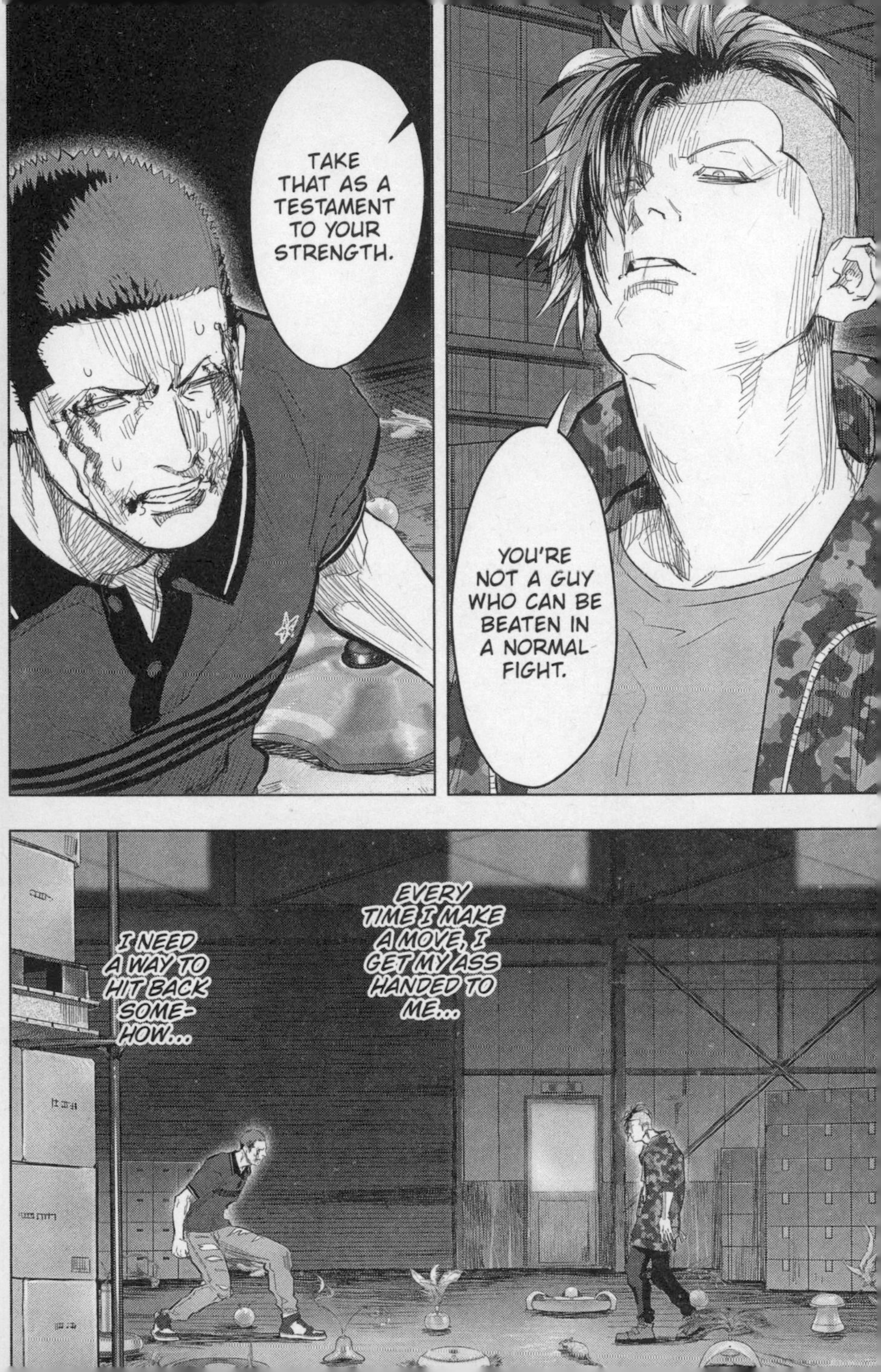
YOU'RE NOT A GUY WHO CAN BE BEATEN IN A NORMAL FIGHT.
TAKE THAT AS A TESTAMENT TO YOUR STRENGTH.
EVERY TIME I MAKE A MOVE, I GET MY ASS HANDED TO ME...
I NEED A WAY TO HIT BACK SOME-HOW...

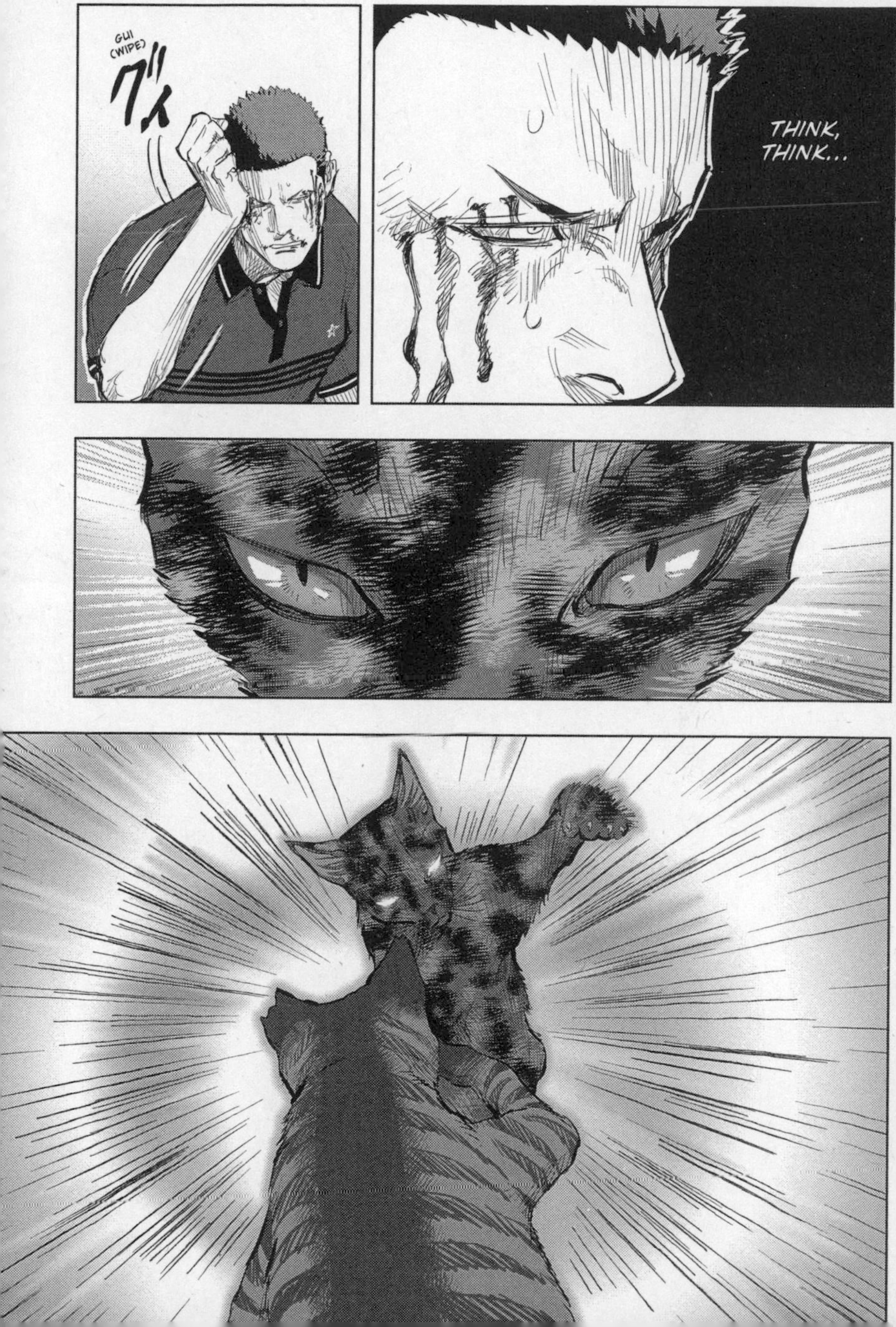
THINK, THINK...
GUI (WIPE)
グィ

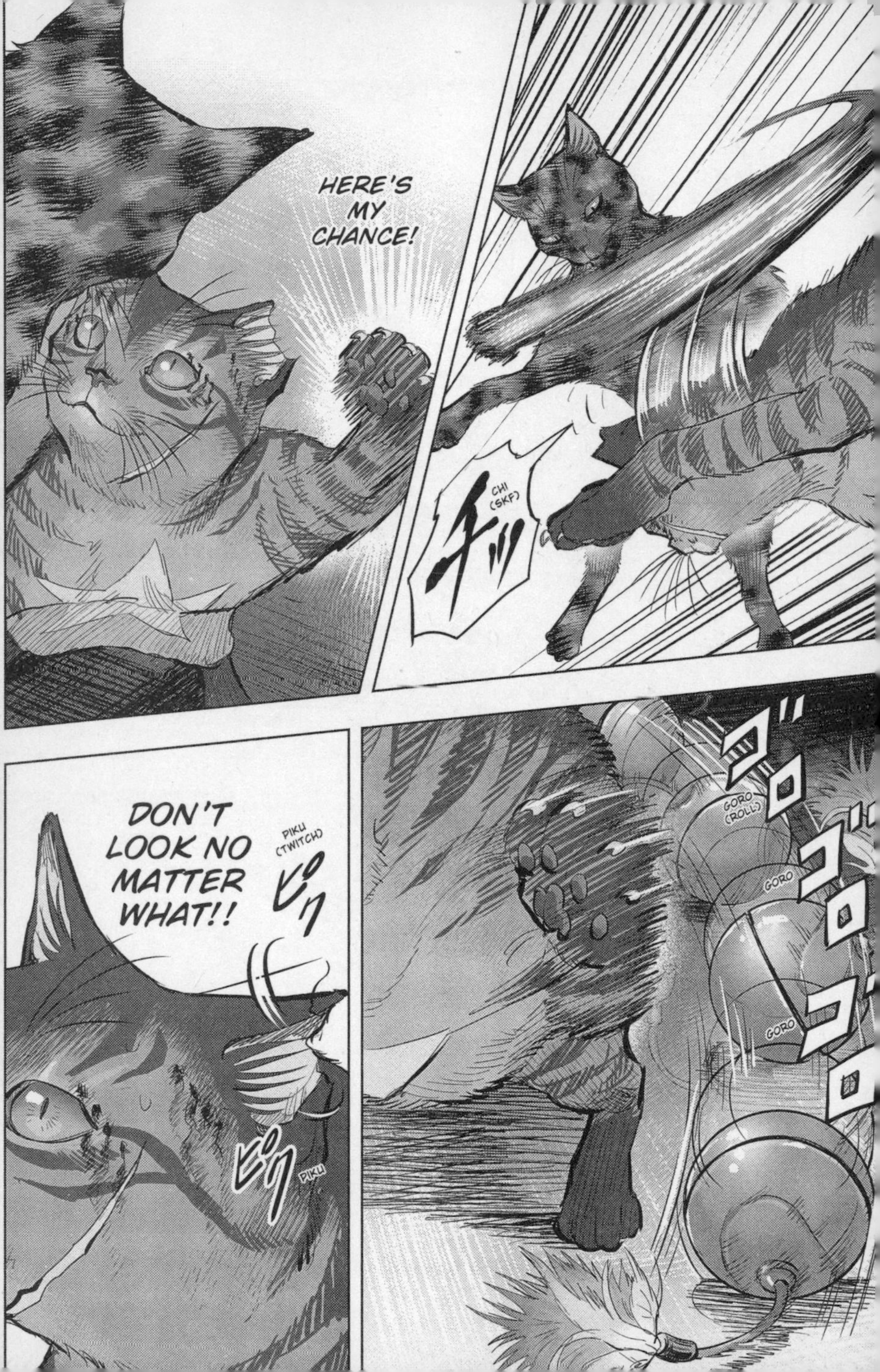
チッ
CHI (SKF)
HERE'S MY CHANCE!
ゴロ
GORO (ROLL)
ゴロ
GORO
ゴロ
GORO
DON'T LOOK NO MATTER WHAT!!
ピク
PIKU (TWITCH)
ピク
PIKU

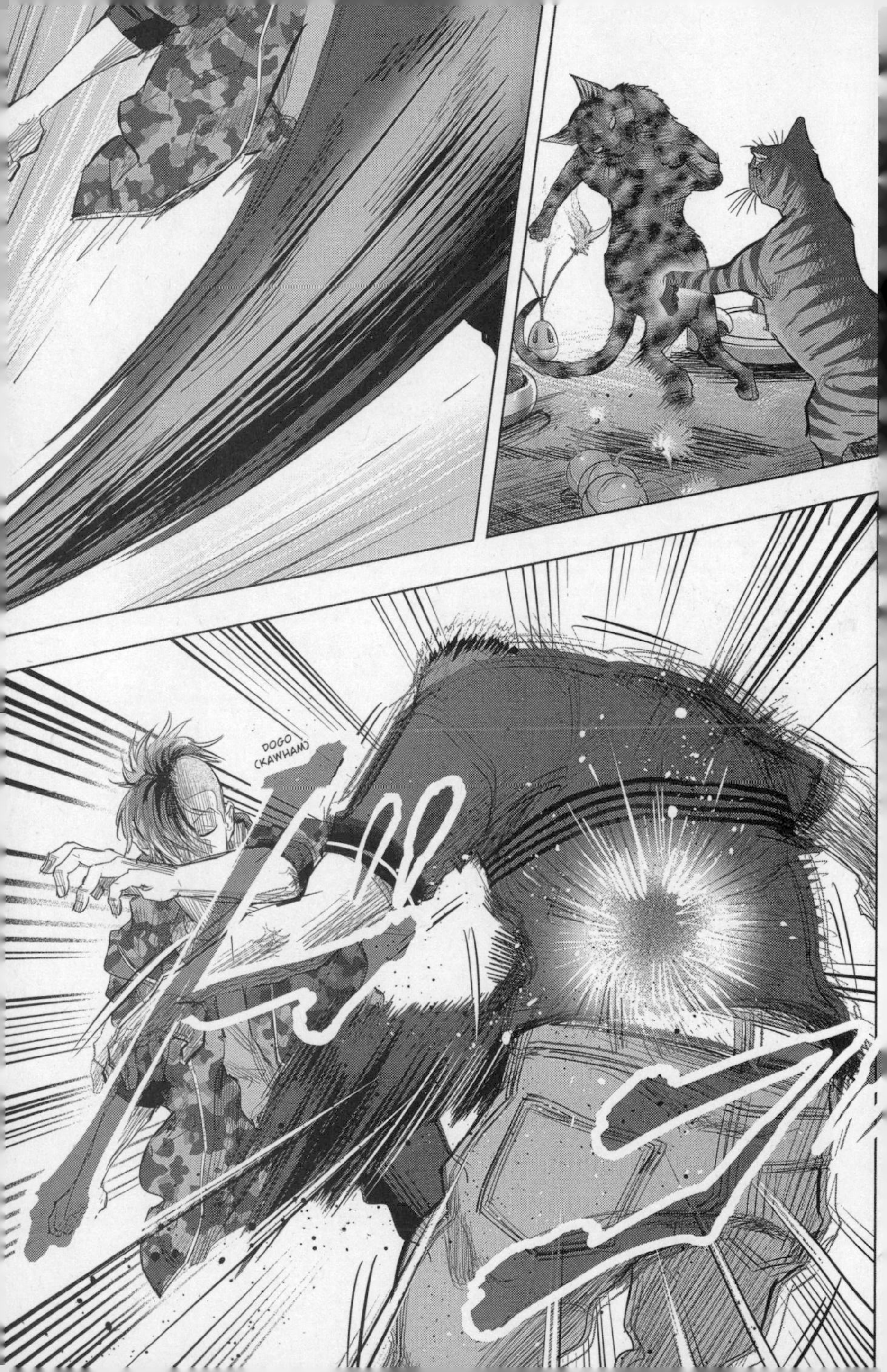
DOGO
(KAWHAM)

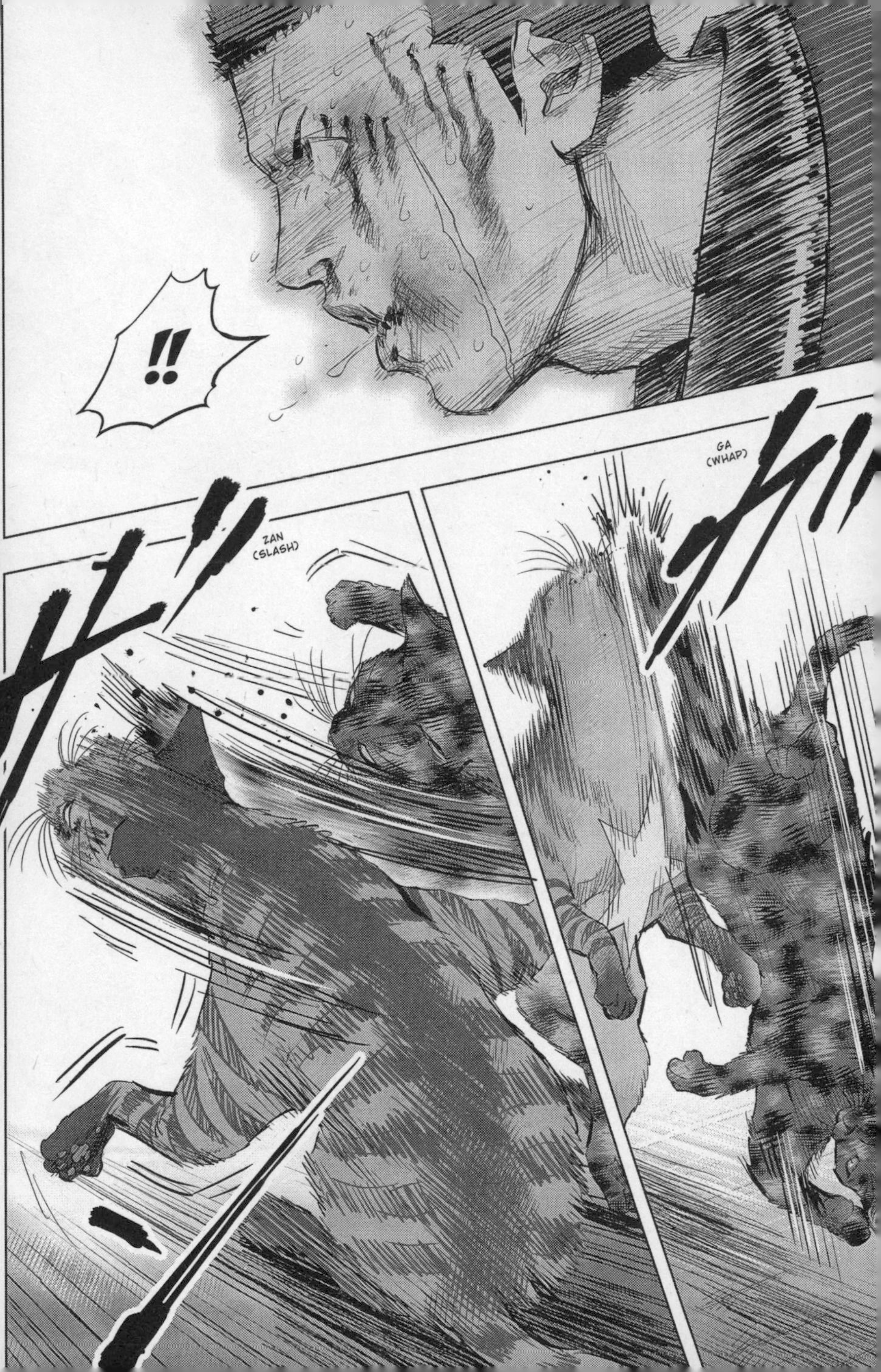
!!
GA
(WHAP)
ZAN
(SLASH)

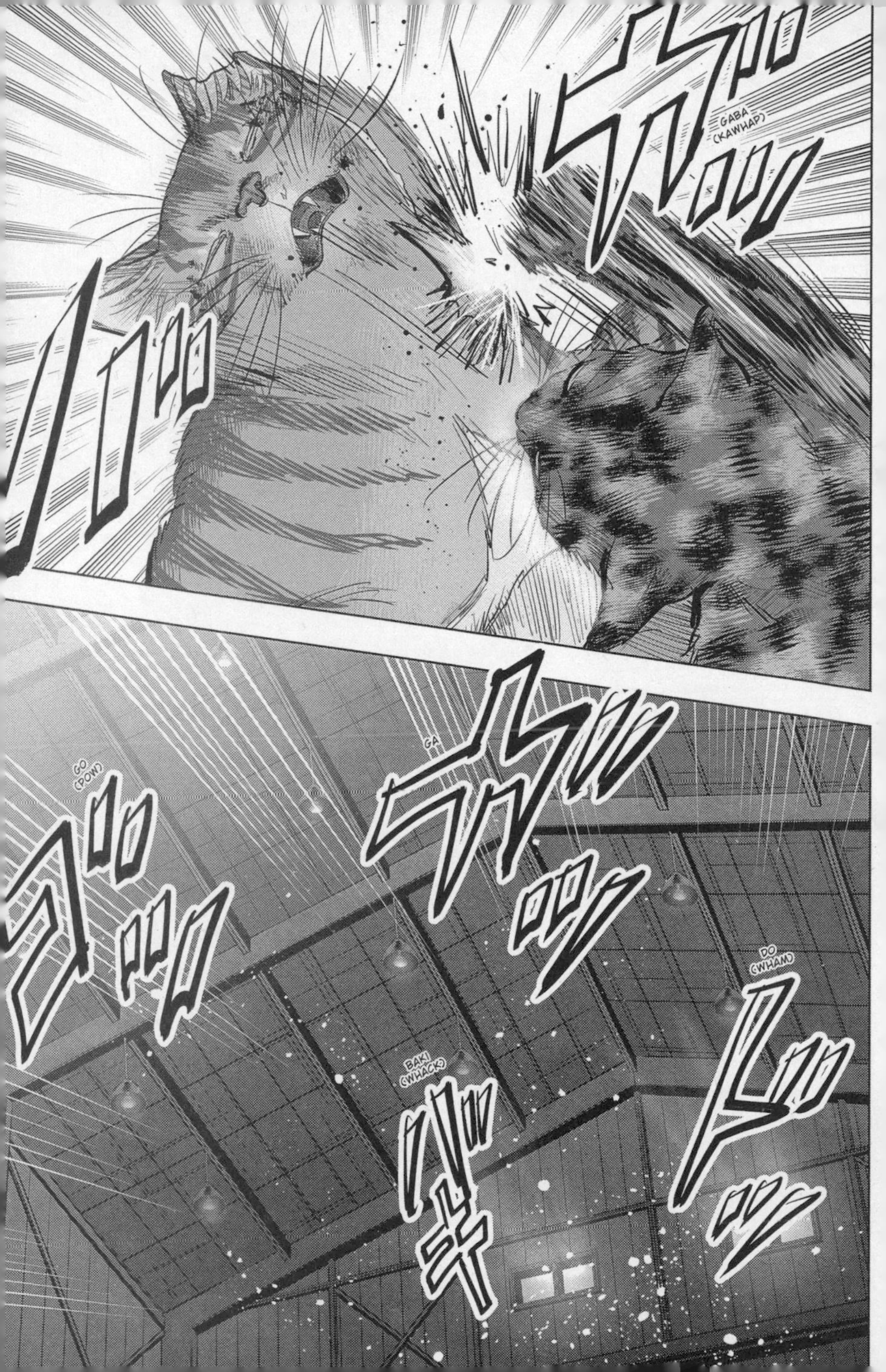
GABA
(KAWHAP)
GA
GO
(POW)
DO
(WHAM)
BAKI
(WHACK)

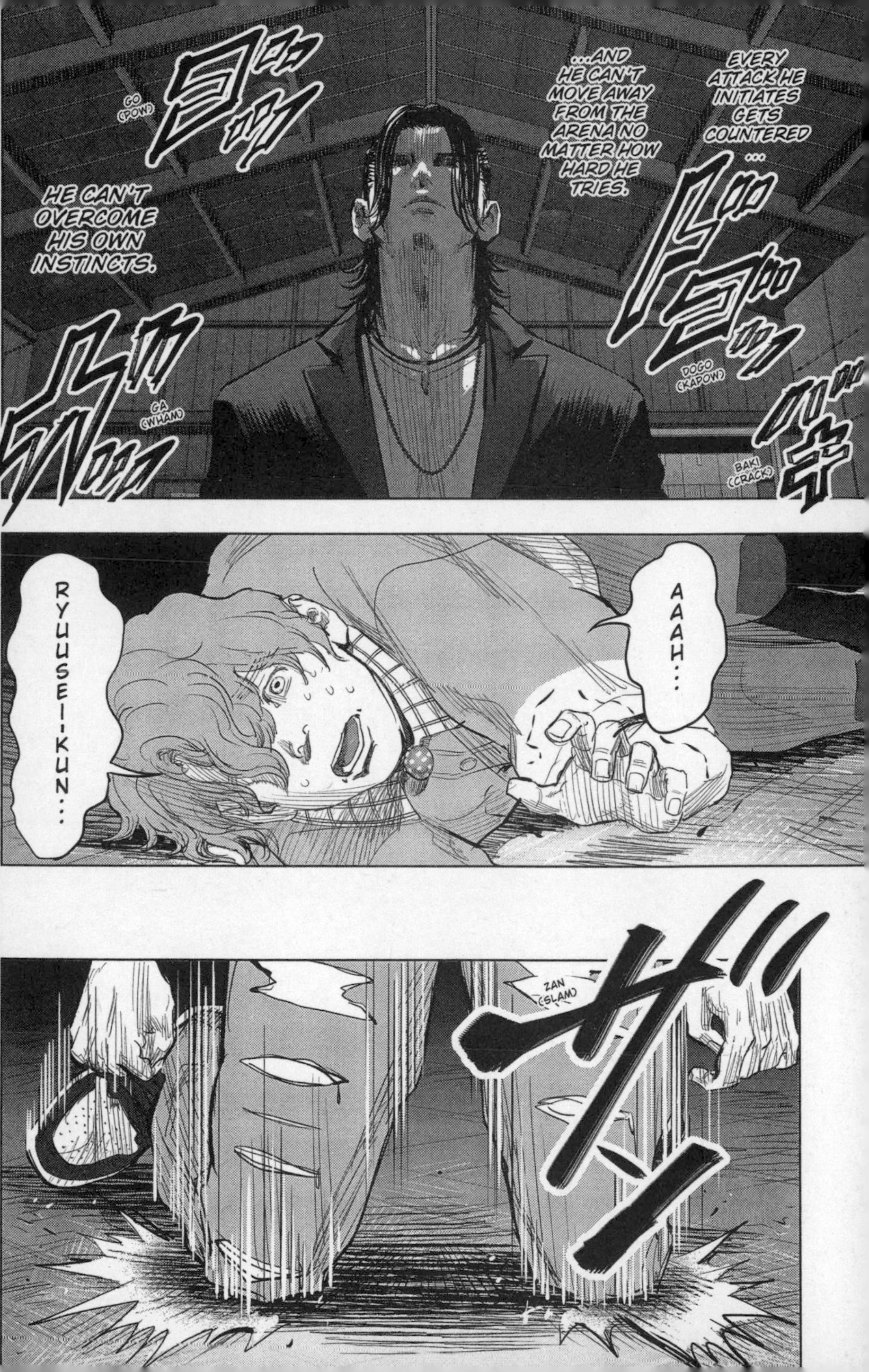
EVERY ATTACK HE INITIATES GETS COUNTERED...
DOGO (KAPOW)
BAKI (CRACK)
...AND HE CAN'T MOVE AWAY FROM THE ARENA NO MATTER HOW HARD HE TRIES.
GO (POW)
HE CAN'T OVERCOME HIS OWN INSTINCTS.
GA (WHAM)
AAAH...
RYUUSEI-KUN...
ZAN (SLAM)

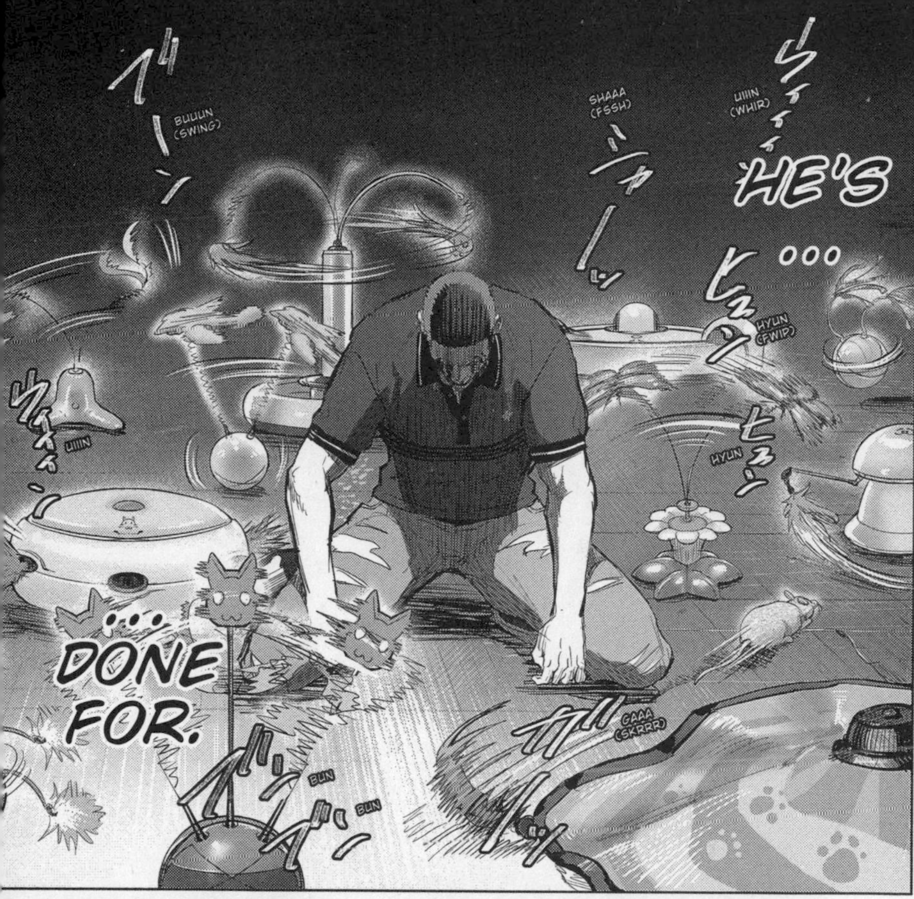
UIIIN (WHIR)
HE'S ...
SHAAA (FSSH)
BUUUN (SWING)
HYUN (FWIP)
HYUN
UIIIN
...DONE FOR.
GAAA (SKRRR)
BUN
BUN

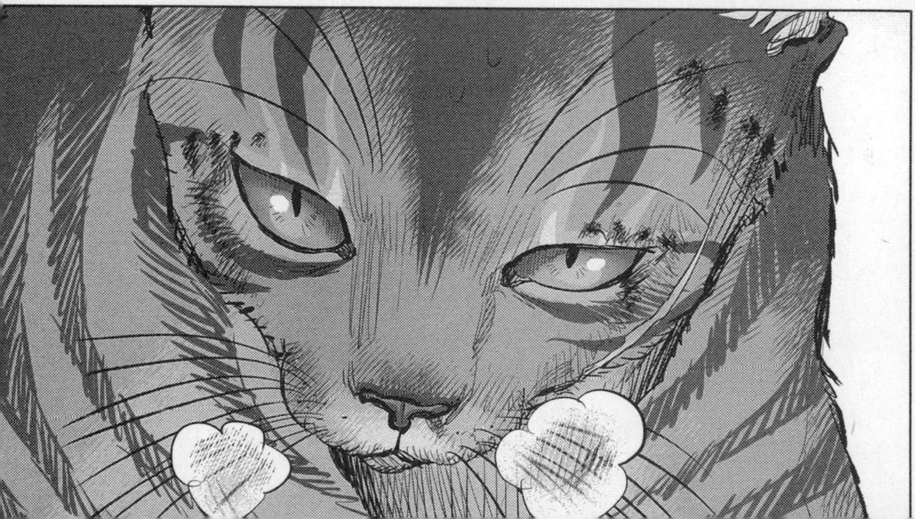

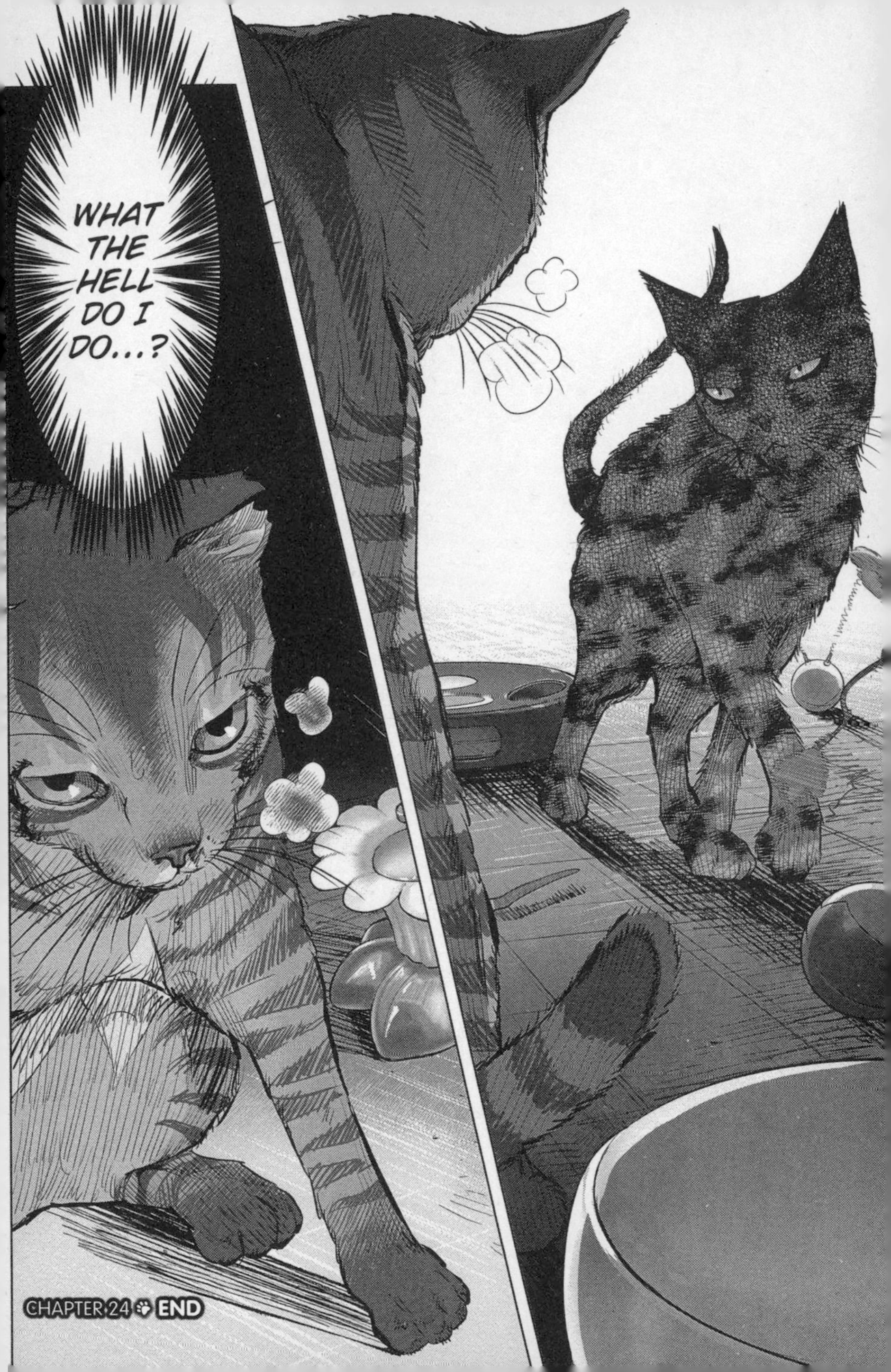
WHAT THE HELL DO I DO...?
CHAPTER 24 END

🐾MR. MOKE

🐾MUGEN

🐾HYOUMA

NYANKEES

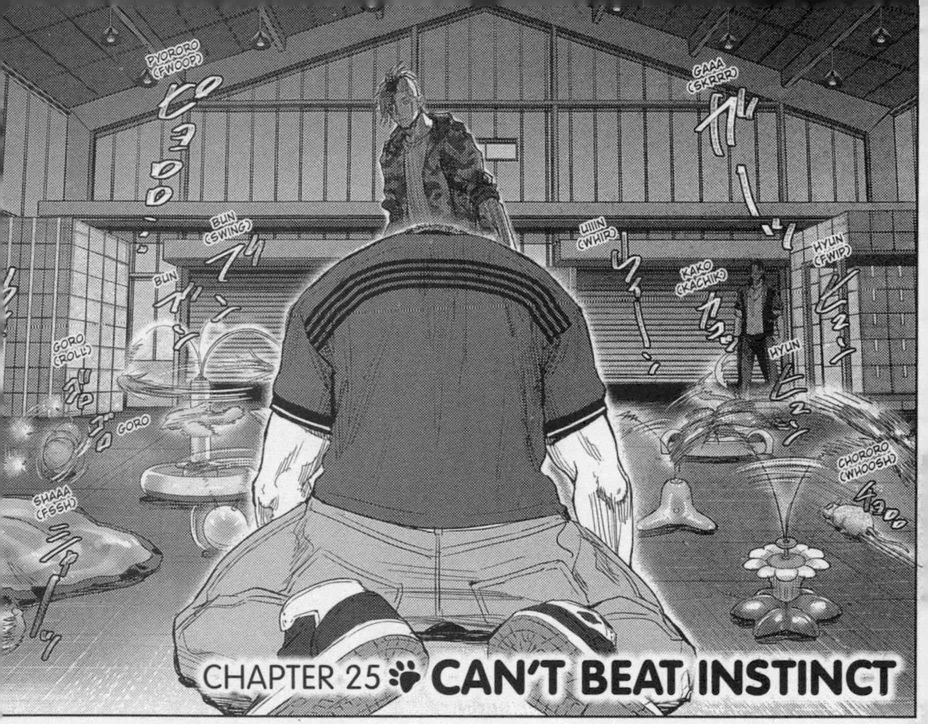
GAAA (SKRRR)
HYUN (FWIP)
KAKO (KACHIK)
WIIIN (WHIP)
HYUN
CHORORO (WHOOSH)
PYORORO (FWOOP)
BUN (SWING)
BUN
GORO (ROLL)
GORO
SHAAA (FSSH)

CHAPTER 25 CAN'T BEAT INSTINCT

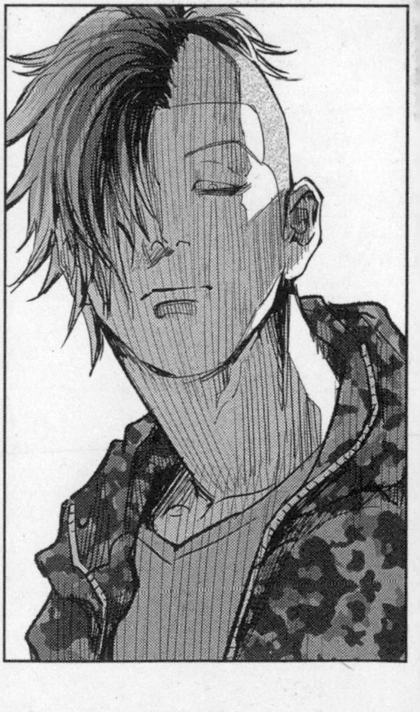

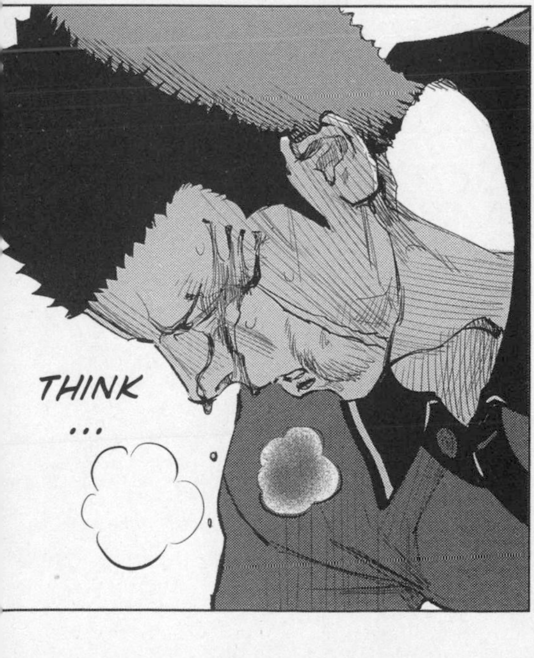
THINK
...

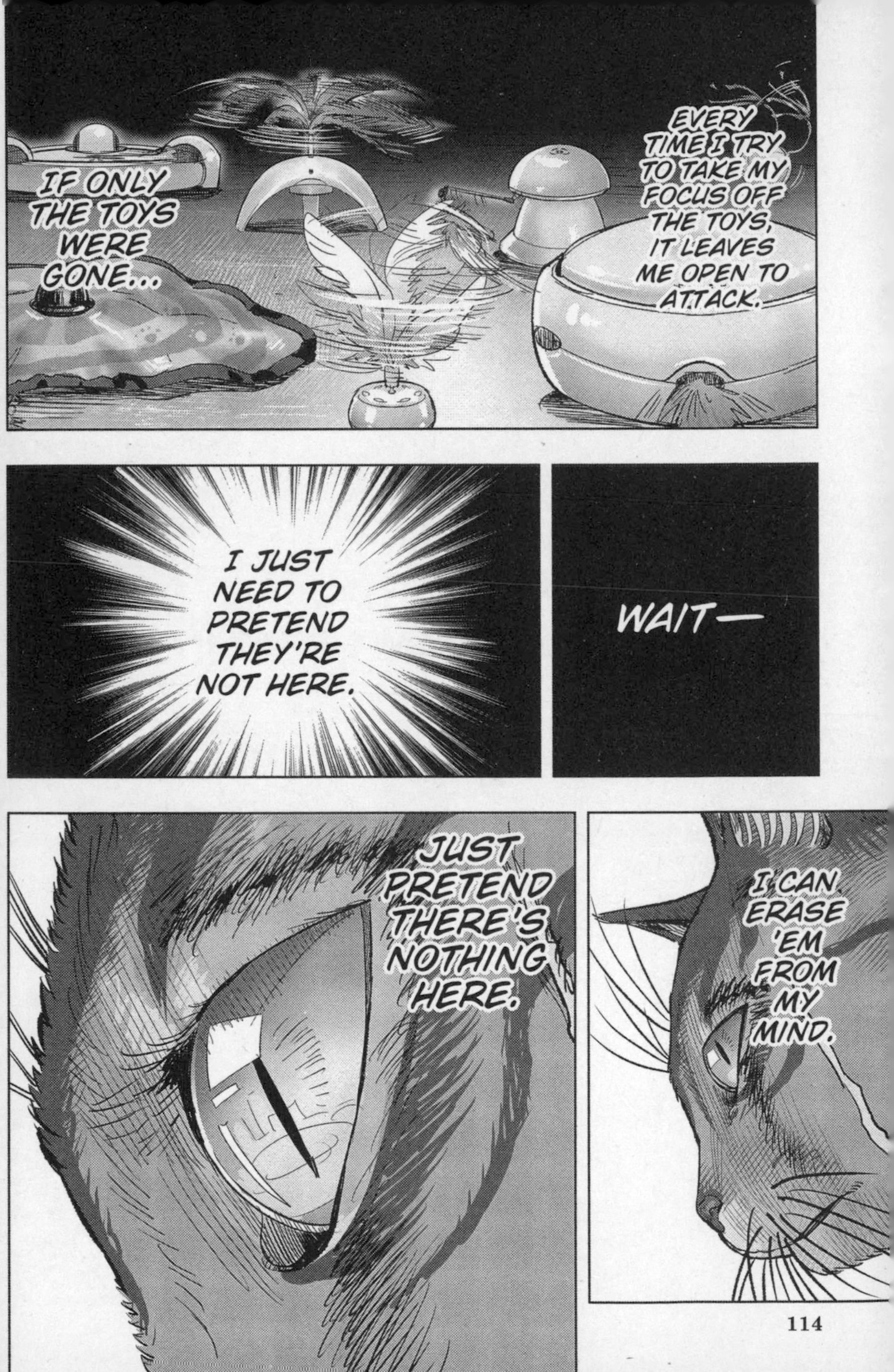
EVERY TIME I TRY TO TAKE MY FOCUS OFF THE TOYS, IT LEAVES ME OPEN TO ATTACK.
IF ONLY THE TOYS WERE GONE...
WAIT—
I JUST NEED TO PRETEND THEY'RE NOT HERE.
I CAN ERASE 'EM FROM MY MIND.
JUST PRETEND THERE'S NOTHING HERE.

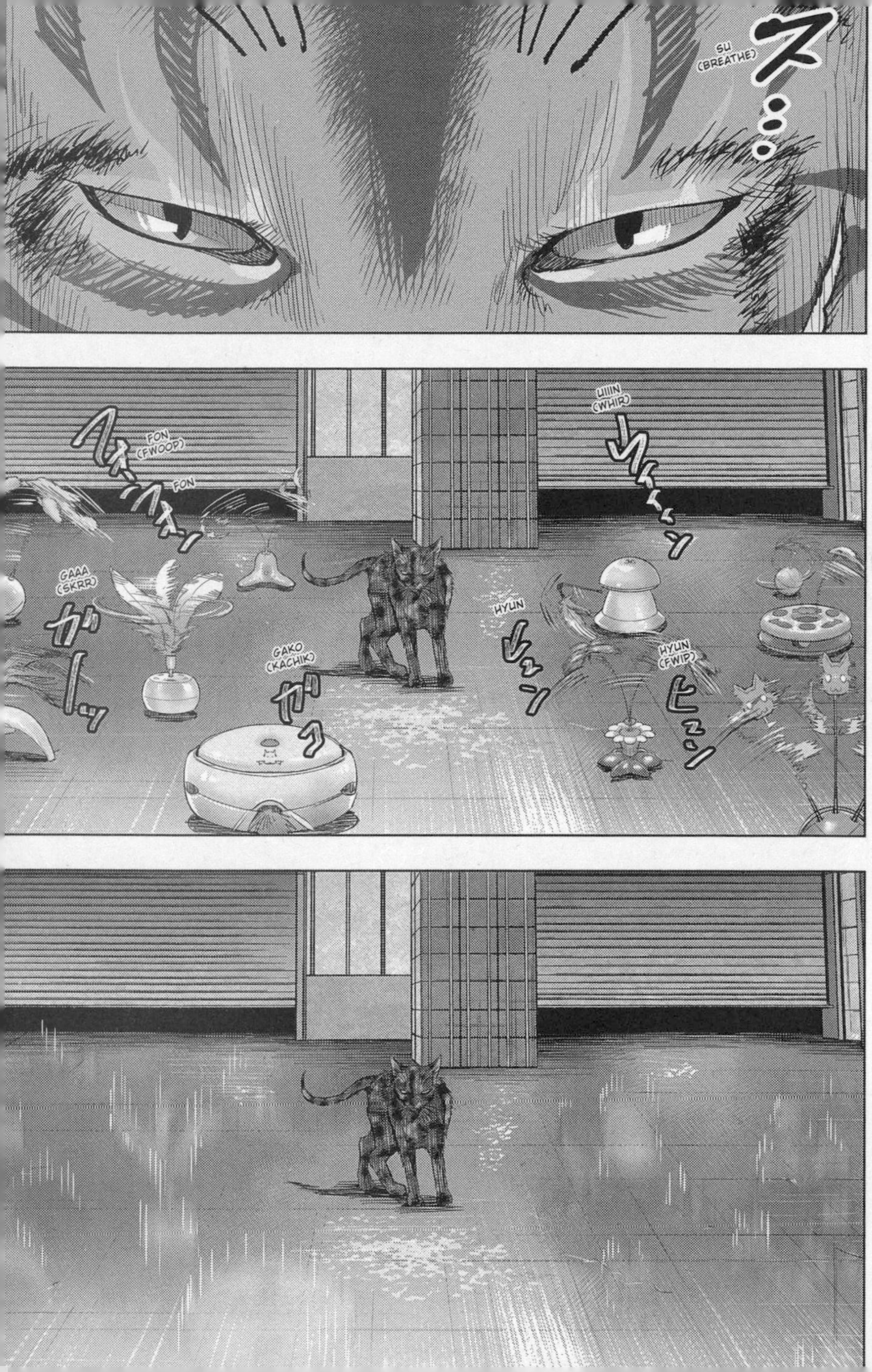
SU
(BREATHE)
UIIIN
(WHIR)
HYUN
(FWIP)
HYUN
FON
(FWOOP)
FON
GAKO
(KACHIK)
GAAA
(SKRR)

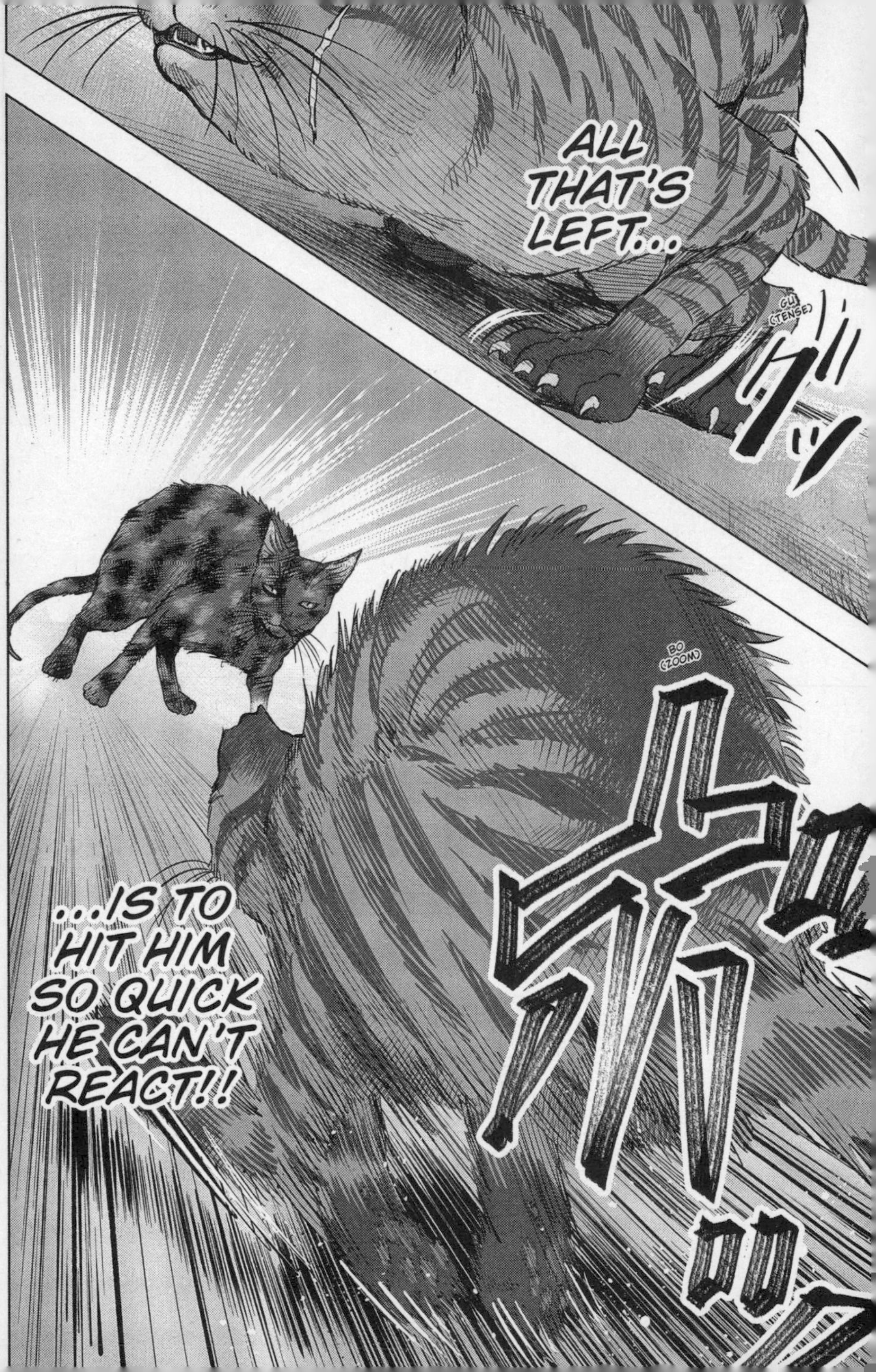
ALL THAT'S LEFT...
GU (TENSE)
グッ
BO (ZOOM)
...IS TO HIT HIM SO QUICK HE CAN'T REACT!!

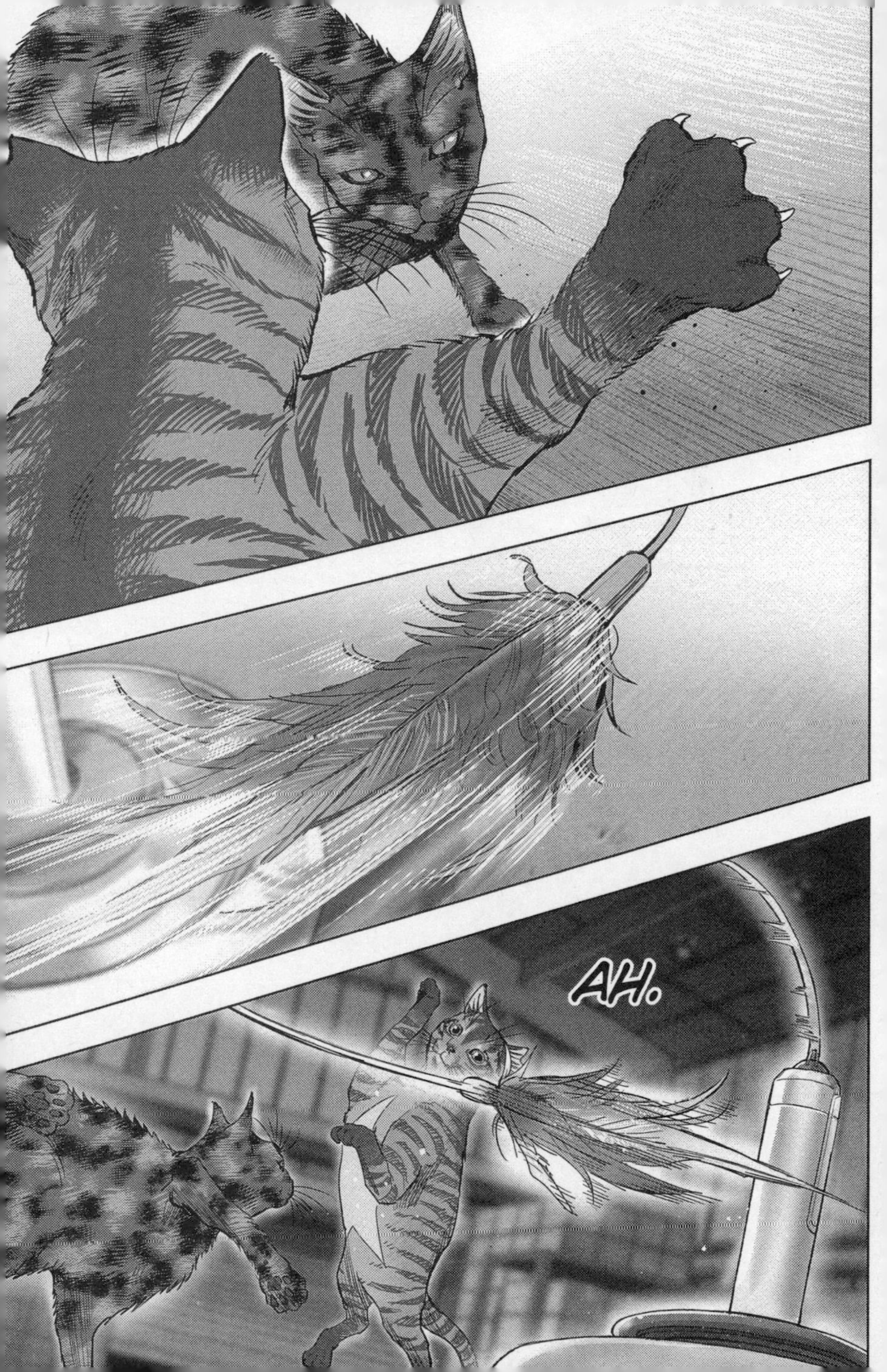
AH.

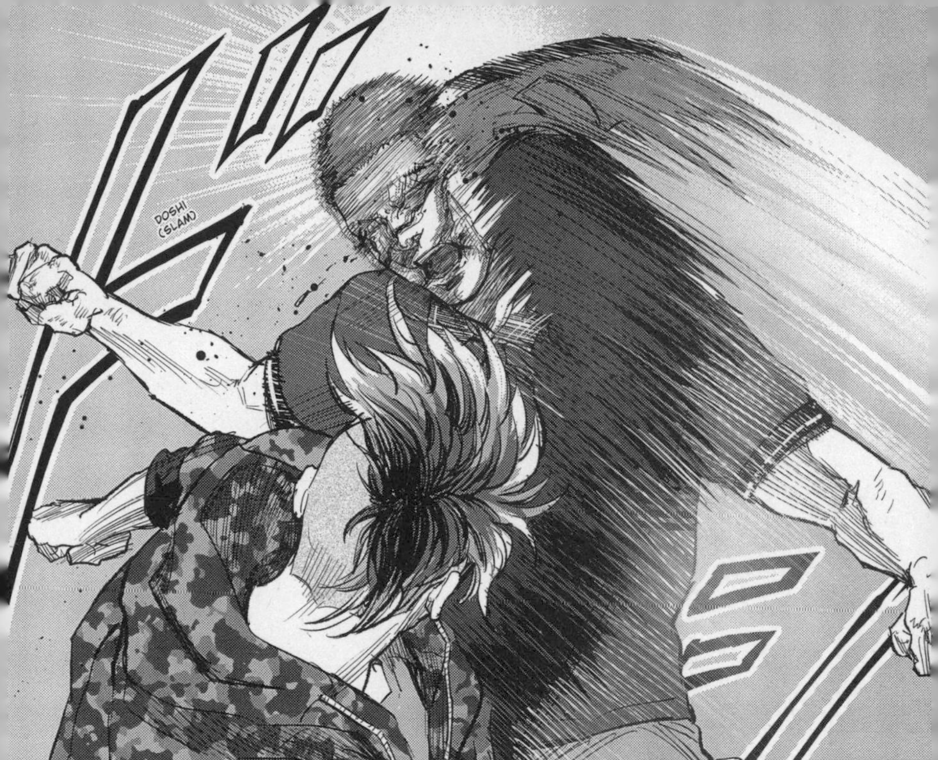
DOSHI
(SLAM)
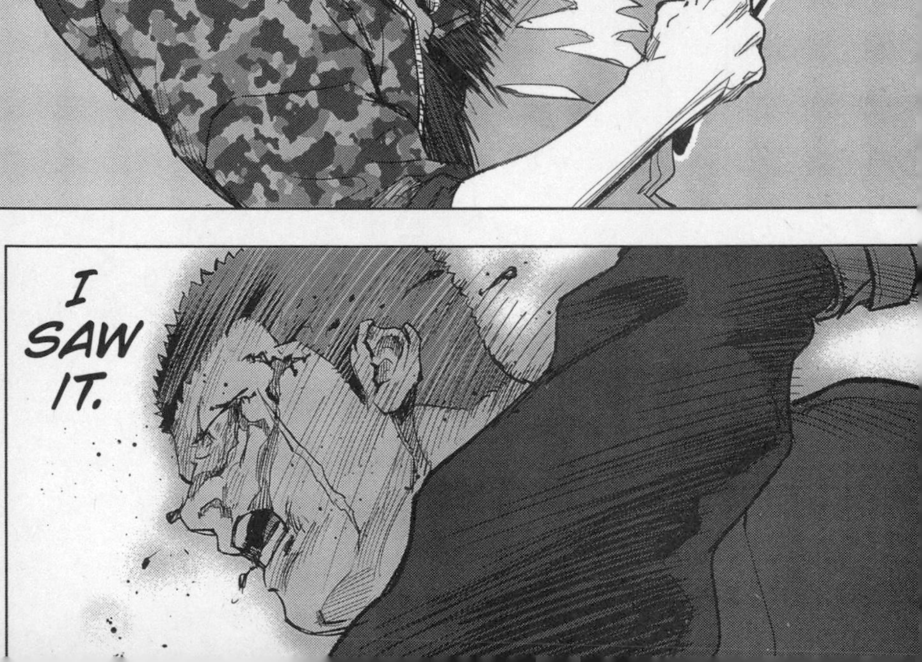
I SAW IT.

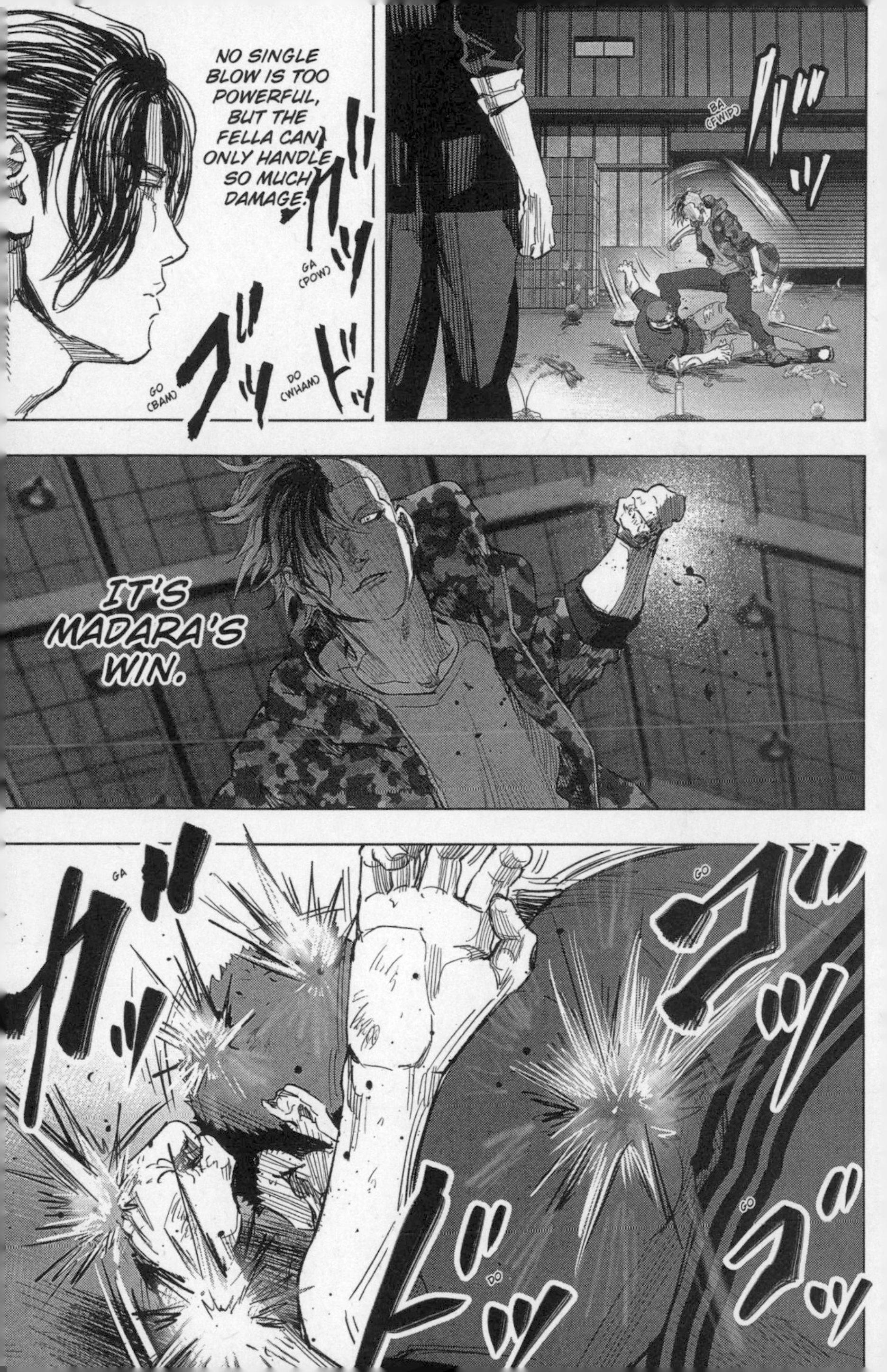
BA (FWIP)
NO SINGLE BLOW IS TOO POWERFUL, BUT THE FELLA CAN ONLY HANDLE SO MUCH DAMAGE.
GA (POW)
DO (WHAM)
GO (BAM)
IT'S MADARA'S WIN.
GO
GA
GO
DO

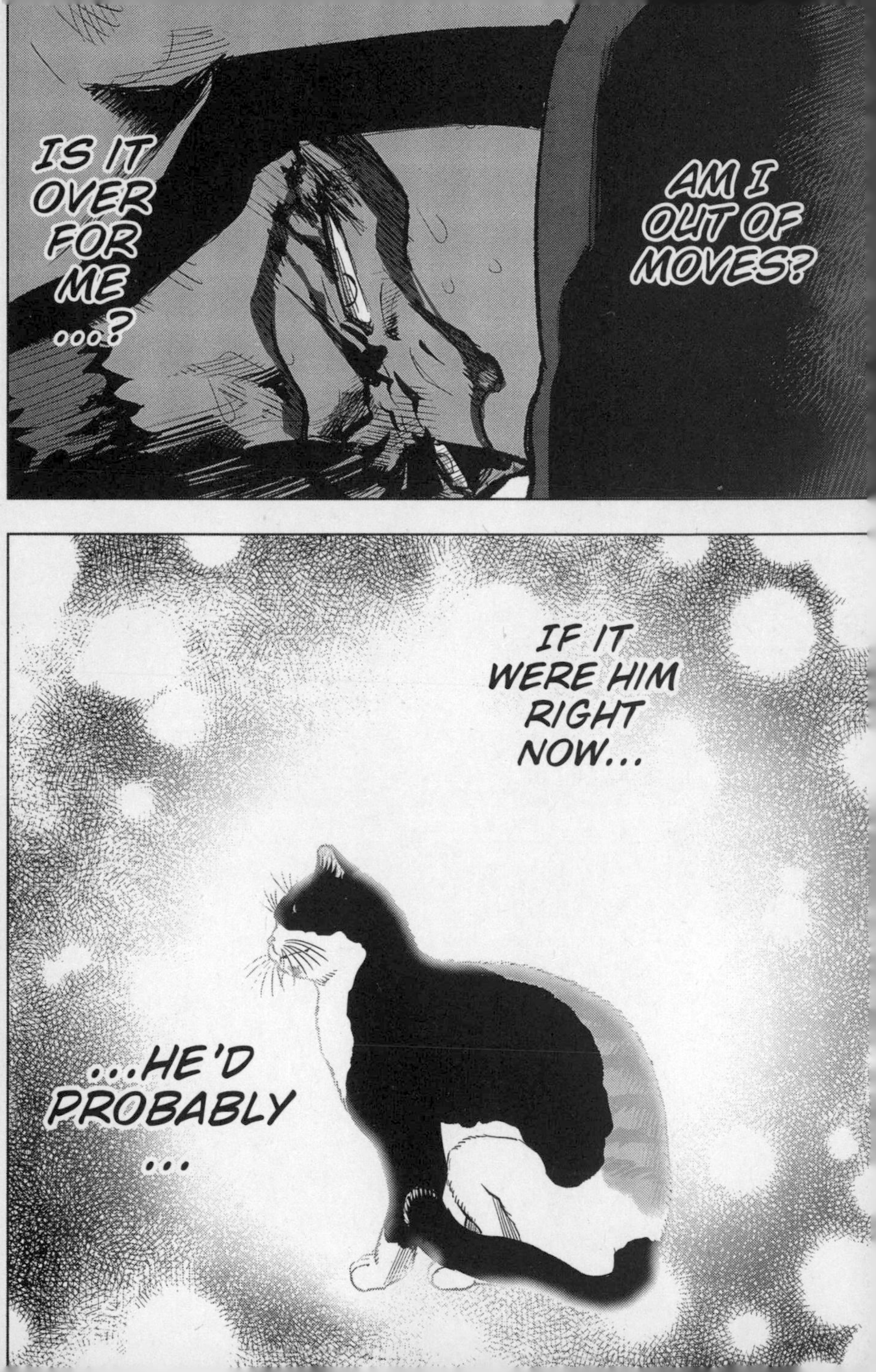
AM I OUT OF MOVES?
IS IT OVER FOR ME ...?
IF IT WERE HIM RIGHT NOW...
...HE'D PROBABLY ...

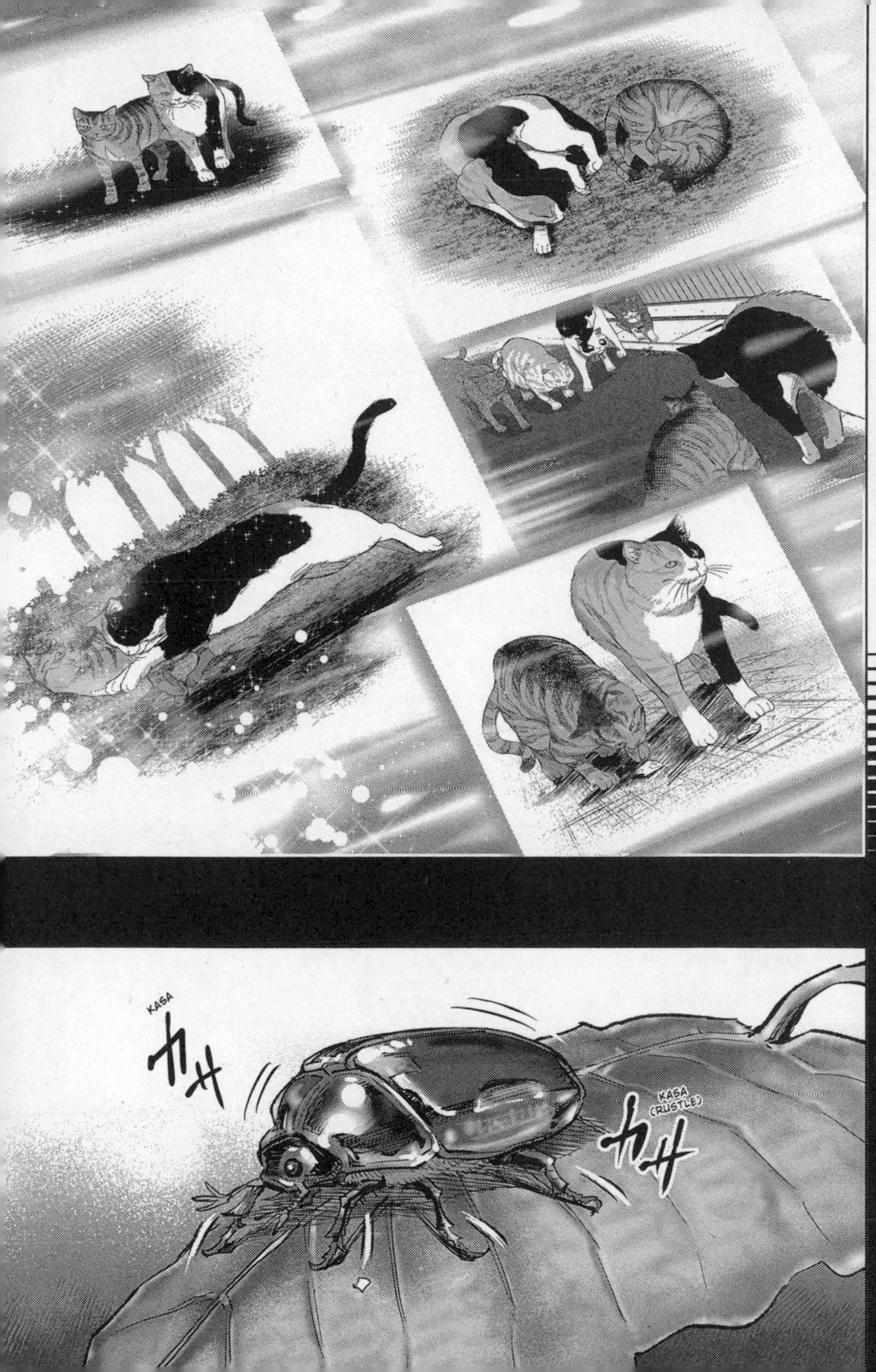
カサ
KASA (RUSTLE)
カサ
KASA

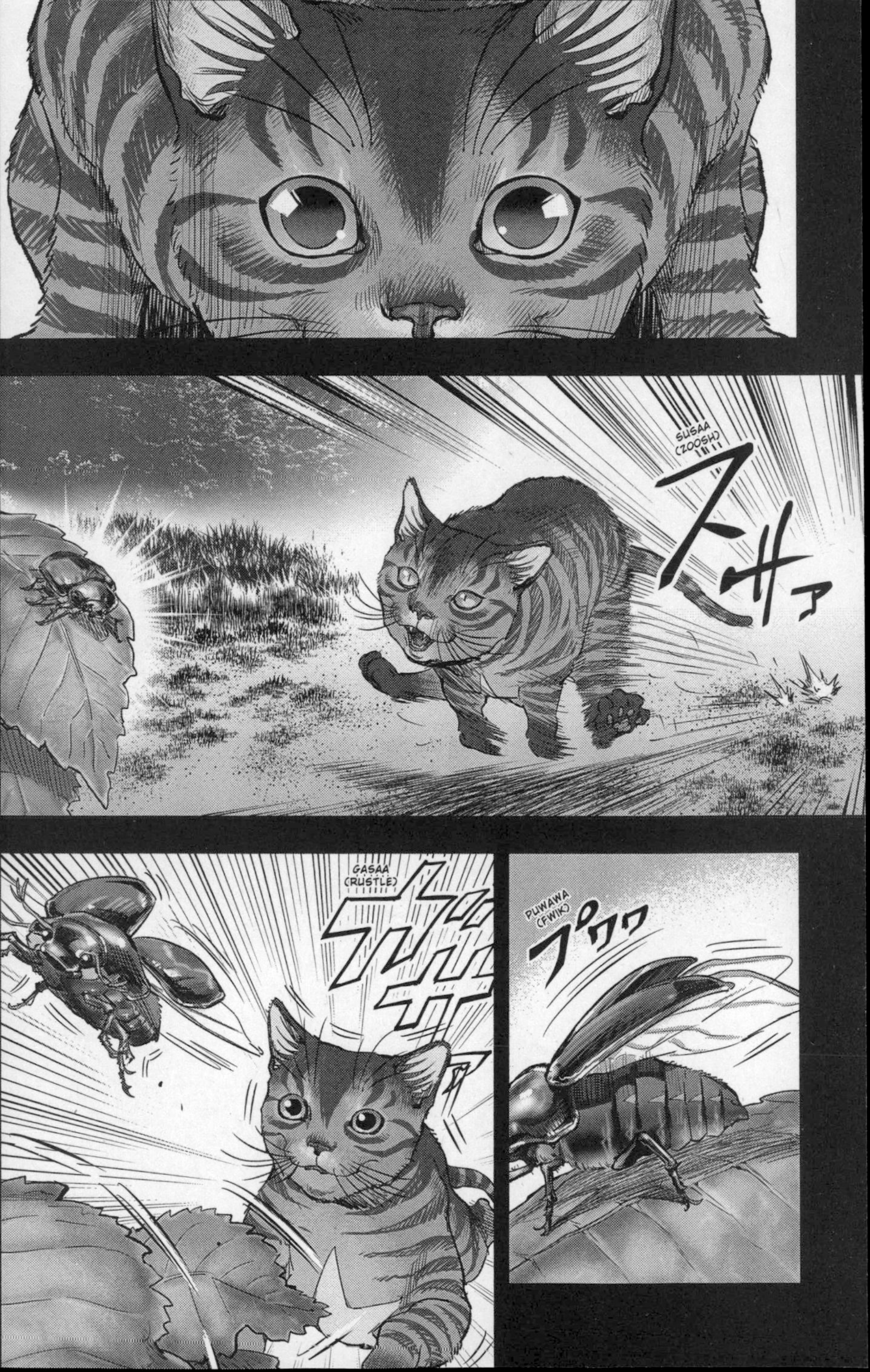
SUSAA (ZOOSH)
スサァ
PUWAWA (FWIK)
プワワ
GASAA (RUSTLE)

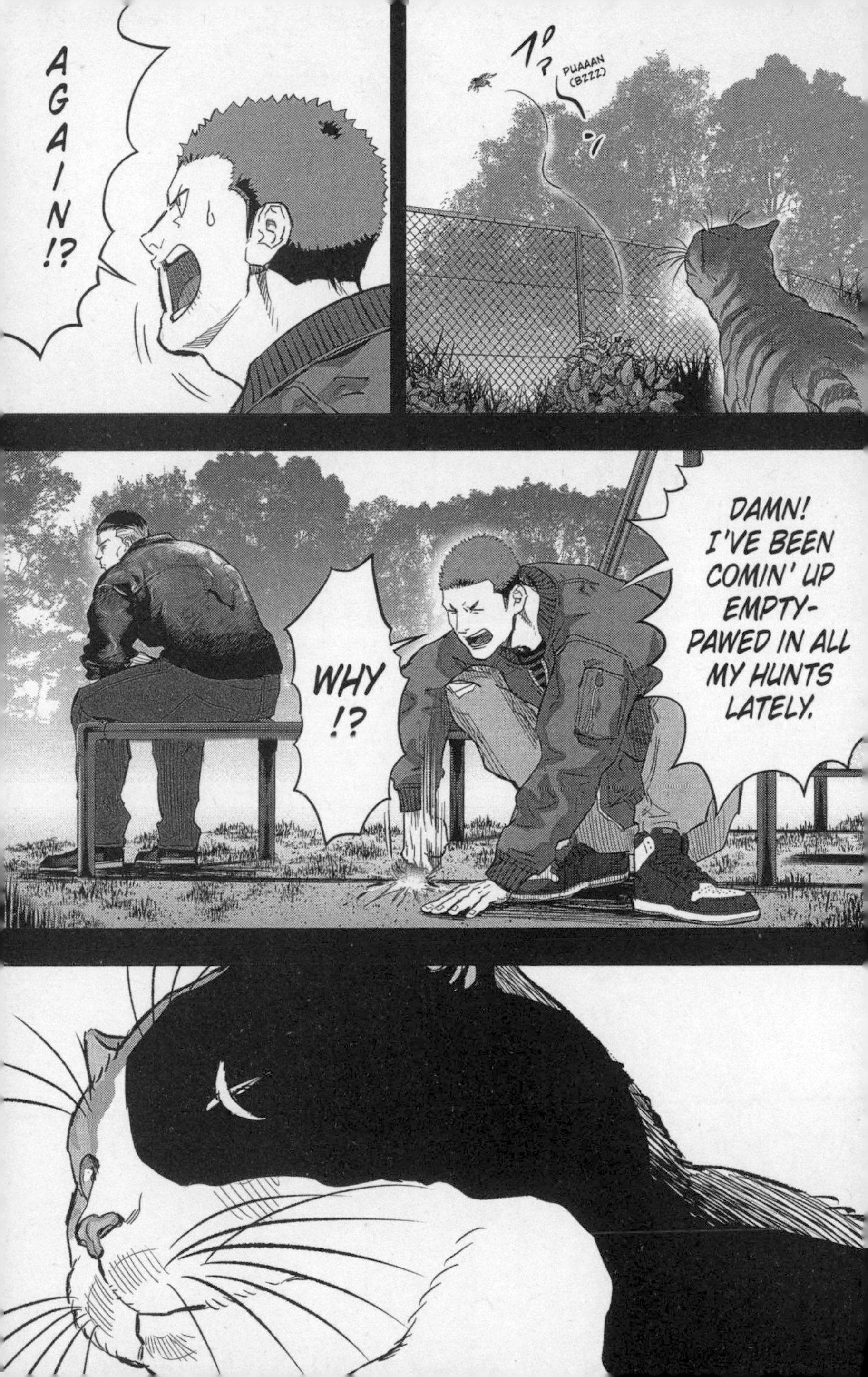
PUAAAN (BZZZ)
AGAIN!?
DAMN! I'VE BEEN COMIN' UP EMPTY-PAWED IN ALL MY HUNTS LATELY.
WHY!?

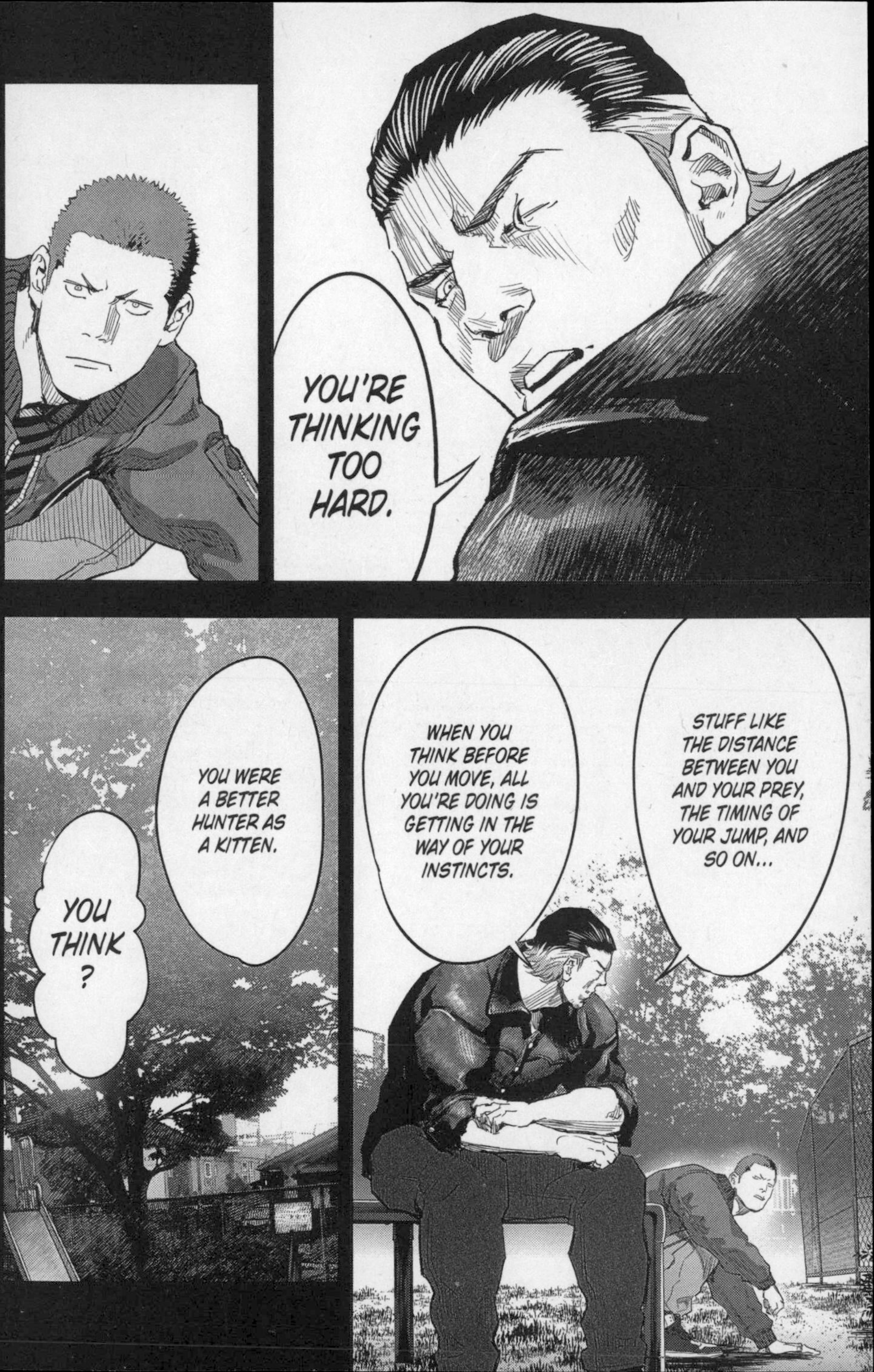
YOU'RE THINKING TOO HARD.
STUFF LIKE THE DISTANCE BETWEEN YOU AND YOUR PREY, THE TIMING OF YOUR JUMP, AND SO ON...
WHEN YOU THINK BEFORE YOU MOVE, ALL YOU'RE DOING IS GETTING IN THE WAY OF YOUR INSTINCTS.
YOU WERE A BETTER HUNTER AS A KITTEN.
YOU THINK?

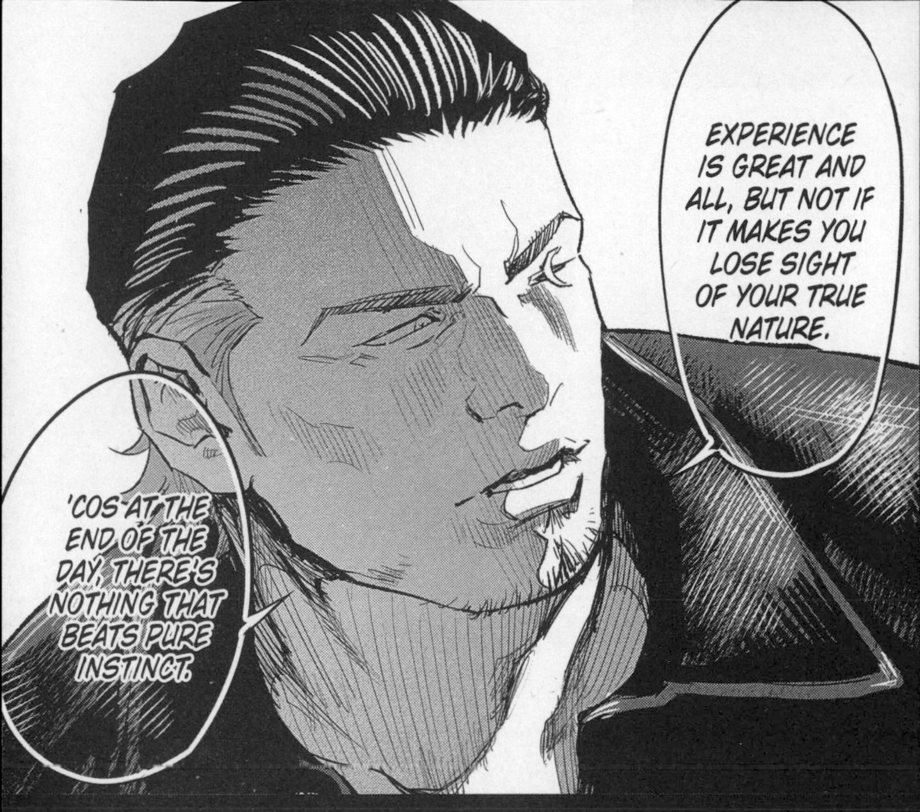
EXPERIENCE IS GREAT AND ALL, BUT NOT IF IT MAKES YOU LOSE SIGHT OF YOUR TRUE NATURE.
'COS AT THE END OF THE DAY, THERE'S NOTHING THAT BEATS PURE INSTINCT.
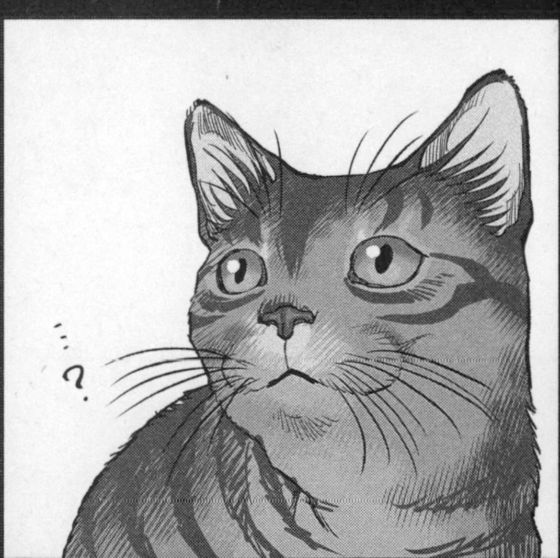
...?
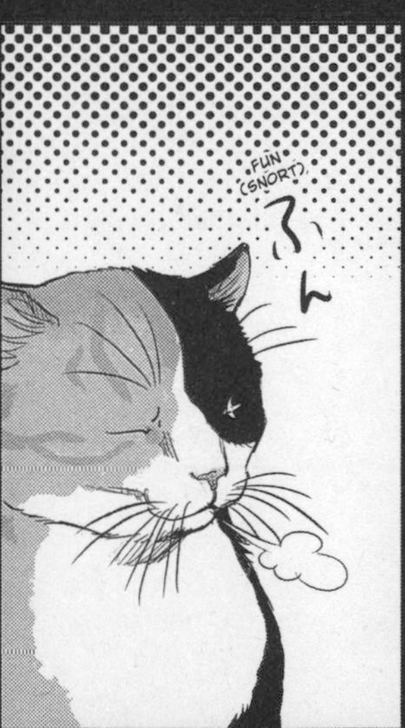
ふん
FUN (SNORT)

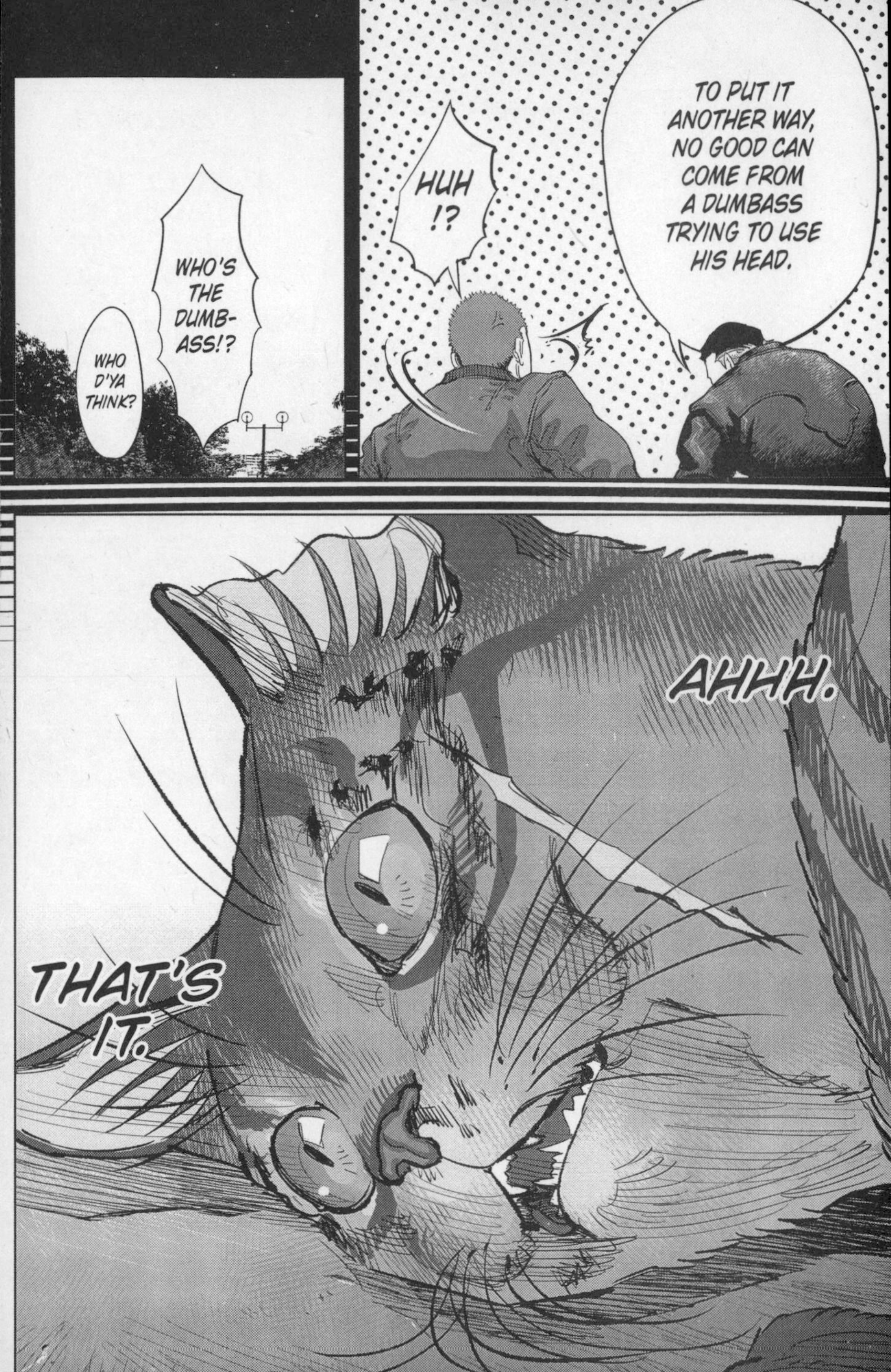
TO PUT IT ANOTHER WAY, NO GOOD CAN COME FROM A DUMBASS TRYING TO USE HIS HEAD.
HUH !?
WHO'S THE DUMB-ASS!?
WHO D'YA THINK?
AHHH.
THAT'S IT.

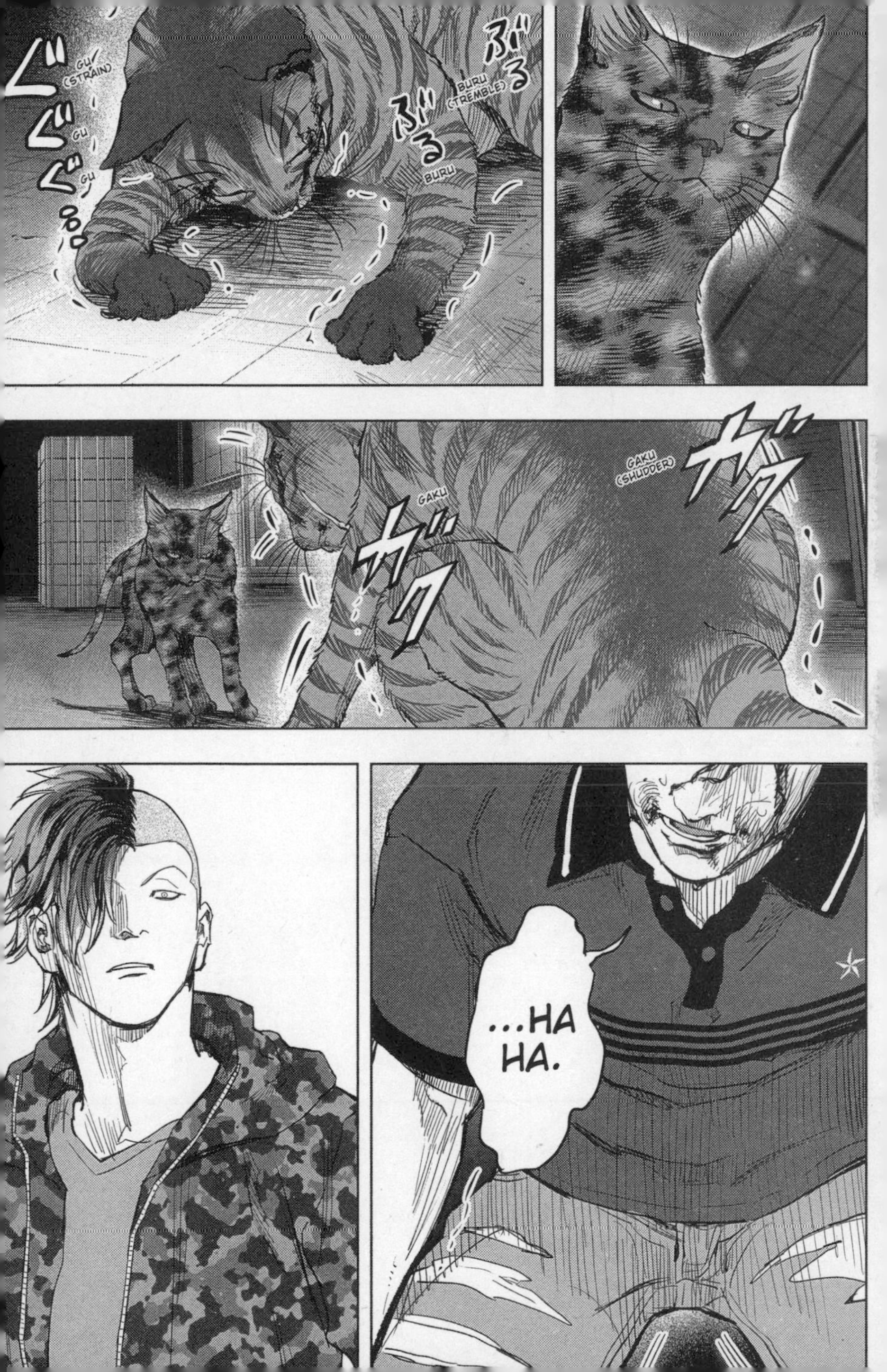

ぶる
BURU (TREMBLE)
ぶる
BURU
ぐ
GU (STRAIN)
ぐ
GU
ぐ
GU
ガク
GAKU (SHUDDER)
ガク
GAKU
...HA HA.

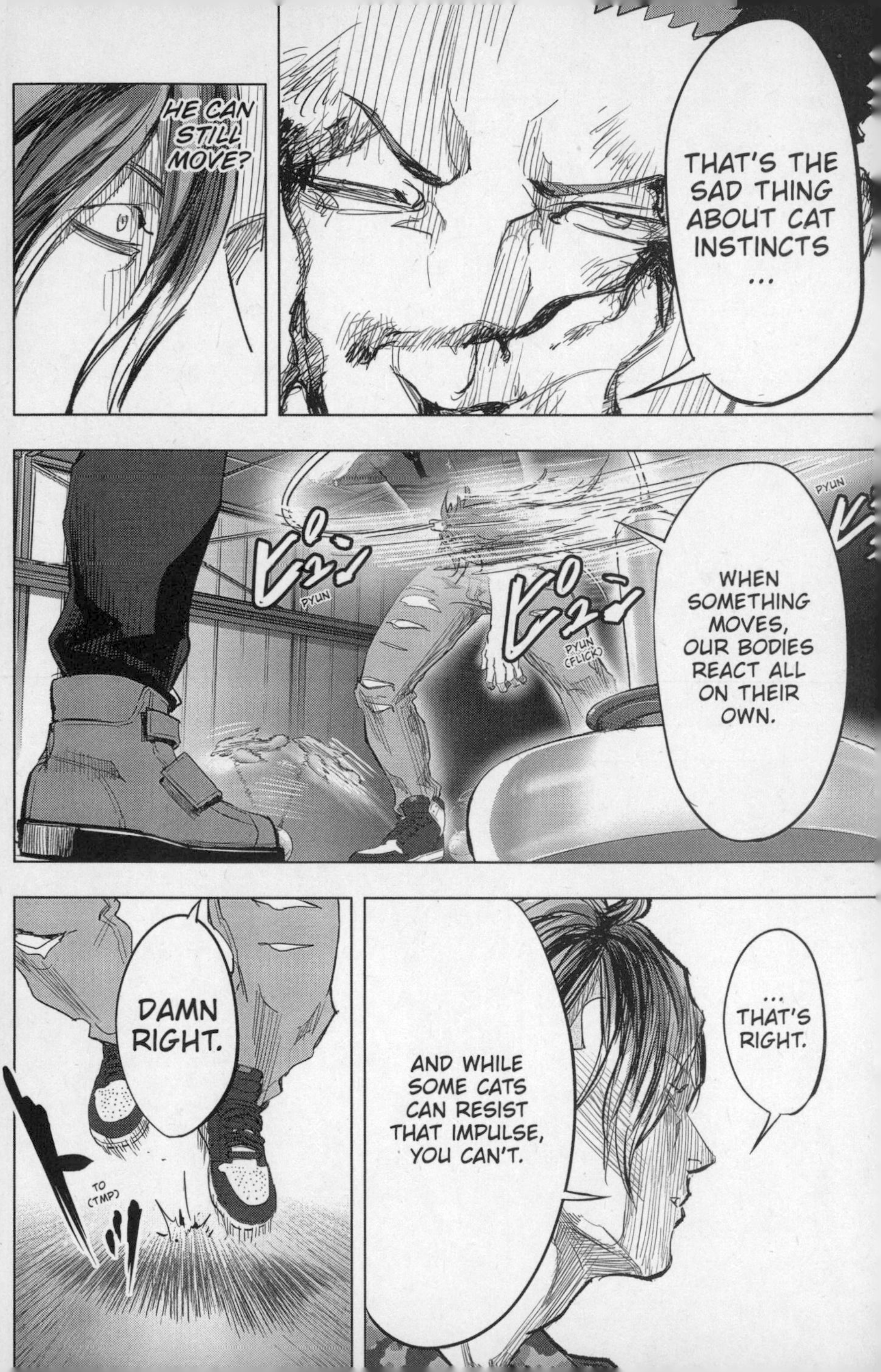
THAT'S THE SAD THING ABOUT CAT INSTINCTS ...
HE CAN STILL MOVE?
PYUN
WHEN SOMETHING MOVES, OUR BODIES REACT ALL ON THEIR OWN.
PYUN (FLICK)
PYUN
... THAT'S RIGHT.
AND WHILE SOME CATS CAN RESIST THAT IMPULSE, YOU CAN'T.
DAMN RIGHT.
TO (TMP)

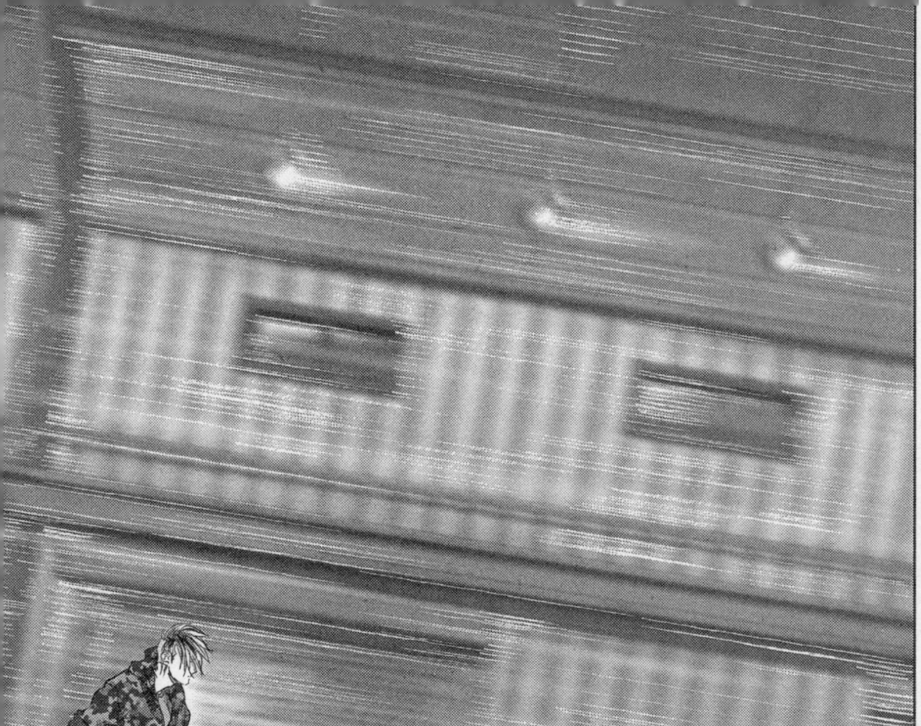

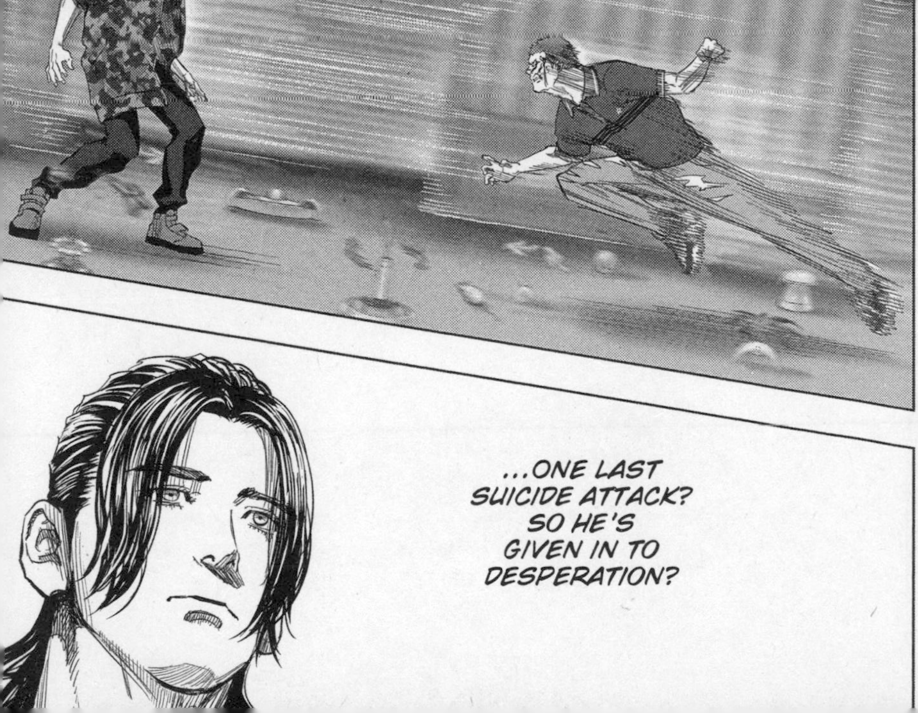
...ONE LAST SUICIDE ATTACK? SO HE'S GIVEN IN TO DESPERATION?

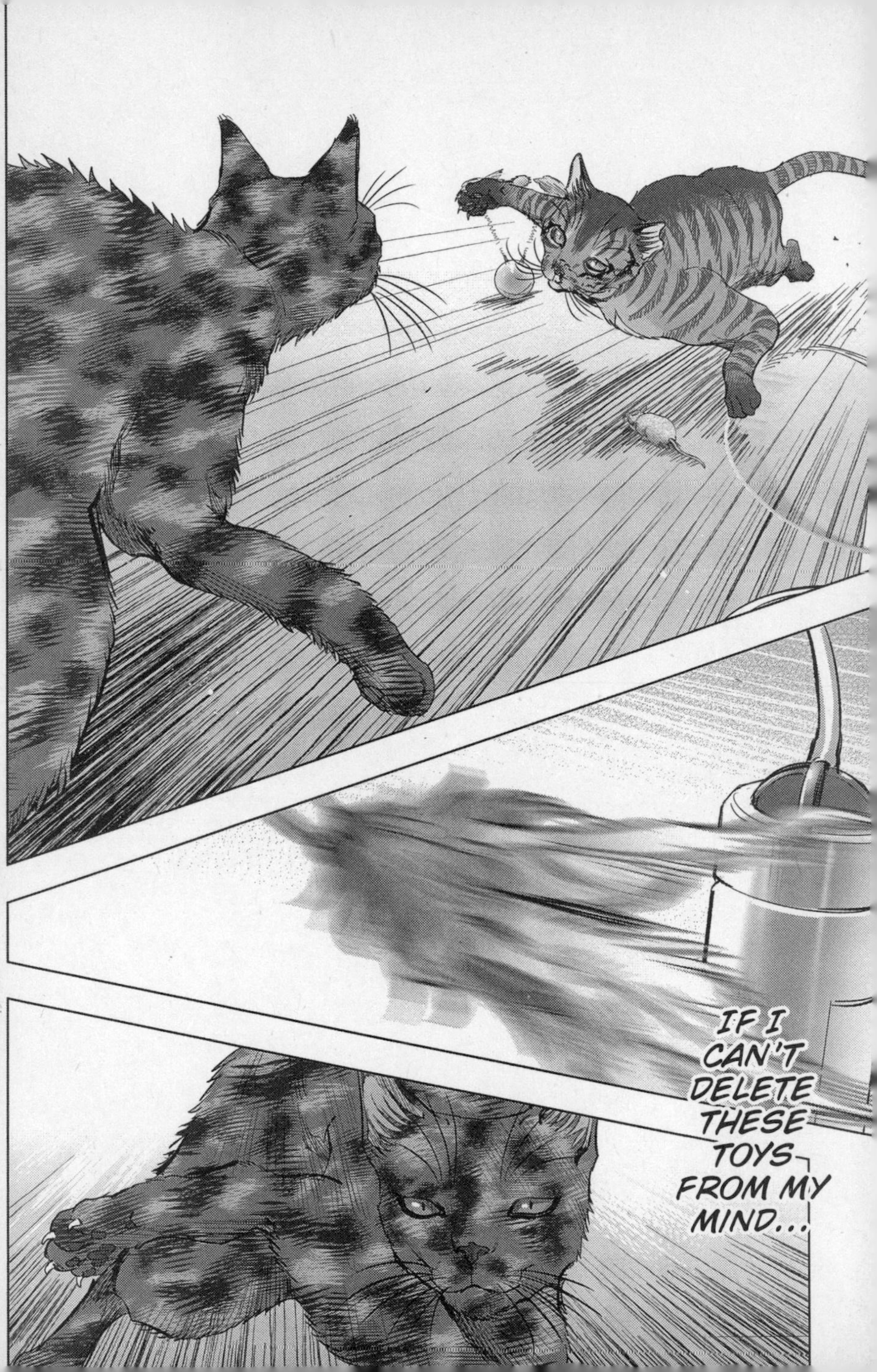
IF I CAN'T DELETE THESE TOYS FROM MY MIND...

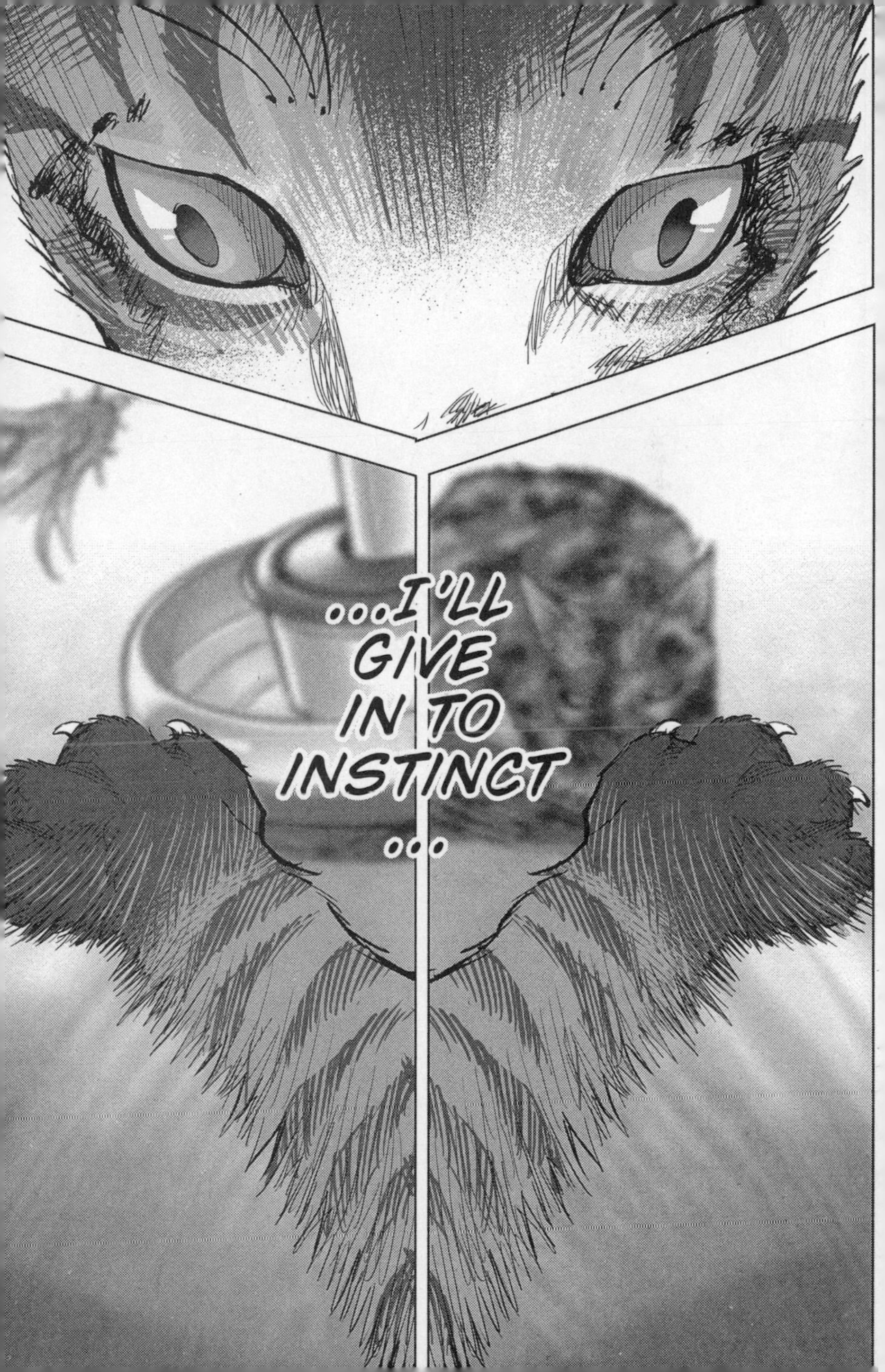
...I'LL GIVE IN TO INSTINCT ...

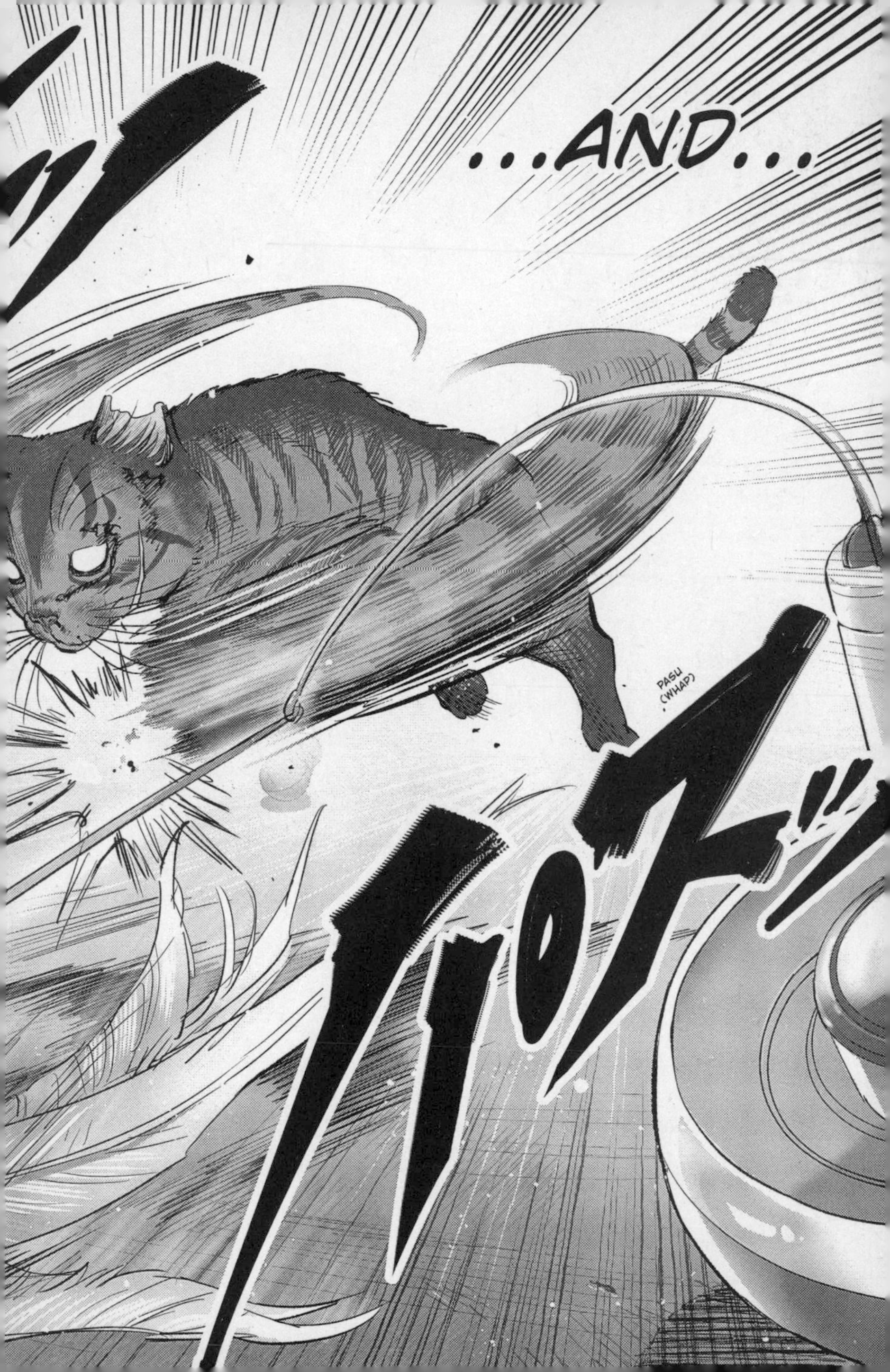
...AND...
PASU
(WHAP)

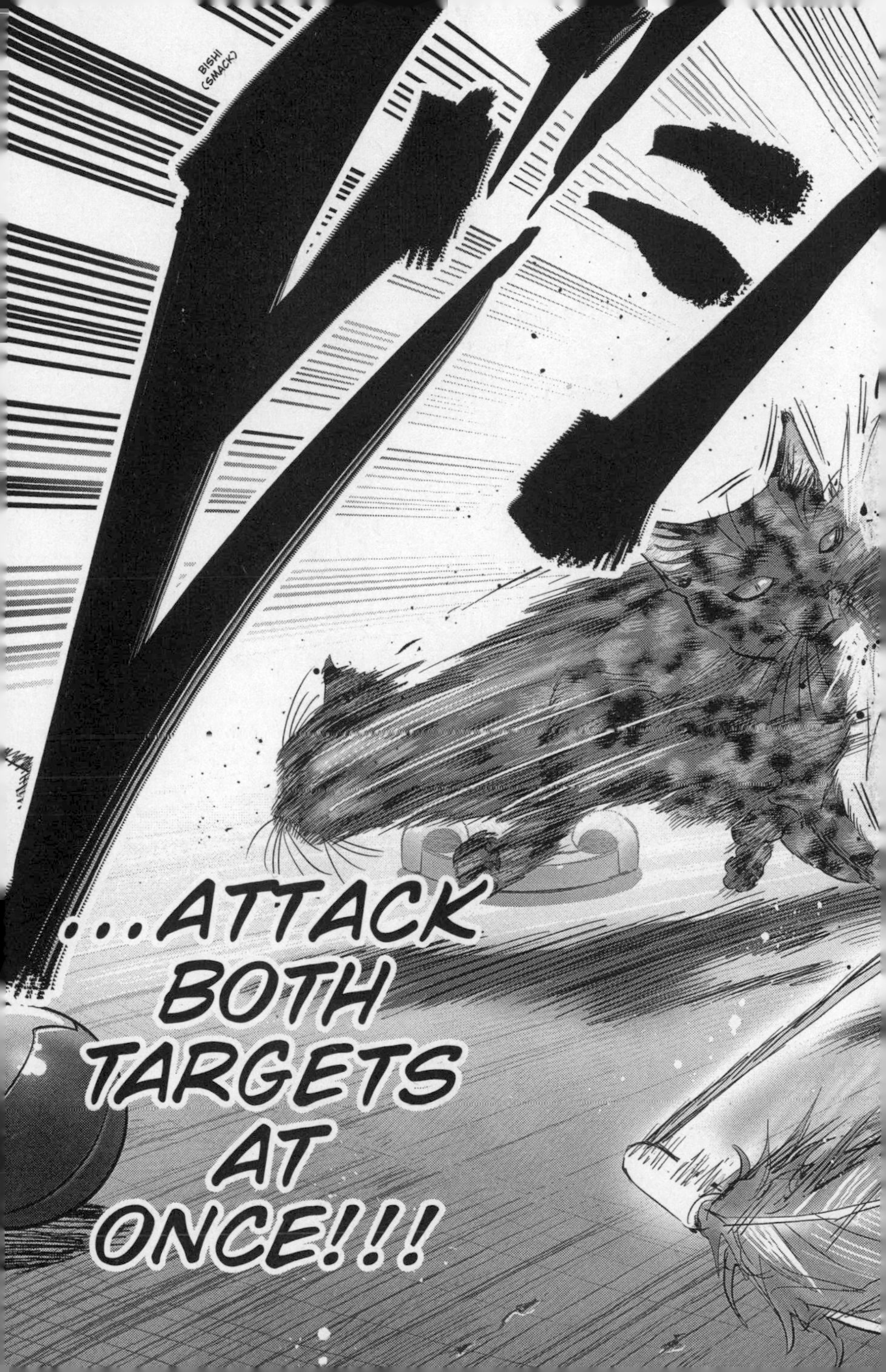
BISHI (SMACK)
...ATTACK BOTH TARGETS AT ONCE!!!

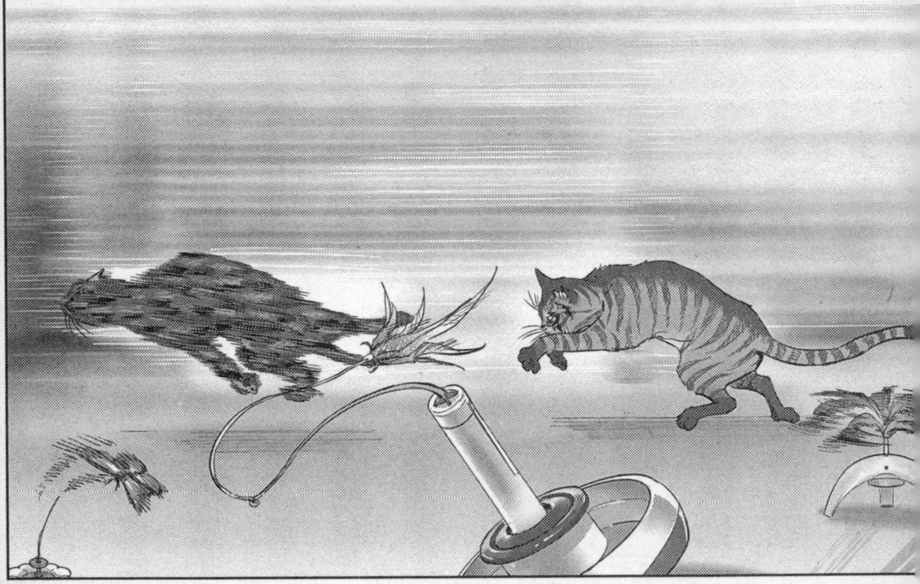

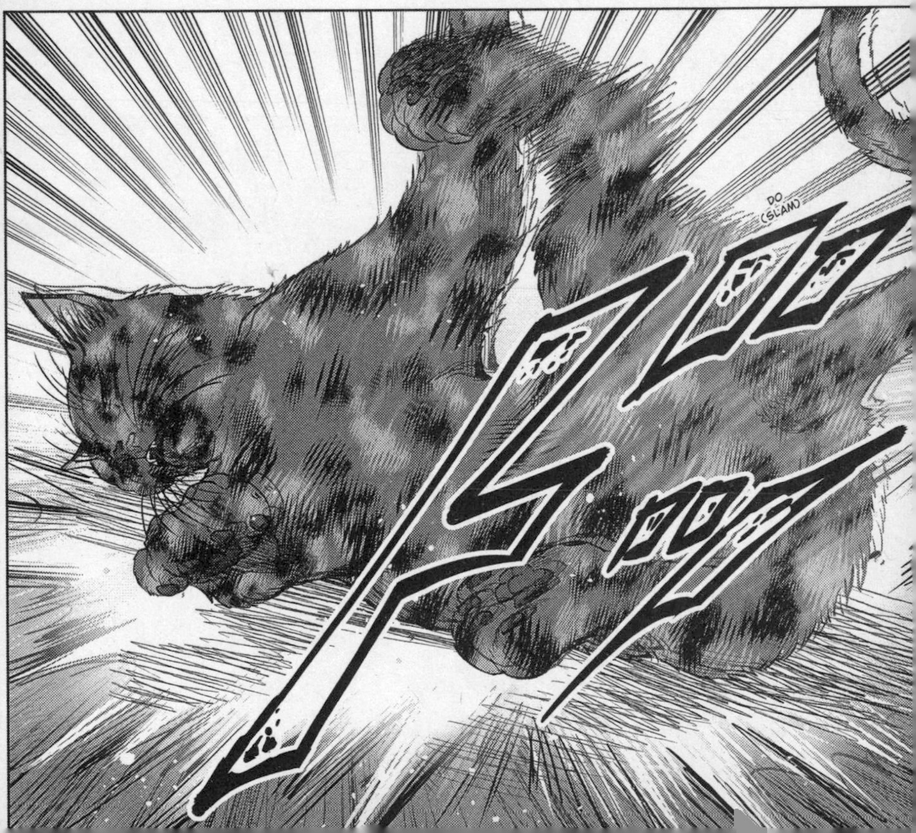
DO
(SLAM)

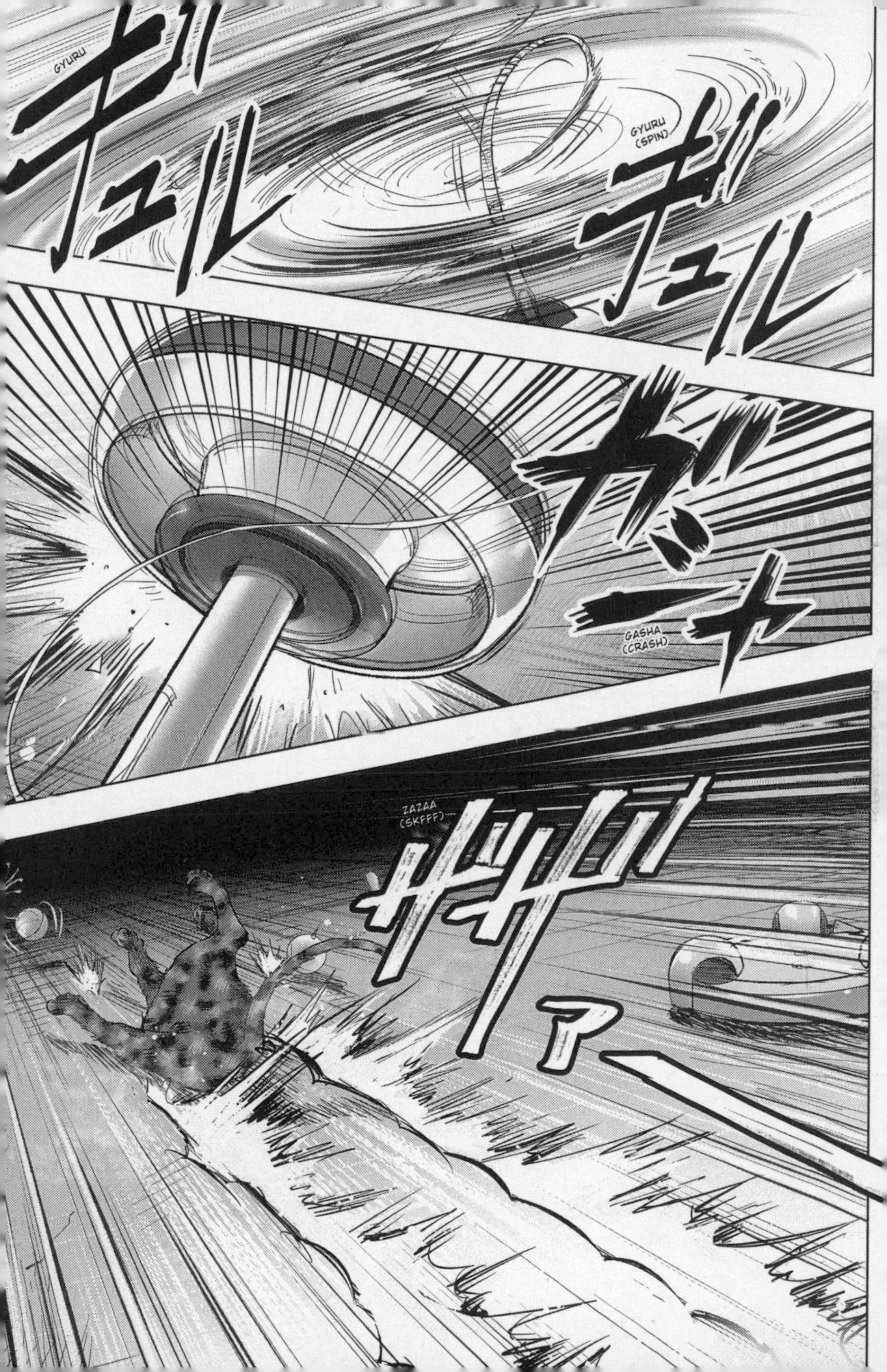
ギュル
GYURU
(SPIN)
ギュル
GYURU
ガシャ
GASHA
(CRASH)
ザザァー
ZAZAA
(SKFFF)

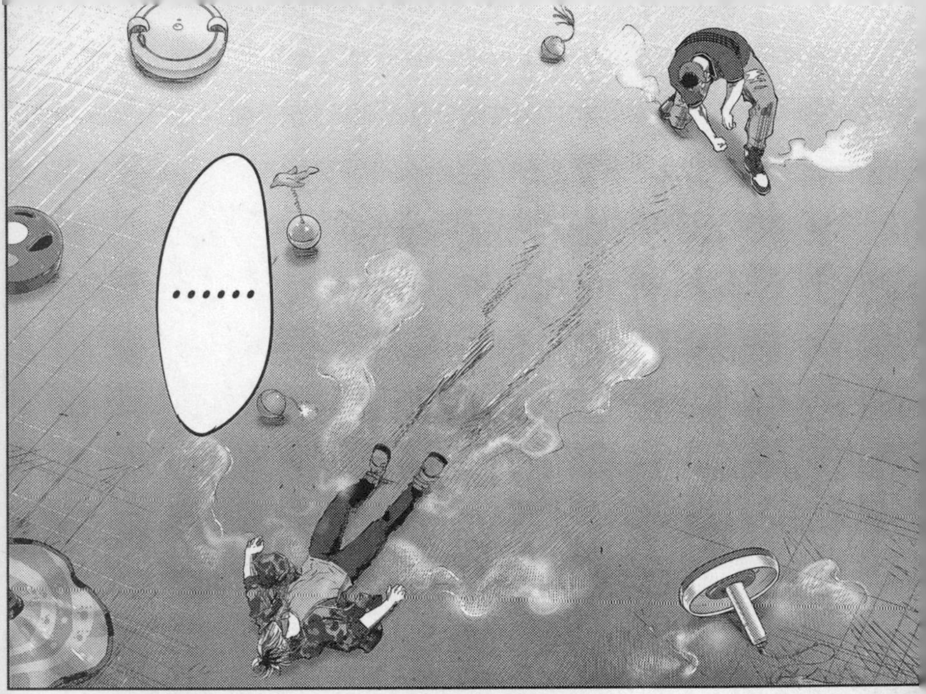
......

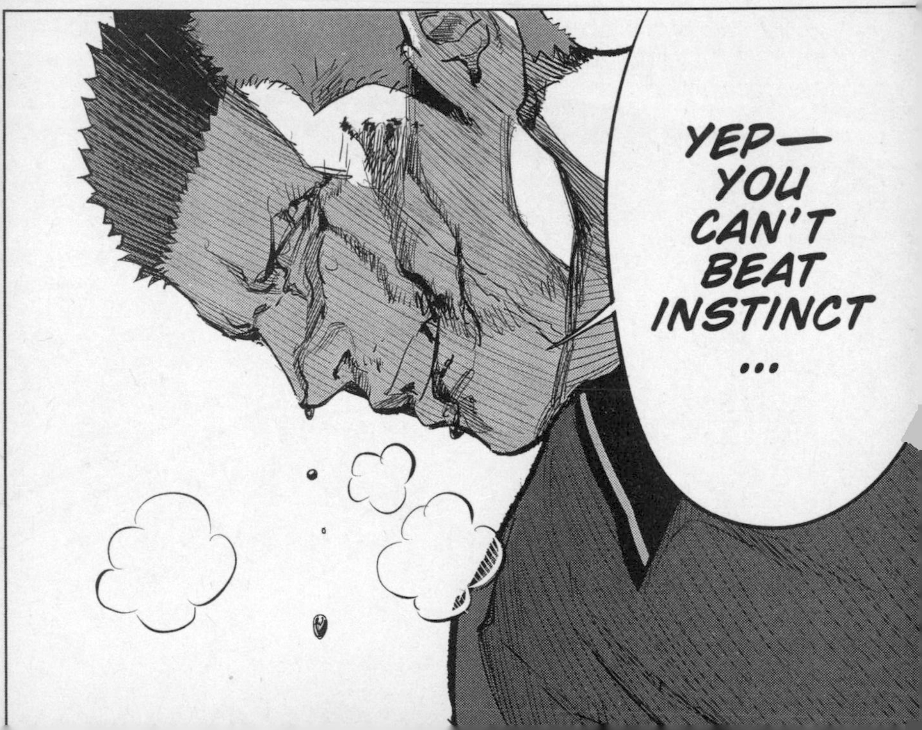
YEP—
YOU CAN'T BEAT INSTINCT ...

RYUUSEI-KUN...!

YOU CAN'T BE FOR REAL.

...

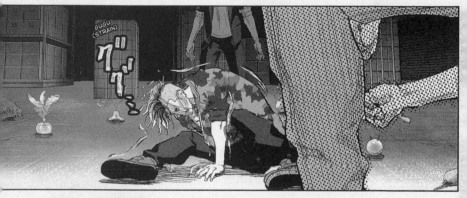

GUGU (STRAIN)

...

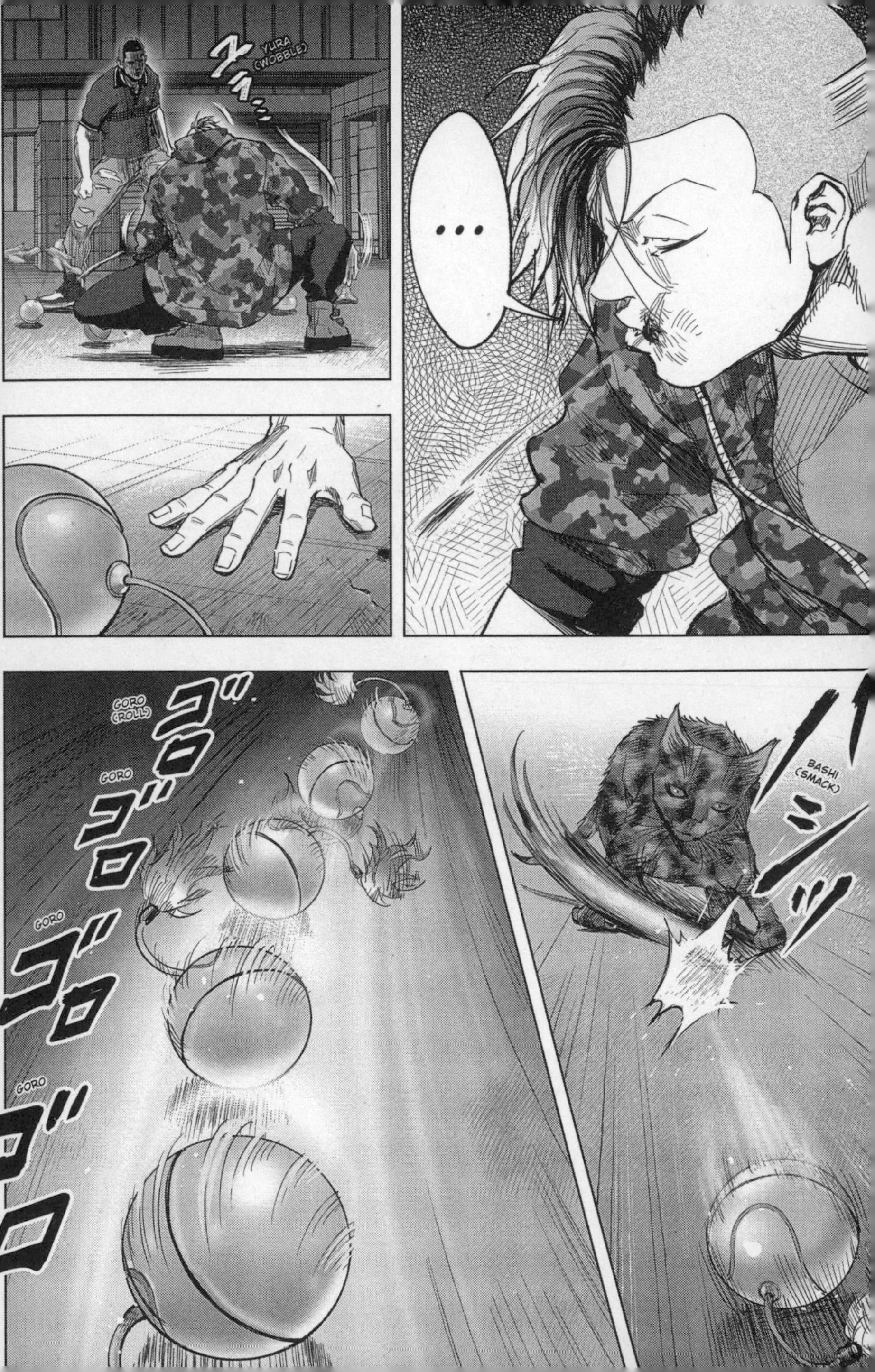
...
ユラ…
YURA (WOBBLE)
バシッ
BASHI (SMACK)
ゴロ
GORO (ROLL)
ゴロ
GORO
ゴロ
GORO
ゴロ
GORO

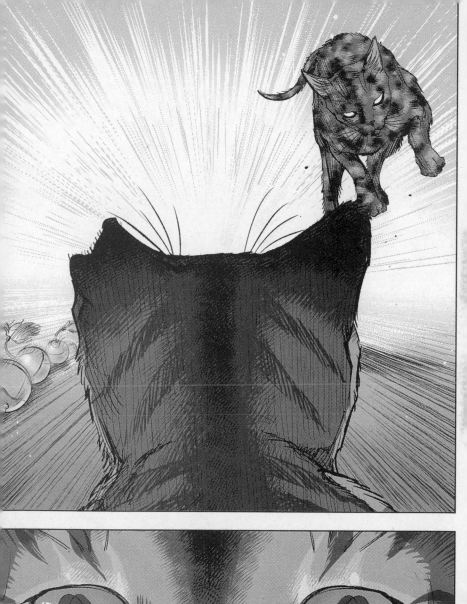
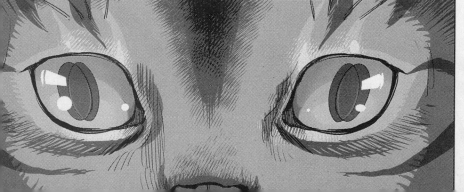

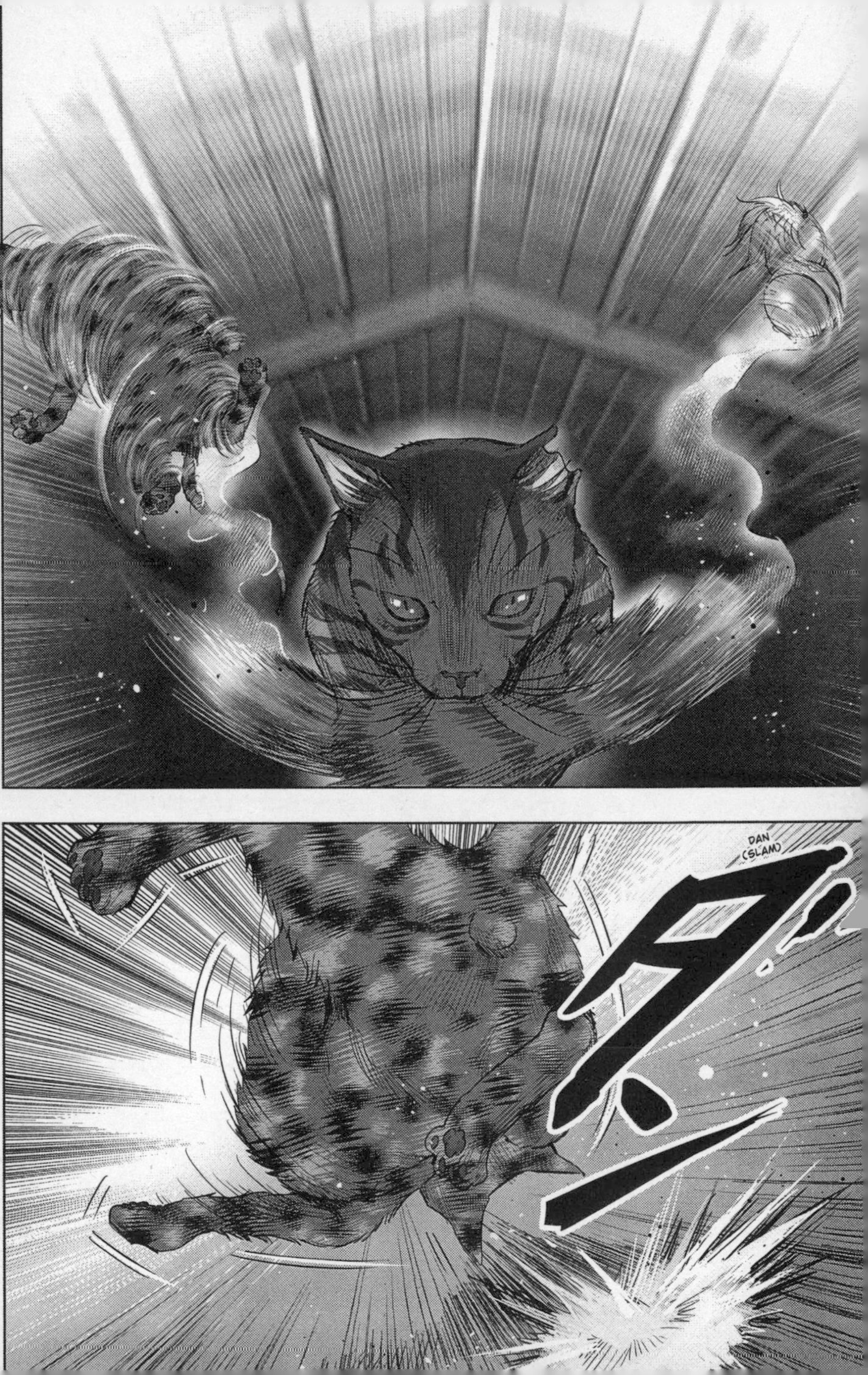
DAN
(SLAM)

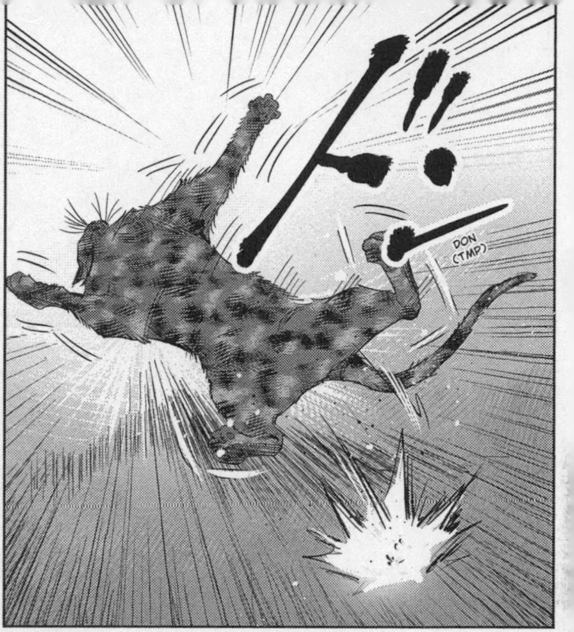
DON
(TMP)
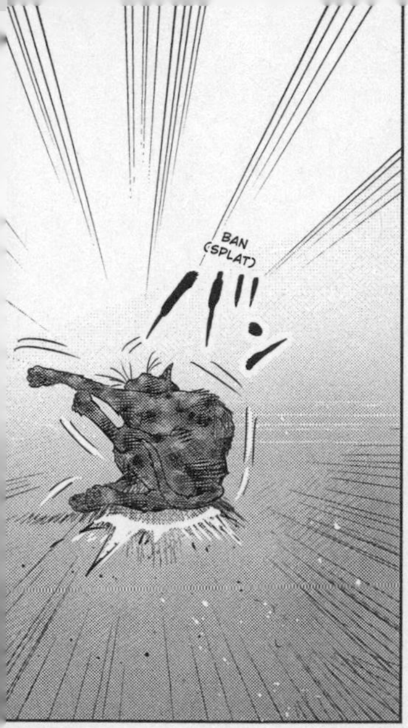
BAN
(SPLAT)
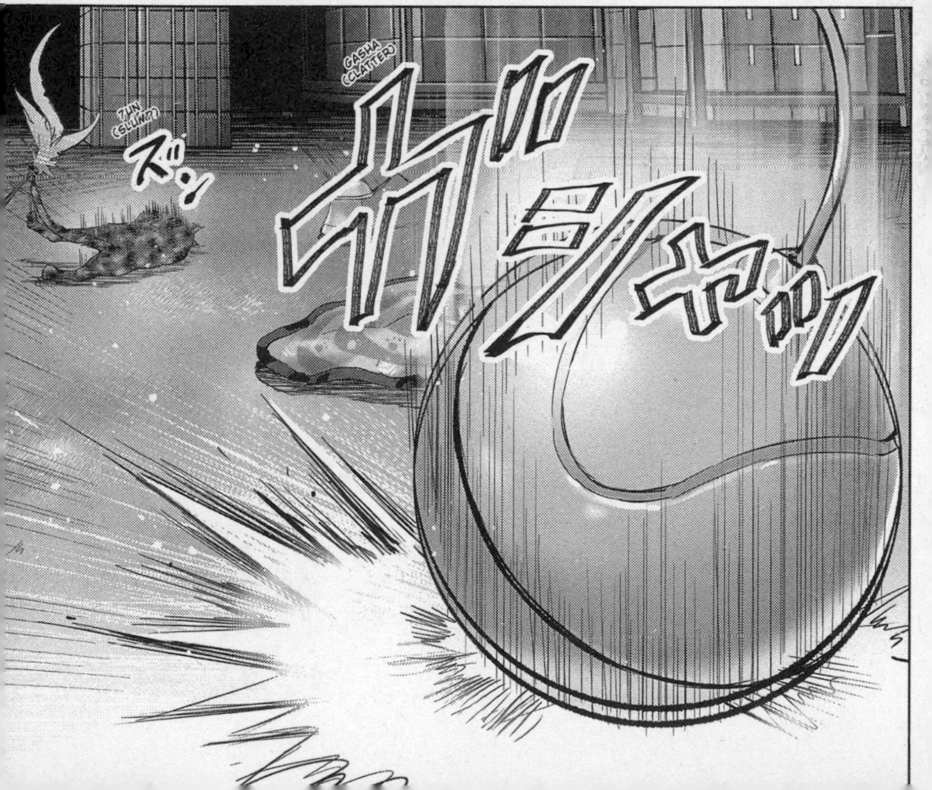
GASHA
(CLATTER)
ZUN
(SLUMP)

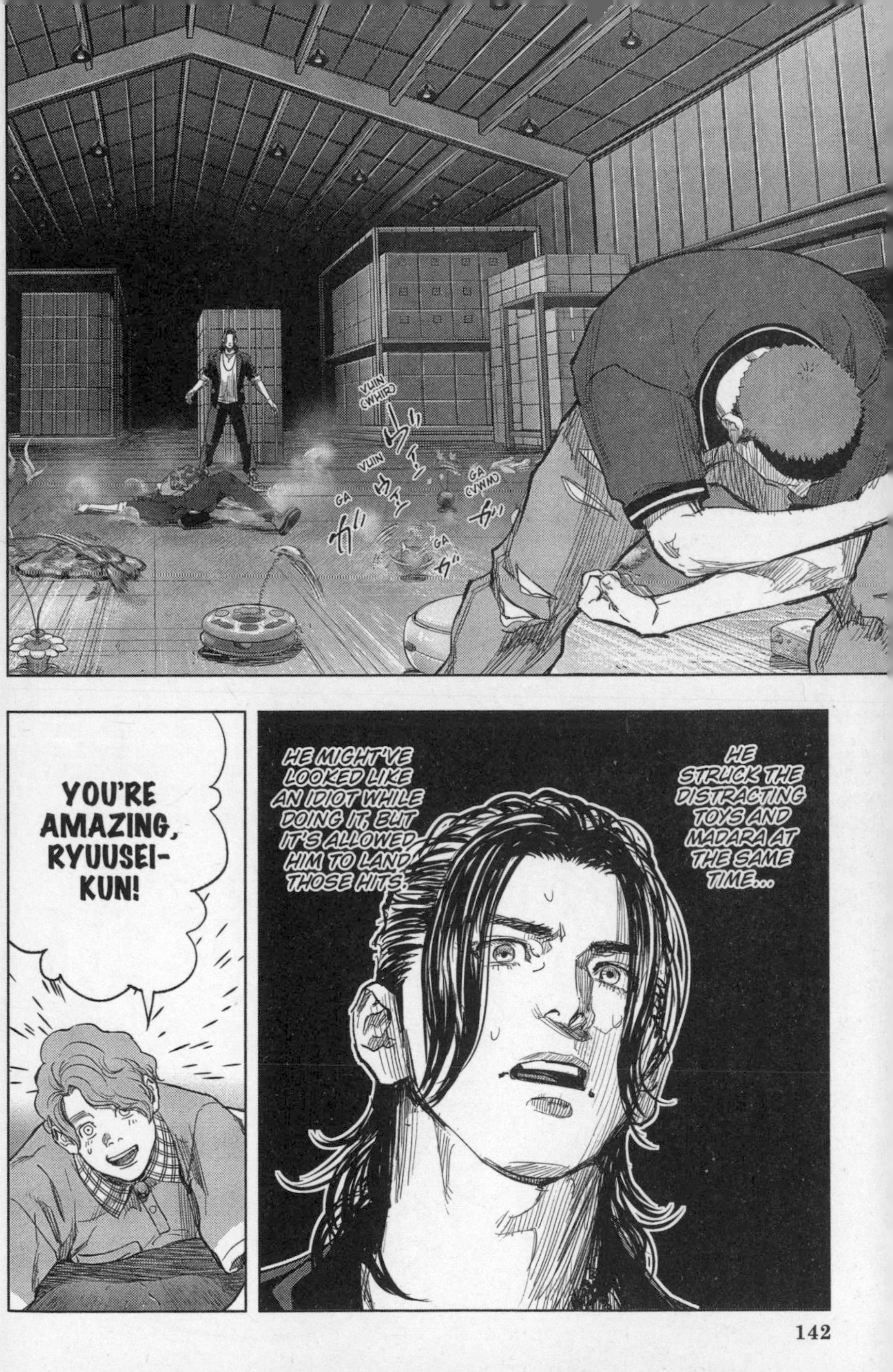
GA (VWM)
GA
VUIN (WHIR)
VUIN
GA
HE STRUCK THE DISTRACTING TOYS AND MADARA AT THE SAME TIME...
HE MIGHT'VE LOOKED LIKE AN IDIOT WHILE DOING IT, BUT IT'S ALLOWED HIM TO LAND THOSE HITS.
YOU'RE AMAZING, RYUUSEI-KUN!

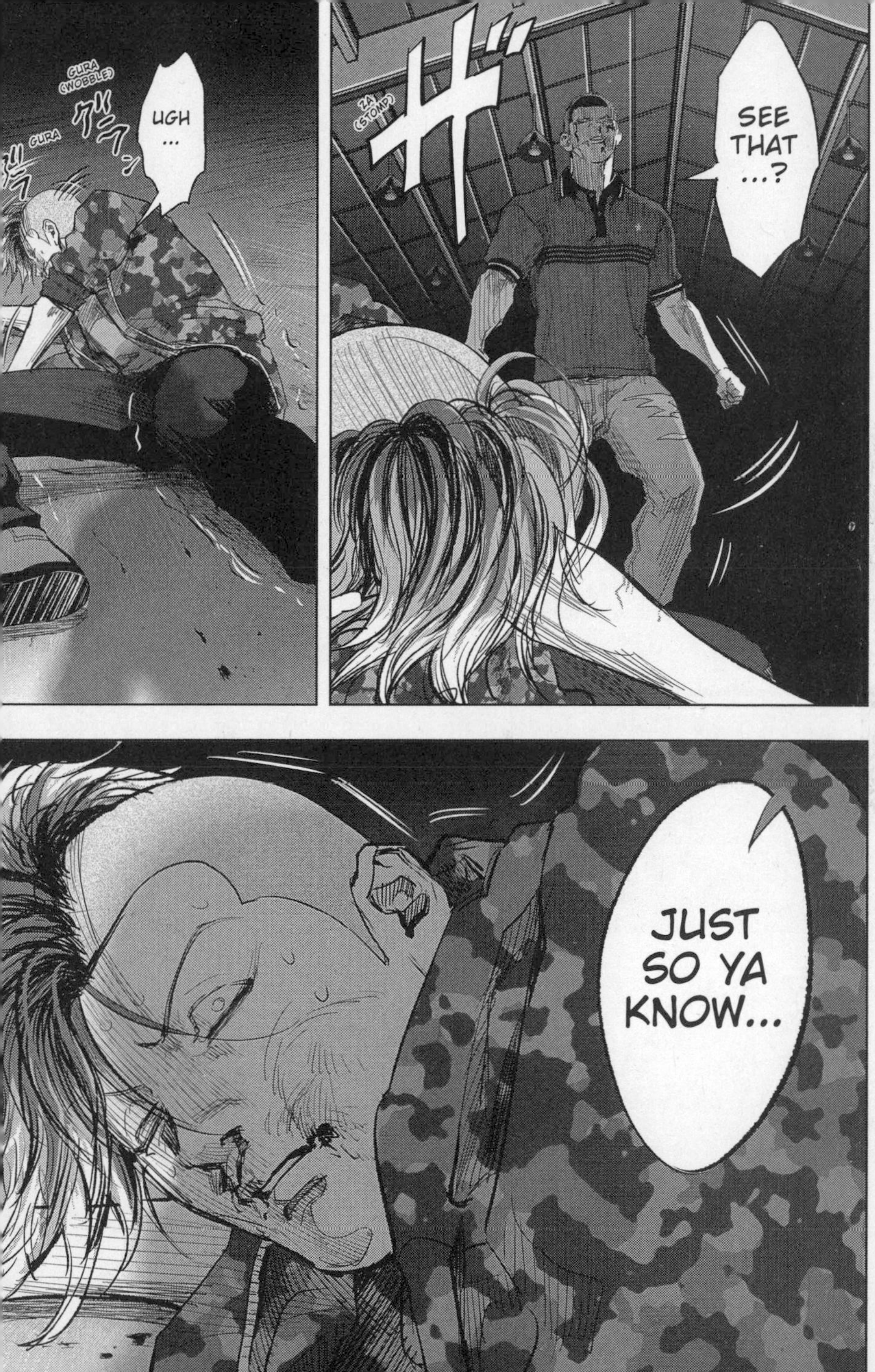
ZA (STOMP)
SEE THAT ...?
GURA (WOBBLE)
GURA
UGH ...
JUST SO YA KNOW...

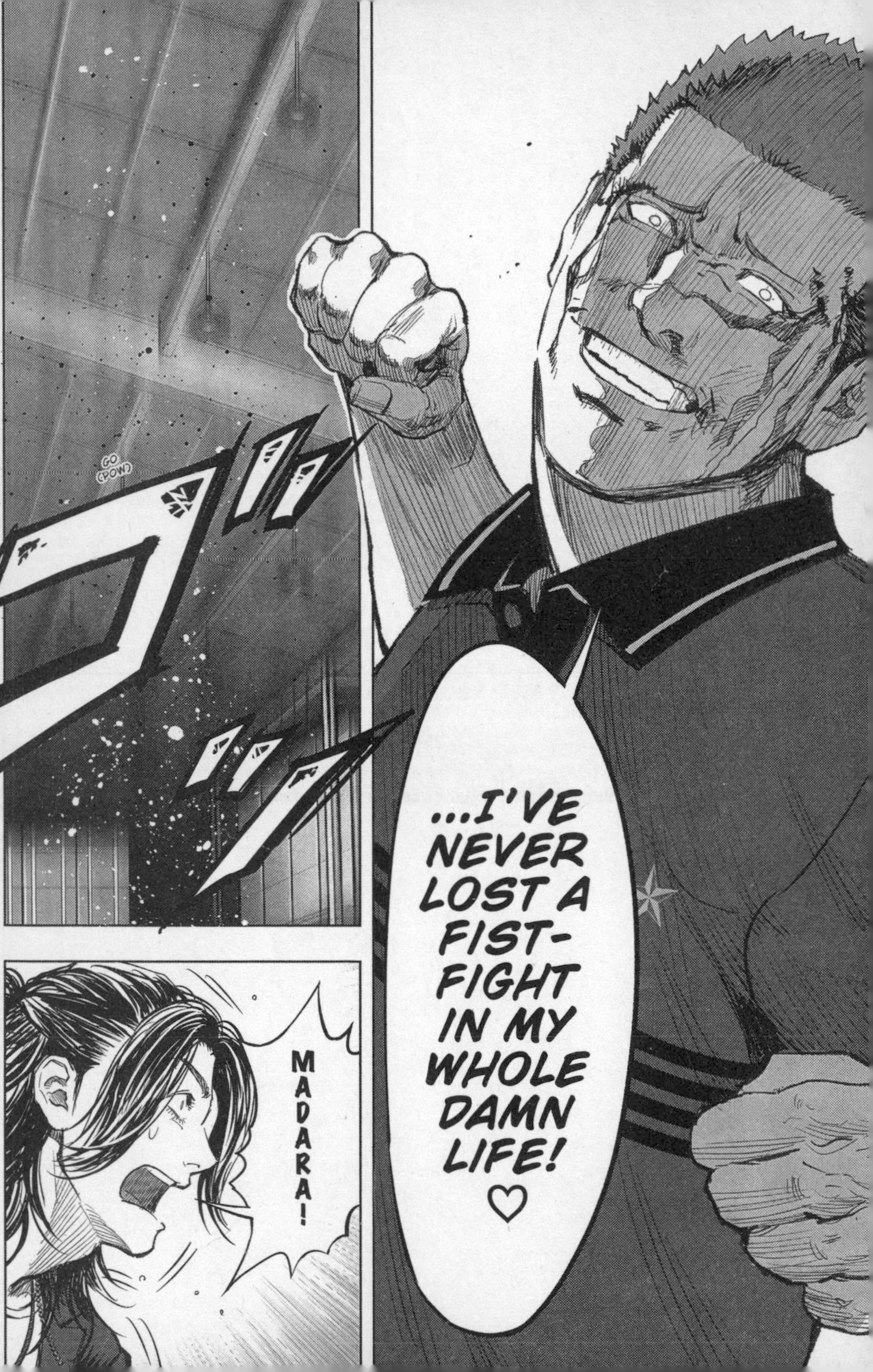
...I'VE NEVER LOST A FIST-FIGHT IN MY WHOLE DAMN LIFE! ♡
GO (POW)
MADARA!

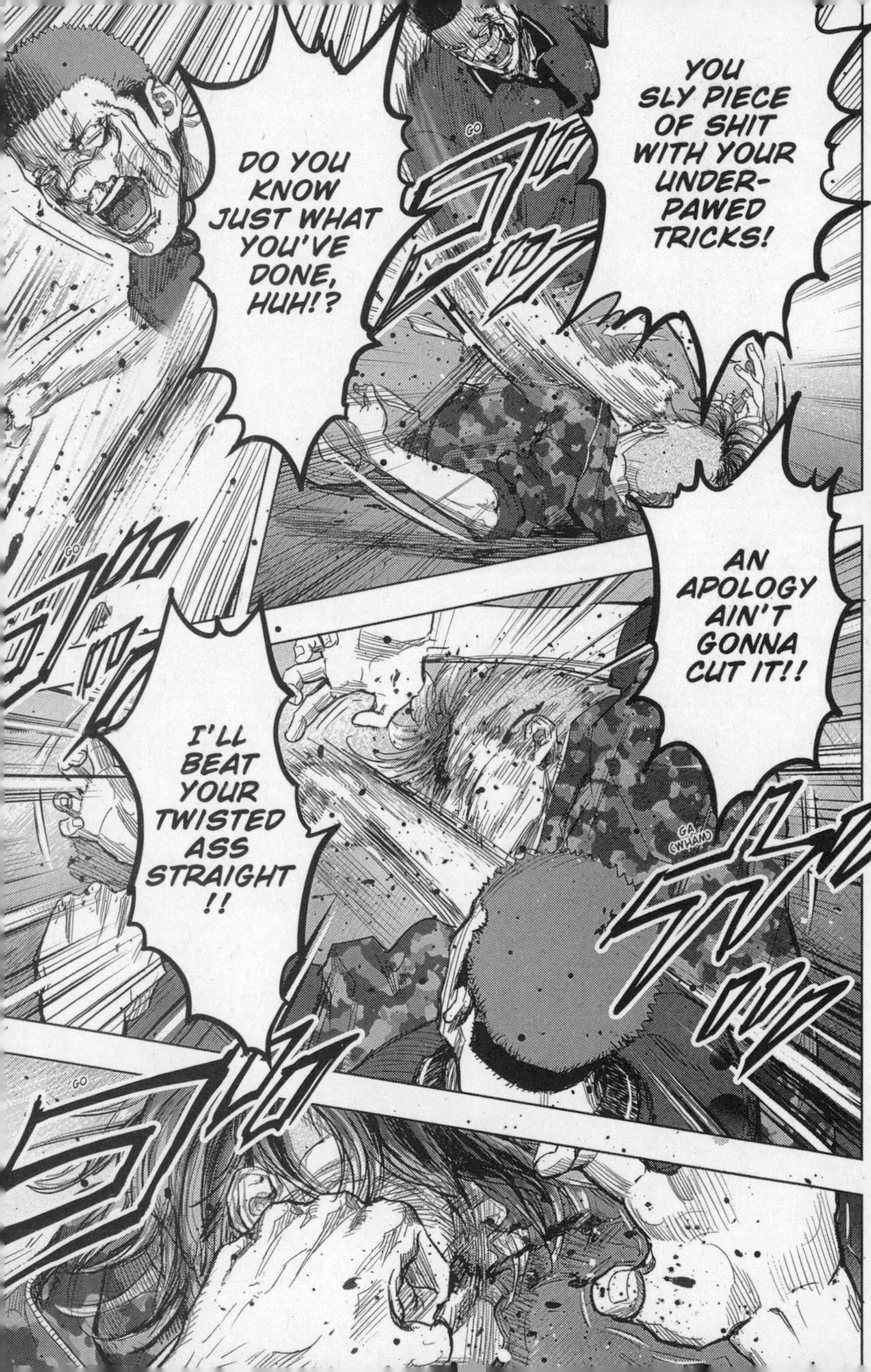
YOU SLY PIECE OF SHIT WITH YOUR UNDER-PAWED TRICKS!
GO
DO YOU KNOW JUST WHAT YOU'VE DONE, HUH!?
GO
AN APOLOGY AIN'T GONNA CUT IT!!
GA (WHAM)
I'LL BEAT YOUR TWISTED ASS STRAIGHT!!
GO

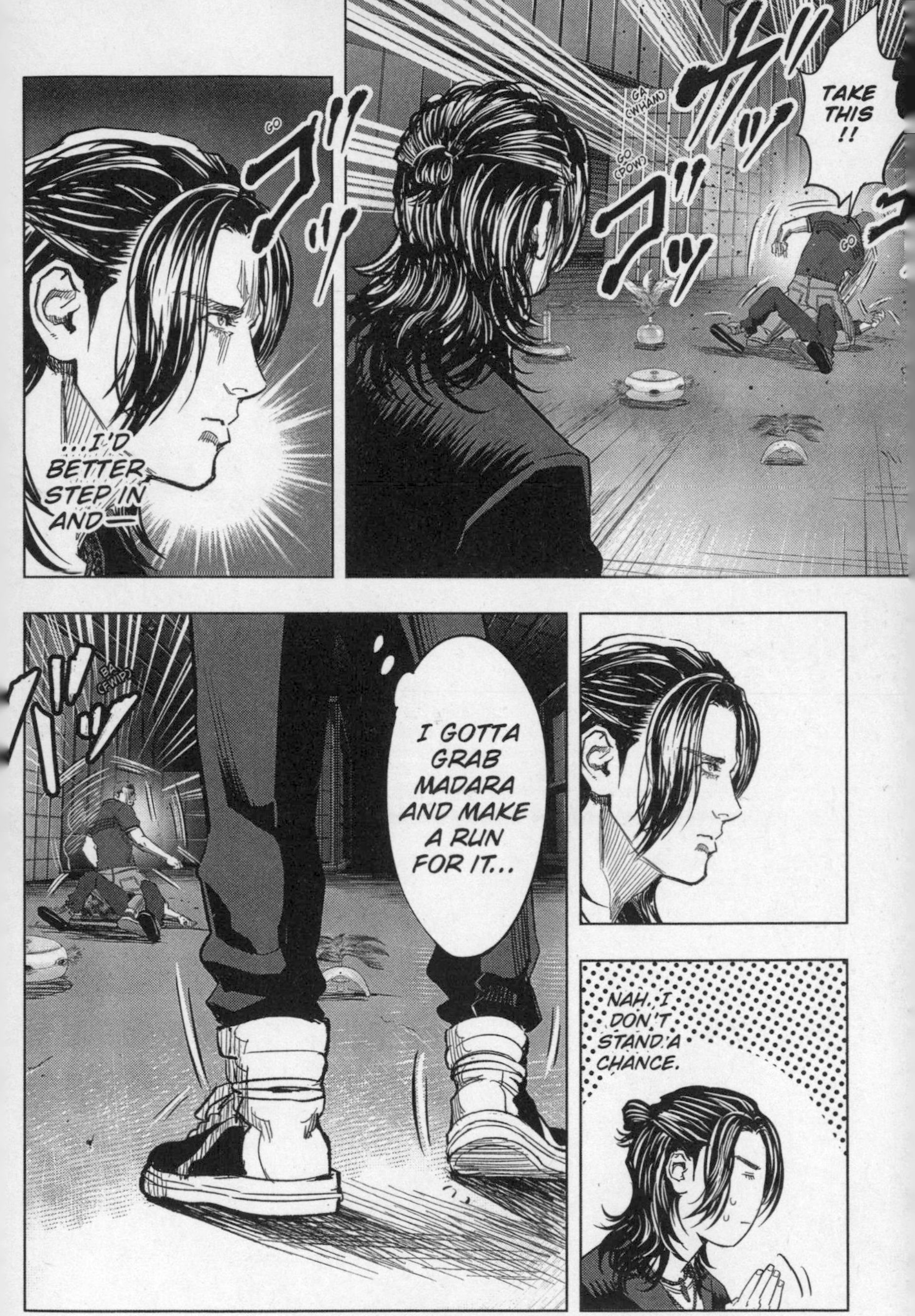
TAKE THIS !!
GA (WHAM)
GO (POW)
GO
GO
...I'D BETTER STEP IN AND—
NAH, I DON'T STAND A CHANCE.
BA (FWIP)
I GOTTA GRAB MADARA AND MAKE A RUN FOR IT...

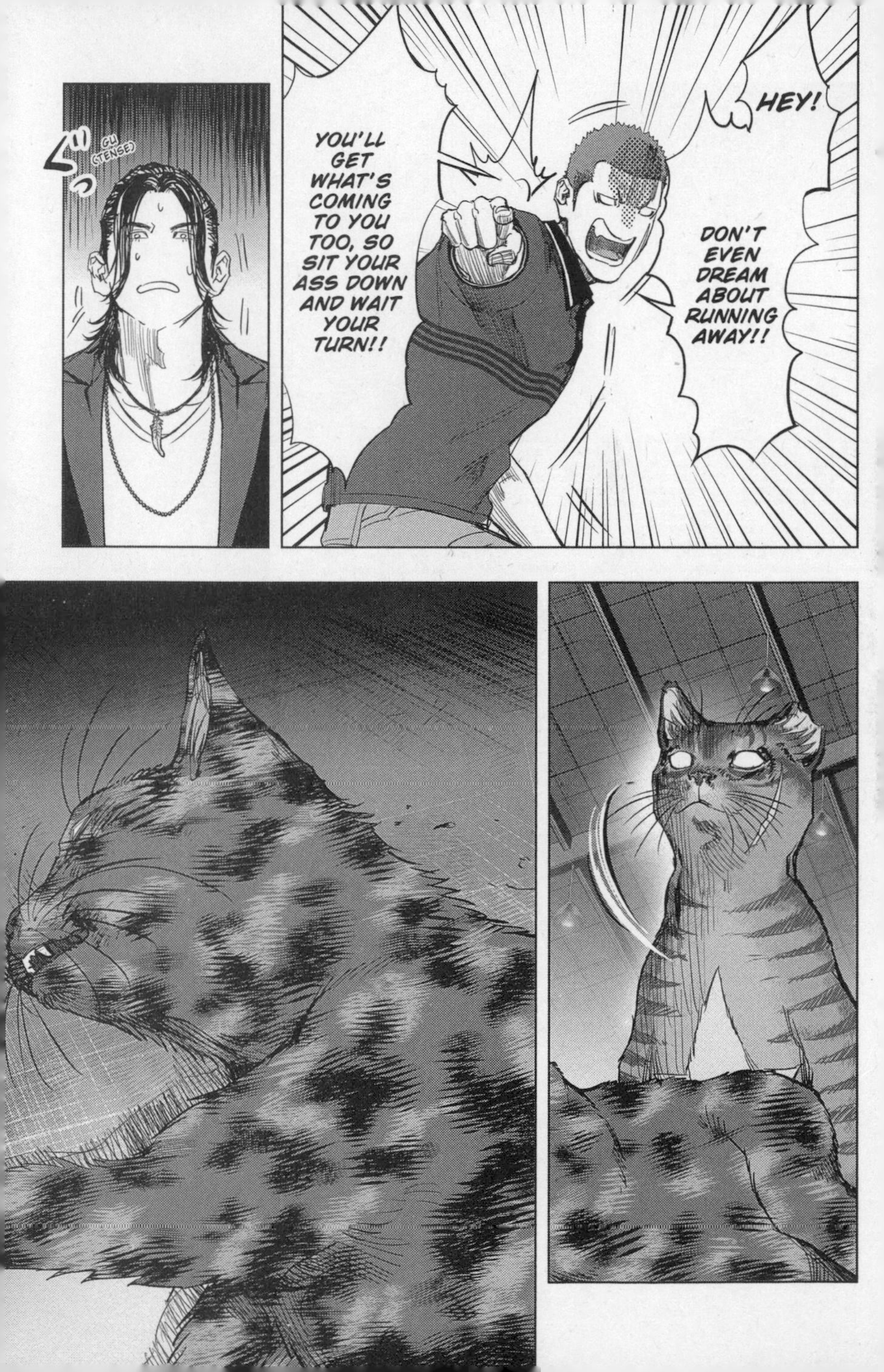
HEY!
DON'T EVEN DREAM ABOUT RUNNING AWAY!!
YOU'LL GET WHAT'S COMING TO YOU TOO, SO SIT YOUR ASS DOWN AND WAIT YOUR TURN!!
ぐっ
GU (TENSE)

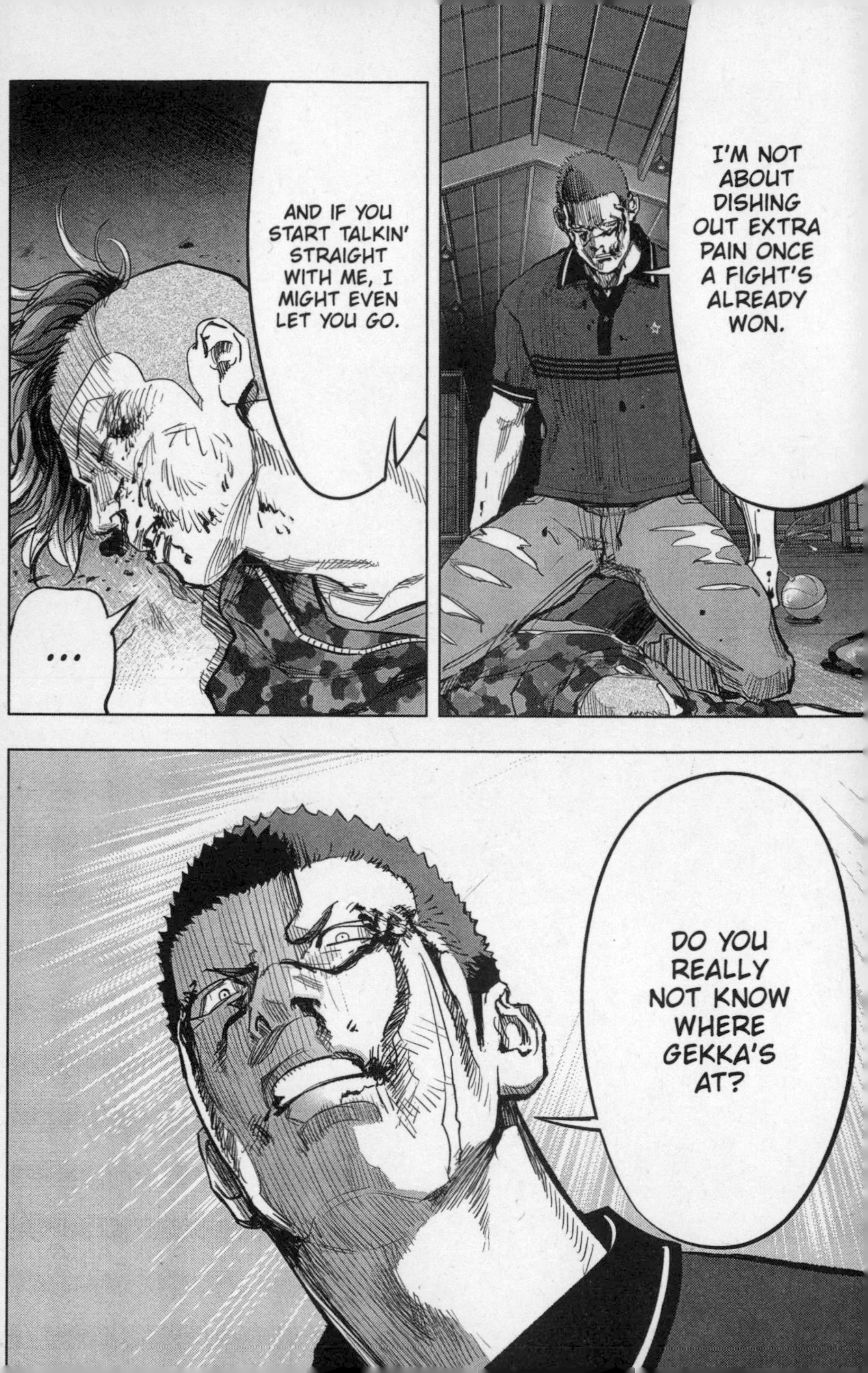
I'M NOT ABOUT DISHING OUT EXTRA PAIN ONCE A FIGHT'S ALREADY WON.
AND IF YOU START TALKIN' STRAIGHT WITH ME, I MIGHT EVEN LET YOU GO.
...
DO YOU REALLY NOT KNOW WHERE GEKKA'S AT?

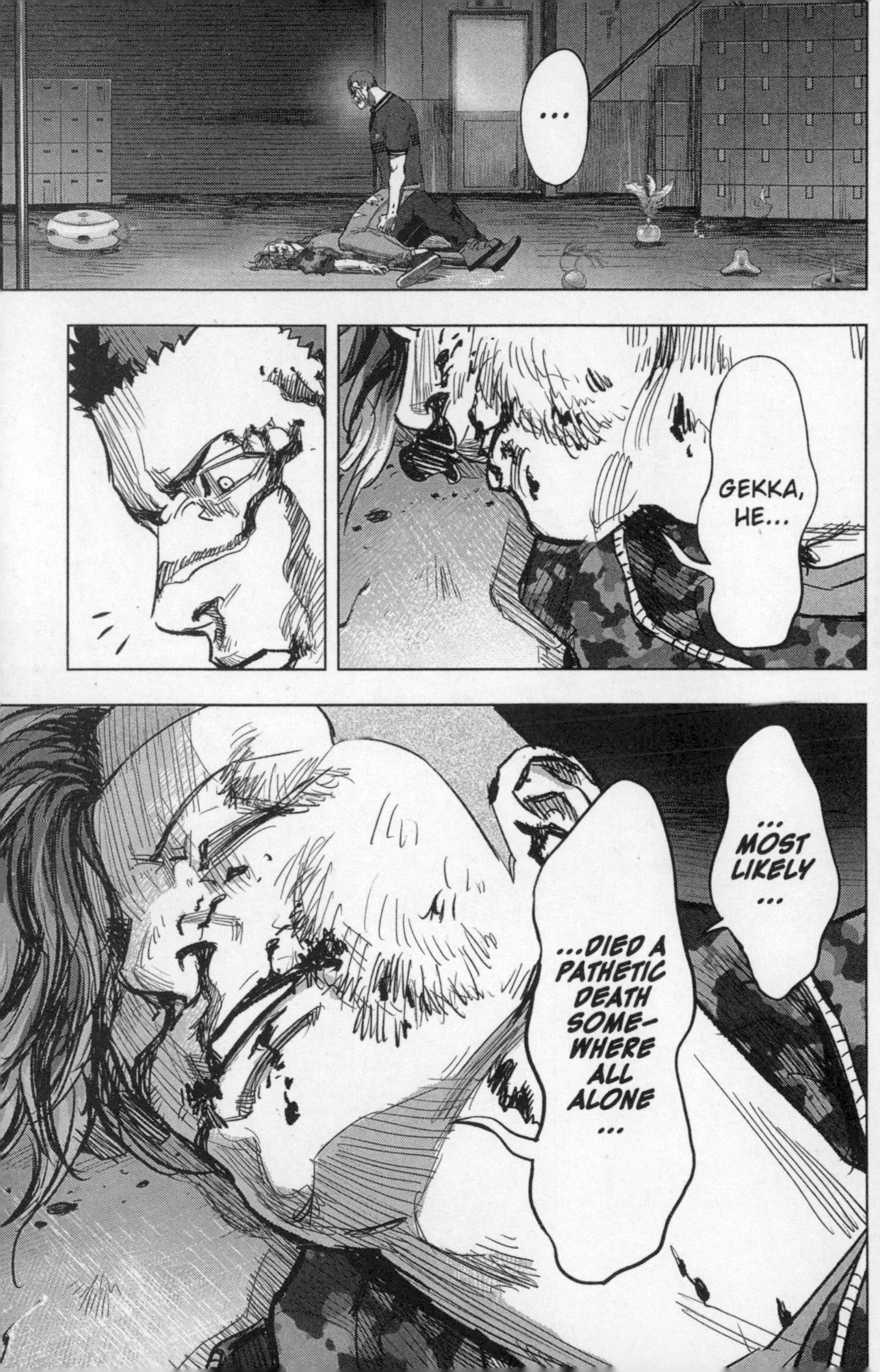
...
GEKKA, HE...
...MOST LIKELY...
...DIED A PATHETIC DEATH SOMEWHERE ALL ALONE...

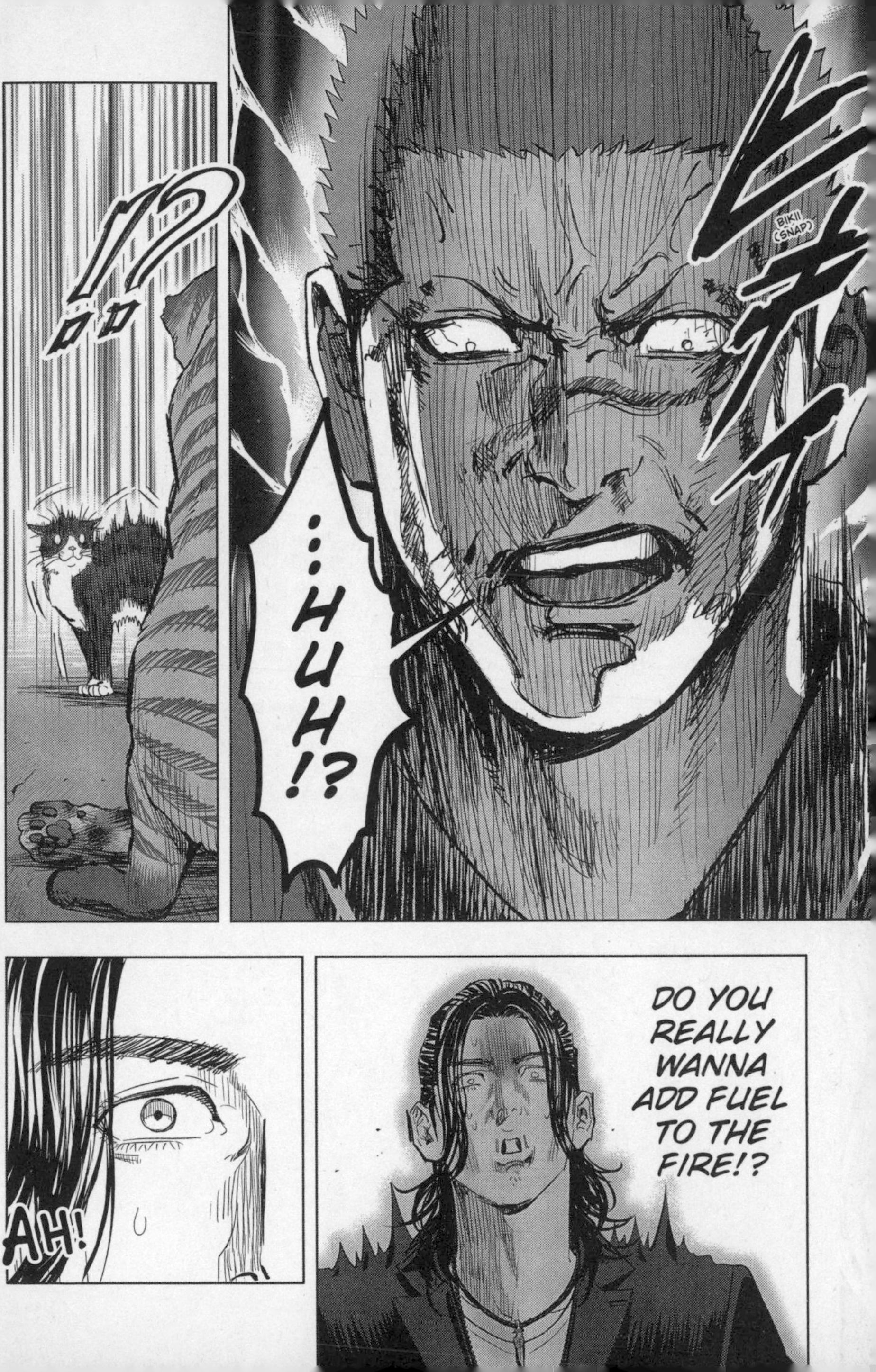
BIKII (SNAP)
...HUH!?
!?
DO YOU REALLY WANNA ADD FUEL TO THE FIRE!?
AH!

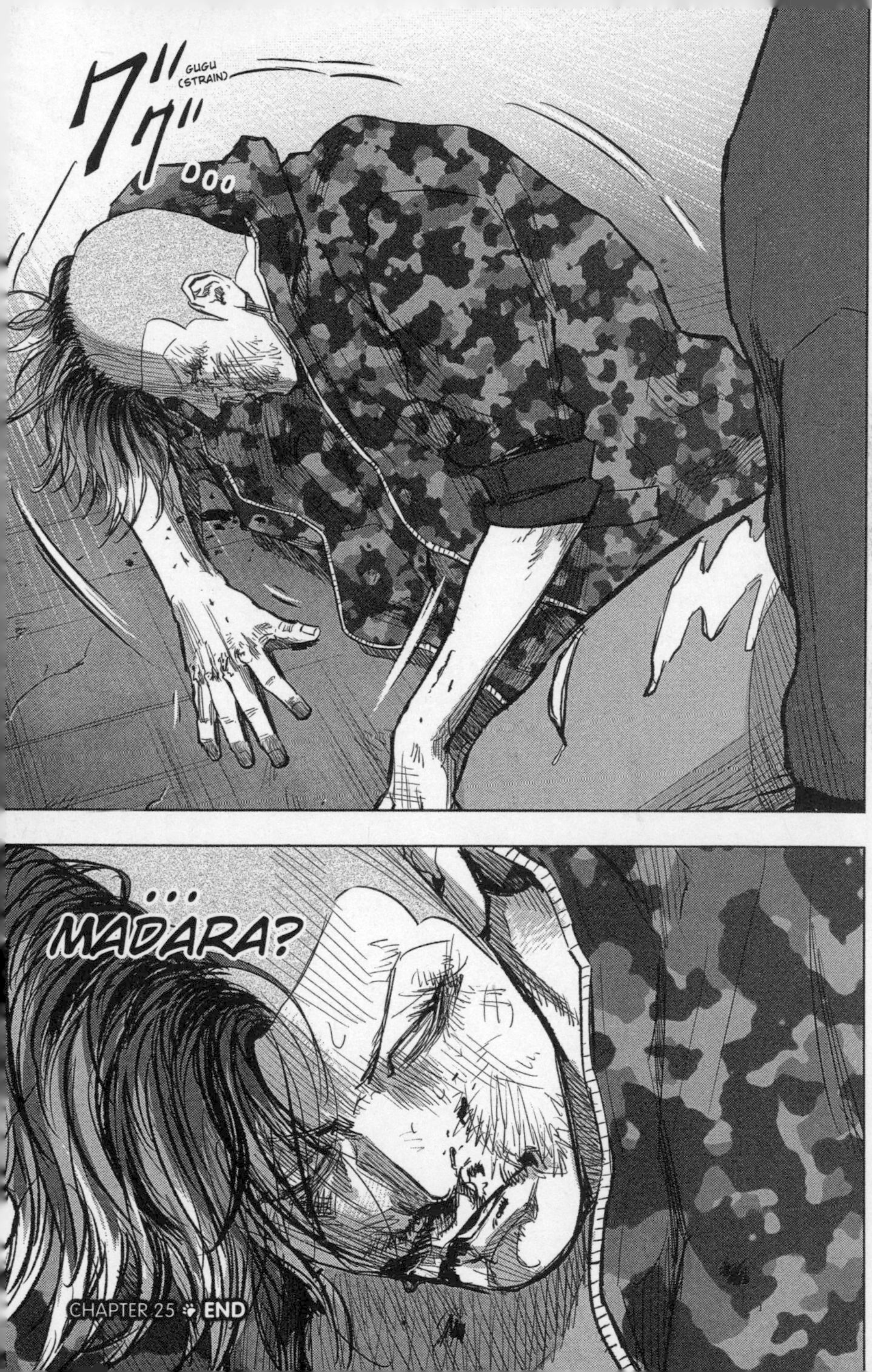
ググ
GUGU (STRAIN)
ooo
...
MADARA?
CHAPTER 25 END

MADARA

HAZUKI

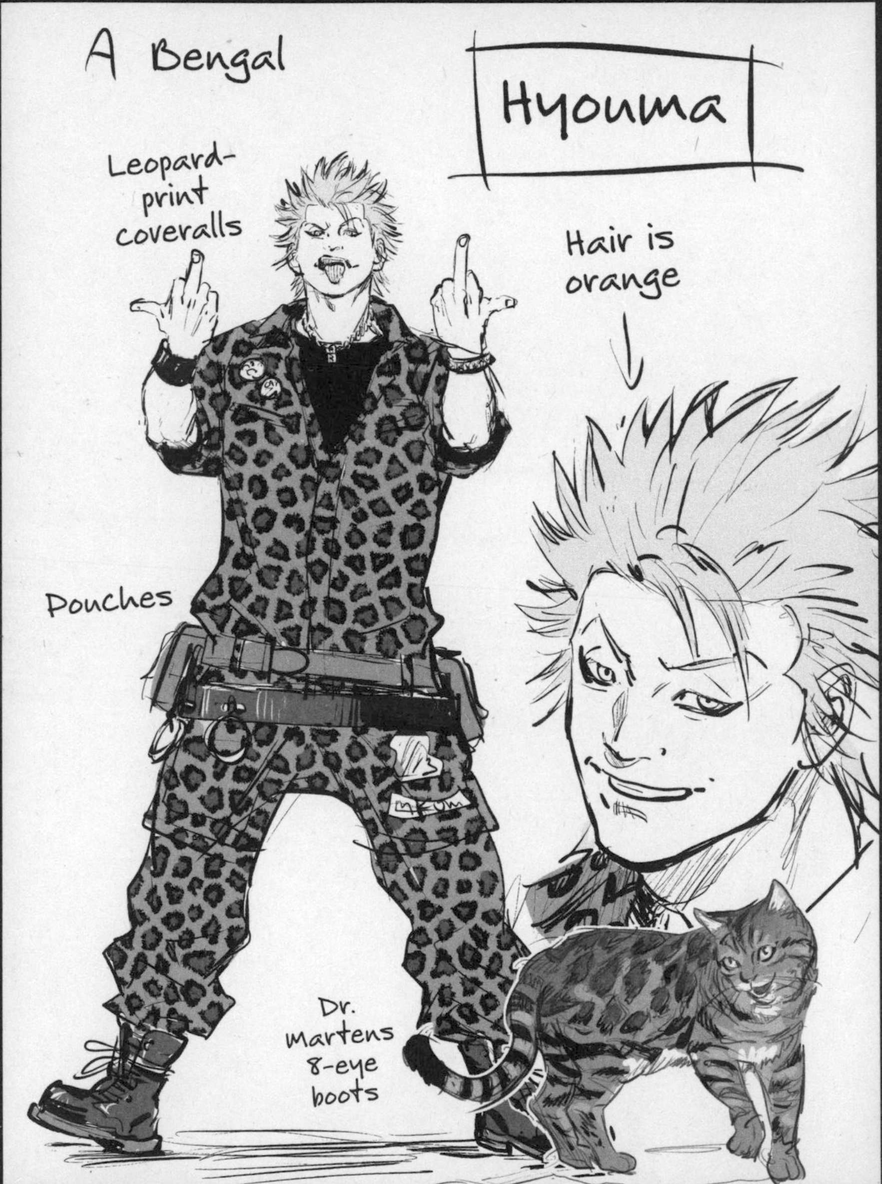
A Bengal
Hyouma
Leopard-print coveralls
Hair is orange
Pouches
Dr. Martens 8-eye boots

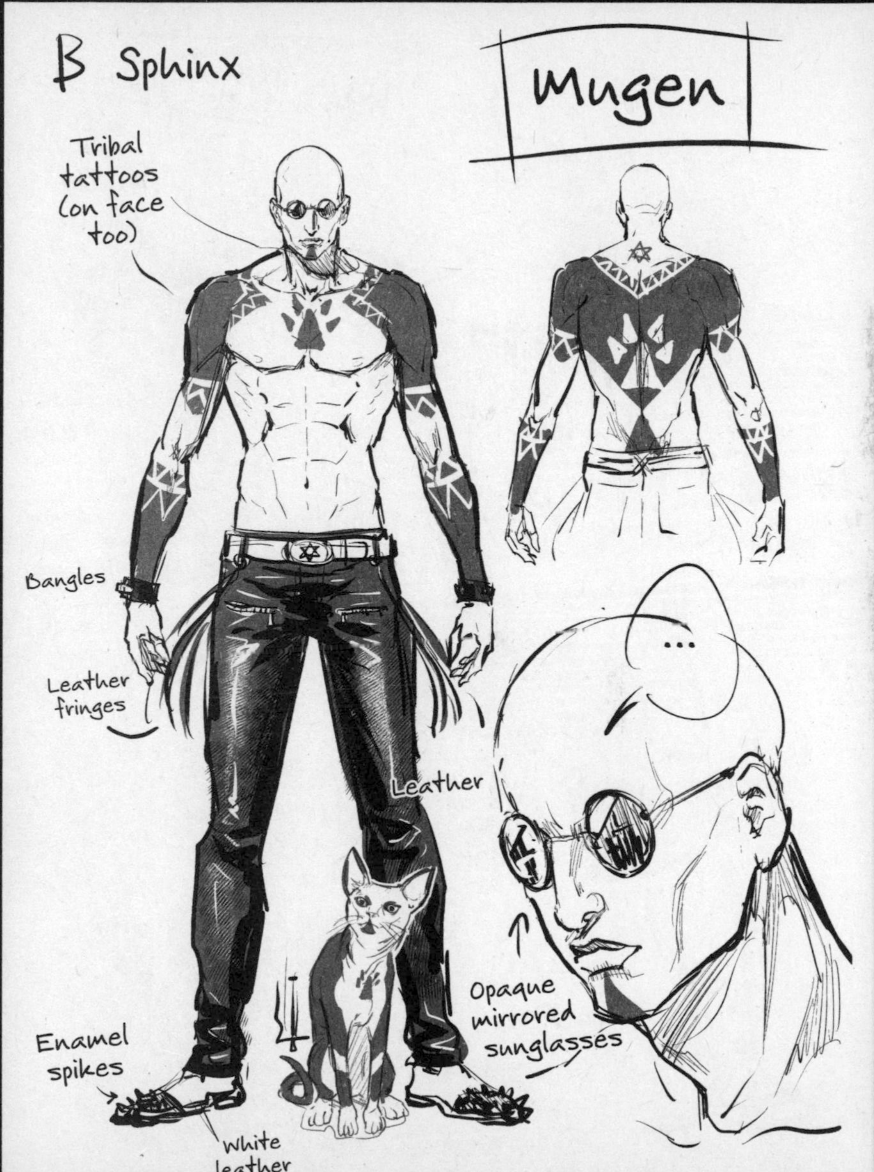

β Sphinx
Mugen
Tribal tattoos (on face too)
Bangles
Leather fringes
Leather
Enamel spikes
White leather
...
Opaque mirrored sunglasses

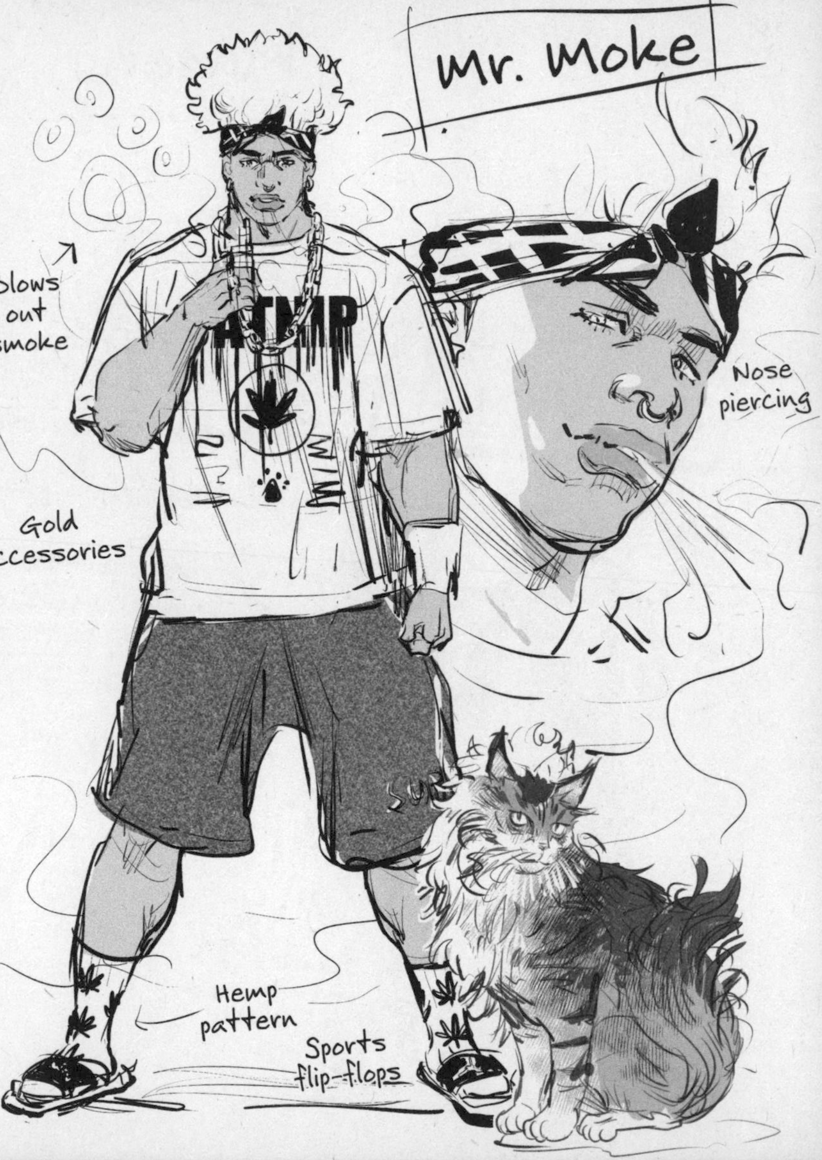
Mr. Moke
Blows out smoke
Nose piercing
ATMP
Gold accessories
Hemp pattern
Sports flip-flops

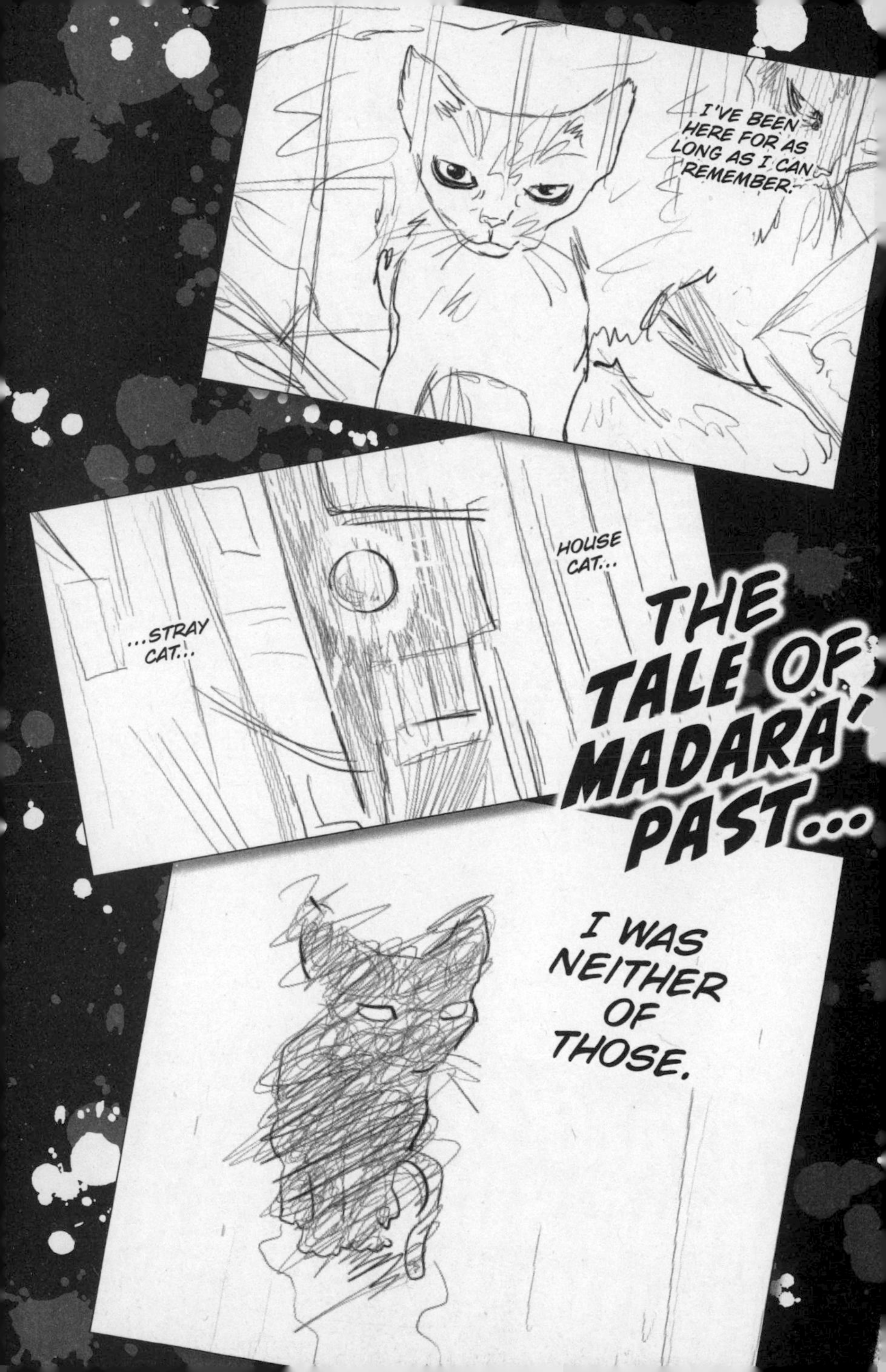
I'VE BEEN HERE FOR AS LONG AS I CAN REMEMBER.
HOUSE CAT...
...STRAY CAT...
THE TALE OF MADARA' PAST...
I WAS NEITHER OF THOSE.

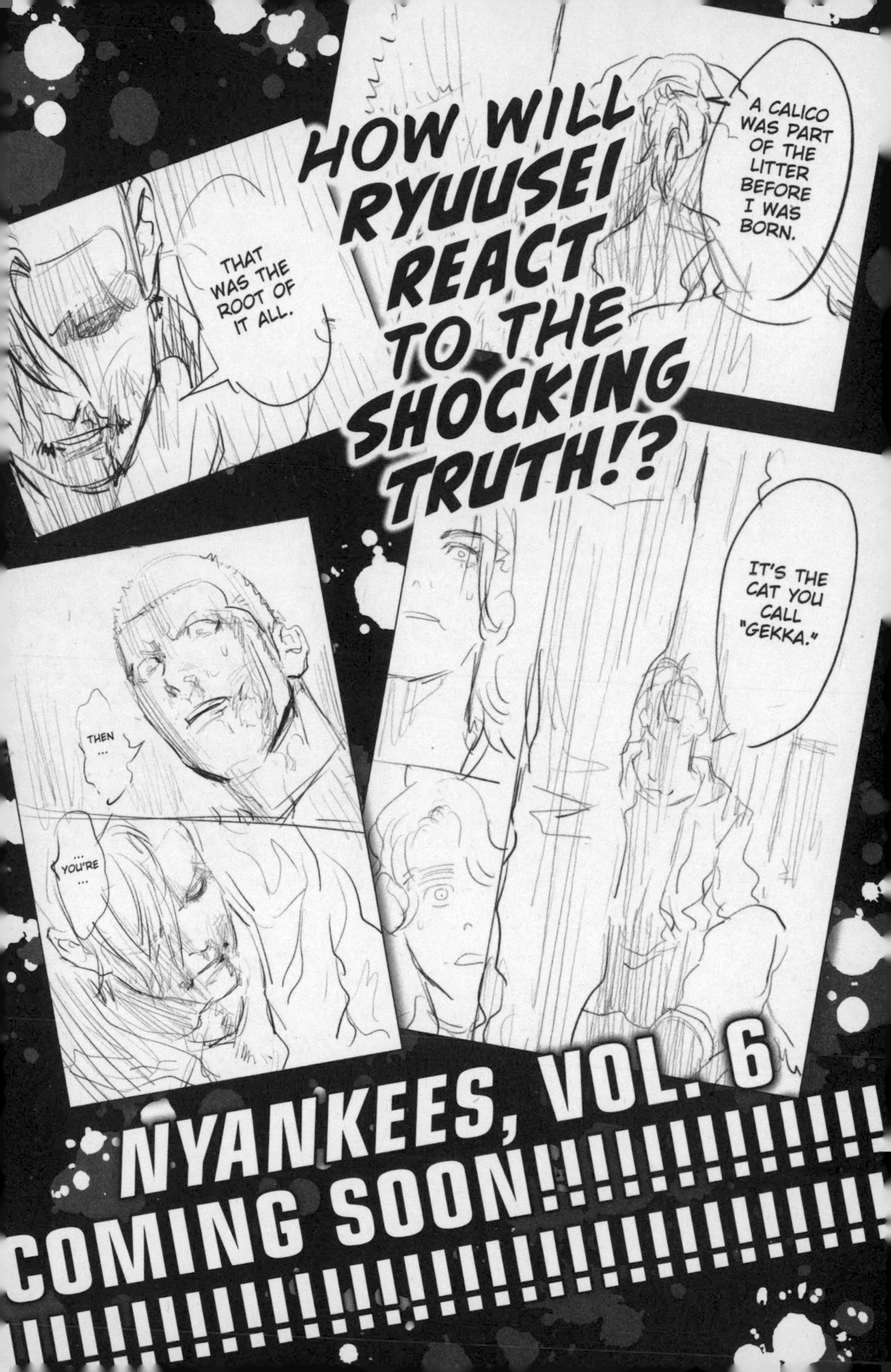
HOW WILL RYUUSEI REACT TO THE SHOCKING TRUTH!?
A CALICO WAS PART OF THE LITTER BEFORE I WAS BORN.
THAT WAS THE ROOT OF IT ALL.
IT'S THE CAT YOU CALL "GEKKA."
THEN ...
... YOU'RE ...
NYANKEES, VOL. 6
COMING SOON!!

TRANSLATION NOTES

COMMON HONORIFICS
no honorific: Indicates familiarity or closeness; if used without permission or reason, addressing someone in this manner would constitute an insult.
-san: The Japanese equivalent of Mr./Mrs./Miss. If a situation calls for politeness, this is the fail-safe honorific.
-kun: Used most often when referring to boys, this indicates affection or familiarity. Occasionally used by older men among their peers, but it may also be used by anyone referring to a person of lower standing.

PAGE 38
Kedama is the Japanese word for "hair ball."

ENJOY EVERYTHING.

YOU SHOULD COME PLAY WITH YOTSUBA TOO!

**Join Yotsuba as she delights in the
things many of us take for granted
in this Eisner-nominated series.**

VOLUMES 1-14
AVAILABLE NOW!

Visit our website at www.yenpress.com.

Hello! This is YOTSUBA!

**Guess what? Guess what?
Yotsuba and Daddy just moved here
from waaaay over there!**

**And Yotsuba met these
nice people next door and made
new friends to play with!**

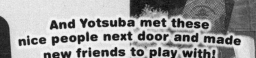

**The pretty one took
Yotsuba on a bike ride!**
(Whoooa! There was a big hill!)

And Ena's a good drawer!
(Almost as good as Yotsuba!)

**And their mom always
gives Yotsuba ice cream!**
(Yummy!)

**And...
And...
OHHHH!**

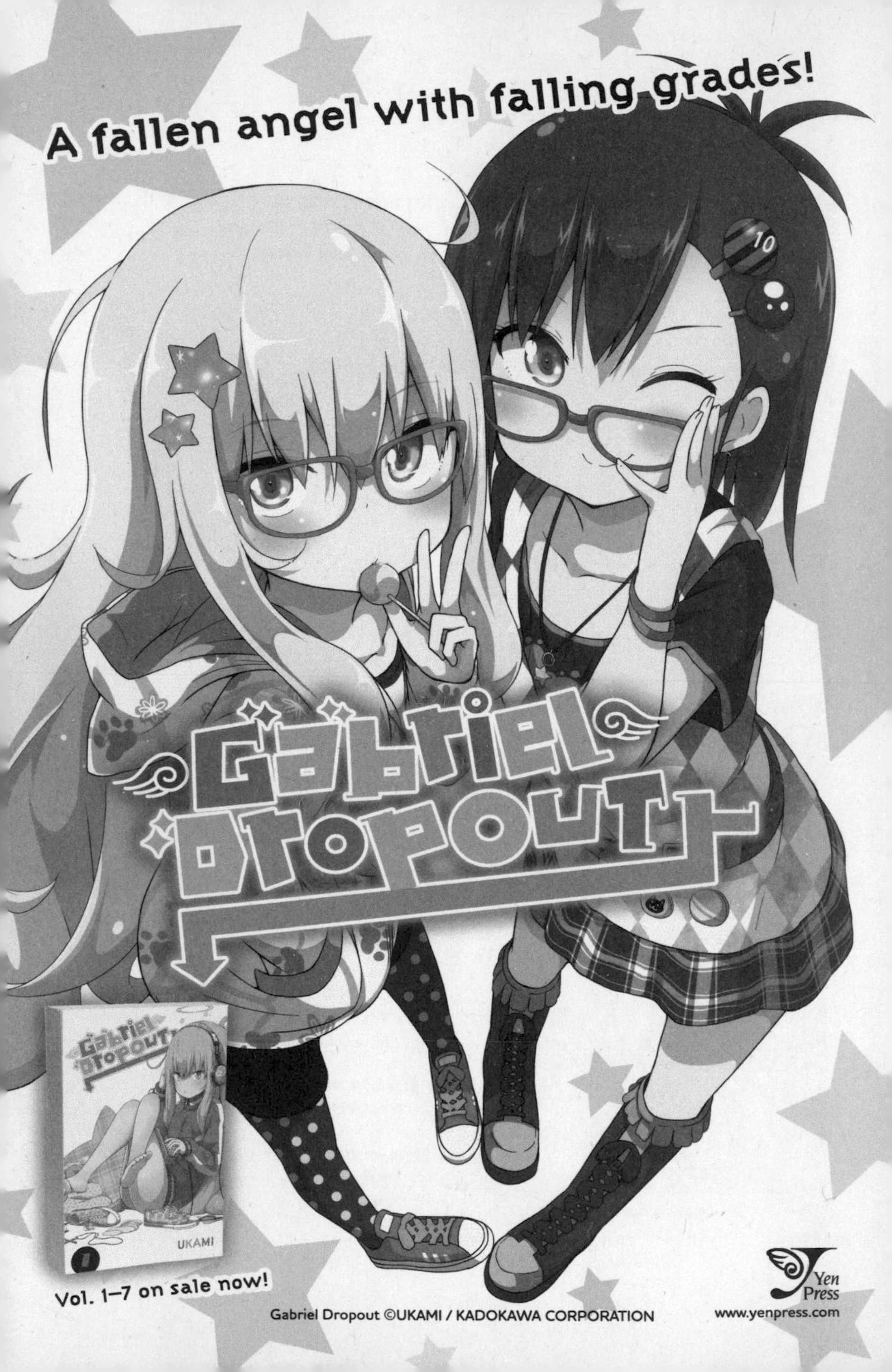
A fallen angel with falling grades!
Gabriel Dropout
Gabriel Dropout
UKAMI
Vol. 1–7 on sale now!
Gabriel Dropout ©UKAMI / KADOKAWA CORPORATION
Yen Press
www.yenpress.com